NOSY BONES

SANDY ST. JOHN

SOUTHPAW PRESS

Copyright © 2019 by Sandy St. John

Southpaw Press

All rights reserved.

No part of this book may be reproduced in any form or by any electronic or mechanical means, including information storage and retrieval systems, without written permission from the author, except for the use of brief quotations in a book review.

This is a work of fiction. Names, characters and incidents are either the product of the author's imagination or are used fictitiously. Any resemblance to actual events, or persons, living or dead, is entirely coincidental.

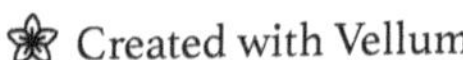 Created with Vellum

~

*For Maggie
I miss you every day*

~

~

...And for Emma
The sweet little spirit who came after

~

I don't like to lie—especially to my friends. And if I am going to tell a lie, I would prefer it to be a pretty little white one, not the monstrous whopper I was about to have to dish out.

Evan and I were sitting in his car on a narrow street, about two miles from downtown Houston. A misty drizzle blurred the windows, falling softly from overweight clouds that hung low in the late-afternoon January sky.

"What do you think?" Evan had asked just moments ago, a giant smile plastered on his face.

I peered through the window again. Maybe it was just the dreariness of the day clouding my thoughts. I squinted a little and tilted my head to the left. No, the house still looked like the slightest breeze would blow it over. The roof sagged ominously in the middle, and the flesh-colored paint peeled off in giant flakes like a bad case of untreated eczema.

"I didn't even know you were in the market for a house," I hedged. "Um, this one is certainly close to where you work, but I'll bet we could find one that doesn't need quite so much work."

His smile faded. "I already bought it." He was staring at me now like I'd just told him his baby was ugly. "I closed on it this afternoon." Uh-oh.

"Oh!" I tried to sound excited. "Wow! That's so exciting." His smile made a tentative comeback while he watched my face. "Evan, I'm so excited for you. Buying your first house is huge." I looked at the nightmare again. Nope, still a mess. "That's an incredible live oak in the front yard," I gushed, latching on to the only positive thing I could find. "And a little paint should spruce it right up."

He reached for the door handle. "Want to see the inside?" His excitement was back, and I pulled my jacket closer around my neck, a sinking feeling coursing through me. Maybe the inside was better than the outside.

Ducking my head against the rain, I hurried up the weed-choked sidewalk after him. Evan was fiddling with the key in the front lock, and I stepped carefully onto a drooping little porch. Traffic sounds caught my attention, and I realized we were just yards from Montrose Boulevard. The dingy back-side of a cinder block building butted up against Evan's property, but I wasn't sure what sort of establishment it was.

"This place has a lot of potential," I said, trying to fill the silence that stretched between us, while Evan jerked and rattled the front door. He grunted something noncommittal and added a little kick to supplement his efforts.

My name is Jessie Gallagher. Evan and I have been friends for years. We used to work together at Astor Oil, forging our friendship under the common abuse of a tyrannical boss. I'd quit my job as a corporate drone several months ago to start my own business, a gourmet dog biscuit company, and after several tough months, I was still enjoying every minute of it. So far, I wasn't rich (well, I wasn't rich from my business; family money was another story). And Evan and I had remained friends.

I pretended not to notice that he couldn't get the door open.

"Dang it!"

Across the street, another small house huddled in the rain. It was similar in structure to Evan's, but that one was well kept, sporting a fresh coat of lavender paint, a neat little square of grass, and rows of purple pansies bobbing velvety heads against the raindrops. I thought I saw a curtain drop as I studied the house, but it was hard to tell through the rain.

With a final grunt, Evan managed to force the front door open, and he flung it wide with a flourish. I poked my head over his shoulder, eager to see the inside. The darkness of the day had crept into the small entry, and I shoved my hand past Evan, probing for a light switch.

"Hold on, Jessie," he said, as I tried to slip past him. "I want to give you the proper tour." He hit a switch, and a dim light flicked on just inside the front door.

We were standing in a small living room, made smaller by a garish floral wallpaper that had been inexpertly hung. Rows of giant tangerine-orange flowers loomed over us, causing me to shrink back involuntarily.

"Whoa," I said before I could stop myself. Evan shot me a look, and I smiled as benignly as I could at him. "It's got hardwood floors! That's great."

"Okay, I know the wallpaper is a little much," he said, squinting his eyes at the uneven rows. "But that's an easy fix, right?"

My eyes were adjusting to the flowers, and I tried to see

past the paper to the potential of the room. The floors could be lovely with a little refinishing, and an unexpectedly ornate crown molding surrounded the room, chipped and dingy for sure, but a nice touch nevertheless. I tried not to notice the slope of the lovely floors, but I was pretty sure if I set a marble down, it wouldn't take long for it to roll its way towards the back of the house.

Evan's eyes were cutting back and forth between watching my face for every little reaction and gazing lovingly at his new house. He was going to make himself sick if he didn't knock it off.

"Yeah, sure. This just needs some cosmetic work."

I inched forward towards the next doorway, anxious to get this tour over with. A short hallway led to a narrow kitchen that did nothing to quell my worries. A wide window over the sink let in the gray afternoon light, and a quick flip of a switch flooded the area with harsh fluorescent rays. Vinyl flooring curled away from the baseboards, leaving a small alley where giant balls of dust gathered and grew. The cabinets boasted a rich avocado paint that matched the seventies-era appliances, and Formica countertops in harvest gold completed the look. As distressing as the cosmetics were, it was the sagging ceiling that held my attention.

Risking Evan's outrage, I couldn't help myself. "Um, so did you have an inspector check this place out?" The silence dragged on until I pulled my eyes away from the ceiling. Evan was gaping at the bulging acoustic tiles like he'd never noticed them before.

"Did I what?" he asked finally, wrenching his eyes away.

I scooted around the droopiest part of the ceiling to take a look out the back door without answering him. Clearly, an inspector hadn't been anywhere near this house. One of the windowpanes on the door had been broken out and covered over with a flimsy piece of cardboard.

"You've got a nice-sized yard out there," I said, peering through dirty panes.

"Yeah! Henry's going to love it," Evan said, sidling up next to me. Henry was Evan's first dog, a sweet little Norfolk terrier who used to belong to the previously mentioned domineering boss. I worried that Evan wasn't quite as good a pet-parent as I would like him to be, but to be fair, this was his first dog, and he really did seem to love Henry. We could work on the finer points as we went along.

I stared more closely into the darkening afternoon. A rotting stockade fence sagged under the weight of overgrown banana trees, separating Evan's yard from the alley of the neighboring strip center. I wasn't sure, but I thought I spied a blue dumpster on the other side, through a gap in the boards.

"What's over there?" I asked, gesturing towards the concrete block building across the alley.

"You're gonna love it! It's one of the reasons I bought this place!" I could hardly wait to hear this. He grinned broadly at me, and for a moment I feared an impending chest bump. "It's a taqueria!"

I turned and looked out the window again so he couldn't see my expression. The dumpster loomed close. Innocuous enough in January, but the Houston summers would surely turn its innards into a noxious stench that wouldn't stop at the fence line. I didn't want to think of what kind of critters it might attract.

"Jess! Did you hear me? It's a taqueria! Okay, I haven't tried it yet, but when have you ever heard of a bad Mexican restaurant?"

I smiled my best fake smile.

"You wanna go over and grab a bite when we're done looking around?"

"That sounds great, Evan. It really does. But actually, I need to get home and work on an order."

"Oh." He turned back towards the kitchen. "I guess we better hurry through this, then."

His phone suddenly erupted in a cacophony of buzzing and beeping. Digging around his pocket, he extracted it and held it to his ear.

"Hello?" His brow furrowed. "Yeah, of course. I'm always there by eight. Why? What's it about? Uh-huh. Uh-huh. Uh-huh. Yeah, I'll be there." He disconnected and shoved the phone back in his pocket.

"What was that about?" I asked.

"It's work. They've got me on this special project." He turned and kept walking. "So anyway, through here I've got the master bedroom and another bedroom that I'm thinking of turning into an office." His voice trailed off as he headed down the hall. I took another quick glance out the back to check out the rest of the yard. Junk littered most of it, and Jurassic-era weeds that were as tall as a toddler ran the length. We would have to get that cleaned up before Henry could go out.

I skirted the kitchen ceiling again and went in search of Evan. He was standing in the middle of what I assumed was the master bedroom, holding his hands up as if framing out where his furniture would go. It was a good-sized room with two windows, one overlooking his non-taqueria neighbor and the other the backyard.

"This is nice," I said, with the first genuine enthusiasm I'd had since this tour started.

"I know. It's way bigger than my bedroom at the apartment." He gestured toward the far wall. "So, I'll probably put my bed over there. The dresser along that wall. And Henry's bed right here." A rumpled blue sleeping bag lay where he was going to put his bed, and a couple of magazines were scattered along the floor.

I looked back at Evan. He was seeing the potential, and looking at his new home in a way that touched my heart. This was exciting. This was Evan's first house. His first home. And here I was being super critical. Maybe I should start looking at the potential with him, and doing what I could to help him fix up the things that weren't perfect.

I opened the closet door, delighted to find a large walk-in closet, which was unusual in a house of this era. Sturdy bars ran down two walls, and the back wall was covered with deep shelves. I squinted into the dimness and took a few steps forward. Dark forms lined all the shelves. It seemed like there were eyes staring out at me.

"Evan?" Through the open door, I could see him still mentally arranging his furniture.

"Do you think I need a nightstand? I don't have one now, but it seems like I should get one. I'm starting to think having an alarm clock on the floor just isn't classy. And maybe I should get a lamp." He glanced at the ceiling. "A lamp would be nice. Then I could read in bed. Not that I read in bed, but I could start." He finally took a breath.

"Hey, have you checked out this closet?" He stepped into the doorway, flicking a light switch on.

"Yeah, it's huge!"

"There's stuff in here." He stepped a few feet in and looked at where I was pointing. I swear, it was like he'd bought this place sight unseen.

"What is that?" His voice rose a couple octaves higher than normal.

"Looks like dolls," I said, keeping my distance. Now, I know there's nothing wrong with people collecting dolls. It's really no different than any other collection, except, well, dolls are creepy. I might be willing to put on some wellies and venture into the backyard where the snakes and spiders lived, and I might even try and help with the bulging ceiling, but Evan was on his own with this problem.

He inched forward and stared at the rows of faces as if afraid one was going to leap out at him. If any of them could, my money was on the mean-looking bride on the second shelf. She was a full head higher than any of her neighbors and had an expression on her face that made me fear for any groom doll that might be nearby.

"What the hell?" he said. "What am I supposed to do with this stuff? I don't know who these people are, but I don't want them in my closet. Get a garbage bag."

"You can't just throw them away," I protested, feeling like maybe we shouldn't be having this conversation in front of our audience. I stepped back into the bedroom and gestured for Evan to follow. As soon as he was out, I gave the dolls a small smile and gently shut the door. "Okay, seriously. Who did you buy this house from?" I whispered.

"I bought it from the bank. It was a foreclosure." He was whispering too. We moved farther away from the closet. I didn't know much about foreclosures, but I was pretty sure they gave you a chance to take your belongings with you when they kicked you out.

"So how come all this stuff is still in here?"

"How am I supposed to know? They told me to come sign

the papers and bring my cashier's check, and I thought that meant everything was done."

"Yeah, I guess," I said. "So, um, this all happened so fast." I tried to make it sound like that was a fun, exciting thing, but he caught my underlying tone.

"I know, but it was like it was meant to be. I mean, look at you. You have that nice little house and Addie loves it. And I don't know. I'm in an apartment. It's not the greatest place, and they're raising my rent, and it just seemed like I need to do something different. And then we got our year-end bonus and I saw this place and..." he trailed off. "Here we are."

I leaned my head against the cool glass of the window. What a mess.

Something rapped sharply on the glass next to my head, and I leapt away from the window, hands flying to my chest in a feeble attempt to restart my heart. I looked out at a puff of orange hair surrounding a crazed white face that was screaming at me through the glass.

"What are you doing in my house? You get out of my closet! You hear me?"

Evan stood open-mouthed at my side, and we watched in silence as the lunatic outside waved her arms at us in angry circles.

"You get out right now! You had no right to change the locks."

"Who is that?" I asked Evan, not taking my eyes off the spectacle. Having a moment to recover myself, I noticed that the initial impression I'd had of a deranged clown wasn't right. It was a woman, her frizzy hair dyed the shade of a construction barrel, and her face made up with an unnaturally pale foundation. Thick lips were painted a bright candy-corn orange, and blue streaks of eye shadow darkened a wide swath between her flaming eyes and her eyebrows. She'd resumed knocking on the glass, and I was afraid the old pane would shatter under the assault.

"Evan?" I stole a glance at his motionless form. His mouth hung open, although it didn't look like he was breathing. "Evan?" I risked a tap on his arm and his mouth closed with a snap, but his unblinking eyes never left the scene outside the window. "Do you want me to call the police?" I reached into my purse and pulled out my cell phone. "I'm calling the cops!" I shouted through the window.

The fuzzy orange head suddenly dropped out of sight, and for a moment I thought maybe she was running away. Edging towards the window, I saw her pick herself up off the ground, where she'd fallen. Either she'd been standing on something to see directly in the windows, or she was at least nine feet tall.

In the gravel driveway, empty on our arrival, now sat an ancient orange VW Thing. The woman rummaged around a junk-filled passenger seat, pulled out a bag, then trotted down the drive towards the backyard. She appeared to be wearing at least two long, mismatched skirts that flapped just above the tops of heavy boots, and a lumpy maroon cardigan that fell nearly to her knees.

I punched 9-1-1 into the keypad but didn't hit send. I felt a little ridiculous calling the cops over this clown impersonator yelling at us through the window.

Evan had raced out of the bedroom, tracking her progress from window to window. I followed along in his wake, rounding the corner just in time to see him run to the back door and slam his body against it as the crazy woman pushed hard on it from outside.

Evan braced himself, shoulder to the door and feet

planted on the slick floor, as the door rattled and bucked beyond him. I dropped my purse and phone and rushed over to help, adding my weight to his while fumbling to turn the lock. Finally with a loud click, the lock engaged and the door stopped moving.

"I want you out of my house!" the woman shouted. She'd backed up and now stood on the far side of a crumbling back stoop. Evan sagged against the door, breathing hard. I peered around the door frame and watched as the woman stomped and turned in a small circle, like a chicken having a fit. I could hear muffled muttering but couldn't make out what she was saying. She caught sight of me and rose up. "Don't think that you're going to keep my things. Those are my belongings and you have no right to keep them from me."

"Maybe she's a squatter," I said. "I saw a story like that on the news. They break into houses and just move in. This family was on vacation, and when they came home, people were living in their house."

"So what am I supposed to do about it?"

"I don't know," I said, suddenly remembering what a legal nightmare that family had gone through trying to get their house back.

"I'll bet she busted out that window to get in," Evan said, running a finger over the flimsy cardboard patch. "I'm gonna board that up. She won't get in that way again." He turned and looked around the empty kitchen. "Okay, I'm going to have to run to the hardware store. I don't have what I need to fix this. I need you to stay here and make sure she doesn't get in again."

A sudden rapping made us both jump. She was back at the door, peering through the window.

"How did you get in my house? Did that bank manager

give you the key? I want you to give it back. He's stupid. He had no right to give it to anybody."

Uh-oh. "I guess maybe that's the previous owner," I said.

"Ya think?" Evan retorted, rather snidely, I thought.

He inched closer to me, crowding into my space and looking over my shoulder out the window. His hot breath puffed against my hair, and I gave him a small shove with my elbow to move him away. It seemed to me that this lady wanted her stuff and her house back, and if Evan had any sense, he'd work something out with her and the bank. The faster he could run away from this deal, in my opinion, the better.

"You should go talk to her," I said. "Maybe it's not too late to give her her house back."

He turned squinty eyes to me. "Thanks for being supportive."

We looked out again. She was muttering and digging through her bag. I wondered how long we were going to be stuck here. Evan's eyes were riveted on her bag.

"What if she's going for a weapon?" he asked. My heart gave a little jump, and I tensed up, ready to throw myself to the floor. "Never mind. She's just getting a Kleenex."

"Okay, I'm gonna count to ten and I want you all out of there," she shouted, her face so close to the glass, she was fogging up the pane. "One."

"Clearly there's been a misunderstanding," I shouted back at her. "Why don't you go home and call the bank manager? I'm sure he can explain everything."

"What are you talking about?" Evan asked, staring at me like I'd lost my mind. "What misunderstanding?"

"This is home!" she shouted.

"Well, I think you need to talk to the bank."

We stared at each other for a minute through the dirty glass, the drizzle beginning to matt her hair down into thick orange spaghetti strands that stuck to her forehead.

Suddenly she jumped. "What time is it?"

I glanced down at my watch. "Four forty-five."

She clapped a hand to her forehead and raced down the broken steps, across the backyard and towards the driveway. Evan ran to the living room, and I followed behind, reaching the front window in time to see her fire up the VW Thing and squeal out of the driveway, the old vehicle belching smoke as it puttered down the street.

Evan and I stared at each other.

"Well, that was interesting," I finally said. Evan's earlier excitement was gone, replaced by a frantic anxiety.

"She can't just come back here, right?" he asked, his cheeks breaking into the red streaks that plagued him when he was stressed. "I mean, it is my house."

"No—no, of course not," I said, trying to sound confident. "And I know you did, but I just want to check—you did do this deal through a bank, though, right?"

"Of course I did it through a bank!" He huffed a little and ran a hand through his dark hair. "Okay, I've got to get to the hardware store. Can you just stay here till I get back? I need you to keep an eye on the place and make sure she doesn't come in again."

I glanced around the empty room. Darkness shrouded the corners now, the lone bare bulb casting a harsh glare like a spotlight on a stage. The thought of staying here alone, even for half an hour or so, made me fidget uncomfortably. I glanced at my watch, knowing it was only about five minutes later than the last time I'd looked.

"You know, I kind of need to get home. I have that order I

need to work on..." I trailed off, feeling like a jerk, but also feeling overcome by claustrophobia in this place. "I'm sure she won't come back. Why would she? There's nothing here for her." Well, there were some creepy dolls and the sleeping bag. "Maybe you could leave her a note on the door and tell her you'll let her clear her things out tomorrow. Right? That would be the only reason for her to come around here."

I inched towards the door, eager to race out into the cool evening air. He still wasn't saying anything.

"Maybe you could put her sleeping bag out on the porch. I doubt very highly she needs her dolls tonight. She can get those later."

"I don't have time to take you home," he finally said, his voice flat. I'd forgotten that he'd picked me up. It felt like days ago.

"That's okay. I can just Uber."

He went and checked all the windows and doors while I arranged my ride. I walked out on the porch with him, feeling terrible how this had gone.

"Call me tomorrow, okay?" I reached over and gave him an awkward hug. "Congratulations on your new house! I'm really happy for you. I'll help you get it spruced up. There's a lot I can help you with!"

"Like waiting till I get back," he muttered, making his way down the porch steps and heading for his car.

I should stay. Not that I thought anything would happen, but it was important to him. Then again, what was she going to do? When my ride pulled up, I got in.

CHAPTER TWO

I hadn't just been blowing Evan off—I really did have a big dog biscuit order I needed to work on. A new doggie daycare had opened in the area, and they were looking for premium dog treats to add to their small retail section at the front. I had other doggie daycare outlets that sold my biscuits, along with some groomers and one of the natural pet stores, but I needed to find more distributors if I was really going to make a go of this.

Normally, I find the biscuit making soothing, but tonight I'd been off my game, burning one batch and mangling the shapes on another. I'd finally given up just before ten, after having put a dozen Barker Street Bones labels on the bags upside down. I cleaned up the kitchen, grabbed a book and went up to bed.

My Border collie, Addie, settled on the bed beside me while I read the same page over and over, unable to concentrate. I finally gave up and turned the light out, hoping to shut my brain off.

By eleven thirty, Addie was up again, pacing around the

bedroom restless and edgy. She senses storms well before I ever hear the first rumble of thunder, and tonight was no exception. By midnight, an unexpected January thunderstorm was directly over us, and the house shook with nerve-jarring cracks. Lightning flashes illuminated the room as if it was broad daylight, and we jumped in unison at each burst of energy. I tried to soothe her as her distress grew, but she retreated into herself, anxiety rendering everything but the storm irrelevant.

Within thirty minutes, the thunder and lightning passed, but the rain continued. Addie finally settled at the foot of the bed, flopping sideways and falling asleep. Her steady breathing was soothing, and I tried to follow suit, but my brain was fully charged with images of Evan's new house.

I felt bad that his big surprise had bombed so thoroughly, and I couldn't shake a creeping uneasiness about how all of this was going to turn out. A lot of people take on home renovation projects. I should give Evan more credit. Okay, he'd seemed surprised by the extent of work the house needed, but with a little time and money, he could turn that little bungalow into a lovely home. The crazy lady in the VW Thing was another matter.

When I finally crawled out of bed at five forty, the rain had stopped, but the streets still reflected the dark sheen of oily puddles. I filled a Kong toy with treats for Addie, bypassing our normal walk, and started to work on my biscuits. I needed to get at least three more good batches done if I was going to be ready with my trial run for the new doggie daycare and still have enough inventory to supply my current distributors.

I flicked on the TV, partly for the noise and partly because I liked to see what dramatic events had taken place overnight.

A defunct Chinese satellite was expected to crash into Earth over the weekend. The flow of guns being smuggled into Mexico was helping fuel the drug violence in the country. And a chicken who'd made her home in Memorial Park was terrorizing joggers. Two anchors, a meteorologist and a traffic guy, laughed like this was the funniest thing they'd ever heard.

I worked through the local news and half an hour into the national morning shows, mixing dough, rolling out bone-shaped treats and lining them up into neat little rows on the cookie sheets. I'd recently invested in a second oven, so I was able to churn out a lot more cookies without nearly as much waiting time. By the time the last batch was out and on the cooling racks, the sun had come up and the streets looked dry enough for a short walk with Addie.

Pulling on my running shoes, I couldn't help but look around with affection at my tidy little townhouse. Everything looked neat, new and sturdy. Cheerful yellow paint glowed on the walls, the hardwoods glistened on the floor, and not one inch of ceiling looked in danger of collapsing. Poor Evan. He would have to spend a fortune on that place to even make it habitable, much less cozy.

As I was putting Addie's harness on, my phone rang. Caller ID indicated it was Evan's work number.

"Hey! How's the new homeowner?" I threw in extra enthusiasm, determined to make up for yesterday's lack.

"Jess." Evan sounded as if he'd run a half marathon.

"What's up? You sound all out of breath."

"I need you to do me a favor." In the background, I could hear phones ringing and someone yelling nearby.

"Wow, it sounds crazy there. What's going on?" Evan worked at Astor Oil, a place I knew well, having worked there seven years myself. Usually there was a steady hum of noise on the trading floor, punctuated periodically by traders shouting back and forth, but that when the market was open. It was way too early for that kind of uproar.

"You're not going to believe this, but they're saying we're being taken over."

"Taken over?"

"Yeah, but that's not why I called. I need you to do me a favor."

"Sure. What do you need?"

"Could you go check on my house? I was going to run over at lunch, but I can't leave. They want me to rerun some of my reports for another meeting this afternoon."

"Is this that special project you mentioned?"

"Yeah. No. Sort of. They never said someone was trying to take us over. It was just supposed to be some special presenta-tion for upper management. But, about my house. I'm just afraid that looney-tooney did something bad after we left last night. Can you go check?" His words raced together.

"Sure, I can swing by. But come on. You don't really think she'd do anything, do you?"

"You saw her, what do you think? She's crazy! Look, can you go all the way around? Make sure she didn't break in again?"

I did a quick mental calculation of my day. I had taken on several dog-walking clients to help keep myself afloat while I struggled to get Barker Street Bones off the ground. Not only did the dog-walking help bring in needed cash, it also kept me active and mentally grounded. But it did take up the better part of my late morning and most of the afternoon. It would probably be best to run by Evan's before my rounds.

"Yeah, okay. No problem."

"Could you go now?" he asked, agitation making his voice crack. "Please? Make sure she didn't break in the back again, or anything? I gotta go. Chip is coming this way. Call me!"

He disconnected with a bang. Addie was sitting like a good girl, staring at me expectantly, and waiting for her walk.

"Hey, how would you like to go for a ride in the car instead of going for a walk?"

The ride to Evan's wasn't bad since the worst of the morning commute was over. I was hopeful that seeing the place in the bright sun would improve its appearance. Or maybe not. Sitting in my car, Addie and I stared out at Evan's new, sad, little house. If anything, the sunlight only high-lighted all the flaws I'd noticed yesterday, and exposed a few more.

How had he thought that this was *the* house to buy? There had to be thousands and thousands of properties for sale all over Houston, most of them in better shape than this one. Maybe he could flip it. Do some cosmetic work and sell it to the next poor sap that wandered down the pike. If he could remember how the bank had offloaded it on him, he could use the same lines on the next potential victim.

I peered into the shadows at the front of the house, looking for signs of the previous owner. Maybe Evan could sell it back to her at a small profit. Or what the heck, maybe he could sell it back to her at a small loss. That would still be better than keeping it. Seeing no signs of life, I inched from the car and closed the door as gently as I could. Freeing Addie from the backseat, I closed that door gently as well. If the lady from yesterday was hanging around, I didn't want to announce my presence.

Traffic on Montrose Boulevard hummed and the smell of empanadas wafted over from the taqueria. I wondered what time they opened as my stomach growled in appreciation of the tantalizing smell.

The live oak tree that graced Evan's property cast dark shadows, and the overgrown bushes guarding the perimeter presented ample hiding places for thugs, robbers or crazy people. I felt better having Addie with me, although truth be told, she wasn't much of a guard dog. Now, if there were any loose sheep in the yard, she would happily round them up.

We strode up the path to the front porch, Addie pulling ahead and racing from side to side as she sniffed the unfamiliar area. Once we were up on the porch and several feet higher than the surrounding jungle, I surveyed the front yard for signs of lurkers. Seeing none, I turned my attention to the front door. I gave the handle a firm yank, halfway expecting the door to swing open, but it was locked. Or maybe it was just stuck. One more push convinced me it was locked, so I pulled Addie down the creaking boards to the living room window. The panes were intact, so no one had broken in, at least not through here.

I rubbed at the window, trying to clear a spot in the dirt, but mostly I just succeeded in smearing it into grimy streaks. Through the streaks, I could make out the living room, pretty much as we'd seen it yesterday.

A sharp tap on my shoulder nearly stopped my heart. I whipped around with a small scream, clutching the leash to my chest while Addie sat passively staring at a young guy in a stylish black leather coat. He reeled back with a shriek that was louder than mine.

"Ahh!" One hand flew to his cheek, the other clutched his chest.

"Oh my God, you scared me," I said to him, watching as he patted the supple leather jacket covering his heart.

"I scared you? Honey, you nearly took the life from me." He was of average height, but slightly built, with thick blond hair mussed in an expensive European cut. Thick lashes surrounded direct gray eyes, and an attractive pink blush crept across his cheeks. "I thought you heard me," he said. "And your animal..." He looked at Addie with the slighted curl of his lip. "Clearly, a well-trained guard dog."

I looked down at Addie who showed no shame at her failure to alert me. She'd shifted her attention from him to a squirrel that was racing down the tree trunk.

"Anyhoo," he said, bringing his attention back to me. "Are you Miriam's—"He tilted his head and stared at me. "Niece? Daughter?" He grimaced. "No. You just couldn't be blood-related. Social worker?"

"Who's Miriam?" I asked. "Is she the previous owner?"

"Previous owner? As far as I know, she's the current owner. Did something happen?"

"Well, my friend just bought this place."

We stared at each other. Suddenly a smile lit up his face. "You mean Miriam sold her house? She's gone?"

"Actually, I think this was a foreclosure. And I'm not sure about 'gone' either. She was here last night, saying this was still her house. I don't think she actually understands it isn't."

His smile dropped. "Sister, if Miriam says it's still her house, it's still her house."

"Well, according to the bank, it's not."

"Your friend is probably going to have to drive a stake through that one's heart if he wants her to go away."

I gave a nervous laugh, afraid he was more than just a little serious. He moved past me, cupped his hands to the window and leaned forward for a look.

"When did she move out?" he asked, peering into the empty living room.

"I don't know. I just found out about this whole thing yesterday."

"Look at that wallpaper," he said, patting his hand against his chest again. "She should spend less time poking her nose into everyone else's business, and more time trying to do something with this place. It's just disgusting." He gave a little shudder and stepped back. "No offense," he added.

"Yeah, it needs a little work," I conceded. "But I think it could be really cute when it's fixed up."

"By the way, I'm Kip Willetto. I live across the street." He stuck out a well-manicured hand.

"Jessie Gallagher," I said, shaking a hand that was soft as a toddler's. "Whoa. How do you get your skin so soft?"

He looked pleased that I'd noticed. "I have a lotion that's amazing! I get it from my stylist. I think he orders it direct from France, but he won't tell me in case I start sending away for it myself. He's afraid I'll stop coming to see him."

I gave my own rough hands an embarrassed once-over. Calluses marred my palms where leashes rubbed daily against my skin. Several scars showed where I'd burned my fingers taking dog biscuits out of the oven, and cracks from the cold weather bloomed red next to my fingernails.

"I can get you some if you'd like," he offered, kindly not mentioning what a mess my hands looked.

"That would be great." Hopefully something this miraculous wasn't going to cost me a hundred dollars an ounce. "I have some work-related battle scars."

He tilted his head like a curious bird. "I'm trying to imagine what a little thing like you could be doing that would rough up your hands."

I laughed. "I have a gourmet dog biscuit business, and I also have a handful of dog-walking clients. Speaking of which"—I glanced at my watch—"I guess I need to check out the rest of the house for Evan, and then get going."

He fell into step beside me as I made my way carefully down the steps and towards the side of the house. Addie trotted ahead of me, eager to explore this place more.

"I have my own business too," he declared, clearly delighted at our common bond.

"Really? What kind of business is it?"

"I make designer pillows."

"That's cool," I said, wondering how anyone could forge a living making designer pillows. I was having a hard enough time with healthy high-end dog biscuits. And those were things people bought all the time. Pillows?

He stood back and let me push past a scraggly azalea bush. Dead leaves, still damp from yesterday's rain, piled ankle deep along the driveway. The smell of mold and rot was almost overwhelming. I glanced back at him, still standing within jumping distance of the porch steps.

"Aren't you coming with me?" The relief I'd felt at not having to check out the rest of the house alone was quickly evaporating as I saw the look on Kip's face.

"And ruin these shoes?" he asked in revulsion. "Oh, I don't think so. I'll just wait for you right here." Well, I had come over here fully intending to do this by myself, so why was I suddenly so reluctant?

"Come on," I said, hitting a sad note somewhere between encouraging and wheedling. "It's not that bad. Look." I lifted a foot to show how clean and undamaged my footwear was.

"You're just darling," he said. "But even that's not enough to get me to go back there. I can only imagine the horrors. I will wait right here for you, though. And if you scream, I shall dash across to my house and dial 9-1-1."

Great. Addie and I continued down the soggy driveway. The leaves were matted down into two grooves, like tire tracks through a forest, and mud squelched under my feet as I walked. Most of the original gravel had been washed away, or covered over with dirt and weeds, and I walked carefully, trying to avoid the hidden potholes. Addie squished along like a tracker in the swamp. She was probably going to need a bath when we were done here. I really should have left her in the car.

To my left, a bungalow similar to Evan's in style, but in much better shape, sat close to the driveway, protected by a sturdy stockade fence. The houses were raised up on high pier-and-beam foundations, the crawlspaces covered over by wooden lattice. Well, Evan's was sort of covered. Most of the latticework was rotted, and holes large enough to admit a feral pig gaped along the base. I hurried along, not wanting to disturb anything that might be nesting under there. The good news for Evan was that he probably wouldn't need to worry about flooding. At least it was something.

I was paying so much attention to the dark spaces under the house that I didn't even notice the orange VW Thing parked around the side. I stopped in my tracks, suddenly on high alert.

The vehicle was parked next to a run-down garage that I hadn't even noticed yesterday. Judging from the vehicle's location, it had been deliberately driven back here so as not to be seen from the street. Maybe Evan wasn't as paranoid as I'd thought.

I crept slowly to the corner of the house holding Addie close to my side. A bird shrilled in a nearby tree, and faint sounds of Mexican music floated past, probably from the restaurant next door. Sounds of traffic muted just about everything else. I didn't hear any heavy breathing or menacing footsteps, so I poked my head around the corner, halfway expecting to get whacked with a two-by-four.

The backyard was empty. At least, I thought it was empty. Patches of knee-deep weeds were thick enough to conceal an entire platoon, but Miriam's vivid hair would be pretty hard to hide. I crept over to the Thing and looked into the open windows. Overnight rain had left the seats wet, and the cardboard boxes that filled the backseat were soggy and stained. Addie stuck her head under the vehicle and sniffed at something so long, that I finally crouched down next to her and steeled myself to take a look. Nothing.

I considered going back and getting Kip but was pretty sure that he still wouldn't be willing to come with me. I turned my attention to the garage, which had an old-fashioned solid flip-up door that looked like it weighed at least a hundred pounds. I gave it a half-hearted tug but was afraid I'd bring the whole structure down if I pulled too hard. To the right was a standard exterior door with small windows near the top. They were too high to see in, so I twisted the knob, surprised to find it unlocked.

Taking a deep breath, I pushed the door in slowly and poked my head into the dimly lit space. The entire garage was stuffed full of what surely must be all of the previous owner's belongings. Furniture was heaped in haphazard piles, and boxes balanced on every surface. Several feet in, couch cushions and pillows had been arranged next to a side window, making a cozy little nest area. It looked like someone had been staying here.

I wondered if Evan had more squatters, or if Miriam had

stayed out here last night after Evan had boarded up the window. But her car was here, so where was she? Maybe she had broken out the window again and was inside. Of course, she could be hiding amongst the piles in the garage. With that thought, I backed out and headed across the yard. Evan had just said to check the house—he hadn't said anything about the garage.

I hop-stepped through the weeds, Addie crashing along beside me, thankful it was January. Most of the scary Texas critters should be hibernating. The back door was locked, and I could see where Evan had not only boarded up the broken window but apparently nailed plywood across the entire thing. So far, so good.

I moved carefully along the back of the house towards the taqueria side. The greasy blue dumpster looked even closer than it had yesterday. Several feet of boards had collapsed, and a hole gaped open to the alley next door. Evan was going to need a whole new fence, or maybe a twelve-foot-high cinder block wall would be better.

I was so busy thinking of what would work best to block that mess that I wasn't really watching Addie. Next thing I knew, she had darted under the house, the leash nearly slipping from my hand as she charged forward.

"Addie!" The opening under the house was higher than I'd thought, and there wasn't anything covering it on this side of the house. Addie seemed to be wrestling with something, and dog-mom panic set in as I tried to pull her back. "Addie!" She ignored me, and I could see her rump jerking backward, looking exactly like she did when we played tug-of-war with her rope. Only I had no idea who, or what, was pulling on the other end.

As much as I didn't want to, I was going to have to reach

under there and pull her out. *Please don't let there be a wild animal under there*, I thought as I squatted down, balancing on the balls of my feet. She was still jerking backward, and as I leaned forward, she slipped back, careening into my side and knocking me completely off-balance.

I fell sideways and forward, one hand landing hard in a slimy patch of muck. Mud coated the knees of my tights, and a sharp pain in my hand drew my attention to a sliver of glass sticking out of the fleshy part of my palm. Seeing the wedge of glass protruding from my skin brought on a moment of wooziness. I pushed myself to a sitting position, took a deep breath and pulled it out, releasing a fresh flow of blood. Well, maybe the blood would keep me from getting any of a thousand diseases probably living in the mud that close to the dumpster. It looked like part of a broken beer bottle.

Just as I was standing up, Addie went back to her attack, grabbing a hold of something and giving it another hard tug. I knelt down again and looked on in horror as I finally saw what she was after. In the dim space under the house, Addie gripped the edge of a thick skirt between her teeth and jerked with all her might, but her forty pounds was no match for what she was pulling.

I recognized the double skirts and maroon cardigan from last night, and I even caught a glimpse of orange hair spilling across the dirt. She looked like a life-sized mannequin that had been left out in the elements before being discarded in a garbage heap. Addie gave another giant pull before slipping backward again. This time, one leg flopped out from under the house, its hiking boot landing with a plop in the mud. It was Miriam under there.

CHAPTER THREE

I flew to my feet and jerked the leash hard, pulling Addie along with me. I felt frantic. My mind lurched from Miriam under the house, to my oozy cut, to the fact that Addie had been pulling at what I assumed was a dead body. Why would she do that? Could she catch anything from doing that? Ugh. I was going to need to brush her teeth when we got home. Was Miriam dead? Might she just be sleeping? I needed some antibiotic cream for my hand. We needed the police.

I was nearly hyperventilating as I rounded the front of the house. Kip was standing on the top porch step. His eyes flew wide at my appearance.

"What happened to you?" he asked.

"Addie knocked me over," I said. "She was pulling at Miriam. She's under the house. I think she's dead."

Instead of dashing across the street to dial 9-1-1 like I'd thought he would, he stood stationary. "Really? Oh my God! This I have to see!" He zipped down the steps and across the front yard, heedless of his precious shoes. "Where? Where is she?" Pushing past me, he skipped around the corner, and down the mud-slicked side yard.

"Kip? I don't think you should go back there. We need to call the police."

"Sure. We'll call in a minute. I've got to see this first, though." He spotted the foot sticking out from under the house and broke into a spirited rendition of "Ding-Dong! The Witch Is Dead." Crouching down next to her boot, he balanced himself with one finger in the dirt. Still humming his little tune, he poked his head into the crawl space and stared into the darkness.

"Kip, come on." I took a few deep breaths and tried to stop my racing mind. I was pretty sure Miriam was dead. I had tried to block it out, but I thought I had seen blood around her. And if she wasn't dead, she surely would have moved when Addie started pulling on her. We needed to call 9-1-1. And not to be selfish, but I was slightly more concerned about my cut, being that I was still alive and could be sickened by dangerous pathogens.

The humming stopped. "She's probably just drunk," he said, lifting Miriam's ankle and giving it a hard shake. "Wakey, wakey, sweetheart," he shouted. Suddenly he paused, his hand still on her leg. He made a guttural sound and snatched his hand away, shaking it convulsively. The leg plopped to the ground. Scrambling to his feet, he rushed backwards towards me, still staring at the outstretched foot. "Oh, that's weird. Her leg feels weird. I don't think she's sleeping it off. I think she's dead!"

"I told you she was dead," I said. "We need to call the police."

Kip turned and faced me, his face visibly paling. "Miriam is really dead under her house."

"Well, actually it's Evan's house." He stared blankly at me. "You know, my friend, Evan. It's his house now."

He turned quickly, mud squelching under his heel, and raced towards the street. "We've got to call the police! That damn bitch actually got herself killed!"

Addie and I ran after him, little chunks of dirt and bits of leaves falling from me like the crust off a French loaf. Kip had disappeared towards the back of his house, and I followed him down a neat little driveway towards the back door. Judging from her swishing tail, this was the most fun Addie had had in a long time.

This house had an actual paved driveway that extended all the way back towards a detached one-car garage. The only thing out of place was the mud clumps Kip had left as he ran. Through the window on the door, I could hear Kip's voice getting more excited and higher-pitched with each word.

"Yes, she's dead! No, I did not check for a pulse. What, you want me to crawl under the house with a dead person? Just send someone!"

He glanced out at me and held the phone away from his head in exasperation. I could hear the voice on the other end from where I stood. He put the phone back to his ear. "What do you mean? I don't know. Police? Ambulance? Just send someone!" He stabbed the off button viciously, cutting off the still-squawking voice. "Stupid cow," he muttered, slipping back out through the door.

The phone began ringing immediately. He threw it inside and slammed the door shut.

"Lord, I can only hope whoever they send is more competent than that woman," he said.

He paced back and forth, muttering to himself. I wasn't sure if he was muttering about Miriam or the 9-1-1 operator. He spotted the mud marring his driveway and stalked into the garage, returning with a broom. He whipped the broom against the pavement, flinging the offending bits side to side until they disappeared. I stood stock-still, afraid if he saw anything flake off me, he'd come after me next.

Once his driveway was pristine again, he replaced the broom and we stood in awkward silence. My hand throbbed where the glass shard had been, and I was convinced I could feel germs seeping through the opening and straight into my bloodstream. Still no sirens. At this rate, I could die of disease before the cops got here.

"Hey, Kip?" He looked at me like he'd forgotten I was there. "Do you have a Band-Aid and some antibiotic cream I could use? I got a piece of glass in my hand when I fell next to Miriam." I held it out for his viewing. "I pulled it out, but I'm afraid of what I might have landed in." I looked at my hand. Were those red streaks already? "You know, germs from that dumpster, or something."

He looked at me in horror. "You cut yourself next to Miriam? Oh my God! Sweetie, why didn't you say so? You know dead bodies leak out everything from their intestines." He shuddered. "And any other fluids they might have had." He gave me a little pat on the shoulder and ran into the house.

I'd been so calm about all of this. Well, mostly. I'd thought the mud I fell in had been from the rain, but it was probably from Miriam's inside fluids leaking out after she died. My breathing quickened into short, shallow puffs. I sat down on the back step and put my head between my knees, trying to keep the blackness from overtaking me. Addie sat down next to me and nuzzled under my armpit.

By the time Kip came back with an armful of first aid supplies, I was still working to stave off the black dots that continued to dance in my peripheral vision. I held my hand out, as if getting it farther away from my body could help stop the immigration of nasty germs into my bloodstream. Kip deposited his load onto the driveway and knelt down beside me.

In the distance, I could finally hear a siren making its approach.

"Okay, let me take a look at it."

It took me a minute to realize that Kip had donned a pair of pink rubber kitchen gloves that reached nearly to his elbows. I felt like a biohazard. I probably was a biohazard.

In spite of the kitchen gloves, he seemed to know what he was doing. I watched him concentrate on my palm. I sucked in a breath when he poured a generous measure of hydrogen peroxide over a cotton ball and dripped it into the open wound.

"Sorry, sorry," he murmured, pouring more liquid onto the bubbling white mess. The sting was less this time, and he waited several seconds before dabbing it with a clean gauze pad. By the time he was done, a small pile of medical waste littered the driveway, and a Houston police patrol car was just squealing to a stop at the curb in front of us. Kip turned back to his first aid pile and extracted some ointment, seemingly unaware of the siren blasting at our eardrums from just yards away. Addie pinned her ears back against her head, and I wished I could do the same.

A uniformed cop burst from the driver's door, glancing

first at us and then across the street to Evan's house, probably trying to verify where the problem was. He was young and good looking, but he seemed rather skittish. I waved my good hand towards the house across the street and shouted, "She's over there," but no one was going to hear me over the racket from the siren. I kept waving and pointing, hoping he would take his edgy, gun-toting self across the street.

Another patrol car approached from the Montrose side, stopping just short of hitting my car. Two officers got out, heads swiveling to take in the scene. One of them was tall and heavyset, and I could see his mouth opening wide as he shouted something to the first officer. The first one hurried to his car and shut off the siren. Apparently it was too late to save my hearing because my ears rang with an annoying high-pitched whine.

Kip seemed unperturbed as he finished spackling my hand with ointment. The grease slicked across my palm, but the throbbing began to subside as he fitted a Band-Aid snugly over the wound.

"There," he said, tossing the wrapper onto his pile of trash. "That should hold you for a while."

Two of the officers headed over towards Evan's house while the big one headed up the drive towards us.

"So, what's going on here?" he asked, his voice surprisingly high-pitched for such a large man.

"There's a body under the house over there," I said, waving again across the street.

"Is that so? Whose body is it?" He pulled a small notepad from his pocket and clicked a pen open in his other hand. Kip began gathering his small mound of trash.

"I believe her name was Miriam." I glanced at Kip expectantly, waiting for him to supply her last name, but he was going about his business as if we didn't exist. The officer stood silently waiting for more. "I don't know her last name."

"And who are you?" He squinted at me from behind puffy cheeks.

"I'm Jessie Gallagher." He flipped the notebook open and started to scratch out a note. I spelled my name for him and then tried to explain how I'd come to find her body. After less than a minute of my babbling, he closed his notebook and stopped writing.

"I'm sure one of the detectives will want to take your statement when they get here." He looked over at Kip who was studiously ignoring him. "You too," he said. He stood for a minute, watching Kip gather up his small pile of biohazardous waste. "You two don't talk until they've taken your statements." Kip shoved the mess into a plastic produce bag and sealed it off with a triple knot before peeling off his pink gloves. A low whistle hummed from his pursed lips. I was pretty sure it was the ding-dong witch song.

The cop furrowed his pudgy face. "What's in that bag?"

"She cut herself by the dead body," said Kip. "This is probably full of dead body germs." He waved the bag towards the officer, who took a startled step back.

"Why don't you just set that down right there," he said, his hand reflexively moving to hover over his pistol.

"Really, it's just some gauze pads and Band-Aid wrappers," I chimed in, holding out my hand so he could see the nice new bandage. "I cut myself when I fell by the body."

The cop glanced towards the street, probably hoping his cohorts would get back and take us off his hands.

"Well, put it down right there. Don't touch it. One of the techs will pick it up."

I glanced at my watch; I was definitely going to be late for my rounds.

Across the street, one of the officers had reappeared and was having a conversation with his shoulder. Another patrol car pulled up, this one in no obvious hurry. They must have confirmed that Miriam was past the rushing stage. Our cop ambled away from us towards the action on the street.

"I'm going inside. Do you need anything?" Kip walked towards his back door, pinching his pink kitchen gloves between careful fingernails.

"No, I'm okay. I need to take Addie home and get going on my dog-walking rounds as soon as I can." Judging by the collection of cops gathering in the street and blocking in my car, I was going to be here a while.

An unearthly yowling shook the other side of the door.

"Okay, then. I guess I'll see you around." He hesitated as the yowling ratcheted up to a wild screech, followed by a thumping against the door.

"What is that?" I asked, catching sight of a flash of black, bursting into sudden view in the window and then disappearing again with another thump.

"Oh, that's just my cat," he said with a nervous laugh. "She doesn't like people much." The screech dropped to a lower, throaty sound that was somehow scarier. The hackles on Addie's back rose up in a black and white wave.

"Wow. I guess not. Well, good luck," I said, backing slowly up the driveway. I didn't want to be anywhere close if that thing burst out the door, and I was pretty sure that I couldn't outrun it. Visions of a spitting furball running up my leg and clawing its way to my hair ran through my mind. Better to go sit on the curb. Miriam was past the point of clawing my hair off.

The door slammed behind Kip, and I made my way to the street, walking as if invisible amongst the choreographed steps of the crime scene investigators and patrol cops as they ran through flawless routines.

A white Harris County Medical Examiner's Office van rolled slowly to a stop, maneuvering between a cruiser and my CR-V, effectively blocking me in completely. Two technicians got out, and I gave up on the thought that I was going anywhere in a hurry.

I walked a little ways up the street and sat down on the curb in front of Evan's next-door neighbor. Addie sat down next to me, seemingly content to just watch the activity. Pulling out my cell phone, I dialed Evan's work number.

"Evan Petty."

"Evan, it's me."

He dropped his voice and I could picture him hunching over the phone. "Are you there? Is my house okay?"

"Yeah, I guess you could say that."

"What do you mean?" he asked. "Did that looney-tooney break into my house again?"

I shifted the phone and examined the bandage on my hand. "I don't think so." I looked up at the collection of cops milling around Evan's front yard. "Did you know the whole garage is full of stuff? I think that lady was storing all her stuff in there. She might have even been sleeping in there."

"Jess, tell me what's going on. I can tell there's something."

"Yeah, you could say that. She won't be bothering you about your house anymore. She's dead. I found her body under the house." One of the patrol cars near me revved their engine and took off.

There was a profound silence on the other end. "Okay. That's great news," he finally said.

Great news? What was wrong with him?

"Evan, she's dead! That's not great news. What's wrong with you?"

"Well, right. Of course not. But at least now she can't do anything to my place." He still sounded way too cheerful. "Are they going to take her away?"

"I would assume the police will remove her." It was like I didn't even know him anymore.

"Okay, well, I've got to go get ready for a meeting. I'll give you a call later." He disconnected before I had time to say anything else. I needlessly poked at the disconnect button, irritated at his attitude. A woman was dead. Okay, sure, she seemed kind of crazy, but that didn't mean I wanted to see her dead.

The sun was warm on my face, and I closed my eyes, leaning into it. Around me, the sound of cars arriving and leaving mixed with the squawk of police radios. They never showed how long these things took on TV, and I wondered if I was looking at a thirty-minute delay or a three-hour delay. I'd give it another ten minutes and then I'd start looking for someone who could take my statement and get me out of here. I needed to get to my dogs.

This whole thing was so weird. How had Miriam gotten under the house? Did she crawl under and die? Or did someone kill her and stuff her under? It seemed like it would be hard to stuff a body under the house the way she'd been positioned. I was pretty sure I'd seen blood though, even though I was trying to suppress that. And she'd looked like a wet ragdoll.

"Ahem. Miss Gallagher?" My eyes flew open to shiny black shoes standing in front of me. I really needed to send Addie off to some kind of guard-dog training. Again, not a peep of warning out of her. Sunlight blinded me from behind the voice's head, and I shaded my eyes and lurched to my feet. My knee was sore from my fall, and I felt ungainly as I brushed dirt off my legs, feeling at a disadvantage with the sun still streaming like a blinding halo behind his head. I shifted a few feet so I could actually see into his face.

"Detective Raines." He held out a hand.

"Jessie Gallagher." We shook briefly.

"My partner and I are going to view the scene and then I'll be back to take your statement. You are the one who found the body, yes?"

"Yes, I am."

Detective Raines was well turned out in a crisp gray suit, pressed white shirt, and baseball covered tie. His haircut was laser-precise and gently gelled so each strand stayed perfectly in place. Dark circles beneath his eyes were the only jarring accent. "Do you know how long this is going to take? I have a dog-walking business, and I'm late for my rounds."

He gave me a level look and promised he'd get to me as quickly as possible. After he left, I was too restless to sit back down, so I walked Addie up and down the sidewalk of Evan's new block. Most of the houses were duplicate versions of Evan's, only his neighbors' didn't look like before pictures of demolition projects. A couple of the original structures had been knocked down and replaced by larger single-family homes that towered close to their property lines. That was probably what should have happened to Miriam's house. Only Evan had come along and stopped the natural selection process. And now that she was dead, he couldn't even sell it back to her.

Back at Evan's, the activity still swirled. A line of crime scene tape had been strung along the far side of the house, and white-booted technicians ducked back and forth under it. If Kip and I hadn't ruined any valuable footprints, this latest crowd surely had. A collapsible stretcher waited on the gravel driveway. I shoved my hands in my pockets and waited with it.

CHAPTER FOUR

I'd explained three times to Detective Raines why I had been poking around the backyard of a house I didn't own. If I was him, I would keep asking too. It just sounded so lame, even to me.

"What exactly did you think the previous homeowner was going to do to the house?" I saw his eyes flick to the saggy little structure.

"I don't know," I explained for the third time. "Someone had broken in through the back door, and Evan thought it was her and he thought she would do it again. He wanted me to check it out." It was the same thing I'd said the first two times.

He finally conceded I wasn't going to give him anything more on that point. I didn't have anything more to give him.

"What time did your friend leave here last night?" We'd also covered this.

"I don't know. I went home. He was going to the hardware store to get something to board up the window in the back door with."

He rocked back and forth on his heels, a quizzical look theatrically plastered to his face. "Can you tell me if Evan Petty had any more contact with the victim after you left here?"

"No, I'm sure he didn't. I mean, he would have said something." Right? I twisted an earring nervously. He had sounded so weird when he'd called me this morning, and again just a few minutes ago. The whole bit about checking this place out really had been odd. I didn't actually know whether or not he had seen Miriam. "I mean, he didn't say if he did or didn't."

"There was a witness who said they saw an altercation between the previous owner and someone on the front porch last night." I stared at him, not commenting. Surely he wasn't referring to Evan. "The victim was shoved to the ground during the altercation. Do you know anything about that?"

My mouth dropped open as I stared at him. Would Evan have assaulted the orange-haired woman? He had been really riled up about her. But shoving her to the ground? That didn't sound like Evan at all.

"I don't know anything about that. Evan wouldn't shove anyone. He's not like that at all." I didn't like where this was going. If Evan had had a run-in with her after I'd gone home, he would have mentioned it. Right?

Detective Raines stared at me for another few seconds. "Could you please tell me as closely as you can what exactly he said when he asked you to come over here this morning?" I was never going to get out of here.

I closed my eyes. "He said he needed a favor. He wanted me to come check his house to make sure"—I hesitated, not wanting to say "looney-tooney"—"that the woman who had accosted us hadn't broken in and done something." He wrote that down.

"So, you came over at what time?"

I glanced at my watch. "I guess it was a little before nine."

"You guess?" His tone was starting to irritate me. I glanced around, wondering where his partner had gone. Maybe I'd rather talk to him.

"Yes. I guess. I'm not sure exactly, I didn't check my watch."

I ran through my next steps: checking the front door, peering through the window, meeting Kip. Then I told him about checking the garage, being concerned about the vehicle in the backyard, and my final leg around the far side of the house. He didn't ask any more questions, so I started blowing past the details, feeling like I was boring him. His pen scratched away on his tiny notepad, however, and when I mentioned the part about Addie pulling on Miriam's body, the writing stopped and he looked up.

"You let your dog play tug-of-war with a dead body?" His voice was tight.

"Well, I didn't know she was pulling at a dead body. I was trying to figure out how Evan was going to keep that dumpster from breaking through his fence, so I wasn't really watching her that closely. *And,*" I continued, feeling defensive, "why would I think there was a body under the house? It's not like we've ever come across that before. Geez. You think I want the mouth that gives me kisses touching a dead body?"

I could tell by his look that he wasn't a dog-kiss kind of guy. He took a few more notes, then turned back a page. "So you fell forward, coming from the backyard towards the front?"

"Yes. Well, forward and sideways."

"And what happened then?"

"Well, my hand hurt and I noticed I had some glass in it, so I pulled that out. But then Addie was still pulling at something under the house and that's when I got down to see what she was doing. That's when she lost her grip and the one leg, um, Miriam's leg came out." A cool wind ran across my neck, and my shoulders twitched involuntarily.

"How did you know the victim's name, if you'd never met her before?"

"Kip told me what it was when we were talking." Detective Raines watched me intently. I could feel my breathing pick up, and for the first time, the reality of what had happened began sinking in. There really was a dead woman under Evan's house. A woman named Miriam, who'd presumably had a family. Someone, somewhere had loved her, and now she was dead. I took a deep breath. "I don't know what happened to her," I said in a smaller voice. "Was she killed? I guess she was killed. Did I see blood? I thought I might have seen blood."

The sun slipped behind a cloud, and I shoved my hands into my jacket pockets, the one still gripping Addie's leash. "We'll have to wait for the autopsy report to determine a definite cause of death."

"Oh, right." I glanced over at the guys with the stretcher. One of them lit up a cigarette, looking like he was settling in for the day. "So there was a chance that she just happened to die under there?" Maybe she'd crawled under the house for some bizarre reason and had a heart attack or something. That seemed better than being murdered.

"When you fell, how did you land?" Clearly, he wasn't going to tell me anything.

"I fell forward onto my hands and mostly this knee." I

held out my hand to show him my bandaged cut. The mud on my knees spoke for itself.

"We're going to need to get a print of your shoes before you go. And they'll probably be taking some samples from your dog. One of the techs can do that when they're through."

"How long is that going to take?" I was bordering on whining, but really. I have responsibilities.

"We'll get you out of here as soon as possible. Please continue with what you did next."

"I looked under the house. I've only seen Miriam once before, last night when Evan was showing me around. But I recognized her shoes and her outfit."

"Did you move the body?"

"I didn't. But, Addie was pulling at her pretty hard. I'm pretty sure she moved her." The guys with the gurney were heading around the side of the house. A cloud of smoke trailed after them. "Then I ran and got Kip, who was still on the front porch."

"He didn't walk around the house with you?"

"No. He stayed on the front porch."

"So, he was never around on the side?"

"Well, he didn't walk around the house with me. But after I found her and I came around the front to call the police, he wanted to go see for himself."

Detective Raines went still. "He went to see?" I shrugged. The detective sighed. "Did he touch anything?"

"I think he poked a finger in the mud when he squatted down to balance himself. And he shook her leg too." His lips were getting tighter and tighter. I looked away, fiddling with a potty bag in my pocket while he scratched furiously at his notepad. I didn't have much to add after that, so he double-checked all my contact information, took down Evan's full name and contact numbers and stalked back to his crime scene. The one that Addie, Kip and I had ruined. I had the feeling that I would be delayed even longer as punishment.

Some of the patrol cars had left, the officers having seen everything there was to see. There was a tempting opening just behind my car, which, if I maneuvered carefully, I might be able to get through. I could drop Addie at home and get to my first dog client in twenty minutes or so. I was ready for some furry love. But I'm a play-by-the-ruler at heart, so instead I leaned against my bumper and took to checking my watch every three minutes. I passed the time trying to come up with housewarming gifts for Evan. I came up with a few ideas, but nothing seemed right. It was hard to shop for someone who had everything. It was even harder to shop for someone who needed so much.

My fingers and toes were getting cold long before I finally spied a police tech with a camera around his neck and a plastic bag in his hand, come around the side of the house. I walked towards him, intent on getting my shoes printed or whatever they needed to do to them, and getting the heck out of there.

"Excuse me," I said, hurrying towards him. "Detective Raines said I needed to get my shoes printed or something before I left. And I don't know, he said something about samples from my dog too. I wasn't sure what he meant by that. Can you help me?"

He kept walking towards a white van, ignoring me like I was an annoying groupie trying to get between him and his tour bus.

"Okay, if it's not you, could you tell me who can help me? I really need to get going. I've got a bunch of dogs waiting for me to walk them. I really need to get to my rounds."

"Dog walker, huh? The shit you deal with's gotta be better than the shit I deal with." He threw open the back door of the van and hoisted his bag into a plastic bin. I glanced inside and looked quickly away, afraid I would see something that would bring on a fainting spell.

"I'm sure," I said, noticing the strained look around his eyes. He couldn't even be thirty yet, but he looked worn around the edges.

"You're the one that played tug of war with the body?"

"I didn't. That would be her." I waved a finger at Addie.

He lifted his camera. "Let me get a few shots of your clothes while we're here. We'll probably be able to match up the mud prints with the impressions we got from where you landed. Then we'll see about the dog."

I felt foolish as I posed for multiple pictures. Once he got going with his camera, he really got going. Pictures of my tights. Pictures of my knees. Pictures of my hands, with and without my new Band-Aid. In case my cut matched up to anything on the victim, I guess. He even dabbed at my hands with cotton swabs before picking his camera back up. And finally pictures of my shoes, both on and off my feet. I was probably lucky he didn't insist on taking all my clothes away in plastic bags as evidence.

Next, he started on Addie. He stuck a swab in her mouth, did a quick rub side to side and pulled it back out before she could bite it off. I wasn't sure why, and I hoped they weren't going to try to pin this on her. Then he brushed some of her hair into a plastic bag and scraped some tape across the bottom of her feet. She doesn't like people touching her feet and she kept jerking them away every time he picked one up. By the time he brought his camera around to get pictures of her teeth, she'd had enough.

"Could you pull her lips back so I can get a picture?" he asked me.

I felt like her. I'd had enough too. I half-heartedly pulled one lip back, exposing a row of strong white teeth. We did both sides, then he asked me to hold her mouth open so he could get a shot that way. Addie clamped her jaws together, and after a short tussle and a lot of camera flashes, the tech seemed to lose interest. I asked if it was okay for me to leave.

"Beats me. I don't need you anymore." That was enough for me. I slipped into my car and turned over the engine, half expecting Detective Raines to come flying after me. I spent an embarrassing few minutes executing a thousand-point turn, but really, if I hit a cop car, I was never going to get out of there.

I was already running late for my dog rounds, and the extra time I needed to take Addie home wasn't going to help. I raced down Montrose towards the museum district. If I hit the lights just right, I could be to my first client's house in West University in about twenty minutes. The first light I hit turned red right before I got there. Great. I glanced at myself in the rearview mirror. Holy heavens. I looked like I'd taken a wild ride on the Tilt-A-Whirl without a restraining device. What had happened to my hair? I tucked some strands behind my ears, but it didn't make much difference. Mud streaked across one cheek, and bits of dried leaves crusted under my chin. Good thing my clients were dogs; they usually didn't care how I looked. A honk from behind set me moving again.

Luckily the lights worked in my favor the rest of the way, and I raced into my driveway, got Addie out of the car, into the house and was back on the road in minutes.

Nelson was my first client, an elderly retriever with a

stately air. I loved him as my own, and I tried desperately not to notice his increasing lameness. He was proud in a way that touched my heart, so during our daily walks, I adjusted my steps to his, and if we only made it to the corner and back in our thirty-minute timeframe, so be it.

He was sitting at the door when I got there, and my heart ached that I'd kept him waiting. His owner left for work early, and generally when I got there, he was more than ready to head outside. He wagged briefly at me, before hurrying out the door. Once he'd visited the nearest bush, he turned his attention back to me. He ran his nose gently up and down my legs, my arms, and finally settled on a spot near my right ear. Sniffling and snorting, he brushed his soft muzzle against the side of my face, conducting a full inspection. And here I thought my clients wouldn't notice my disheveled appearance.

It was much the same at the rest of my stops. Apparently I was a treasure trove of scents, the likes of which these guys hadn't smelled before. My lateness was instantly forgiven when they sniffed the odors wafting from my body. I couldn't smell anything, but by the time I got to my sixth dog, I was getting paranoid about what exactly they were smelling. Kip might have washed my hand, but something else seemed to be all over the rest of me. If it wasn't so chilly, I might have taken a hose to myself. As it was, I could barely wait to get home and into a hot shower. Just two more dogs and I'd be done for the day.

Just as I thought I might make it through the day without anyone seeing what a mess I was, I walked into the next house. "Whoa, what happened to you?" a voice croaked from the couch. I jumped, not expecting anyone but Blue, the active Siberian Husky that I walked every day, to be there. I'd only met Blue's owner, Dan, once—the day he'd hired me. He shouldn't be home in the middle of the afternoon.

My hands flew reflexively towards my ratty hair, and I smoothed it back to no effect. Then I noticed how terrible he looked.

"Oh, I didn't expect anyone to be here." He was lying on the couch, a plaid blanket pulled up around his chin, and an assortment of sickroom items clustered on the coffee table in front of him. "Whoa, what happened to you?" I echoed.

He gave a feeble laugh and coughed into a wadded-up tissue. "I think I have the flu." Blue sat placidly at his side, head within inches of his owner's hand. "Somehow I think your story might be better."

He'd collapsed back against his pillows, but his eyes were still traveling over me, halfway crinkled with amusement. I took no comfort in that. What I had seen in the twenty square inches of rearview mirror had been bad enough. I glanced down at the front of me and brushed vigorously at a mud stain on my jacket. Nope, it wasn't coming out quite that easy. Blue moseyed over and began an intense investigation of my knees, just like all the dogs before him had.

"I think you've got a stick in your hair." I brushed back what remained of my ponytail, and felt a rough twig snarled towards the back.

"Oh, geez." A warm heat crept up my neck, no doubt mottling my skin, as if I didn't look bad enough already. He was still watching me like a kid waiting for story time. Only I wasn't sure how he'd feel about having someone who fell over bodies having a key to his house. "It was something stupid," I said, glancing around the room to avoid his intense stare.

"Trouble with a dog?"

"No. No, nothing like that." Blue was focused on my shoes now, his nose snuffling up the dust from the laces. "Just a little mishap at a friend's house. I'm really sorry I'm late."

"Oh, don't worry about it. He's fine. I'd ask if I could get you something, but it took me most of the day just to make it this far. Although, you look like you could use a drink. Or a bath." He tried to smile again, but I could see he'd used up what energy he had.

"Okay, I guess I ought to get Blue out."

"Yeah, thanks." He closed his eyes and looked like he might die while I was gone. I hooked Blue's leash on and dashed out the door. The last thing I needed was to catch what he had.

Blue and I raced up and down the streets of his neighborhood as I tried to burn off his excess energy. Even though Dan was currently the color of plumbing putty, I'd been jolted as I remembered how good looking he was. Okay, maybe not right this second, but still. I tried to think of something witty to say when I took Blue back in, but I couldn't think of a thing.

Thirty minutes later, I'd only come up with, "Okay, hope you feel better," but when we went in, the couch was empty except for a few dozen tissues and the crumpled blanket. I unhooked Blue's leash from his collar and slipped out the back door.

My last stop was thankfully uneventful, and I was home a little before five, feeling wrung out and exhausted. I could tell I'd woken Addie up from a good nap. She'd probably been sleeping since I'd dropped her off earlier. She came over and began sniffing at my shoes as if she'd forgotten our adventure this morning.

"I think you and I need to get cleaned up, Addie."

Addie hated baths, but the thought of her under the house with Miriam's body made me immune to the sad face she turned my way when she realized the bath was meant for her. I lathered her up with her best organic lavender shampoo and rinsed her twice, dog hair swirling around the hair trap I'd placed over the drain. After drying her off, I went to work on her teeth with her chicken-flavored doggie toothpaste.

Once she was done and the tub was clean again, I scrubbed myself under a hot shower, but tension still knotted the muscles in my shoulders and neck, and my hand was throbbing from my cut. Maybe a nice glass of wine and a hot soak would do the trick. I trotted downstairs for a glass of sauvignon blanc while the tub filled with steamy water. Addie stared at me with the look of a dog that hadn't been fed in three weeks, so I filled her bowl and carried everything upstairs to my bedroom.

I sank into the steamy water while Addie poked her head into her bowl and began picking out tasty crunchies. I lay back, closed my eyes and tried to clear my mind. The rhythmic sound of Addie's chewing was soothing. Crunch crunch crunch crunch swallow. Crunch crunch crunch crunch swallow. As she picked her way through the bowl piece by piece, I found myself counting along to the beat. My breathing slowed and I took a long sip of wine.

A vision of Miriam's leg flopping into view pushed into my mind, and I pushed it out. *Focus on your muscles relaxing. Slow breaths. In and out. In and out.* Dan's warm eyes danced into my mind, and I didn't push that thought out. Had I not noticed how attractive he was when I first met him? I couldn't remember. How could I not remember?

Frances, my grandmother, had insisted I take on some

dog-walking clients when I'd first started my gourmet dog biscuit company. She felt that it wasn't good for me to be cooped up alone everyday rolling out dog treats, and this also generated some cash until my business was up and running. It had only been a few months, and slowly but steadily my sales were picking up on the biscuits. My days were full with baking, packaging, finding new distribution channels, walking my doggie clients and spending time with Addie. At some point, I might have to give up some of my walking clients to focus more time on keeping up with sales, but so far, I'd been able to balance both.

But back to Dan. If I recalled correctly, he was the grandson of one of Frances's friends. They'd put me in touch with him, we'd talked on the phone to arrange the terms of Blue's walks, and I'd swung by to meet Blue and pick up the key on a Saturday afternoon. How had I not noticed his gorgeous eyes? I vividly recalled seeing Blue trot across the backyard when I'd arrived, admiring his beautiful eyes, his luscious gray coat and his long, lanky legs. His mouth was open in a friendly smile and his tail waved good-naturedly over his muscled flanks. Dan, I'd barely noticed. What was wrong with me that I would pay more attention to a dog than his gorgeous owner?

I was just trying to figure out how I could pry some information out of Frances about him without raising any flags when the doorbell rang. Addie ran to the top of the stairs and barked. Good dog. I closed my eyes. *Go away*, I thought. *Whoever you are, go away.*

After the third ring, when the banging started, I realized whoever it was wasn't going away. I flung myself dripping from the tub, ran a towel up and down and pulled on some sweats. "Stop it! I'm coming!" I shouted. Good grief. I pounded down the stairs, Addie running ahead. I flung open the front door without even looking through the peephole. That kind of obnoxious behavior could only be one person —Larry.

Larry was my next-door neighbor, and I'd had some trouble with him before. He had his finger pressed against the doorbell and was beating on the door with his opposite hand. He nearly fell across the threshold when I opened the door.

"What are you doing?" I shouted at him, irritation filling me. So much for my relaxing bath.

He pushed past me and flung himself down on my new couch. I'd had to throw my old couch out after a particularly nasty incident with Larry a few months ago. Addie stood across the coffee table from him, hackles raised and a low growl rumbling in her throat. I felt like that myself.

"Did you call the homeowner's association about my signs?"

"No." Last week, Larry had stuck a parade of No Pooping signs along the small yard that fronted his house. There were probably twenty signs along a fifteen-foot stretch.

"Well, someone did, and I don't appreciate it." He stuck a hand down the front of his sweatpants and scratched at something out of sight. I gave an involuntary shudder. "It's my property and I have the right to put up any signs I want."

"It wasn't me. Is that all you came for?"

He wiggled his bottom further into the soft cushion. "And what gives you dog owners the right to let your dogs take a dump anywhere they want?" He squinted his eyes at Addie, as if she were to blame for all his doggie doo problems. She squinted back, pinning him against the couch with her full-on Border collie stare. He squirmed and looked away.

I sighed. Larry and I had been down this road before. I was apparently the only dog owner he knows, so he tended to take out his frustrations on me.

"No one has the right to leave dog poop in your yard. Houston has a leash law, so no, they can't just leave it, they have to pick it up."

"But they don't! I'm telling you, since I put the signs up it's gotten even worse." He sighed and rolled his flabby belly sideways, throwing one soft leg over the other. Another couple of minutes and he'd have his feet up and be asking for a beer.

"Well, I'm sorry about that. Maybe if you catch them in the act, they'll pick up." Oh, wait. He'd tried that approach a couple of months ago. In fact, he'd set traps for the offenders. The neighborhood certainly didn't need a repeat of that. "Anyway, I don't want to keep you."

"Don't worry. You're not keeping me from anything." He sank down a little farther. "Hey, you got any beer?"

"No."

"You got anything to eat? I don't really have anything at my house."

"No." Did I just say that? I don't have food? I was raised better than that. I rubbed a hand over my eyes. "I mean, I have some food, but I'm really tired and I've had a long day and I found a dead body, so I just really want to relax and go to bed early."

He rolled his eyes and blew out an exasperated breath. "Dude, fine. Whatever. What kind of food do you have? I'll just take it with me."

I threw a can of Chunky soup (expiration date about a year and a half ago), a frozen bag of corn, and an opened bag of Fig Newtons that I didn't even remember buying into a plastic grocery bag and shoved it at his chest.

"Okay, here you go. This should get you through the night." He gave a dramatic sigh and lurched to his feet. "Oh, and make sure you boil the soup really well before you eat it." I didn't really like Larry, but I wasn't out to kill him either.

"Great. Thanks." He shuffled to the door, his sweatpants wedged into the crack of his bottom. "If you find out who complained about my signs, I'd appreciate if you'd let me know." Thrusting out a hip, he reached around and worked vigorously to clear his wedgie before walking out the door. Just one more thing burned into my brain, threatening nightmares for the night.

CHAPTER FIVE

The next morning Evan called, just as I was gearing up for my dog-walking rounds.

"Hey." He sounded flat and tired. "I need you to do me a favor."

Oh boy. "Like what?" I really didn't feel up to any favors.

"I've got an inspector coming to the house this afternoon, and I don't think I'll be able to get there in time. Do you think you could go by and let him in?"

The annoying thing about having your own business is that people think you're available at any time to do things for them. I didn't want to go to the house.

"What time's he coming?"

"He's supposed to be there at three. I would be there, but I've got a meeting I can't get out of. I just need you to let him in." He paused. "Oh, and I need you to come get the key. I can't leave the office." I rolled my head around, feeling the tension building in my neck muscles.

We agreed that I'd come pick up his key now. It was pushing it, expecting me to meet the inspector at three and still have time for all my clients. If I skipped lunch and raced from one house to the next, I could probably just make it. My mood was not improving.

I'd worn something cute, hoping that Dan would still be home and feeling a little better, but when I got to his house, Blue came trotting out from the bedroom alone. Judging by the additional dirty dishes on the coffee table, Dan was still home, but probably sleeping. Blue and I took our walk, and then he disappeared back into the quiet bedroom when I brought him back inside. I was disproportionately disappointed but didn't have time to hang around.

By the time I got to Evan's house, it was three fifteen, my blood sugar level was falling, and my mood was falling with it. Hungry and tired is not a good combination for me. Luckily, the inspector wasn't there yet, so I let myself in. Maybe being able to take a fresh look around without the pressure of Evan's watchful gaze would make things look better.

I wandered through the living room, squinting at the harsh wallpaper. Okay, wallpaper is an easy fix. And the floors really could be nice with some work. So the living room wasn't a total write-off. The kitchen, on the other hand, would have to be gutted. The sagging ceiling was even worse than I remembered. One small poke could bring the whole thing down. The floors were crusty with grime and curled away from the baseboards like rotted lemon peels. I marveled that Evan had seen this room and still made an offer. Of course, I'd seen his apartment, and cleanliness wasn't his strongest character trait. But still, this went beyond disgusting.

I backed away from the kitchen, wondering when the inspector was going to show up. This place made me feel claustrophobic. A small laundry room opened off the kitchen, and I stepped in to check it out. At least Evan would have a place to do laundry. It was something. The washer and dryer looked moderately new, so hopefully they worked, and he could at least save on that expense. A small window looked out at the taqueria over the fence. An employee stood outside the back door, smoking a cigarette and talking on his cell phone, and as I watched, another employee came out with a bulging bag full of garbage and heaved it into the dumpster. I wondered if Miriam had stood at this window watching the goings-on in the alley. A sudden chill swept across my arms. Probably a gaping hole in the wall somewhere.

There was so much work that needed to be done around here. I wondered how much Evan had budgeted for repairs and remodeling. The main bedroom was by far the best room in the house. The windows overlooked the driveway and backyard, letting in a lot of natural light. And the ceiling didn't look at all like it was going to collapse. I opened the door to the closet before remembering the inhabitants. Dozens of eyes glinted at me from the dark, and I slammed the door shut. Evan was going to have to do something with those dolls. The thought crossed my mind that maybe they killed Miriam, and I hurried back towards the front of the house, impatient for the inspector to get there.

The screech of a branch against the window made me jump. I might have even let out a small shriek. This just wasn't like me. I'm usually so steady. Something about the vibes in this house made my nerves tingle.

I looked out the front window—no sign of the inspector yet. I paced from window to window, imagining what it had been like for Miriam living here. I really didn't know anything about her except that she'd been inordinately fond of this house. Just goes to show, there's no accounting for taste.

As I waited, a low-riding red Mustang screeched to a stop in front of the house next door. The passenger door flew open and a slender teen extracted herself from the depths of the car. She was dressed entirely in formless black clothes that hung in limp folds from her bony frame. Her hair was a shocking shade of pink, and her face looked as if someone had recently sucked all the blood out of her body. She turned suddenly, staring in my direction, and I wondered if she could see me. Feeling unaccountably like a peeper, I drew back towards the shadows of the room.

Within seconds, the car peeled out, and I took another glance around the window. The girl was standing stock-still, continuing to stare. I felt foolish, so I popped out the front door and onto the porch. Might as well be neighborly, even though these weren't my neighbors. I waved and called, "Hi!" but she just narrowed her eyes at me and went up the walk, banging the door behind her as she went in.

Okay, then. I sat down on the front steps. Better to wait outside anyway. If I hadn't had my jeans on, I would never have risked being impaled on the bottom by a giant wood splinter, but as it was, it felt good to sit down. I'd just closed my eyes to review my mental to-do list when I heard a diesel engine. Finally.

But when I looked up, it wasn't an inspector but a small shuttle bus. This one said "Sunny Ridge Senior Center" across the side, and as I watched, it pulled up in front of the house, hitting the curb and nearly taking off the back bumper of my car. I leaped to my feet, cringing as I waited for the crunch of collapsing metal. Instead, the bus stopped with a squeak, and a bevy of waving arms flapped at me from inside.

I squinted at the tinted windows, trying to make sense of this. Finally, the door swung open and Kip emerged from the driver's seat, decked out in a black striped suit, gray fedora, and chipper red ascot. He clapped his hands together and gave a little squeal of delight as I approached.

"We are in luck today, ladies and gentlemen! This is the one who *actually found the body*!" He flung his arm towards me as if presenting the world's most amazing dancing bear. A chorus of clapping and cheering greeted me, and the little bus bounced on its wheels. I took a step back and gave a small wave.

"What is this?" I asked Kip as, from within the bus, the small crowd surged forward.

"Be careful!" he called, rushing to catch a thick-set older woman as she missed the first step off the bus. "This is the first ever Miriam Murder Tour, courtesy of yours truly!"

"You might want to rephrase that," I told him as he helped the rest of his group off the bus. There were six in all, five women and one small man. Every one of them was beaming with excitement and fully loaded with all sorts of paraphernalia. As they gathered around me, two of them pulled cameras out and began snapping pictures of me, the flashes causing spots to dance in my vision.

"This is Jessie..." Kip paused, clearly forgetting my last name.

"Gallagher," I said.

"This is Jessie Gallagher. She's the one that found Miriam dead under the house yesterday." There was a smattering of applause and a few more pictures. "Jessie, I'd like you to meet my grammy and her friends." He led a tiny woman in a floral house dress and a thick cable knit sweater forward. She shook my hand with bones so fragile I feared I would break one. Her eyes were bright, and her white hair even brighter. An oversized patchwork tote hung from her shoulder, bulging with what looked like a bowling ball. I was surprised she had the strength to haul around something that heavy.

"It's a pleasure, dear. My Kip told us all about how brave you were yesterday." She patted me gently on the arm, and a warm feeling swelled in my chest, like I'd done something more noble than find a dead woman.

"This is Miss Potts." Miss Potts was taller than Grammy, but equally bony. She wore a thick purple suit, bisected by a wide belt that made her resemble an ant. I tried not to stare at the headlamp that protruded from the middle of her forehead. Maybe they were going spelunking after their murder tour. She flashed wide teeth at me and waved awkwardly.

"Mr. McNeil." Kip waved a hand at the only man of the group. Mr. McNeil grunted a little by way of greeting but was really too busy trying to fit a round metal disk onto the bottom of his cane.

"Hi," I said. Mr. McNeil didn't look up.

A short chunky woman rolled a neon red walker past Mr. McNeil, nearly knocking him over.

"I'm Esther Staskywicz. It's a real pleasure to meet you. Miriam has been a pain in our patooties for years. I just wish I could have seen her under the house with her legs sticking out." I didn't bother to tell her that just one leg had been sticking out. And that only after Addie had pulled it out. She barked out a laugh and turned towards Kip. "Do it again, sweetie. Sing that song for us."

"Maybe later." He looked embarrassed.

Mr. McNeil began rumbling in a raspy voice, "Ding-dong, the witch is dead. Which old witch? The wicked witch."

"Not you. Kip does it better," said Mrs. Staskywicz, waving a hand to shush him.

"And finally, we have Mrs. Liddell and Mrs. Johnston," said Kip, presenting the last two members of his party. Mrs. Liddell was decked out in a pink polyester pantsuit that made her look like a popsicle. She had a bulging fanny pack strapped to her waist and a pair of binoculars and a camera dangling from her neck. Mrs. Johnston was a little thicker and wore a mint-colored sweat suit mostly covered by a long black trench coat. She dragged a wheeled suitcase behind her. No telling what she had in there. All in all, this group looked like they were ready for anything.

"Okay, gang. Listen up," said Kip, clapping his hands to get their attention. "We're going to follow the path that Jessie followed yesterday on her journey of discovery." But like a group of unruly kindergartners, no one was paying him the slightest attention. They wandered off singly and in pairs. Mr. McNeil, having finished his cane project, produced a heavy-duty set of earphones from somewhere and began wandering towards the far side of the driveway. It finally dawned on me that his cane was actually a metal detector. Mrs. Johnston pulled her suitcase across the uneven yard behind him, struggling to keep it upright, and Mrs. Staskywicz pushed her walker gamely along behind.

"Mr. McNeil. Mrs. Johnston." Kip's voice rose as he tried to get through to his errant members. "Mrs. Staskywicz, please! This way! The tour is going this way."

But either they couldn't hear him or they were choosing not to, because they continued across the rocky yard towards the far side of the house.

"That's not the way she went," screamed Kip. "You've got to come this way! The tour is going this way!"

I felt a little sorry for him, and I guess the others did too, because the remaining three lined up dutifully and followed him as he walked slowly backwards down the pitted driveway to the backyard. "Well, I would have gone with her, of course, had I known she was going to find a body. Not that I'm into 'finding bodies.'" He gave a giggle as he bracketed the phrase with his fingers. "But I wouldn't have let her go alone. Although, to be fair, she did have that dog with her."

Murmurs of encouragement seemed to soothe his frustration with the other tour members, and I could hear him getting more animated as they disappeared around towards the backyard. I considered following along, curious as to his take on yesterday's events, but a white pickup cruised slowly past, pulling alongside the curb next door. Finally, the inspector.

He stopped at least fifteen feet before he reached me, staring open-mouthed at the house behind me.

"You bought this?" he asked.

"Oh, no! Not me," I said, mortified that he would even think that. "My friend Evan did."

He glanced down at his clipboard. "Evan Petty, right?" He looked up at the house again. "Wow."

"I know." We both stood staring for a few moments. I could hear Kip's group getting rowdy in the backyard, and the back end of Mrs. Staskywicz was just disappearing around the corner. "Where do you want to start? There's actually a little tour going on in the backyard right now."

"A tour?" He looked at me like his day just couldn't get better than this.

"Yes. Well, I actually found a body under the house

yesterday, and the guy across the street brought his grand-mother and some of her friends over on a 'murder tour.'" He started taking notes in the margin of his form. "You're not writing that down, are you?" It struck me belatedly that maybe I shouldn't have mentioned that. But what the heck? It wasn't really like I could make this any worse than it already was.

"I have the feeling I'm going to be taking a lot of notes at this place." He seemed like a guy who loved his job. At least one of us was having a good time. "So someone was murdered here?"

"I'm not actually sure how she died. It was the previous owner."

"She probably got an estimate on what it would take to bring this place up to code." He took a couple more notes. "I'll start on the roof. Work my way top to bottom. I think I'll probably be here awhile." He headed back towards his truck. "Too bad your friend didn't call me before he closed."

That's what I thought too. I left him to gather his gear and went towards the backyard to see how the tour was progressing. I could hear the commotion before I even rounded the corner.

"Let me see it! I saw it first."

"No, you didn't. Mr. McNeil found it, it's his."

"Ouch! You rolled over my foot. Do you have to take that suitcase everywhere we go? Does she have to take that suit-case everywhere we go? It's a nuisance."

And finally Kip's voice, competing for control. "Okay, folks! Why don't you let me through here? I'll hold it and we can take turns looking at it."

The group was bunched together, close to where I'd fallen over Miriam. Mrs. Staskywicz brought up the rear, struggling to get her walker over the uneven ground. "Let me through. Let me through." Like a battering ram, she jammed the wheels into the back of Kip's legs, trying to get past him.

"Please, people. Let's calm down and take turns. Mr. McNeil, let me see what you've found."

"Oh, it's probably nothing but an old bottle cap," muttered Mrs. Liddell. Or was that Mrs. Johnston? Pink popsicle, I think it was Mrs. Liddell. She pushed her way past the crowd and back into the yard.

"Mr. McNeil, if you let me hold it, then everyone can take a look." The headphones had been knocked askew on Mr. McNeil's head, and he glowered at Kip, clutching his treasure tightly in his palm.

"You can hold it when I'm darned ready for you to hold it, sonny."

"Oh, just give me that," said Mrs. Staskywicz, shoving her walker forward again and reaching for Mr. McNeil's hand.

"You get away too!" said Mr. McNeil, swinging his metal detector in front of him. Unfortunately for Kip, he was standing between them, and I saw the round metal end connect solidly with his shin.

"Oh! Ow!" He hobbled sideways, falling against the fence. "Ow!" The fence sagged under his weight, and I was sure he was going to fall through, but he managed to grab a handle of the walker on the way down and caught himself. Mrs. Staskywicz wasn't so fortunate—down she went falling on her well-padded fanny.

We all rushed forward to help her up, and Mr. McNeil took the opportunity to race away, tucking the metal object into his front pants pocket.

The ladies seemed to be setting Mrs. Staskywicz to rights, so I made my way over to Kip, who stood alone, rubbing his shin. His jaunty smile was gone, and I thought I saw tears welling at the corners of his eyes.

"Your tour seems a little out of control," I said.

"You noticed?" He glanced sideways at me. "I wondered why the activities director was so hesitant to let me take them out."

We looked over to his group, which seemed to have settled down. Mr. McNeil had righted his headphones and was moving slowly along the fence line. Mrs. Staskywicz roosted on the seat of her walker, watching him, her heavy brows drawn together. I had the feeling she was plotting how to get the metal object from him. Two of the ladies had opened the suitcase and extracted a measuring tape, a sketch pad and a fistful of colorful markers. One was measuring distances from various points and calling off numbers to the other one, who was designing a complicated diagram on the sketch pad.

"They seem like they're having a good time," I said. "It's probably way better than what the activities director usually plans."

"It is a good idea, isn't it?" He looked around. "And we haven't even hit the highlight of the tour yet—where Miriam's body was found. Do you think you could tell them about how you found her? It would really mean a lot to them."

"Was Miriam a member of the senior center?"

"Well, she came to some of the activities. Like my grammy. Grammy goes on Tuesdays for painting, and Wednesdays for scrapbooking. Thursday they usually have a potluck lunch that's a big hit. And Fridays they play canasta. And of course the computer room is always open. Grammy likes to go early because it gets crowded. She's started her own blog."

"Really? That's great. You'll have to give me a link to her website, I'd love to read it."

I heard a scraping noise on the roof and saw the inspector inching his way along on hands and knees, tapping the shingles in front of him before easing his weight forward. You'd never get me up there.

"I've got to tell Grammy you want to read her blog! She's trying to increase her readership, but so far it's been a little slow. She's going to be so excited!" He looked across the backyard. "Grammy? Grammy!" Kip took off at a trot. "Where is she?"

I did a quick head count but only saw five. Lord, if one of them fell, we'd have to call out Texas EquuSearch to find them in these weeds.

CHAPTER SIX

"Grammy? Grammy!" Kip yelled, sounding more like a glee club girl than a grown man. The other seniors stopped what they were doing and stared at Kip.

"Did we lose someone?" asked Miss Potts, reaching up and turning on her headlamp. "Where did you see her last?"

"She's around front," said the inspector from the roof. "Saw her go that way a couple of minutes ago."

Kip raced around the corner and I followed at a slower pace. I figured the odds of him returning everyone to the senior center in one piece was sitting at about fifty percent.

But before I even turned the corner, Kip had gotten out in front and was herding Grammy towards the backyard. His arms stretched out to either side, fingers wiggling as he shooed her along in front of him, the gay man's version of a full court press. Grammy clutched her tote bag to her chest as if the weight were becoming too much to handle. For a moment, I thought I saw the bag move as if something was trying to kick its way out, but that thought raced out of my head when I heard Evan's voice behind me.

"What the hell is this?" His fair cheeks flamed red and his straight dark hair fell uncombed over his forehead. His normally wrinkled work khakis looked even worse than usual, and his shirttail half protruded from his waistband.

"Hi, Evan," I said cheerfully, trying to distract him from the crowd of seniors milling around his backyard. "How was work?"

His eyes had settled on Mr. McNeil and he squinted, trying to make sense of what he was looking at.

"The inspector is here," I said, continuing on like nothing was happening. "He's up there on the roof." I waved a hand vaguely above my head. It was enough to distract him momentarily.

"Hey there," hollered the inspector. I guessed he could hear pretty well from his perch. "I'm almost finished up here. We can go over what I'm seeing when I come down."

"How's it looking?" Evan asked.

"Well, how about we talk about it in a few minutes after I'm finished?" His hesitation struck me as a very bad sign. But then again, what did I really expect? I was surprised he hadn't already fallen through.

"So, I guess I'll be going, then, since you made it." I was still worried about what he would do to Kip's murder tour, but really, I was sure Kip could handle it. Okay, maybe not, but I was going home anyway.

Evan turned his gaze back to the seniors. "Who are these people?" he asked me in a slightly calmer voice.

"The guy in the black suit with the red ascot is your neighbor Kip Willetto."

He shot me a look. "Ascot?"

"The others are his grandmother and some of her friends."

"What are they doing here?"

I stole a glance around. No telling what they were doing at this point. Miss Potts came over and knelt beside us, shining her headlamp into the dimness of the crawlspace.

"Is this where you found her?" she asked me, shifting awkwardly. Her skirt was really too tight for her to be crawling around on all fours.

"No, actually she was around the far side, over that way." I put out a hand to help her back to her feet. She brushed off her knees and trotted off.

Luckily, I was saved from Evan's death stare by a sudden commotion on the far side of the yard. I had the same feeling you get when you see an accident about to happen, when everything shifts into slow motion, but there's nothing you can do about it. I watched, as if removed.

Mrs. Liddell was screaming at the top of her lungs and running towards us as fast as her comfort-soled shoes could carry her. The binoculars and camera slammed against her chest as she ran. Mrs. Johnston had abandoned her suitcase and had hauled herself up onto the seat of Mrs. Staskywicz's walker, while Mrs. Staskywicz pulled on a handle with one hand and tried to push her friend off with the other. Miss Potts had disappeared around the far side of the house, with Kip hard on her heels. I think he was shrieking the loudest.

But what really caught my attention was Grammy. She stood solidly on her little bird legs, trying to control her now out-of-control patchwork bag. Something in the bag was yowling and fighting to get out. She finally lost the battle, and a gray cat burst from the bag, pushing off against her chest like a sprinter bursting from his blocks at the sound of the starter pistol. He raced across the yard to where Mr. McNeil stood near the fence, beating his metal detector against a thick stand of weeds.

"I gotcha, you giant bastard!" Mr. McNeil shouted. The cat stopped short of the swinging metal detector and crouched immobile, his eyes focused on something I couldn't make out. Finally, from out of the weeds, a giant rat rumbled toward a hole in the fence. His thick, greasy body moved with an easier grace than you'd expect from something that huge. I felt a scream rise up in my throat, and I nearly made a break for Mrs. Staskywicz's walker, sure I could knock both women out of my way in order to climb up on the seat.

The cat turned and raced away from the rat. He ran straight to Grammy, who had been warbling, "Howard! Howard!" in a thin, reedy voice over the din. He clawed his way up her floral housedress to her shoulder, where he perched, hissing and spitting.

Mr. McNeil gave chase after the rat, still swinging. "I'm gonna get you, you giant varmint!" I had to give him credit. Mr. McNeil was the only one not frightened out of his wits by that thing. Next to me, Evan had gone white-faced. His jaw hung open, and he clutched at his chest like he might be experiencing a heart attack.

Finally, the rat pushed its way through the opening and disappeared from sight. Probably back to the dumpster and its mutant family and friends.

"I gotta tell you, that's one of the biggest rats I've ever seen," said the inspector from the roof. "My God! It had to weigh at least three or four pounds." Evan still hadn't moved. "You know, I hate to tell you this, but where there's one, there's bound to be more."

Mr. McNeil had given up the chase but was clearly

buoyed up by the experience. I had the feeling he was enjoying this tour more than the others.

"Did you see that thing?" he shouted to no one in particular. "Reminds me of the ones we used to see in Korea. Not as big as the ones we had over there. No, not by a long shot. Did I ever tell you about the time I woke up with a rat as big as a dog sitting on my chest?" He was making his way over to Mrs. Staskywicz and Mrs. Johnston.

"I told you we'd see a giant beast," said Mrs. Johnston. "I told you this morning."

"It's true," said Mrs. Staskywicz, looking in my direction. "Dotty has a gift. When she has a vision, it's usually always bang on!"

"Well, I guess you don't need me anymore," I said to Evan. He was still immobile, but at least a little color seemed to be creeping back into his face. "Let me know what the inspector says." I began inching my way towards the side of the house. Really, I just wanted to shimmy up Evan's back and make him piggyback me to the safety of my car. "Evan?" I shouted, hoping to break him out of his spell.

"What? Oh, yeah. Thanks for coming over. I'll call you tomorrow." He still wasn't making eye contact. Not a good sign. But also not enough of an issue that I was going to stick around and worry about it.

"Good luck," I said and raced towards my car.

Kip sat hunched in the driver's seat of the Sunny Ridge bus. I gave him a little wave, but he had the same haunted look that Evan did. Maybe they had more in common than I'd originally thought. Maybe they could bond while forming a community rat watch.

I paused a minute, wondering if he was going to be okay getting all his seniors back to the senior center. Then I glanced down the driveway to where two of them had just discovered the unlocked door to the garage and, with cries of delight, had raced inside. He was never going to pull them away from all this fun.

My house was an oasis of serenity when I got home. Neat and orderly, everything in its place, nothing in view that might harbor a giant rat family. No dumpsters, no Triassic-era weeds, no taqueria anywhere in the neighborhood. Nothing but Larry's stupid signs.

Once inside, I changed into my fluffy slippers, made a cup of tea and perched in front of my computer. Addie brought along an old rawhide and settled at my feet. I'd been so distracted by Evan's issues, that I'd been neglecting my own world. Barker Street Bones was doing okay, but I really needed to come up with ways to expand it. I'd been selling my treats mostly through grooming salons and doggie daycares, but if I really hoped to make a go of this, I needed to find additional distributors.

The problem with the internet is that you can have the best intentions in the world and still go horribly off track. I started out searching for recently opened doggie daycares and dog groomers, but before I knew it, I'd veered off onto more enticing subjects.

I hadn't known that Gambian pouched rats had escaped from an exotic animal breeder in the Florida Keys in the late '90s. How had I had been unaware of this fact? And who was to say they hadn't made their way from Florida to Texas since then? The average rat weighs three pounds, but they can grow up to nine pounds. I'll bet one of those rats living in a taqueria dumpster could get to be nine pounds.

That led me to looking up rat extermination in Houston. It seemed to me that the amount of poison they would have to put out to kill something that large would also be enough to kill Henry. This was even worse than the house falling down. I would have to strongly suggest to Evan tomorrow that he was just going to have to stay in his apartment until he either returned this lemon to the bank or sold it to a developer. I hadn't asked what he'd paid for it. He should have paid a discount to the land value, because of the costs of clearing it.

As it turned out, I didn't have to wait until tomorrow. At nine thirty, my phone rang. I'd gone to bed nearly thirty minutes earlier and was propped up on my cushy feather pillows enjoying a new mystery that I'd picked up last weekend. Addie raised red-rimmed eyes towards the phone, obviously irritated at the noisy intrusion.

"What am I going to do?" moaned Evan without preamble.

"Can you make the bank take it back?" No sense beating around the bush. If he'd asked me my opinion before he'd gone and bought the danged thing, he wouldn't be in this mess.

"What? What are you talking about?"

"Aren't you talking about the house and the inspector and your giant rat?"

"No, I don't know what I'm going to do about this presentation I'm supposed to have done for the meeting tomorrow. Why would you say that about making the bank take it back?"

Whoops. "What presentation?"

"I told you already. About the takeover?"

"Oh, right." I let him ramble on for what felt like hours about all the complexities of what they expected him to pull together. I have to say, having left Astor Oil several months ago, all my interest in anything going on there had dwindled to zero. My thoughts drifted back to a housewarming gift. I wondered how much it would cost to get one of those junk companies to come pick up all the garbage in the garage.

I suddenly became aware of a prolonged silence. "Are you even listening to me?"

"You're having to try and calculate the ROCE, and you don't have any of the info you need." Thankfully, some of his words had stuck in my short-term memory.

"Right, so anyway, I just don't know how they can expect me to pull this together tonight." Time to move on to what I really wanted to know.

"So, what did the inspector say?"

"Um, I don't know." He hesitated long enough that my antennae went up. "He had some stuff that he said I need to get checked out. I don't remember exactly."

"Oh. Did he find any more rats?" I elected not to bring up the Gambian giant ones I'd been reading about. Exterminators probably charged more for exotics.

"Not exactly," Evan said. "But he said he can see signs they've been in the crawl space, and probably the attic. And maybe the kitchen." He sighed some more. "So I've got to get an exterminator before I can move in. I guess I'll see if one can come tomorrow, because I have to be out of my apartment by Saturday."

There was no way that house would be habitable by Saturday. What was he thinking? I'd cut the conversation short at that point, fearful that he'd ask if he could stay with me until his house was ready. While, yes, we were friends, we weren't really "can I stay at your place?" kind of friends. Good grief. The thought alone was enough to make me want to pull in the shutters, turn off the lights and pretend no one was home.

I felt more balanced the next morning. After last night's conversation, it was clear that Evan had no intention of walking away from his monstrosity, so I needed to get behind him and do whatever I could to help out.

The skies were clear and blue as I raced through my day collecting money for sales made, replenishing inventory, taking notes regarding customer comments and chatting with all the owners and managers. My business relied on relationships as much as maintaining a quality product, and I enjoyed both sides of the enterprise. I stopped for a quick sandwich, then hit the pavement with my dog friends.

Dan was home once more, propped up on his pillows, and I tried to tell myself that I didn't care in the least about his warm brown eyes. He looked tired, but maybe a shade less deathly than he'd been on Wednesday.

"How are you doing?" I asked, rubbing a wildly wagging Blue.

"I'm okay," he said, not sounding like he meant it. "But I feel bad that this guy's been dying for some exercise and I just can't do it."

"That's what I'm here for," I said, trying to maintain my balance. Blue had jumped up, paws on my chest, and was leaning into me as he tried to lick my ear. "I can tell he's full of it."

"I think it's the cold. He just loves it." He coughed into a tissue, his lungs sounding like they needed a good cleaning with a wet-vac.

I leashed Blue up, and we escaped into the germ-free air. I didn't need any part of whatever that bug was, and yet it was so tempting to linger and perhaps get to know Blue's owner a little bit better. As far as I knew, there was no Mrs. Dan. Why hadn't I thought to bring him some soup?

Dan was the first decent guy I'd met in ages. I mean, I'd met him that one time before, but now here he was looking terrible, and inexplicably, I was drawn to him. I'm not sure what that said about me, but psychology aside, I couldn't deny the attraction.

My last boyfriend had been a long time ago. In fact, when I thought about it, a really long time ago. My parents had loved him, and if you were into smug entitlement, a name recognized all over Houston, and someone who wore navy blazers everywhere, well, he was the perfect guy.

By the time I'd realized what a self-centered ass he was, nearly two years had gone by. I'd been worried about my judgment ever since. How could it have taken me so long to notice what a jerk he was? I liked to think I'd been swayed by my parents' opinions. The only one who hadn't liked him, but who had been too polite to say anything, was Frances. She told me later that had it progressed, she would have told me what she thought, but she had faith that I would see it for myself. And I had.

I raced along beside Blue, trying to come up with clever things to say to Dan when we got back. Unfortunately, I couldn't think of a thing. I really *was* out of practice.

When we got back, Dan had straightened up his little invalid corner and looked slightly more animated. At least he was sitting upright. Blue raced over and jumped up on the couch beside him, digging energetically at the blanket and stomping in circles on the cushions.

"Geez, I thought I'd burned off a little more energy than that," I said as Blue's tail whacked Dan across the face before the big husky plopped down.

"It's okay," Dan said, reaching for another tissue. "That's what he does before he settles down."

"Lord. That's quite a routine." I wondered what the couch cushions looked like under the blanket. Dan laughed for a second before a cough overtook him and he began to hack. I stood there awkwardly for a minute before Dan waved a hand at me.

"Thanks for coming," he choked out as he went into another spasm.

"Well, I hope you feel better," I said. "I'll be back tomorrow. Same time, same place." Did I really just say that? How lame. I raced out the door and was halfway to my car before I remembered that it was Friday, and I actually wouldn't be back tomorrow. What had happened to the poise that had been drilled into me since birth?

Mercifully, I made it home after my last client without embarrassing myself further. I changed into heavy sweats, pulled on my slippers and padded to the kitchen. The cold weather I'd enjoyed all day now chilled my bones, and fatigue began settling into my muscles. I was too tired to cook anything ambitious, but spaghetti was still within my abilities; nothing like a giant bowl of pasta on a cold night. I love Friday nights relaxing at home with Addie. That's not pathetic, right? And really, judging from my deteriorating social skills, maybe it was good that this made me happy.

If Dan could see me now. Exciting hot chick on a Friday night.

CHAPTER SEVEN

I'd fallen into the best sleep I'd had all week when the doorbell rang, eliciting fearsome barks from Addie and effectively jolting my heart into overdrive. Who would be ringing my doorbell in the middle of the night? I glanced at the clock. Oh, it was only nine thirty. I rolled out of bed and crept to the window. Evan's car was in my driveway. Addie had stopped barking and was whining and wagging at the top of the stairs. Evidently, she knew who was here too.

She raced to the door and bounced up and down at the threshold. I had to guess Evan had brought his dog with him. Sure enough, when I opened the door, the whiskey-colored terrier raced in, wriggling in delight.

"Hey, Henry," I cooed, reaching down to scoop up the small dog. I hadn't been sure that Evan was up to taking proper care of him, but so far he was still alive and seemed quite happy.

Addie, both happy to see him and jealous of me holding him, waffled between jumping on Evan and jumping on me.

"Hey, Evan," I said once the initial chaos began to settle.

"What's going on?" He was holding a plastic grocery bag that bulged at its fragile seams and a round green dog bed.

"Hi, Jessie. Sorry to barge in this way. I didn't wake you, did I?" He was staring at me in an odd way. Belatedly, I put a hand to my hair and felt a tangle of strands poking out in all directions.

"No, not at all!" I said, my voice rising.

"Oh. Then I like your hair," he said, suddenly nervous. "Um, anyway. I was hoping I could leave Henry with you tonight. The movers are coming first thing in the morning, and I'm afraid Henry might run out or get stepped on or something."

I set the dog down and he raced off, sniffing for changes since the last time he'd been here. Addie stuck close to his heels, making sure he didn't try to take anything that was hers.

"Sure. I'd love to have him. I think Addie's missed him." Henry had his head under the couch and his back end stuck in the air, tail wagging madly. He emerged with an abandoned Kong and barely had time to register his find before Addie knocked him flat with a paw and snatched the toy from his jaws. With a ferocious baring of her fangs, she carried the Kong off to the far corner of the kitchen.

"Yeah, I can tell," said Evan, kneeling beside Henry and running his hands quickly over him, obviously checking for injuries.

"She didn't hurt him," I said, feeling suddenly defensive. Sheesh, she'd barely touched him.

Evan squinted his eyes at me. "You will keep an eye on them, right? I mean, I know Addie's a little..." He paused. "I don't know, possessive or something? But I really don't want her to hurt Henry. He's so much smaller."

"Evan." I took a patient breath. "You know I would not let anything bad happen to Henry. Was I not the one who saved him? Was I not the one who gave him to you? Trust me, I will not let anything happen to Henry."

"Okay, fine." He thrust his plastic bag at me. "I've got some of his food and a few of his favorite toys. He gets a quarter cup for breakfast, and I should be able to pick him up before his dinner tomorrow."

My mind flashed to the giant rat prowling through Evan's new backyard.

"What about the exterminator?" I asked.

"They're coming tomorrow too. Sometime after ten. So by midafternoon, I should be set." A glimmer of his original excitement flickered in his eyes.

Henry hung over the back of the couch, grinning at me.

"Do you think you'll have time to work on cleaning up the backyard tomorrow?" I asked. "I could help you. I'm just worried about Henry getting cut on some of that trash out there."

"I don't know. It's going to be pretty hectic. And the exterminator wanted me to clear all the garbage out of the garage so he can bait in there too." He ran a hand through his hair before bending over Henry, scooping him off the couch and cradling him against his chest. "I mean, if you could help me a little, maybe we could get somewhere."

"Great!" I said brightly, trying to get into the mindset that this could be a fun way to spend my Saturday. "I'll just come over to your new place in the morning." I considered the cut on my palm. It was nothing short of a miracle that my hand hadn't already swelled up with infection. I couldn't assume I'd be so lucky next time.

"Great," he echoed. "Do you think you could be there by

ten, just in case I'm not there with the movers yet? Then you could go around with the exterminator." Exactly what I wanted to do.

After Evan left, it took a while for the dogs to settle down, and even longer for me to get back to sleep. But we made it through the night without any bloodshed and only relatively minor scuffles.

Once it was light, I took the two of them for a walk long enough to wear them out so they wouldn't kill each other while I was gone. Or rather, long enough to take the edge off Addie's attitude. There's no question she loves being an only dog. Luckily, Henry would be going with Evan to his new home tonight.

I loaded my car with all the gear I thought I might need for decluttering and weeding Evan's backyard, including a full first aid kit, stretchy trash bags, a long metal weeder, a cushy kneeling pad and enough bug repellent to get me through the Amazon jungle with nary a bite. Forget the fact it was January, I wasn't taking any chances. I also threw in a broomstick to poke at the thicker patches in the hopes of scaring away any vermin.

Then I raided my closet, looking for protective clothing. I opted for flannel-lined jeans and wellies, hoping that this would deflect any snakebites. A thick canvas shirt that came down to my knees also seemed perfect for today's events.

I pulled my hair into as tight a ponytail as I could—so tight, in fact, that I could feel it stretching the skin alongside my eyes. I pulled the tail through the back of a baseball cap and went to work on my cut hand. I poured liquid skin over the still-open flesh, covered it with a bandage and gauze and then taped all the way around. That should hold it. If not, I did have the first aid kit. To top it all off, I brought out my leather gardening gloves. Too bad they didn't reach to my elbows.

It was almost nine when I pulled up in front of Evan's. Morning sun dappled the front yard, and the wind blew dead leaves into piles along the curb. The neighborhood was quiet, the cold probably inspiring everyone to hang out in their warm jammies, lingering over steaming coffee and reading the paper.

Feeling virtuous, I unpacked my gear, leaving the first aid kit on the front seat for easy access. I needed a plan of action. The side yards were almost as bad as the back, but the back-yard was where Henry would mostly likely end up once Evan fixed the fence and closed off the access to the street. So, I would start in the back and work my way from one side to the other.

Plunking my supplies on the crumbling back steps, I surveyed the jungle. Mr. McNeil had unearthed the giant rat close to the dumpster side, so perhaps I would start on the side by the goth girl's house. Obviously the rats and snakes could be hiding anywhere, but I really preferred to avoid the dumpster area. Evan could deal with that.

I picked up the bug spray, closed my eyes and held my breath while I covered myself with its toxic fumes. Once I was dripping, I grabbed my broomstick and began slashing at the weeds hoping to frighten away any creatures that might be lurking. "Yah! Yah!" I shouted, sounding more like I was driving cattle than rodents.

I made it all the way to the far corner without anything leaping out at me. So far, so good. Adjusting my thick gloves, I set my sights on a two-foot-tall semi-spiky-looking thing near the fence. Kneeling on the soft pad, I poked my weeder into the dirt. The ground was harder than I'd expected after the last week's rain. I pushed harder and grabbed a hold of the stalk near the ground, giving it an experimental pull. Wow. This thing was in there good. Bracing myself, I pushed farther into the dirt, shoving the handle side to side to help break up the roots. Once I was sure I'd broken most of them, I took a hold of the thing with both hands and pulled as hard as I could, throwing my weight backwards. Dang. It didn't even move.

I moved to the other side of it and repeated the process, stabbing and thrusting the weeder into the dirt determined to break this monster. I could feel my face reddening with the effort, and sweat broke out under the brim of my hat. I gave the plant another pull, and when it barely moved, I started stabbing at the dirt with great slashing motions.

I was hacking away at the dirt like Jack the Ripper on speed when I heard a derisive laugh behind me. Glancing over my shoulder, I saw the pink-haired goth girl, decked out in black, arms crossed over her chest, laughing. Gripping the weed, I gave a tremendous tug. My gloved hands raced along the spiny stem, tearing leaves off but having no effect on the stem. I fell backwards, landing hard on my butt as the weed bounced back up.

Goth Girl snorted behind me and slowly clapped her hands. "Good work," she said in a snarky tone.

The sarcasm alone was enough to make me want to beat her with a thorny branch. I took a breath and turned to study her. Today she was in a long faded sweatshirt that draped to midthigh, black tights and pink Converse sneakers that made her feet look huge. Her hair stuck out in clumps, and up close I could see metal spikes that pierced her cheek. I had to look away.

"You live next door?" I asked. I heaved myself to my feet and brushed the dirt off my butt.

"Smart one, aren't you?" She walked past me and began poking around the yard.

"Is there something you need?" I halfway wished one of the Gambian giant rats would jump out and take her down.

"Did you buy this dump?" She picked up my broomstick and poked idly at a rock.

"No, a friend of mine did," I said. I felt defensive on Evan's behalf in spite of the fact that she was only saying what I thought.

"Why would anyone buy this dung hole?"

I put down my weeder, afraid of the sudden urge to drive it into the back of her neck.

"With a little work, I'm sure it can be fixed up really cute," I said. "So did you just come over here to be rude, or was there something you wanted?"

She shot a quick look at me. "I wanted to see where Miriam died." What was it with these neighbors? First Kip and now Goth Girl. Evan was surrounded by ghouls.

"Why would you want to do that?"

"Because it's cool." She looked at me like I was a complete idiot. "I've never seen the place where someone was shot to death. I wondered if there was a lot of blood."

"How do you know she was shot?" Maybe she'd actually seen something.

"The cops were here yesterday. I heard them talking." I looked at the stripped weed that I still hadn't managed to get out of the ground. This was going to take longer than I'd thought. I readjusted my gloves and went back to work, hoping she would lose interest and wander back to her crypt. "So where was she?"

"I just don't see why this matters to you," I said, pulling up a few smaller weeds just to give myself a mental boost.

"God, what's your problem?" she snapped. "Whatever. Fine, be like that. I'll know when I see it."

I wondered when Evan was going to get here. She drifted listlessly towards the back of the house, calling softly, "Miriam...Miriam..." The soft whisper raised goose bumps along the back of my arms. I clutched the weeder tight in my hand, although it probably wouldn't be much help if Miriam actually did answer. *Don't be stupid*, I told myself. *You saw the guys with the coroner's office. You saw the gurney. You were here two days ago when Kip and his murder tour were running all over the place. There was no Miriam here then, and there's no Miriam here now.*

"Miriam..." Goth Girl disappeared around the far corner of the house, closer than she knew to where Miriam had died. The whispering stopped, and I tried to go back to work, but I found myself listening. I finally hopped to my feet and followed her.

Turning the corner, I stopped short when I saw the pink Converse shoes poking out, toes up, from under the house. She was almost exactly where Miriam had been when Addie found her.

"What are you doing?" I thought I was calm, but maybe I was shouting just a little bit, because as I leaned down, she sat up suddenly, banging her head rather hard on the underside of the house.

"Oh my God, she was here! Miriam was right here." She scrambled crablike out from under the house. "She's still here!" She shot out, banging her head once more before she totally cleared the edge. Grabbing my arm, she lost all the teenage attitude she'd had just moments ago. And frankly, she was freaking me out.

I backed away from the death space towards the backyard. She clutched at me, afraid I was going to leave her. With my free hand, I patted at my heart, trying to slow down the pounding she'd started when she said Miriam was still here.

"What do you mean, she's still here?" I whispered.

"She's still here. I can feel her." Her eyes were wide and she plucked furiously at my arm. "What are we going to do?"

Evan needed to run, not walk, away from this house.

CHAPTER EIGHT

R esisting the urge to run screaming to my car, I grabbed the girl's shoulder and gave her a shake. "Miriam is not here. She's dead." Maybe I could stay with Frances tonight. Just in case the nightmares got the best of me.

"I felt her under there. You don't know." Her voice faltered. "I felt her." I kept waiting for her to suddenly jeer at me, "Aha! Gotcha!" but she didn't. She let go of my arm and began picking at her sweatshirt sleeve until I could see a hole developing along the seam.

"What do you mean, you felt her?" Like watching a scary movie, I wanted to cover my face with a pillow and look away, but this girl had my full attention. She looked over her shoulder, then leaned in closer towards my face as if expecting Miriam to be eavesdropping behind her.

"I don't know how to explain it." She took a deep breath. "Sometimes when I'm out places, I'm aware of other beings around me. Like, you know."

"Er, not really," I said. Just when my goose bumps had

begun settling back into smooth skin, she got them up on end again. "You mean like ghosts?"

Her head whipped around again, looking behind her, then behind me, her eyes finally settling on something over my left shoulder. As much as I tried, I couldn't keep from looking. The only thing I saw was the same weed-choked yard. And a few moving shadows, but I was sure that was from the wind blowing tree branches. When was Evan going to get here?

"I know this sounds crazy. It doesn't happen very often, and I don't see anything, I just feel them." She started picking at her sweatshirt sleeve again. "Whatever. Never mind. You probably think I'm a freak."

"No, not at all," I lied. I had to hope she was a freak or I wasn't going to sleep well for weeks. "How did you know that's where Miriam's body was?"

"I told you, I felt it." Her attitude was making a comeback. It was comforting, in a way.

From the street, the squeal of brakes and rumble of an engine broke the creepy atmosphere. Goth Girl followed me to the front yard. A twenty-foot moving van was trying to angle into the driveway. Up and over the curb, he took out several branches of the live oak before crunching to a stop.

Evan pulled up in his car at the curb, scowling at the broken branches on the drive. He brightened when he saw me and made a beeline right to my side. And in a totally unexpected move, he put his arm around my neck and pulled me close to him.

"Hey, babe," he said loudly.

"What are you doing?" I pulled back, put off by the unexpected, and frankly unwanted, intimacy. He leaned closer, playing idly with my ponytail. The doors to the moving van opened and out popped three of the buffest, best-looking guys I'd seen in a long time. Not your average movers. The truck was pristine. Well, with the exception of the new scratches from the tree. I'd expected Evan to go with a more budget-friendly company. In fact, I'd anticipated a rattletrap, belching smoke with plenty of dings, and a couple of slipshod movers wearing stained coveralls. But these guys had cute uniforms with matching sweaters, boot-cut jeans, and adorable motorcycle boots.

I looked again at the truck. "Three Bucks & a Truck" was emblazoned in bold orange letters against a pale yellow background. Evan started twirling little circles on the back of my neck.

"Three Bucks and a Truck?" I asked him. "What is this? A gay moving company?"

I heard a door slam, and Kip soared across the street like a sailboat with hurricane-force tailwinds.

"Jessie! Darling, so good to see you again." He nearly knocked me over as he air-kissed my cheeks. "Who are your friends?" He ran a hand along his perfectly mussed hair. His eyes held the same look that Addie's got when staring at a liver treat. I halfway expected him to start drooling.

"This is Evan Petty. Didn't you guys introduce yourselves the other day? When you were here with your murder tour?"

"You had a murder tour here?" asked Goth Girl. I'd forgotten she was there. "Will there be another one? I want to come. How much is it?"

Kip waved her away with a flick of his fingers. The movers had arranged themselves around the back door of the van and were consulting a clipboard. Evan draped an arm around my neck and pulled me up against his chest.

"You look hot, babe," he said loud enough for the patrons of the taqueria to hear. "I'm really glad you're here."

I pushed him off. "Stop it! What's wrong with you?"

Kip had wandered away towards the movers. "Hi, boys," he said with a little tilt of his head. "Can I get you something to drink? It certainly looks like hard"—he paused dramatically—"work."

I turned back to Evan. "So, how'd you find these guys? Is there something you want to talk about?"

His face flushed crimson and he leaned in close. "I thought it said 'Three Bucks *for* a Truck.' I mean, I didn't really think it would be three dollars, but I thought it was going to be cheap. I was in a hurry. You know how busy I've been." He glanced over at Kip, who was laughing and running a hand up and down one of the mover's arms, and his gaze slid quickly away. He reached out for my ponytail again. I slapped his hand away.

"Stop it. Good grief. They're here to move your stuff, not marry you."

Goth Girl snorted. "Homophobe," she said to Evan.

"And who are you?" he snapped.

"I'm the non-homophobe who lives next door to you. I also wouldn't have bought this cesspool." She gave a disgusted glance at the house. "Oh, and by the way, did you know Miriam's still here?"

Oh, geez. I needed to get her out of here. That was the last thing Evan needed to be hearing about right now. "What?" he asked. The white part of his eyes was starting to be the predominant color; I needed to do something fast.

"Wynne!" From next door, a neatly dressed man approached. His khakis sported a military precision crease, his hair was just shy of being a buzz cut, and the shirt under his jacket looked as if it held enough starch to stand on its own. "Wynne, honey. Come on. Your mom and I are ready to go." He spotted the hole in her sweatshirt sleeve, which had gotten quite large in the last several minutes. "What happened to your shirt?"

"I'm not your honey, you perv," she said. She stomped past him and clumped back to her house, pushing past a blonde woman at the door. I didn't care who the perv was—he had mercifully knocked her off her Miriam course.

"Kids," he said, laughing ruefully, as if we understood how difficult it was to raise teenagers. "Hi, I'm Brian Barbieri. You've obviously met my stepdaughter, Wynne." We shook hands all around, and Evan and I introduced ourselves. "That's my wife, Tiffany." He waved to the blonde woman who was scowling at us from the front path. Interesting hair. In a style more suited to a four-year-old, she'd pulled her highlighted strands into a ponytail that sprouted like a fountain from the top of her head. She gave it an impatient shake.

"Hi," she said in a monotone. "Come on, Brian, we're going to be late."

He flashed us a quick smile. Even his teeth lined up with military precision. "I'll be right there, hon. Come meet our new neighbors."

"Oh, I'm not moving in," I said quickly. Maybe a little too quickly. "Just Evan is."

"Oh, sorry. My mistake." He gave Evan a little wink. "Not yet anyway."

A roar of laughter came from the Bucks' truck. "Well, we better see how they're getting on," I said to Evan.

"Brian, let's go," Tiffany said, flouncing away from us towards their driveway. She wore a purple miniskirt with tights and a cropped rabbit skin jacket.

"Right behind you, babe," he said, giving us another smile and turning to follow his wife. He paused and turned back to us. "Oh by the way, I was just wondering...did the last owner leave anything behind?"

Evan huffed. "She left a whole bunch of junk. The garage is stuffed with it."

"Anything in particular you're looking for?" I asked.

"No, no," Brian said. "Just wondering. You know, so many charities need so much these days. I thought there might be things to donate."

"It's all going to the garbage," Evan said.

"You're not even looking through it?"

"Brian, come on," Tiffany was already in the car.

"Nope," Evan said. "I don't have time to deal with it. If anyone wants it, they can take if off the curb."

In spite of Evan's protests, I left him to deal with the movers while I headed back to my weeding. I needed to clear at least one monster weed successfully before calling it a day. I felt better with all the activity going on in the house. If Miriam's ghost popped out at me, there were at least five people within shouting distance.

I worked steadily for about half an hour before Evan came around the house looking for me.

"They're just about done," he said. "Do you mind coming around front with me?" He kicked uncomfortably at a rock. "I'd just really like it if you'd come with me when I settle up with these guys." He dipped his head and looked away. Red spots stained his cheeks, and he shoved his hands in his pockets and rocked back on his heels.

I heaved myself to my feet, feeling tightness in my lower back and legs. Poor Evan. The least I could do was save him from the gay Bucks with a truck.

We walked around front. Two of the guys were already hoisting themselves into the cab of the truck. The third one scratched away on a clipboard, glancing up at us as we approached. I stood back while Evan wrote out a check for payment, not wanting to intrude.

As soon as he got his receipt, he raced up onto the porch. I followed him, more in the interest of not getting run over. Several tree branches later, and another new scar on their beautifully painted truck, the Bucks rolled away. I followed Evan into the house, shoving the door closed behind me.

Piles of boxes lined the walls, and the heavier furniture had been positioned in the way the Bucks thought it should be arranged. Not bad. Well, the arrangement wasn't bad; the furniture itself could stand to be replaced. However, with all the necessary projects to be done around the house, Evan would probably be living with this furniture until he was ninety.

Evan stood in the middle of the room, his head swiveling back and forth. "What do you think about the couch over here?" he asked, already pulling on an end in an attempt to drag it to the far wall.

"I kind of like where they put it," I said. "It delineates the space nicely."

He paused, leaving it at an awkward angle. "Really?"

"Yeah, it creates a nice little walk-through to the kitchen."

He pushed it back but still looked doubtful. He seemed to favor lining the furniture up along the walls, as if to be ready for square dancing in the middle of the room at all times.

"Do you want to start clearing out the garage?" I glanced at my watch. "I thought the exterminator was supposed to be here."

"Oh, yeah. He called and said he couldn't make it out till

this afternoon." He paused, looking up from the box he had just opened. It looked like a box full of empty beer cans.

"You moved empty beer cans?"

He gave me a flat stare. "They're not just empty beer cans," he said, huffing at my ignorance. I thought he was going to elaborate, but he didn't. More than likely, there wasn't anything more to say. Reluctantly, he closed the lid. "I guess we should see how much we can get out of there before he gets here," he said.

It had taken both of us lifting and straining to shove the garage door into the open position, and I still had major concerns that it might fall and kill one of us. But once it was up, we both stepped back and stared. I hadn't fully appreciated how stuffed with junk it was when I'd looked in earlier. Boxes balanced on furniture. Furniture balanced on boxes. There seemed to be no rhyme or reason to the order. We stood staring at the mess, trying to find a place to start.

"How do you want to do this?" I finally asked, as Evan began gingerly picking his way forward.

"Everything goes," he said forcefully. "Everything." He tugged a sagging box from the top of a pile. It toppled sideways, a heap of floppy clothing spilling out. He kicked out at a sweater. "This is going to take forever."

We tried to figure out what was going to be the easiest way to handle this and finally decided there was no easy way. So, we just began pulling and carrying things to the curb.

"You're sure you don't want to look through any of this?" I asked, picking up a shoebox full of papers. I'd already hauled five boxes out unopened, and I was starting to have concerns we could be throwing out something valuable. Opening the shoebox, I riffled through a stack of junk mail circa 1987.

"Here's a credit card application," I said. "Montgomery Ward. Does that even exist anymore?"

"She doesn't need credit. She's dead."

He dragged a neon yellow beanbag chair across the gravel. He had a point. I hauled the box to the curb and tossed it with the others. I was starting to work up a sweat, and the urge to sit down was overtaking me. I crossed the garage to where Evan was trying to decide which box to grab next.

"I think we need a break," I said. He must not have heard me come over, because as I spoke, he jumped and let out a small yelp. He looked terrible. Dirt streaked his face, and his hands were gray with it. But it was the wildness in his eyes that was most disturbing. "You okay?" I asked.

"Yeah, yeah. You scared me is all." He ran a filthy hand through his hair. "What time is it anyway?"

I glanced at my watch. "Almost twelve."

"Really? Wow, yeah. Do you want to go to that taco place and have some lunch?"

My stomach rumbled just thinking of food. We went inside to wash as much of the grime off our hands as we could. Evan wasn't sure where his soap or towels were.

"Give me a minute," he said, heading for the kitchen. "I'm sure I can find it."

I poked around the living room for a few minutes, trying to get a feel for how the room might look after he unpacked. It was going to be tough making it look good until he got that wallpaper down. I headed for the kitchen to see what was taking so long. Evan was on his hands and knees, his head stuck into a lower cupboard.

"What are you doing?" I asked, trying to peer in behind

him. He reared back, knocking his head solidly on the wood frame.

"Holy crap. You scared me. Don't sneak up on me like that." He rubbed his head.

"Sorry. What are you doing?"

"I was looking to see if there was any soap under here, but it's dark and I put my hand in something."

"What kind of something?" I bounced on my wellies, ready to run.

"I can't tell exactly," he said, lowering his hand and looking at it.

"What is it?" I leaned forward trying to get a look in the dim light. Small dark beads dotted his hand. We leaned closer, our heads nearly touching. Evan pinched his thumb and forefinger together.

"Kind of soft," he said slowly.

I moved away, grimacing. "Evan, I think they're rat turds. Ew, ew, ew!"

"No!" Evan threw the offending material onto the floor. Or at least the pieces that didn't stick to his hand. "Oh, geez." He scraped his hand against the counter, dislodging the rest. That was enough for me. I raced for the living room. Time to collect my things and head home to disinfect.

"Hey, wait," Evan yelled. "You're not leaving, are you?" He ran after me, his hand still flapping at the end of his wrist.

"I was thinking I should go home and check on the dogs." I glanced at my watch to bolster my claim. Oh, wow. It was actually later than I'd thought.

"Oh." His shoulders slumped forward and he looked forlornly at the floor. "I thought we were going to the taqueria." I looked at the brown spots dotting the floor. Those giant rats probably lived at the taqueria as well. Shoot, they'd probably originated at the taqueria.

He looked pleadingly at me.

It took us fifteen minutes to find the box with the soap in it. I wouldn't let Evan touch anything for fear he would spread rat contamination from his hand to the boxes, so he pointed at various boxes that he thought the soap might be packed in while I opened them, did a quick rummage and moved on. When I did find it, mercifully, it was antibacterial.

It was another five minutes before Evan was sufficiently disinfected and ready to head next door. I'd take the time to wash my hands and rebandage my cut, but there wasn't much I could do about my outfit. Normally I wouldn't be caught dead dressed like this in public, but really. We were going to a taqueria.

It wasn't as bad as I'd imagined it would be. Okay, it wasn't exactly Brennan's, but it wasn't horrible either. A bar ran down the left side of the space, most of the shelves lined with tequila and beer. I didn't see a bartender, but then again, it was pretty early.

Evan had moved to a counter at the back, where he stood studying the posted menu. He was ready immediately.

"Beef burrito, please," he said to a short Hispanic woman behind the counter. "And a Coke." She looked expectantly at me. I was still studying the menu, trying to pick out something that was less than three thousand calories.

"How about a taco salad, hold the shell, with grilled chicken and dressing on the side. Oh, and no cheese, please." She looked at me like I'd said something inappropriate but punched it into her register anyway.

"Something to drink?" she asked.

"Just water, please."

Evan shot me a disappointed look. "I thought you were going to try something good."

"What's wrong with a taco salad?"

"No shell? No cheese? Geez."

We paid the lady and she slid a yellow maraca painted with a big red number twelve across the counter at us, followed closely by two plastic cups, one large and one small.

Evan grabbed the big cup and headed to a soda dispenser in the corner. I got the maraca and my water and followed him to a table near the windows.

"This place is great," he said, looking around and sucking a mouthful of Coke through his straw. "I don't know why you didn't get a burrito. Or tacos."

"I wanted something a little lighter," I said, giving the maraca a little shake. Seeds inside rattled against the gourd. I shook it again, enjoying the sound. "Very cute," I said, wanting a maraca of my own. I could get into this thing. A lady a couple tables over looked up from the book she was reading and gave me a frown. I put it down on the table and dropped my hands into my lap.

"So. You never told me what the inspector said."

Evan took another drink then swiveled his straw in a circle.

"You know. The normal stuff." It must be bad. "There's some stuff I need to get fixed. But still, with the deal I got from the bank, it should turn out okay." His enthusiasm wasn't quite as high as it had been earlier in the week.

"Is there anything major you need to get done?" Like replace the roof and gut the kitchen and kill the rats.

"He gave me a list of things I should have checked out. Like maybe there are some spots on the roof that need a little work. That kind of thing. I'll just have to find a handyman or something." Oh, boy. He probably needed a contractor and a twenty-man crew. "And some of it I can do myself." I squinted across the table at him. "Well, there is some stuff I can probably do myself," he said.

Luckily our food came at that point, delivered by a tall Hispanic man in dress pants, a white button-down shirt and a brightly colored floral tie. He slid our meals in front of us.

"Is there anything else I can bring you?" he asked, picking up our maraca and surveying our table. He turned and waved a finger at a young man standing near the counter, and with a scowl, he jerked his head towards our table. The teen jumped into action, grabbing a basket full of chips and a bowl of salsa and hustling to our table.

"Awesome," said Evan, pulling a chip off the top. "This is great! Are you open every day?" he asked, dipping the chip into the homemade salsa and popping it in his mouth.

"Every day," said the man, who I was guessing was the manager.

"Awesome!" repeated Evan, nearly swooning with delight. "I just moved in behind here, and this is so close! I just can't believe how lucky I am."

"Well, welcome. I look forward to seeing you regularly. I'll have to set you up with the next-door neighbor discount." He smiled, flashing smooth white teeth. "I'm Diego Lopez. If you ever need anything, please don't hesitate to let me know."

I flashed to the dumpster and the broken fence.

"Evan Petty," said Evan, wiping his hand on a napkin before sticking it out and shaking. "And this is my friend, Jessie Gallagher." I waved. "There's a next-door neighbor discount?" Evan asked, sounding more amped up than I'd heard him in weeks.

"I'm sure I can work out something for my new neighbor."

"Well, I don't want to get you in trouble or anything. But that would be awesome!" I really needed to get Evan a thesaurus.

Diego looked over and gave me a wink. "I'm pretty sure the owner wouldn't mind."

"You own this place?" Evan was sounding more and more like a preteen groupie coming face-to-face with her favorite boy band.

"Awesome," I said, just to preempt Evan from saying it again.

Diego laughed. "Please, I don't want to keep you from your meal. Enjoy."

Evan pulled his plate closer, hovering over the steaming mound. "Look at this thing!" he said, closing his eyes and inhaling deeply.

I did look at it. Honestly, if he ate one of those every day, it wouldn't be long before he doubled in size. With all the money he was going to spend on the house, I doubted he would have enough left to replace his wardrobe.

The salad was good; all the ingredients were fresh and the chicken was tender and seasoned perfectly. If Evan would make some healthier choices, this might not be a bad place for him to eat. I really wanted to hear more about what the inspector had found, but after a couple more questions, I realized the answers were going to be given around a mouthful of mashed burrito, so I resigned myself to eating.

"Have you heard anything more from the police about Miriam?" I asked him after most of the burrito had disappeared.

"Yeah, they came by yesterday. I wasn't home. They called

me at the office." He used the last bit of his flour tortilla to soak up the grease that had leaked out from the back end of the burrito. "They just kept asking me the same questions that I already answered."

"Really? Like what?"

"You know, like what happened when that crazy woman came back after you left. When did I last see her? What time did I leave? Did anyone see me leave? Was there anyone at my apartment who saw me come home? Like that."

"Evan, do they think you killed her?" I stared across the table at him, wondering why he was so nonchalant about it.

"How could they think I killed her? I had nothing to do with it."

"Okay, yeah, but they don't know that. And you had a fight with her."

"It wasn't a fight exactly." He picked a broken chip from the basket.

"Well, they told me you shoved her."

"I didn't shove her!" His voice rose enough that people looked over. "She just, like, fell down."

"Okay, but you can see why they're asking you questions. I don't suppose anyone at your apartment can vouch for you?"

"I don't know. Not that I know of. But maybe there're security cameras or something." He pulled the last chip out of the basket.

"Did they say anything else?"

"They said she'd been shot. They asked if I had any guns." He pushed his plate away and patted his belly. "That's really all I know." He sounded remarkably disinterested that someone had been shot to death under his house. I thought of Wynne's creepy voice saying, "She's here." I gave myself a little shake and looked around the taqueria. Hard to imagine ghosts wandering through here.

I shoved the remaining lettuce leaves around the bottom of my bowl. "You've got some interesting neighbors," I said, changing subjects.

"Yeah, that Brian guy seems pretty cool." He looked away from me and fiddled with the salt shaker.

"His stepdaughter is a little strange." I pushed my plate away. "She wanted to see where Miriam was killed."

"You didn't let her come on my property, did you?"

"I didn't exactly invite her," I said. "She just showed up."

"Well, I don't want any more people tramping around my property," he said. "I mean, what the hell was that guy doing the other day with all those old people? What if one of them fell and broke a hip? I'm not going to be responsible for someone getting hurt on my property when they're trespassing."

"Look, Wynne just showed up. She seems morbidly fascinated with this murder. I don't know what to tell you. I mean, look at her. Does she look like your average teen? Not hardly."

I glanced around the restaurant, noticing for the first time that we were the only customers left. Diego stood behind the counter, writing furiously on a clipboard. He didn't seem to even notice our conversation heating up.

"What time is it?" Evan asked, also noticing we were the only ones left from the lunch crowd, such as it had been. He hopped out of his seat before I even had a chance to check my watch. "I gotta go. That exterminator should be here soon. Do you want to see if we can get some more of that junk out of the garage before he gets here? Then maybe he can at least start on the garage even if he has to come back later."

I sighed, thinking longingly of a hot shower and some quiet time with the dogs. "Maybe a little more."

Evan turned to Diego as we reached the door. "Thanks, Diego! You've got the best food in town."

"Thank you," he said solemnly. "It was very nice to meet you. I look forward to seeing you often."

A truck with a huge plastic rat hunched on top of the cab cruised slowly down the street as we walked back. A long pink tail hung limply down the back side of the truck, looking a little more true to life than I cared for.

"Looks like your exterminator," I said as the truck cruised past. "You'd better catch him." Evan sprinted after the truck, waving his arms and shouting.

In the short amount of time we'd been gone, a smattering of people had shown up and were pawing enthusiastically through the junk at the curb. I turned up the driveway, looking into the garage, dismayed at how much stuff was still stuffed in there. Maybe Evan should just put up a sign that said "Free" and let folks take away what they wanted. It would save us the trouble of having to haul all this out.

He returned with the rat truck following him into the driveway. Two of the women at the curb took one look at the truck and dropped the items they were holding. Murmuring cries of disgust, they race-walked for their cars. But as even as they pulled away, another pickup truck took their spot. A burly man hoisted himself out of the driver's seat, caught my eye and jerked his head towards the junk pile.

"Okay?" he grunted.

"Yeah, sure. Take anything you want," I told him. "In fact, if you want, you can look through the garage and see if there's anything in there you'd like. Take it all." I waved a magnanimous arm.

He grunted again and followed me up the driveway. I ushered him into the garage, trying not to stare at the giant pistol tattoo that took up most of the back of his neck. Maybe I shouldn't have been so quick to invite this total stranger onto Evan's property. Two more men and a tiny lady followed, darting into the garage before I could change my mind. I stood there awkwardly as they began digging through the piles like gerbils working their way through new bedding. Evan wasn't going to like this. But then again, he was the one who'd said it all had to go. I was merely helping out.

Evan was standing near the exterminator's truck, talking fast and gesturing wildly with his hands. I inched past, giving him a quick wave to let him know I was leaving, and pointed to the garage, mumbling that there were some people going through Miriam's things. I was pretty sure he didn't hear me.

CHAPTER NINE

Addie and Henry were overjoyed to see me when I got home. We went through the usual greetings with only a few low growls. Leaving my boots in the garage, I ran upstairs to take a quick shower.

I'd considered calling Frances to see if she wanted to go out to dinner, but as the afternoon ran on without word from Evan, I discarded those plans. There was last-minute, and then there was last last-minute. We were definitely into the last last-minute phase.

At five, my doorbell rang, causing Henry to leap from his perch on the back of the couch and race towards the door, earsplitting yelps echoing off the walls. Addie ran for the door as well, flattening her ears against the side of her head, trying to defend her hearing. Evan pushed his way in as soon as I opened the door, scooping Henry up as he passed.

The duffle bag slung over his shoulder gave me a slight pang.

"So, is the exterminator done?" I asked brightly.

He threw himself dramatically down on the couch, dropping the duffle on the floor. "Not really," he said, not looking directly at me. Henry put his paws on Evan's shoulders and licked his chin in greeting.

"Oh." Addie sat primly at my feet and looked up at me, as if anticipating a bad reaction on my part. "What does that mean? Does he have to come back?"

"He said he hasn't seen such a bad infestation in a while," Evan said. "So he laid down some poison and he set some traps. He wants to come back and see if he can find the nest. He kept talking about this nest. I don't know." He leaned back against the cushions.

My brain whirled through what I knew about rat extermination. It wasn't much, but the idea that he laid down poison brought my gaze right to the twelve-pound furball squirming in Evan's lap.

"Where did he put the poison? I mean, you have to be concerned about Henry eating it." I trailed off when Evan shot me a look of disgust.

"I know that," he said, clearly irritated. "He put it in the attic. He wanted to lay some under the house, but I said no, because obviously Henry could get under there. So he laid the traps under the house." He took a breath. "And in the attic. And all around the kitchen and the laundry room."

I shuddered, thinking about all the dead bodies that were going to pile up overnight.

"He wants to come back Monday, clear the traps and check the bait." Both of us glanced at his duffle bag. A moment of silence dragged on for half a beat too long.

"Oh, so do you need a place to stay?" I asked, like an idiot just seeing the point.

"Do you mind? That would be great. I guess I shouldn't have moved out on the last day of my lease."

"It's no problem," I lied, feeling his presence seeping around the room. What was wrong with me? This was my friend. He just needed a place to stay for a couple of nights. A good person wouldn't even bat an eye. "You're always welcome."

"Great!" He jumped to his feet and grabbed his bag. "Where should I put my bag?" I have two bedrooms, but I'd converted one into a small home office. He knew that. Surely he wasn't suggesting he stay in my room. I stared unblinking at him.

"Don't you have a spare room?" he asked, his voice suddenly unsure. He'd been through my house before. But then again, guys don't always remember domestic details the way women do.

"I have an extra room, but it's an office. Remember?" A slight flush had begun to creep up his cheeks. "But you can definitely stay on the couch if that's okay. And you're welcome to the spare bathroom upstairs. You know where it is."

"That'd be great," he said, swinging his bag over his shoulder. "You won't even know we're here."

We made it through the first evening fairly well. Well, mostly. Evan said he wanted to take me out to dinner as thanks for my hospitality. We ended up at the Black Lab, an English pub on Montrose, where we ordered beers and burgers. We'd come here fairly often when we'd worked downtown together, commiserating about our work woes over pints. So within a couple of minutes, we'd settled back into our comfort zone.

By the end of the first pint, Evan started talking a little more about what the inspector had shared. I guess the list had been exhaustive, detailing every item that needed to be addressed. Evan hadn't read through the whole list yet, hitting his mental limits at page three. But really, it wasn't hard to pick out the big-ticket items just by looking around.

By the second beer, he'd decided to blame both Miriam and the bank for this mess.

"How the hell are they allowed to sell a house that has that many problems?" he asked, taking another gulp of his beer. "I mean, really. Is that legal? How come I get stuck with this shit?"

I was saved from answering by a waitress in a khaki skirt slapping down two plates: chargrilled burgers surrounded by mounds of spicy, crispy fries. I picked up a fry, dragged it through the ketchup and popped it in my mouth. Fabulous.

Conversation was put on hold as we plowed through our food. I'd only made it through half my burger when Evan sat back and patted his stomach.

"Wow," I said, slightly alarmed at the speed with which he'd packed all that food away.

He looked at all the fries still piled on my plate. "You going to eat those?" he asked.

Actually, I had been planning on it, but on second thought, I really didn't need all of them. "No. Help yourself," I said, sitting back against the hard booth.

He leaned forward and pulled one loose. "Okay, so back to what I was saying. Your father's a lawyer. Do you think you could ask him if what Miriam and the bank did was legal?"

I took a long sip of beer. "I don't know that much about real estate, Evan. But I think the fact that you didn't get an inspector in before you bought it..." I trailed off.

"I know I didn't get one at first, but I've got one now, and he's telling me there's all kinds of things wrong with that place. You can't tell me they didn't know that!"

I traced a line in the water beads on my beer glass.

"You know they knew!" he pushed. *Don't say it,* I told myself. *Don't say it. He's spending the night and this would not be a good way to start.* "They shouldn't be allowed to sell a property that has so much wrong with it." He sat back with a pout.

I took another sip of beer, delaying any response. He kept right on going. "Right? Right? There have to be laws against that. Do you think your father could look into it? I mean, I'm not sure what kind of fee he charges..." He trailed off, but just for a second. "Well, it can't be that much just for looking into something like this. At least I would think it wouldn't."

Did he even need me in this conversation?

When we got back to my house, I ran upstairs to check my answering machine, and by the time I got back downstairs, Evan had stretched out on the couch and commandeered the remote control. He flipped aimlessly from channel to channel, finally coming to a stop at a basketball game.

I flopped down in my oversized armchair and kicked my legs over the side. Addie came over and sat directly in front of me, giving me the eye.

"What's the matter?" I asked her. "Do you need to go out?" She continued to sit and stare. In Addie's world, that's a no. "Do you want to go to bed?" That elicited a tiny wag, but mostly she continued to stare. "You had your dinner, what's the matter?" The thing about Addie is that she's very good at answering questions; the problem is, they have to be yes/no type questions.

"Whoa!" Evan screamed from the couch. "Did you see that?" Addie and I both flinched at the unexpected outburst. Within a second she was back to staring at me, while simultaneously darting quick glances towards Evan. Oh. She didn't like him being here.

I leaned forward and rubbed her ears. "I don't like it

either, sweetie," I whispered. "But it's only for a day or so." Border collies are smart. She gave me a skeptical look and headed for the stairs.

I leaned my head back and closed my eyes. The next time Evan screamed, "Whoa!" my heart only lurched a little bit. "Did you see that? Jess! Look. You're not even looking."

I raised my lids. "Sorry. I'm not really into basketball." He stared at me like I'd just told him I wasn't really into bathing.

"Really? Oh." He picked up the remote and ran his fingers slowly over the buttons. "Have you ever really watched it? Maybe if you watched it and I explained some of what's going on..." He trailed off hopefully. I closed my eyes again.

"I know how basketball works," I said.

"You're not even watching."

"I'm listening." The sound of a commercial, nearly double the decibels of the program, assaulted my ears. "But, could you turn it down just a tad?" I asked.

The volume declined infinitesimally. My thoughts flitted to Miriam living in a rat-infested house. How has she stood that? How could you sleep wondering if a rat was going to run across your face? I shuddered at the thought.

"Are you even listening?" Evan's voice broke through the noise from the TV.

"I was just thinking about Miriam."

"Okay, whatever. But the Rockets are only down by three. I think you'll want to see this."

"What do you think happens to us when we die?" I interjected. Not that I expected any kind of deep and meaningful answer from Evan, who considered whether or not to use steak sauce a thought-provoking question.

"I don't know. You see a bright light and you go towards it," he said, giving me more thought than I expected. "I always pictured it kind of like a train tunnel. And you know—you run towards the train."

"Do you think anyone ever gets stuck here?" He was quiet for a minute, the silence between us filled with whistles and rubber soled shoes screeching on the polyurethane glossed hardwoods. The crowd roared. I opened my eyes and peered at him.

"I don't know. I guess I never thought about it," he said, lowering the volume again. "I guess I'd rather think that we go right to heaven. I mean, my grandparents died, and I'd hate to think they're just stuck here." He looked side to side as if fearful one of them might tap him on the shoulder.

"But what about if you're murdered? Do you think your spirit could get stuck here?"

"You mean like Miriam?"

"Well, yeah. Do you think she crossed over?"

He turned the volume back up. "Yeah. I'm sure she's gone."

I was going to tell him what Wynne said about Miriam still being there, but really, what would be the point? Mostly, I was hoping for reassurance that ghosts aren't possible, but Evan probably wasn't my best option for spiritual advisor.

I endured another ten minutes of court sounds before excusing myself and disappearing up the stairs. He didn't even notice I'd left, although Henry raised his head and gave me a wag.

I didn't sleep well, the feeling of another person permeating my house so completely that it kept waking me up every time I drifted off. Addie wasn't much help either; she insisted on nudging me with her nose periodically to remind me of the intruders lurking downstairs.

The morning wasn't much better. Normally I would

wander downstairs on Sunday morning and hang out drinking coffee in my jammies while watching the news until Addie pestered me into going for a walk. Today, I was trapped in my bedroom.

Cracking my door, I listened for sounds of life downstairs but heard nothing. Seven o'clock. I flopped down on the bed beside Addie. She settled in for the long haul, concentrating on grooming her perfectly white paws. I stared at the ceiling.

Seven ten. I popped back up and crept to the door again. Addie didn't even look up. She knew. Nothing going on downstairs. I paced to the window and checked the weather. Cold air brushed my cheek through the glass as daylight began creeping up the street.

By seven forty-five, I'd stopped caring whether Evan was still asleep. Time to get this show on the road. I opened my bedroom door and let Addie fly through. From downstairs, I could hear Henry whimpering with excitement. I crept down the stairs, hoping Evan was decent.

"Hey, what's happening?" He sounded croaky. "Oh, hey, Addie." I poked my head around the stairs. Addie had landed full on Evan's chest and had pinned him down while she slapped her tongue all over his face. I couldn't be sure yet, but he looked clothed.

"Hey," I said, sounding overly bright, even to myself. I raced through the living room and opened the back door to let the dogs out.

"What time is it?" He lurched to a sitting position and rubbed his eyes like a little kid.

"It's almost eight. Did you sleep alright?" I couldn't tell if his mangled appearance was because he'd slept so hard, because he hadn't slept at all, or because he always looked like this in the morning.

"Yeah, I guess so. What time is it?"

Addie burst through the doggie dog at full speed and launched herself straight at Evan. I guess she'd gotten over her disapproval of our visitor sometime during the night. He went down with a grunt. Outside, Henry sat at the far edge of the patio, terrified of the swinging flap of the doggie door. I opened the door and he raced in.

"I'm going to take Addie for a walk. Do you want me to take Henry too?" I ignored the time question, since I'd already answered it once.

"Sure, if you don't mind."

I hooked up the dogs and headed out, leaving Evan to get himself in order. The walk wasn't fun. Henry insisted on pulling ahead, which infuriated Addie the alpha dog. She strained to get in front of him, resorting every few yards to banging sideways into him and throwing his little frame off balance. Within five blocks I'd had enough and turned to go home.

Evan was nowhere to be seen, but I could hear the shower running upstairs and his voice belting out some off-beat interpretation of "Thriller." Yikes, I thought I couldn't sing. As soon as I unleashed the dogs, they leaped onto the couch, jumping and digging in the sheets and blanket that lay tangled there. A dirty sock hung over the back and a T-shirt poked out from under. It was like a high school kid had moved in with me.

I headed into the kitchen to make coffee. The comforting burble had just begun when the phone shrilled through the quiet morning. Who would be calling me this early on a Sunday morning?

"Hello?"

"Is this Jessie?"

In the background I could hear a clamoring of voices.

"Is it the right Jessie this time?"

"Did you find her?"

"What time is she coming?"

"Hello?" I said again. It sounded like Kip's group of seniors. "Kip?"

"Oh, thank heavens, I found you at last! Do you know how many people I've woken up trying to find you? Honey, you would not believe how cranky people can be in the morning."

"No doubt," I said, wondering how he'd found me at all.

"Anyhoo, I'm sorry for the short notice, but we were wondering if you would join us for brunch? Mrs. Johnston had a feeling we needed to bring you over."

I wasn't sure how to feel about that.

"What kind of feeling?" I asked, even as I saw an opportunity to get out of the house. "Actually, never mind. Just tell me when and where."

Turned out, I was already late. I grabbed Addie's bowl and kibble, and we raced back upstairs to my bedroom. I poured her an extra big breakfast, which she daintily worked on while I took a lightning-fast shower and threw together a brunch-worthy outfit. I was ready to go before Evan was done in the guest bathroom. I didn't even want to know what was taking him so long.

"Hey, Evan?" I yelled at the closed door. "I have to go out. Addie's already been fed, so don't let her trick you into any more food, okay?"

The door cracked open and a cloud of steam billowed out. "Yeah, okay," he said. "See ya later."

I swung by the grocery store, picking up a half dozen fancy jellies and a gift bag. At the last minute, I tossed in a jar of cashews for Mr. McNeil and a packet of cat treats for Grammy's cat, just in case he was attending. I figured in an emergency, I could toss the treats in one direction while running the opposite way. I'd seen Howard move, and I had no delusions that I could outrun him. In spite of this, I had the uneasy feeling that I wasn't entirely prepared to spend a morning with this crowd.

CHAPTER TEN

It didn't take long to find Mrs. Liddell's house; Kip's directions had been perfect. She lived on a quiet street, not far from the University of St. Thomas. Small bungalows lined the street, set back nicely behind shaded lawns. A huge brown Chrysler Imperial was parked half up on the curb and half in the street, stretching along the length of the house that I was looking for. I could only guess this behemoth thing belonged to one of the seniors.

I had to circle the block twice before I found a space I could get my car into. Okay, so there were several spaces closer, but I'm not the best parallel parker in town. I trotted down the block feeling anxiously late, even though I hadn't known I was invited till just a little while ago.

It didn't help that as I approached the house, two heads bobbed in the window and I heard someone shout out, "She's here!"

"'Bout time," came the gruff reply from somewhere in the house. Had to be Mr. McNeil.

"I'm so sorry I'm late," I said, trying desperately to

remember who was who. Now that they'd changed clothes, I couldn't rely on my pink popsicle and trench coat hints.

"Oh, it's fine! It's fine," said someone that was either Mrs. Liddell or Mrs. Johnston. The other one was also either Mrs. Liddell or Mrs. Johnston, I was pretty sure of that.

"Thanks for having me," I said, proffering the gift bag and stepping into the house. We shuffled in a threesome down a long hall as the ladies cooed over the bag, and my thoughtfulness, and remarked on how sweet I was.

The hall ran the length of the house, dumping us out into a sunlit kitchen. It was remarkably large for a house of this age, and a spacious breakfast nook spilled farther out into a sunporch.

"This is really nice," I said, taking in the festively set tables and surfeit of food overflowing the countertops. A row of paper lanterns had been strung along a hutch, and a giant philodendron festooned with ribbons took up the middle of the table. Everyone wanted to fuss over me, and you'd have thought I'd brought a bag of precious stones instead of jellies the way they carried on. The noise level rose appreciably.

In spite of the size of the room, it felt crowded as the group jostled and maneuvered for prime space. Mrs. Staskywicz perched on her walker seat overseeing the kitchen, while at the same time blocking egress from the kitchen area to the table. Mr. McNeil was trying to push past her carrying three dozen eggs. Kip was wearing a tall paper chef hat and a vintage pink gingham apron.

"Sweetie, I am just over the moon that you were able to join us. Would you like a mimosa?" He waved a wooden spoon toward a nearly empty pitcher on the table. "Miss Potts! We're almost out of mimosas! Could you please...?" He was drowned out by a commotion as Grammy skidded into the room chasing after Howard, who had apparently smelled the treats I'd brought and was trying to climb up, well, either Mrs. Liddell or Mrs. Johnston.

"Mrs. Liddell," Kip shouted. "What are you doing to that cat?" Okay, that was Mrs. Liddell, so the other one must be Mrs. Johnston.

"I'm not doing anything to him. Jessie brought some cat treats." She reached into the bag and pulled out the treats. The cat mewled piteously as he stretched up the length of her thigh, trying to reach the bag.

"Just give it one already," said Mr. McNeil, finally shoving Mrs. Staskywicz out of the way. "He's hungry. I'm hungry. I don't know why we're eating so late today." He continued to grump as he pushed past Kip and made his way to the stove.

Everyone settled into what seemed like a well-practiced, if not well-orchestrated, routine. Miss Potts produced a new pitcher of mimosas, which I have to say seemed a bit stronger than anything I'd ever had before. Perhaps that explained why she and Grammy kept dissolving in fits of giggles every time they looked at each other.

Kip and Mr. McNeil took their places in the kitchen, Kip at the waffle maker and Mr. McNeil over a giant fry pan, where he was whisking up all of three dozen eggs. I watched mesmerized as the yellow mound grew bigger and bigger. There was no way this group could eat that many eggs.

Mrs. Liddell had taken her position next to Kip and was garnishing the waffles with strawberries and powdered sugar as he produced them. She must have the patience of a saint, and seemed unruffled as Kip critiqued, criticized and fussed at her over every strawberry placement. It wasn't until I saw her refill her mimosa glass that I understood where her patience was coming from.

By the time the food was ready, I was lightheaded from hunger. My mimosa had hit my empty stomach hard, and I needed something to try and absorb it with. Everyone bumped around the table like kids playing musical chairs. I slid into the closest empty one, only to have Grammy stand beside me and bleat, "Kip! Kip!" until he came over and gently moved me halfway around the table. Mr. McNeil had just been getting ready to sit down, until Kip waved a finger towards a card table that had been set up with two chairs.

"Why do I gotta sit there?" Mr. McNeil asked, staring pointedly at a large platter of bacon that sat directly in front of us. Kip picked up the bacon and led Mr. McNeil to the card table, much like what I do when I want Addie to follow me somewhere.

Finally, when everyone was seated, Kip raced around the kitchen distributing waffles and dishing out heaping mounds of scrambled eggs. After refilling everyone's glasses, he finally slid in across from Mr. McNeil at the card table.

"A toast. A toast," he said, raising a glass.

"To food," said Mr. McNeil, taking a sip of his drink and biting off a piece of bacon.

"To Jesshie," said Miss Potts, clinking glasses with Grammy. Grammy nearly fell off her chair, her tiny form shaking with laughter.

"To Jessie," everyone chorused.

The spread was as good as anything you'd find in a restaurant. I was reaching for my first bite of egg when Howard popped up onto my lap, shoving himself between me and the table. I sat back, shifting my legs, hoping he'd jump right back down.

"Oh, Howard," said Grammy, smiling at him. "Look, Howard is toasting Jessie too."

Howard most certainly was not toasting me. He had turned his backside towards me and was kneading his claws into my thighs while waving his bottom directly in my face. I looked away, uncomfortable at the proximity of his personal parts. Stomach rumbling, I pushed down on his hindquarters, hoping he would at least lie down so I could eat. But every time I pushed him down, his backside would levitate up again, like a fast-rising bread dough.

"Oh, look," Grammy exclaimed over a bite of egg. "Howard's made a friend." Everyone murmured approval while continuing to eat.

"Hey, Howard," I whispered. "How about you go take a nap or something?" I slipped a hand under his ponderous belly, hoping to lift him to the floor, but he turned and flattened himself against my legs.

Okay, fine. Maybe I could eat over him.

Mild chatter started up around the table, various conversations going on at once. It was obvious that this group spent a lot of time together, and I settled into the peaceful atmosphere, determined to reach my meal. As I leaned to the right for my first bite of eggs, Howard rose up again, this time brushing his nose against my chin.

Why wouldn't this cat let me eat? I looked around the table, hoping someone would notice my plight and help, but no one did. Time for Howard to get down. I reached gingerly around his middle, determined to drop him to the floor. His sharp little teeth flashed white, pressing against the skin of my arm before I could blink. I jerked my arm back, resisting the urge to throw Howard as far as I could.

We were at a stalemate. The food on the table was disappearing around me faster than I would have thought these seniors could pack it away. Meanwhile, Howard fixed me with a glare and settled in to clean his private parts while balanced on my legs.

"Don't you like your waffle?" asked Mrs. Johnston, hostess-concern etched on her face.

"Oh, it's lovely," I said. "I'm just..." I tried again to reach past Howard, whose rear leg was stretched out like an oversized drumstick while he licked himself with long, steady strokes. I'd nearly managed to stab a chunk of waffle when he swatted out at my arm with a front paw. How he managed to balance with all this was a testament to his athleticism.

"Howard, you get down," Mrs. Johnston said firmly, fixing him with a steely glare. "My word, poor Jessie hasn't had a bite of food." Howard ignored this, and I sat back helplessly in my chair.

Miss Potts, now feeling no pain, took the opportunity to throw a grape at Howard's head. I was amazed she was able to strike her target, and with a yowl of protest, the cat launched off my lap and disappeared around the corner. Finally. Glancing around the table, I noticed everyone was almost finished with their meals. I pulled closer to the table and bolted my food in a very unladylike way. The eggs were outstanding, if a little cold. Light and fluffy, with a hint of butter, they perfectly complemented the waffle, which was also light and fluffy. I noticed the bacon had never made it all the way around the table, and a quick glance showed that it was still on the card table in front of Mr. McNeil, where he was working his way steadily through the pile.

"Arthur! You never passed us the bacon!" said Mrs. Staskywicz. "I knew we were missing something." Mr. McNeil hunched closer and snagged another piece before Kip grabbed the plate and handed it across to the ladies' table. A plate of biscuits materialized from somewhere, and two of my jelly jars were opened and passed along with the biscuits. By the time we were done, I felt like I needed to lie down and rest.

Instead, I got up and helped Kip clear the dishes, over the protests of the hostess. It seemed the least I could do. Meanwhile, the group was transforming the table. I wasn't sure what was coming next, but a Yahtzee game, a deck of cards, and a large cardboard box appeared, along with another pitcher of mimosas. Good thing I'd padded my stomach with so much food.

I wondered briefly what Evan was doing, then promptly forgot as I was ushered back to the table, where they'd jammed in the two extra chairs from the card table. I was squished between Mrs. Staskywicz and Grammy. Unfortunately, Howard decided to reappear on Grammy's lap, where he insisted on swiping at me with half-extended claws.

"He loves you so much," cooed Grammy, kissing his gray head.

"I see that," I said, pressing farther away.

"Okay, everyone!" said Kip, clapping his hands. "We agreed that today would be a good day to continue our investigation into the Miriam Murder Mystery. Mrs. Liddell and I"—he paused to bow to Mrs. Liddell—"have thought up something that might generate some new ideas, since we seem to have stalled this week."

They'd been investigating Miriam's death? I looked around at the circle of earnest faces. Mr. McNeil and Mrs. Johnston had pulled notebooks out and sat forward, looks of intense concentration on their faces. Mrs. Liddell took a pack of three-by-five notecards from the cardboard box in front of her.

"Now, take a card, but don't look at it," she said, handing

the stack to Grammy. Grammy took a card and immediately turned it over.

"Suspect: Next-Door Neighbors," she read out. "I don't want this one."

"I said, don't look at it," snapped Mrs. Liddell. "Fine, put it back and take another one, but don't look at it." She fixed Grammy with a steely gaze. Grammy pulled another card and placed it facedown in front of her, passing the deck on to me. I pulled a card from the middle and put it facedown in front of myself.

"So, we thought it might generate ideas if we all took a random card which represents either a suspect, a motive or a miscellaneous idea, and just say what comes to mind when we see it," Kip explained as the deck made its way around the table. "Who wants to go first?"

Grammy's hand shot up like a know-it-all first-grader.

"Excellent!" said Kip with pride. "Grammy, please turn your card over, read out what it says, then just say everything that comes to mind. Don't try to think too hard. We want impressions."

Grammy dumped Walter on the floor, grabbed her card and held it out at arm's length. "Suspect: New Owner," she read slowly, her fluffy white brows knitting together. She shot a sideways glance at me, then looked back at Kip. "Maybe I could have my other card back."

"No, it's fine," he said patiently. "Jessie is not the new owner. Remember? It's her friend who's the new owner. We decided not to include her on a card this time. Remember?"

"Wait, you all think I might have killed Miriam?" I asked, a faint flush heating up my cheeks.

"No, sweetie, of course not!" said Kip, placing his hand

across his heart, as if that would make him sound more sincere.

"I think she might have," said Miss Potts, tipping her glass back and catching the last drop on her tongue. "I mean, really. Who elsh do we have?"

"What about you?" I asked Kip. "I mean, you live right there. You had more opportunity to kill her than I did! I wasn't there. I don't even know her."

"Knew her," said Mrs. Staskywicz. "Being that she's dead now."

An awkward silence descended on the table, broken only by the scratching of Mr. McNeil's pen across his pad. "Didn't know her," he mumbled as he wrote.

"Okay, everyone, let's just start over," said Kip. "Jessie, we wouldn't have invited you here if we thought you'd killed Miriam."

"Sure, we would have," said Mrs. Staskywicz. "Miriam was horrible. Anyone who knew her must have thought about it at one time or another." Murmurs of assent went around. "So, don't be upset," she went on, leaning over to pat my arm. "You have a unique perspective that we think could help us."

When she put it like that, I felt a little better. I settled back in my chair. "Okay, I'm sorry," I said. "I shouldn't have gotten upset."

"So, it's still my turn?" asked Grammy, looking around. Assured that it was, she tapped a finger against her lips, deep in thought. "The new owner probably thought he was going to be stuck living with Miriam if he didn't kill her. So, maybe he did. Because he was probably going to be stuck living with Miriam if she hadn't died."

No one could argue with that. Not even me.

"Jessie? Do you want to counter that?"

"Well, yes. I don't think Evan could kill anyone." Frankly, I sounded insincere even to myself. And he had been under a lot of pressure. The seniors exchanged glances amongst themselves, like they'd been discussing this before I'd gotten here. I got the feeling I hadn't changed anyone's mind.

"Okay, nice rebuttal," said Kip. "Jessie, it's your turn. Read out your card and then say anything that comes to mind."

I flipped over the card. "Motive: Theft," I read. "I don't know what that means."

"She took things," said Mr. McNeil.

"Oh, she did!" said Mrs. Johnston. "She was kicked out of the senior center for stealing. She took people's pills, money, books, magazines. Remember when she stole Betty's necklace? The one her grandkids gave her? That's what finally got her kicked out."

"Oh, okay," I said. "So definitely that could be a motive for killing her. Maybe she stole something incriminating. Or maybe someone came over to get their thing back and snapped when she wouldn't give it to them." I thought about all the junk in the garage and wondered if we should be looking through the stuff before we threw it out. "You know, there's a whole bunch of stuff in the garage that Evan is throwing out. I wonder if we should be looking through it. Maybe there's a clue in there."

A wave of excitement went around the table. Mrs. Liddell pushed back, her chair nearly toppling over. "I'll get the suitcase," she said as everyone began to shift. I hadn't meant now. And I really hadn't meant this group. Kip and I exchanged panicked glances.

"Hold on, everyone," he said, half rising. "Hold on! This is a great idea. Mr. McNeil, can you please make a note of this? But I think we shouldn't just stop what appears to be a good process for working this case. I think we need to press on. Then we can make a list of action items, and maybe split them up."

Low-level grumbles indicated their displeasure, but everyone settled back down.

"Jessie? Any more ideas on the theft motive?"

"I don't know. It sounds like you knew a lot of the things she took, but do we have a way to know if there was something in particular that someone would kill for?"

We did not.

We moved on to Mrs. Staskywicz. "Motive: Nosiness. I got a motive too. I think you should have shuffled these better."

"It doesn't matter the order," grumped Mr. McNeil. "She was a nosy broad. I can see where someone would kill her for that."

"Remember how you said she would watch out the window and spy on all your visitors?" Grammy chirped, looking at Kip. "That really annoyed you."

"Yes, well, I wasn't the only one she was spying on," said Kip, a little less gently than normal. "She spied on everyone in the neighborhood."

"Do you think there was anything she could have found out about someone that would make it worth killing her?" I asked.

"You said she scared off your one boyfriend," Grammy said. "Remember? The cute one you liked? Wasn't he some kind of senator, or something?"

"No, he was a law student," Kip mumbled. "And he didn't want his family knowing anything. Miriam popped out from behind a bush one evening when he was coming over for dinner. Started asking him all kinds of questions. And I never saw him again." He gave a deep sigh.

"She shtole shtuff," said Miss Potts, holding her glass to her eye to see if there was anything left in the bottom. "And she made your boyfriend dishappear."

There was a moment of silence while everyone slid glances at Kip.

"Oh! I'm getting something," said Mrs. Johnston, breaking the silence. "Yes. Something is coming through." She closed her eyes and swayed back and forth.

"Dotty's having a vision!" said Mrs. Liddell. "Arthur, write down what she says!"

"I see snow," Mrs. Johnston said, in the tone you used at middle school sleepovers when you were trying to scare your friends. "Bags and bags of snow. There's something inside."

"Bags of snow. Something inside," said Mr. McNeil, scratching away on his pad.

"Bags of white. Snow. Or ice." She paused. "White ice. Darkness inside," Mrs. Johnston went on. Then her eyes popped open and she reached for her mimosa. "That's it."

That was it? Didn't seem very helpful to me.

"Darkness in the snow?"

"Bags of snow and rice?"

"No, she said ice, not rice."

"Where is this? Who has bags of snow?"

"Bags of rice makes more sense."

The others peppered Mrs. Johnston with questions, but that was the extent of her vision. She had nothing else to give us.

We continued around the table as everyone turned over their cards and threw out thoughts about the topics. The bank manager got a lot of attention, as people weighed in on how much Miriam had harangued him, in her ever-desperate attempt to save her house. It seemed she visited the bank regularly, making scenes on almost a daily basis. Mrs. Liddell had been with her on one such visit. They were supposed to be going to the grocery store, but Miriam insisted on stopping by the bank.

"I was mortified," she told us. "They thought I was with her. Well, I was with her, but I wasn't crazy like she was. But it was very embarrassing."

"It seems like the bank manager had more to be afraid of from her than Miriam did from him," I pointed out.

"Unless he just snapped," said Mrs. Johnston. "Everyone has a limit."

Miss Potts snorted, although I wasn't sure she was actually following the conversation.

"What happened that she lost her house, anyway?" I asked. "It seems like she lived there a long time. Why did she fall behind?"

"She lost her job—oh, when was that?" Mrs. Staskywicz said. "Last year? Eight months ago? Whenever it was, she was so upset. She got another one, I think a couple of months ago, but it wasn't the same. I don't think she made very much."

"Didn't she have any family?" I asked.

"Not that she ever spoke of."

"She mentioned that sister once," said Mrs. Liddell. "Mona? Moira? Something like that. But she said she was crazy."

"Takes one to know one," said Mr. McNeil.

We sat in sad silence for a few minutes, suddenly reminded this was more than a murder mystery game.

Suddenly, Miss Potts, whose head had been lolling forward on her long neck, sat bolt upright. "What?" she shouted. "Is it my turn?"

"You already went," said Grammy.

"Oh." She looked around the table, eyes finally lighting on the mimosa pitcher. "Is there any more left?"

"No," said Kip, deftly moving the pitcher behind the philodendron so she couldn't see it anymore.

"That's a shame," she said. Grammy grabbed the pitcher and refilled her own glass and then mine.

"Hate to waste things," she whispered to me.

I began to get slightly fuzzy around the edges as I sipped my drink. As we worked through the cards, I got the sense that we weren't going to solve this today.

Everyone seemed to have their favorite theory.

Kip thought it was the goth girl next door. He didn't have a motive other than she probably did it for fun. Never mind where she'd gotten a gun. He was sure all her friends had them.

Mrs. Staskywicz thought it was a stranger. "She lived near that busy street. And behind that restaurant. Maybe she was mugged."

Miss Potts managed to focus long enough to declare it was Betty from the senior center, in the library with a rope. Because of the necklace. We ignored the library and the rope, and someone else pointed out that Betty was in Minnesota visiting her daughter and had been there since before Christmas.

Mr. McNeil was convinced it was tied to the dumpster. He wasn't sure why, but he felt like maybe she'd been harassing the restaurant owner and that fellow had had enough.

Grammy agreed with every theory, and Mrs. Liddell said she did not have enough evidence to make an informed decision. Mrs. Johnston was unusually quiet, perhaps hoping no one asked why she couldn't just get a vision and solve this thing.

As for me, I had no idea.

"Okay, everyone!" Kip said as everyone seemed to be winding down. "We need to come up with some action plans. Let's each take someone to investigate this week. Maybe we'll make better progress that way."

I glanced around, feeling like perhaps this wasn't a great idea, but everyone else was clearly enthusiastic.

"Who do I get?" asked Grammy, bouncing excitedly in her seat.

"I thought you could team up with me," Kip said. He looked sideways at me. "And we could take the current owner."

Grammy stuck out her lower lip. "Why can't I have my own person?"

"You don't want to be on my team?"

Grammy sat silently, running a finger along the side of the table.

"Okay," Kip said. "Why don't you investigate me? It seemed like you had some concerns about me earlier."

Grammy beamed. "Okay! I have Kip!"

"Mr. McNeil, can you make a list of who is investigating what?"

Mr. McNeil hunched over his notebook again. "Yep."

"You're investigating Evan?" I asked, still stuck on that point. "I thought we were past that."

"No, we're past you. None of us think you did it."

"How exactly are we supposed to be investigating?" I asked, thinking Evan was going to love having Kip skulking around his property.

"I would think each situation will call for a different approach," said Kip primly. "Okay, who wants the neighbor girl? I would have taken her, but I can't bear to be in her presence. Mrs. Liddell?"

"Well, okay. I'm not sure how to investigate a teenager, but I'll try."

Kip rubbed his chin and stared off into space. "Well, actually the whole family over there. Do you think you could take the whole family?"

Mrs. Liddell looked doubtful. "I guess so," she said.

Miss Potts looked around the table. "What are we doing?"

"I know," said Kip. "You and Miss Potts can team up since it's a whole family."

"What? What's a whole family?" asked Miss Potts.

"Don't worry about it," said Mrs. Liddell. "I'll tell you about it tomorrow."

"I'll take the restaurant guy," said Mr. McNeil before he could be assigned someone. He scratched it onto his paper.

"Who does that leave?"

"The bank manager, maybe her coworkers and persons unknown," said Kip.

"I'll take the bank!" said Mrs. Staskywicz.

"Maybe you could try to pick up something on persons unknown," said Kip to Mrs. Johnston.

"Which leaves the coworkers." They all turned and looked at me.

"Okay," I said. "I'll take her coworkers. But I don't know where she worked."

"Wasn't it some kind of party place?"

"Yes, she told us once. It had a funny name." They all looked around at each other, squinting in concentration.

"It was a warehouse."

"Marty's Party Warehouse?" I asked. Marty's Party Warehouse had been around for years. I remember going there myself as a teen, but it had been eons since I'd even thought of it.

"Yes! That was it. That's where she was working for the last few months."

I found it hard to imagine that anyone from Marty's Party Warehouse had shown up at Miriam's house on a random stormy Tuesday night and shot her to death. But, hey, if that was my assignment, then that was my assignment.

CHAPTER ELEVEN

By the time I got home, I realized how tired I was, mostly due to too many mimosas and too much food. I'd nearly forgotten that Evan was staying with me, and a small wave of disappointment washed over me as the thought of curling up on the couch with Addie and a good book faded away.

I pulled into the driveway, having to swing wide to avoid a car that was half blocking my way. Ignoring an urge to gently ding it on my way past, I settled for a mild curse, grabbed my bag and headed for the house. I heard manly shouts rising and falling in unison. Poking my head out the garage, I glanced towards Larry's. No doubt one of his friends was the driver blocking my driveway. Worst neighbor ever.

My door swung open, and one of the revelers came out. It wasn't Larry's party. The unknown guy pushed past me, cell phone pressed to his head.

"Babe, what's your problem?" he whined into the phone. I walked into my house and slammed the door shut behind me. A half dozen guys sprawled around the living room and a couple more were shoveling food into their mouths in the kitchen. I glanced around for Addie but didn't see her. Henry, though, spotted me, let out a bark and flew across the room towards me.

None of the guys even looked my way.

"Where's Addie?" I shouted to no one in particular.

"Whoa!"

"Dude!"

"Did you see that?"

"Watch this! Watch this!"

My heart sped up a little. What if she'd gotten out? I scanned the room for Evan but didn't see him. Larry was sprawled on the couch, but the rest of these guys I'd never seen before.

I raced up the stairs, hoping she was hiding in my room. Rounding the corner, I nearly mowed Evan down as he came out of the bathroom. He grabbed me by the arm and looked nervously towards the stairs.

"Jess. I am so sorry. I'm not sure what happened. This..." He waved a hand towards the stairs. "I thought it would be nice if you and I watched the game together. I ran out to get some food and some beer, and I was going to surprise you. I mean, I wanted you to know how much I appreciate you letting me and Henry stay here." He ran a hand through his hair. "Anyway, I just thought it would be nice. But when I got back, your neighbor came over, and the next thing I knew, all these people were coming in." He ran a hand through his hair again, looking on the verge of a nervous breakdown.

"Where's Addie?"

He scrunched up one eye thoughtfully. "I don't know. I think she's hiding. Maybe in your room?"

I pushed past him towards my bedroom. "Addie?" I called,

racing into my room. She wasn't on the bed, not at the window, no sign of her in the en suite bath. "Addie?" My voice took on a wobbly octave. I dropped to my knees and peered under the bed. She couldn't fit under my bed, I knew that.

Last place to look—I threw myself across my reading chair, looking over the back into a small corner space she sometimes retreated to. And there she was, staring at me with accusing eyes.

"Addie!" I reached down to touch her fur for reassurance. She gave me a baleful look, put her nose down on her paws and looked away from me. Oh boy, was she ticked. "What's the matter, sweetie? Are those stupid boys downstairs bothering you?" A roar erupted from my living room. "Well, they're bothering me too," I cooed at her. "Let me see what I can do."

Evan had disappeared. I was guessing he'd made his way back down into the fray. A guy I didn't know was coming up the stairs as I went down.

"Can I help you?" I asked.

"Yeah, I'm going to the bathroom."

"There's a powder room downstairs." I edged toward the center of the stairs blocking his ascent.

"Yeah, but Bruce was just in there and it stinks like you wouldn't believe. I'm not going in there."

"Well, it's your only option."

He grunted at me and rolled his eyes, but when he saw I wasn't either kidding or moving, he turned around and thumped down the stairs.

I wasn't feeling friendly.

The mood in the living room had ratcheted up to frantic, and I gathered the Texans were close to scoring. Most of my visitors were pushing and elbowing for space in front of my obviously too-small-for-a-football-party TV. Evan was scooting around the room, putting coasters under drinks and picking up empty chip bags off the floor.

I walked unnoticed to the kitchen, where I stood staring at the mess. Every surface was covered with beer cans, bowls of dip, chips, cheese, grocery store cookies and peanuts. Trails of salsa and dip snaked across the kitchen tiles and onto the hardwoods of the living room. What was wrong with these guys? I tamped down my anger and began cleaning the food and goop off the floor. If I could stop them from trampling this onto my rugs, at least it was something.

Henry hunched in the corner of the kitchen, shooting furtive glances at me. What was that about? I walked over and he turned away from me, little jaws chomping faster as I approached. Oh good Lord. He'd managed to snag an entire bag of beef jerky and was busy ripping through as many as he could before he was discovered. I reached down and snatched the few that were left and then took the one he held tightly between small paws.

Clutching the jerkies in my hand, including the one Henry had been chewing, I muscled my way towards the center of the group and tossed them onto the coffee table. It only took a minute before they were all snatched from where they landed. Larry grabbed the one covered with dog saliva and shoved it in his mouth. It wasn't much, but it made me feel slightly better.

"Awwww!"

"Dammit!"

"What the hell?"

"Ya freaking moron!"

I guess they didn't score.

"Yo, get me another beer, will you?" A pudgy, baby-faced guy waved an empty beer can at me as I passed.

"Oh sure, no problem," I said as I headed back to the kitchen. Pulling a trash bag out of the pantry, I began clearing the counters.

The pudgy guy strolled in. "Beer?" he asked.

"Oh right." I grabbed some wadded-up napkins and swiped at a blob of dip. He stood watching me, waiting for me to get his drink. He was going to be there a while.

"Hey, Woody. Bring me a beer while you're up," Larry hollered from the living room.

"Wanna know why they call me Woody?" he asked, leaning past me to open the refrigerator.

"No." I headed into the living room with my trash bag.

It must have been halftime, because everyone was milling around, talking and drinking. Two guys tossed M&M's at each other, trying to catch them in their open mouths. Another had taken off his shoes and socks and was intently picking lint out from under a toenail. Evan hovered around the edges, keeping an eye out for dripping cans and dropped snacks. This clearly hadn't worked out right at all.

Woody tossed a can to Larry, who caught it and popped the top, foam shooting up and bubbling over his hand onto my couch.

"Larry!" I said. "Are you kidding me? I mean, what is all this anyway?"

"Hey, don't blame me," he said, grabbing one of the toe-picker's socks and wiping at the spill. "Your friend invited me."

"I didn't, actually," Evan said, his voice so low he could hardly be heard. He was wringing his hands together in a way that made me think he was going to need some anti-anxiety meds soon. I stomped back into the kitchen.

"Pretty sure you did," Larry said. "And while you're up, make yourself useful and bring us some chips and dip, would you?"

The kitchen had cleared out, and I sank down on the floor against a cabinet. Only about another hour and a half to go. I didn't care who won the game, I just didn't want any overtime.

I glanced under the kitchen table, surprised that Henry hadn't found his way over to me. Generally, anytime I sat down, Henry raced like a missile for my lap.

"Henry?" He was still in the corner behind the table, but standing with his back to me. That was weird. I crawled a little closer. "Henry?"

Ba-ooou. Ba-oooo. Oh, no. I flew to my feet, intent on getting him outside. *Acckk.* Too late. The beef jerkies were back. Along with a whole lot of other disgusting-smelling things. Bile rose up in my throat. Good Lord. Were they trying to kill this dog? You don't give dogs—what was that? Looked like an entire bag of cheese puffs. I scooped him up and raced him out the back door. His sides were still heaving. I set him down on the grass, where another torrent of junk food made its return. Well, it was probably better that he was getting it out of his system.

Frustration stirred in me at Evan. He hadn't been watching this dog. How had he not paid attention to what Henry was up to? He was a terrible parent. Henry was lucky to still be alive if this was the kind of care he'd been getting. Maybe he'd taken on more than he could handle with a dog and a new house. On top of what was going on at work.

The wind had picked up, and I crossed my arms in a vain

attempt to stay warm. I wouldn't be able to stay out here long. Henry hung his head and looked at me with miserable eyes. I wondered if this warranted a trip to the emergency veterinary clinic. He waddled over and put a paw on my leg.

The back door opened and Evan poked his head out. "There you are," he said, sounding chipper.

"What all has Henry eaten today?" I asked, trying to keep my tone level.

"He had his breakfast earlier. And, I don't know. Maybe if someone dropped a chip or something, he might have eaten one of those."

Henry started licking his lips with quick little darts of the tongue. Uh-oh.

"Are you sure?"

He began walking towards the grass. *Ba-ooouu. Ba-oooooouu.*

"Oh my God! What's he doing?" Evan asked, bounding out the door and slamming it shut behind him. "Is he okay?"

Acccccck. A smaller puddle of goo landed close to the other one.

"Oh my God!"

"Yeah, exactly. I don't know if he needs to get to an emergency vet clinic or not. Why weren't you watching him?"

"I was," he protested, then stopped. The evidence was damning. "Is he going to be okay?" Panic lurked in his eyes, jolting my own worry to a higher level.

"I don't know. I don't know what all he's gotten into. When I got here, he'd eaten almost an entire bag of beef jerky. From the looks of what's come up, it seems like he got into some cheese puffs or something. And who knows what else he's had. If he's had any chocolate, that could kill him."

Evan started running a hand up and down through his hair, making it stand on end. "Jessie, what do we do?"

"Well, for one, you've got to learn to watch him! Evan, dogs have to be watched. You can't expect him to know what's good for him and what could kill him." I took a breath. "I'm not entirely sure you're ready for a dog."

Silence descended like a muggy fog, leaving a chill in its wake.

"Is that what you really think?" he finally asked. "One mistake and you're ready to judge me like that?" His lips tightened, nearly disappearing inside his mouth. Red streaks ran down his neck and his hands clenched in tight balls at his side. Maybe I should have taken a more roundabout approach to this.

"Evan." I bit my lip, searching for words. "Look, I'm sorry. But really." I glanced over at Henry, who was nibbling on some grass. "They're a lot of work. I know that. And with your new house, I'm just not sure you're going to have a lot of time for him."

A puff of wind raced across the patio, blowing a pile of dead leaves towards the wall. Evan stood staring at his feet. I waited, wanting to back down. Wanting to say I didn't mean it. Wanting everything to be right.

Finally he shifted, staring hard at the patio, pointedly refusing to look at me. I had to lean close to hear his words. "One of the reasons I bought this house was so I could have a home for him. My apartment wasn't a good place to have a dog. I wanted somewhere with more room, somewhere with a yard where I could throw a ball for him. I know it needs work. I know it's kind of a mess right now. But it's our house. It's his and my house." Henry trotted over to Evan and put a paw on his leg, looking up. He couldn't have planned that any better.

"And maybe I don't know as much about dogs as you do, but I'm trying." He looked up at me, his cheeks flaming. "I am trying to be a good dad for him. I know I screwed up today, I get that!" I didn't need to lean close anymore. The people three doors down could probably hear him. "But I love that little guy and I would never do anything to hurt him. I have never had anything that means as much to me as he does!"

Before I could respond, he stomped through the door, slamming it behind him. Henry waffled between navigating the doggie door to follow Evan or staying behind with me. He whined in frustration.

"It's okay, boy," I told him, feeling tears collecting at the corner of my eyes. He trotted over and leaned against my leg. Sliding down onto the flagstones beside him, I gathered him onto my lap and held him tight. I just wanted what was best for him. But Evan was my friend, and what he'd said rang true. Maybe he wasn't taking care of Henry in the same way I would, but it didn't mean he wasn't taking care of him. Then again, look at what had happened today.

I sat on the cold stones until my back began to ache. Henry settled sadly onto my lap and lay with his wheat-colored head hanging over my leg. The sounds from inside rose and fell as the game dragged on. I knew I'd have to go in eventually, but I wasn't up for it yet. If only I could magically transport myself upstairs to my room where I could wallow in comfort. Tonight was shaping up to be long. I wondered what Evan and I would find to say to each other.

Finally, I couldn't stand the cold anymore. Shifting Henry off my lap, I struggled to my feet. The crowd had thinned and a quick head count showed a hardy five remaining, making the most of the beer and eats. Evan sat alone at the kitchen table, running one finger listlessly around the top of a beer can. Henry ran over and crawled up into his lap, his legs hanging awkwardly over the sides.

"How much time is left?" I asked no one in particular.

"About four minutes. Game's pretty much over. Texans can't win."

Larry lurched from his place on the couch, screaming at the TV. "You moron!" he shouted. Too late, he remembered the bowl of cheese dip that had nestled in his lap and it flipped sideways, landing upside down on my new couch. Orange goo blobbed out from under the upturned bowl. "Oh shit," he said, picking the bowl up from the bottom. He waved it backwards, flinging whatever hadn't already dripped out onto the back of the cushion. "Oh shit," he repeated, finally turning it right side up.

I stood rooted, watching the cheese spread like thick lava across the fabric towards the crack between cushions. Larry placed the bowl in front of the edge and began scooping the mess towards the bowl, as if brushing crumbs off a counter. Only instead of crumbs, it was a thick, gloppy mess that he was applying like spackle to my sofa.

A guy with spiky red hair sprang into action, running with a roll of paper towels and a spatula that he'd found somewhere, and he started dabbing at the mess, trying to get it off the cushion. Standing the spatula on its side, he tried to block the forward flow of cheese towards the crack. It was a nice try, but I knew it was too late. Those cushions would bear the mark of this day. My new couch. The one that replaced the other one that Larry had ruined. How ironic. If I'd been in a better mood, I might have laughed. As it was, it took everything I had not to start screaming.

They were still working, or rather Spiky Red was still working—Larry had turned back to the game when someone else came over with a beer and plopped himself down into the middle of the cheese.

"Aww, man," he shouted, springing back up. "What the hell?"

"Dude, what's wrong with you?" Larry yelled back, waving a paper towel at him. "Can't you see we're working here?"

We're working here. He was priceless.

"Look at what you did to my pants!" The first one wasn't giving an inch.

"Well, you sat in it," Larry shot back.

"You could have said something." They were still going at it when I dragged myself upstairs. I went into my bedroom, shut the door and locked it. Maybe I would come out and try again tomorrow.

Addie crawled out from behind the chair, hopped up on the bed and hung her head over the side. I could hear voices rising downstairs as Larry and the cheese-sitter continued to fight. I closed my eyes and hoped that they wouldn't tear up any more of the place before they left. Whenever that might be.

CHAPTER TWELVE

W hen I finally emerged from my bedroom, the cold winter dusk had begun gathering around the corners of the house. Concern for Henry was what finally propelled me off my bed. As it turned out, he was lying right outside my bedroom, curled in a sad little ball.

"Oh baby," I said, dropping down beside him and gathering him in my arms. "I didn't realize you were here. Why didn't you let us know?" He felt chilled, so I grabbed one of Addie's blankets off her bed before wrapping him like a baby and holding him in my arms.

I carried him against my chest as I tiptoed down the stairs, cool air creeping around my ankles. Addie followed at my heels, unusually subdued for her. The living room was silent as I poked my head over the banister and peered around the corner. It looked empty.

I wondered where Evan was. I shuffled through the dim light towards the kitchen, hoping I wouldn't break an ankle on a stray beer bottle. Flicking on the overhead kitchen lights, I stared in surprise. The place was spotless. Every chip, every beer bottle, every dish—gone. I peeked in the dishwasher, hoping my dishes weren't actually gone. Empty. Biting my lip, I moved to the cabinets. There they were: sparkling clean, albeit put away in different places.

I backtracked to the living room, throwing on lights. Not a coaster out of place. Wow. I hadn't expected this.

The sofa didn't look as good, but I could see how hard someone had tried. The fabric showed damp stains, and the nap stuck up in stiff, spiky angles off the cushion. An orange glow radiated like a lopsided sun from the middle cushion, the fabric color completely changed. What kind of chemical cheese had that been? Maybe I could just flip it over. Nope. The cheese had leaked underneath and the same funky glow streaked across the other side as well.

I sighed and sank down on the carpet, a ripple of depression fluttering through my chest. I felt terrible about how the day had gone with Evan. Okay, I was still upset about what had happened with Henry, but when I thought about the whole situation, I could see how it had gotten away from him. Larry was not a neighbor for beginners. He must have sensed a weakness in Evan, and the rest was history. I reached for my cell phone and hit Evan's number. He wasn't answering, and I went to voicemail.

"Hey, Evan. It's me. Look, today was kind of a mess. I really appreciate you cleaning this place up, you did a really great job. Um, I have Henry. He's okay. I wasn't sure if you're coming back tonight? Anyway, let me know."

I prowled restlessly around the house all evening, but I never heard back from Evan. I finally gave up, took the dogs and went to bed.

By morning I felt better, determined to get myself back on track. I had a lot to do this week, most of it related to my business. I'd come too far to be distracted by trifling fallouts now. With a little effort, I was able to relegate Evan and his mess to the bottom of my list.

With that in perspective, I threw on some warm clothes, ran down the stairs and turned on the burner under the tea kettle. The dogs raced out the door while I pulled ingredients from the freezer for the day. I should have defrosted the liver last night, but I hadn't thought of it. Well, today I was done with the drama and back to business.

I flew through the day, happy to be back to my routine. By the time I was done with my morning baking, rows of Barker Street Biscuits lined the countertop and I was feeling pleased with myself. My dog-walking rounds were relaxed, as most of my clients tended to be a little less exuberant on Mondays after busy weekends with their families, so all in all, a good start.

I was driving home from my last client when I thought about my investigative assignment. It seemed that now might be a good time to check out Marty's Party Warehouse. I couldn't imagine that they would be crowded on a Monday afternoon. Maybe I would find out something from Miriam's coworkers.

It took a little longer to get there than I'd expected, mainly due to construction and early rush-hour traffic. I couldn't remember the last time I'd been here. It must have been sometime in high school, and the area had changed a lot. New shopping centers had replaced old warehouses, and massive apartment buildings helped explain the increased traffic I was seeing.

But when I rolled into the gravel lot, it was like stepping back in time. Marty's Party Warehouse hadn't changed one bit. Still a hulking old brick warehouse with boarded-over windows and a chain-link fence. I was actually surprised the fire department hadn't closed this place years ago; it just seemed like a fire trap ready to ignite.

There were more cars in the lot than I'd expected for a Monday, although when I entered the building, I didn't see anyone. But that was pretty typical for Marty's. Rows of cheap party merchandise wound their way around the cavernous space, and once you made the first turn it was like getting lost in a multi-tunneled cave.

But it was the smell that hit my olfactory nerves and whisked me right back in time. The collection of smells at Marty's was unique to this place. A mix of artificial flowers, rubber masks and damp cardboard, with an overriding aroma of dust, which smelled exactly as it had the last time I was here. You would think it might have changed, but clearly it hadn't.

I resisted the urge to wander through the store. The last thing I needed was to lose an hour and come home with a string of turkey lights for Thanksgiving or a dozen faded plastic sunflowers. Instead, I made my way across the uneven plywood floor towards a row of cash registers.

Two ladies were stringing red heart-shaped lights over a romantic little Valentine's Day display. A tiny table was set for two, and teddy bears sat staring at each other across a festively set table.

"Aww, that's adorable," I said as I walked up, thinking perhaps I needed some red heart-shaped lights before remembering I didn't actually have anyone to share Valentine's Day with.

They turned and smiled at me before one turned back and finished adjusting the string to her liking. "Thanks. Valentine's is one of my favorite holidays." I could have guessed that judging from her headband that sported two red hearts bouncing on springs with every movement.

I suppressed the urge to argue about the commercialization of romance and the pressure it put on people, both in relationships and out. Instead, I smiled back and said, "I know! Mine too."

"Can I help you with something?" the other one asked, noticing that I didn't actually have anything to check out. She was a little older, with long gray waterfall braids that flowed gracefully over her shoulders and laugh lines that made her look like she'd be fun to hang out with.

"Well, maybe," I said, suddenly regretting not having prepared anything in advance. "I wanted to talk to someone about one of your coworkers? I mean, I'm not even really sure what I'm trying to find out. This is going to sound kind of weird, but we're trying to figure out what happened."

I realized I was rambling.

"Okay," said Valentine Girl, sounding doubtful. "What do you mean 'what happened'? And who are you talking about?"

"Yeah. It's about Miriam. I don't, umm, even know her last name, but she was kind of tall, with orange hair." I trailed off as they exchanged a look.

"Miriam hasn't been in. I'm not sure if she stills works here."

"Oh," I said, suddenly flummoxed. They didn't know. "Well, yeah, I guess not. She was killed last week."

"Oh, no," said the older woman. "Was it a car accident? I never did think that car she drove was safe."

"No," I said. "Actually, she was killed. Shot."

They both gasped, and the younger one raised her hands to her cheeks in classic astonishment. "Shot! Oh my gosh! That's terrible. Do they know who did it?"

The other one recovered more quickly. "I guess they don't if you're looking into it. Are you a family member?"

"No." I hesitated. "I only met her once, but some friends of hers are trying to help figure out what happened. I guess this could have been a random killing, but it just doesn't seem like it was. So, we're trying to see if we can figure out what was going on in the days or so leading up to her death."

A lady carrying a basket full of football-themed tableware approached hesitantly. "Can I check out?"

Valentine Girl took her basket and led her to the closest register. The other lady reached out and gently touched my elbow. "Let's go talk over here." She steered me to a small alcove that had been hollowed out by stacks of boxes and separated from the public space. An assortment of folding chairs led me to guess that this was where the employees took quick rest breaks while remaining close to the registers.

We sat down and she leaned forward. "I'm not sure if there's much I can tell you that would help."

"Yes, I'm not even sure what I'm asking. I guess, did you work closely with her? Was there anyone who might have wanted to kill her? Was there anything going on that she talked about that might have seemed relevant now, in light of her being killed?"

"I probably worked as closely with her as anyone here. We were on a lot of the same shifts."

"What was she like?"

The women looked at me, honesty warring with the desire not to speak ill of the dead. "She was different."

I smiled. "Yes, I only met her once, and that seems like a good word."

She shifted in her chair. "She was difficult too. She wasn't very good with the customers, but she was fine working on the floor, restocking. Well, mostly."

"What do you mean?"

"She was loud. And kind of brash. And she liked to pop out at people and scare them. Sometimes she put a mask on. She thought they liked that."

I thought of her orange head appearing in the window. "I'm guessing people didn't really like that."

"No. No, they didn't. The manager finally convinced her to stop that. We'd gotten some complaints." She looked up at me. "But I guess this isn't very helpful."

"You never know," I said. "I'm sure the police are looking into it. I guess they haven't been here, then?"

"I haven't heard anything about it, and believe me, if they had been here, we'd have heard about it. No. No one knew anything about this. It's sad, really."

"When's the last time she was in?" I asked.

"Let's see." She closed her eyes in thought. "I guess the last time I saw her was last week. Tuesday, maybe? She wasn't working, but she came in right as we were closing up." Her eyes widened. "It was strange. She was very upset. She wanted an advance on her paycheck."

This must have been where she was heading when she left Evan and me. A tingling ran up my neck as I imagined her last hours.

"Is that something they do here?" I asked, thinking I couldn't even have gotten an advance on my paycheck at Astor Oil, and they had a lot more money in the bank than Marty's Party Warehouse.

"No. I've never even heard of such a thing. The manager was already gone, so she was asking me about it. I told her that I didn't think that was possible. Then she got more agitated and started asking if she could borrow money. Said she was going to lose her house. It was very uncomfortable."

"I hate to say it, but she'd already lost her house. It had been foreclosed on."

She looked stricken. "Oh, that's terrible. I had no idea. This just happened Tuesday?"

"I don't know the exact timing," I said. "But I think it had been sold at auction before that. I get the feeling she maybe didn't understand that it was final until Tuesday." I flashed to her wild hair and clown-inspired made-up face, screaming at me and Evan to get out of her house.

"Well, it was kind of a scene," she said. "We had an older couple in here, and I think they gave her some cash, but she just kept saying she needed more. I thought she was having a breakdown of some kind. And then when she didn't come back to work, we all just figured she'd snapped." Her eyes filled with kind tears. "I feel really bad now."

I felt bad too. I mean, she'd seemed like a lunatic, and if she hadn't been killed, I had the feeling Evan would have spent the next few years trying to convince her she had to move on. But nevertheless, it was hard to think of someone losing everything they had like that. Even worse was thinking about the way she'd been killed.

It seemed like I wasn't going to learn much more. I really hadn't learned anything at all, except where she'd gone after Evan and I had seen her. And the fact that she was suddenly desperate for money. It made me wonder where else she might have gone that night, and who else she might have approached. A leaden feeling in the pit of my stomach made me feel like I was on the right track, but I wasn't sure how to chase down her movements beyond this. Maybe one of the seniors would come up with something.

Evan had left a message on my machine while I was out on my dog-walking rounds and said he would come by after work to pick Henry up. He sounded distant, distracted and somewhat chilly. I took some deep breaths and tried to get back to my earlier optimism, but I was feeling a little less buoyant.

True to his word, Evan swung by just before six. I had already fed Henry, and that fact was pretty much the whole sum of our conversation. He never looked me in the eye, and I had already packed up Henry's food, treats and bed, so there wasn't much to do once he was there. He had left his small duffle in the living room, so he picked that up with everything else.

When he was gone, I was left with an odd let-down feeling. I like my relationships to be happy. I like everyone to get along, so this discord with Evan left me feeling put out. And yet, the whole thing with Henry really bothered me. I couldn't help but worry about the little guy.

CHAPTER THIRTEEN

Tuesday went by, and Evan never called. Maybe Henry had been poisoned by rat bait and he couldn't bring himself to tell me I'd been right. Or he was so busy with work that he hadn't had any time to spend with Henry, and he was again afraid to tell me I'd been right. At any rate, I was convinced that Henry was suffering in his new home.

Wednesday morning, I headed towards a bagel shop on Montrose. Convinced I couldn't live without a chocolate chip bagel and a cup of hazelnut coffee, I was suddenly just up the street from Evan's. It wouldn't hurt to drive by and see if anything looked amiss.

Feeling slightly like a high school stalker, I secured my coffee in the beverage holder, threw the bagel on the passenger seat, and drove the few blocks to Evan's. Hopefully he'd already left for work; I'd be embarrassed to be caught spying on him. Or, I could say I'd brought him a bagel as a peace offering.

Two minutes later I was cruising down the street, eyes fixed on the front of Evan's house searching for signs of...

signs of what? I wasn't sure. The driveway stood empty, so he must have already left for work. Well, I could at least take a peek in the window and make sure Henry was still alive.

The porch sagged and groaned as I went up the steps towards the living room window. I waited for Henry's ferocious little bark to cut through the quiet morning air, but all was quiet from the house. I leaned over, cupping my hand against the glass to see past the glare. The furniture remained where the Bucks had left it, and unpacked boxes were stacked along the wall. I guess Evan hadn't had much time to do anything. But where was Henry? I went to the next window and repeated the process. There was a little more glare on this window, but I was finally able to make out a little patch of fur in a sunbeam near the front wall. Henry?

Panic welled up in my chest. Why wasn't he moving? Oh no, the rat poison. "Henry!" I cried out. "Henry, are you okay?" I tapped on the window and squinted into the room. The fur moved. "Henry!" I would kick the door in if I had to. Mentally, I raced ahead. I could get to the vet in about fifteen minutes if I flew through a few lights. I rattled the doorknob and was finally rewarded with a bark. He was alive.

I ran back to the window. Henry stood up and stretched, looking suspiciously at me through the window. "It's me, baby," I cooed, wishing I could scoop him up.

"It's me, baby," came a voice directly behind my head. I twirled around, startled by the closeness of it.

"Holy crap," I said as Kip took a quick step back, grinning at me wickedly.

"I thought that was you," he said, twirling a cashmere scarf that was draped nonchalantly around his neck. "You haven't been by at all this week."

"Yeah, Evan and I..." I trailed off and turned back to the

window. "It's a long story." Henry stood staring at us, tail hanging still. Why wasn't he wagging? "Are you okay, sweetie?" I asked.

"Are you talking to the dog?" Kip asked, leaning towards the window with me. "Hey, pookie," he crooned in a high-pitched voice, wiggling his fingers at Henry.

"I'm worried about him," I said. "He's not acting right. Look at him. Normally he'd be jumping and barking and wiggling, trying to get to me. But look. He's just standing there."

He looked. "I think I prefer this to what you just described." He looked again. "Looks fine to me."

"No, he's not normal. I'm worried about the rat poison."

Kip squealed. "Oh my God! I still haven't gotten over that thing that Mr. McNeil found. I was so afraid that there might be more than one of those things running around the neighborhood. I've been positively afraid to go out alone at night." He bopped the edges of his scarf together for effect.

"Evan had the exterminator come by Saturday. He was supposed to lay down poison and put rat traps out. That's what I'm worried about. What if Henry got into some rat poison?"

Kip caught his lower lip between his teeth. "Oh." He leaned towards the window. "Hey, sweetie!" he called. "Are you okay?" He tapped on the window with a delicate nail. I leaned in next to him. Henry stood staring at us like we were crazy. Or like he was beseeching us for help. It was one or the other.

"Hey, what's going on?" Wynne materialized at the side porch rail, a new purple streak cutting through her hair.

"We're trying to see if Henry is okay," I said.

"What's wrong with him?" she asked, pulling herself over the rail.

"Hopefully nothing," I said. "But he's acting weird, and I'm worried about whether he might have eaten some rat poison."

"Where's the lame-o who lives here?"

"I think he's at work."

"Aren't you supposed to be in school, little girl?" Kip asked.

"What's your problem?" she asked. "Unlike your new neighbor, I'm woke."

"Nice hair," he said under his breath.

She ignored him and peered through the window. "It's probably just Miriam," she said, staring at Henry, who was watching the gathering crowd outside his window with nary a growl.

"What do you mean?" I asked, immediately wishing I hadn't.

"She's probably hanging around here scaring the shit out of him. Dogs are sensitive to ghosts. Don't you know anything?" She scowled at us and plodded down the steps, kicking her way to the street.

Kip gave a nervous giggle and clutched his scarf close to his chest. "Good luck with your dog dilemma," he said, backing away from the window. "I have a fabulous new design I'm in the middle of, or I'd stay and help you."

"Hey, wait," I said, not wanting to be left alone. Kip glanced back from the curb. "Um, has everything been okay around here the last couple of days?" Kip was anchored to the street, so I moved towards him, not wanting to shout.

"What do you mean?" he asked.

"I don't know. Have you seen Evan around? Has he been out walking Henry? You know, normal things like that."

He gave furtive glances up and down the street, then motioned me closer. "I don't know," he whispered when I got close. "I don't know your friend at all, but he seems like he's been acting strange to me."

"Strange in what way?" The same goose bumps that had run up my arms when Wynne had talked about Miriam hanging around now raced down my spine.

"Well, you know he's my assignment. So I have sort of been watching him, although I haven't been able to question him yet about his alibi."

"Oh for Pete's sake. Evan didn't kill Miriam."

Kip raised an eyebrow at me. "Okay, sweetie. Anyway, he hasn't been around that much, but when he is here, he stands at that front window, just staring out."

I looked back at the front of the house. That was weird. "He just stands there?"

"Yes. And then sometimes he pulls back fast like he doesn't want to be seen, but mostly he just stands there. And stares out." We both looked back. "Gotta run. Toodles," he said, blowing me an air-kiss from the far side of the street. "Come back soon. Maybe you could move in after they take your friend to the funny farm." And with that, he twirled and sped away.

Maybe Evan was having a breakdown. He had been under a lot of pressure lately. First the potential buyout at work, then the disaster of a house he'd bought, and then I'd gone and told him he wasn't fit to raise a dog. Oh, and the ghost. A shadow blew across the sun, further darkening the gloom of the yard. Poor Evan.

I trudged reluctantly back onto the porch, wishing I could

get Henry out of there, but not wanting to linger any longer myself. I looked in the window, but he was gone. Tapping and calling didn't bring him back, and I knew the other windows around the side were too high to see into.

Giving up, I headed home, cranking up the heat to try and ward off the chill that I'd gotten in the short time standing outside Evan's.

Addie sniffed at my shoes when I got home. Ghosts couldn't stick to your shoes, could they? If only Wynne would stop showing up and freaking me out.

Warming my bagel and coffee in the microwave, I took the plunge and dialed Evan's work number.

"Evan Petty," he shouted into my ear.

"Hey, Evan, it's me," I said, pulling the phone slightly away from my head. "What's going on?"

"Jessie?" He was still shouting. "Hey, I'm really busy."

"Oh, okay. Sorry to bother you. I just wanted to check in and see how everything was going." I listened to a moment of silence.

"Look, I need to talk to you." Now he was whispering. Furtive, even. Maybe he was losing his mind.

"Sure. Anything," I said, talking in even tones.

"Not here. Not now. Can I come by after work?"

"Of course," I said. "And Addie would love to see Henry. Maybe you could bring him too. I think she's missing him." I glanced over to where she had taken up position on the couch. Nestled in on the side away from the cheese stain, she'd flipped onto her back, poked her legs in the air and was snoring softly. Okay, maybe she didn't miss Henry that much, but I did. And I was going to miss him more if he died.

"Yeah, that'd be great," he hissed into the phone. "I'll be there around six." He hung up. Well, the conversation certainly hadn't made me feel any better. I grabbed my laptop and squeezed in next to Addie, trying to avoid the orange area. I'd have to address that issue another time. Right now I wanted to see what I could find out about mental breakdowns.

Thirty minutes later, I'd concluded that Evan was in trouble. He had the classic high-stress triggers for nervous breakdowns. Death of a loved one. Okay, Miriam wasn't exactly a loved one—in fact, he'd been delighted initially when he'd found out she was dead. But still, someone died. Post-traumatic stress that could have been caused by seeing that nasty rat. Heck, I was suffering a little post-traumatic stress after seeing that rat, and I didn't even have to live there. Employment stress. The whole idea of losing his job just when he had a new mortgage to pay was pretty terrible. At any rate, he was under a lot of pressure. And he was acting weird.

Slamming my laptop shut, I ran upstairs to get ready for my day. I'd already blown through any extra time I might have to make extra biscuits. Maybe I could get a couple batches ready to go between my last dog-walking round and when Evan showed up.

At five thirty, my doorbell rang and Evan puffed through the door carrying Henry in his arms.

"Is he okay?" I asked in alarm, seeing Henry's head hanging limply over Evan's arm.

"Yeah, I think so," said Evan, setting him on the couch. Addie raced over and gave him the once-over, sniffing him from tail to nose, finishing up with a nose-bop to his head. He barely noticed.

"Are you sure? He doesn't look well." I glanced around the kitchen for my car keys, ready to scoop him up and head to the Gulf Coast Emergency Vet clinic. Evan plopped down on the couch next to him, heedless of the orange stain. Addie gave Evan the once-over as well. She finally retreated a few feet away and sat very erect, staring at the two of them.

"I think he's depressed," Evan said, letting his head loll back on the cushion. They looked like a pair of rag dolls, with no stuffing.

"Depressed? Are you sure he didn't get into any rat poison?" He cut his eyes to me, and it wasn't pretty. "Well, I'm just asking because he looks sick. And you *did* just have an exterminator over there laying down rat poison." I hated feeling this defensive, but really. The dog looked sick.

"We haven't been sleeping well." He threw an arm across his eyes and blew out a deep breath. "I think Henry is afraid of parts of the house."

I thought back to all the stuff I'd read on mental breakdowns.

"Has he told you that?" Voices in the head. A very bad sign.

Evan's neck straightened with a jerk. "What? Of course he hasn't *told* me that. But he acts really weird in certain parts of the house. I can tell he doesn't like it." He shut his eyes again, looking defeated. I moved to the kitchen and covered the bowl of biscuit dough I'd been working on with plastic wrap. I had the feeling Evan needed some undivided attention. But by the time I'd put it away and returned to the living room, both Evan and Henry were sound asleep on the couch.

Addie and I exchanged a glance, and I shrugged my shoulders, retreating back to the kitchen. Addie stayed to keep an eye on them. I could roll out the biscuits without making too much noise. I hated to wake them, since they both looked so pathetic.

Two hours later, I'd finished my biscuits, cleaned the

kitchen and still they hadn't stirred. Evan's head had tumbled backwards and his mouth hung open so wide I could have tossed a cookie in without hitting a lip. Henry was sleeping, but not quite as peacefully. Twice I'd heard him growling and making little yipping noises while he slept. Poor baby was having bad dreams.

Well, bad dreams or not, I was getting hungry. I'd fed Addie an hour earlier, and even that hadn't stirred anyone. Normally Henry was more attuned, snapping to attention anytime the food bag crinkled. But not tonight. Poking my head in the freezer, I eyeballed the contents. Nothing that would suffice as dinner for two. I grabbed my cell and put in an order for Chinese.

Twenty minutes later, the doorbell woke the sleeping duo. Henry leapt from a deep sleep and raced into attack mode, flying off the couch and racing for the door. The racket scared Evan awake, and he gave a little scream before sinking back into the cushions and blinking in confusion at his surroundings. I pretended I didn't hear the scream and went to get the food.

We dished up the Hunan beef and General Tso's chicken over sticky white rice and sat down at the kitchen table. I poured a couple of beers and we ate in silence. Evan still looked half-asleep.

"So how's work going?" I asked, starting with an easy topic.

"I don't know," Evan mumbled over a mouthful of chicken.

"Do you think you'll really get bought out?"

He sighed. "My luck, we probably will."

Silence descended again. I wondered when he was going to get to whatever it was he'd wanted to talk to me about. I ate until the sodium started stretching my stomach. Evan finished his beer, and I retrieved another couple of bottles from the refrigerator.

Halfway through the second beer, he finished pushing rice around his plate and sat back.

"Remember when we were talking about crossing over?" he asked, staring into his beer.

"Yeah, you said you're supposed to go towards the train." I smiled at his imagery of going towards the light, but he wasn't smiling with me.

"And you asked me if I thought maybe Miriam had gotten stuck because she'd been murdered?"

"Yeah," I said slowly.

He finally looked up and stared me right in the eye. "I think she's still here."

CHAPTER FOURTEEN

First Wynne and now Evan. They were determined to ruin my sleep. I gave a quick involuntary look around my kitchen.

"Not right here." Evan sighed at my denseness. "She's still at my house. I know it sounds crazy." He took another sip of beer. I did too.

"I don't think it sounds crazy," I said. "But tell me why you think she's still around." I didn't want to put any ideas in his head that weren't already there.

"Henry is terrified over there," he said. "At first I just thought it was because it's a new place. But then I noticed he wouldn't go near the laundry room. I mean, he's freaked out everywhere, but he won't go anywhere near that room." I did a quick mental sweep of his house, and cold chills raced up my arms. The laundry room sat right over where Miriam had died.

"And it's not just like he won't go in there. He'll sit staring at the door with the hair on his back all standing up. It freaks me out." That freaked me out too. I made a vague noncommittal noise.

"Remember that first day I took you over there? And we heard someone outside? It's like that sometimes. I think I hear something, but when I look out, I don't see anything." Well, that would explain what Kip had been seeing. At least he wasn't having a breakdown. That was the good news.

He looked me straight in the eyes and I could see his fear.

"Oh, Evan. You should have called me." I felt terrible. Acting like a jerk and telling him he wasn't a good dog dad.

"And said what?" he laughed. "I bought a haunted house?"

"Well, if it's Miriam, it wasn't haunted when you bought it." He gave me a wan smile. "So what are we going to do about this?" I asked.

"I'm not sure," he said. "And I hate to ask you this, but do you think you could keep Henry for a few days? I'm worried about him."

"Of course!" I said. "The poor little guy. I hate thinking of him being scared while you're at work all day."

"Yeah, me too." Belatedly, I thought that I should feel bad for Evan having to spend the night there alone. Maybe I should invite him to stay too. But then the feeling passed. A ghost couldn't actually hurt a person. Right?

"Do you think she'd go away if her killer was caught?"

"Probably," I said, thinking about it. It made sense. It was certainly as good as anything I could think of. "Have you talked to the police again?"

"Yeah, they called me at work. Asked if I had any more information. Like what kind of information would I have that I didn't before?"

"I guess they haven't found who did it then."

"Guess not. They did tell me they estimated she'd been shot around midnight. Or at least sometime after the storm started. I guess they thought maybe that might trigger something for me. But like I told them, I was at my apartment."

"So, she was definitely shot?"

"Yeah. They told me she'd been shot in the back and then crawled under the house where she got shot again."

We sat in silence digesting that. How horrible.

"I'm surprised no one heard the shots," I said. "Then again, the storm that night was so bad."

"Yeah, Henry was terrified."

"So was Addie." It had been good timing for the killer. You had to wonder if it was lucky or planned that way. Although no one knew the storm would be that bad or that loud.

Evan rubbed his face, the circles under his eyes standing out, the rest of his face looking pale in the bright kitchen lights. "I guess I need to get going."

He nearly broke my heart as he swept Henry into his arms and held him tenderly, whispering softly into the dog's floppy ear. Kissing him gently on the head, he set him back down on the couch. He was acting as if he'd never see him again. A flash of foreboding shot through me.

"Do you want to stay here tonight? You can sleep on the couch and just get up early to go to work."

He stood waffling, obviously weighing the ghost-free comfort of my house versus the terrifying prospect of spending another night in his haunted house.

"Have you ever felt her?" I asked, speaking before considering how inconsiderate it was to freak him out further. His eyes widened in alarm.

"What do you mean?"

"Nothing," I said. "I mean, it could just be that Henry doesn't like the laundry room. And there's a lot of stuff that could be blowing around your yard. You know there's a lot of junk out there. I'm saying that maybe this is nothing."

"You're right. I know," he said, looking unconvinced. "It's probably those things." He shuffled slowly towards the door like a death row inmate heading for the chamber. "Thanks for the offer. But I should go." The dogs looked up as he went out the door. Henry didn't even try to follow.

As he walked out, he turned back. "Oh, I forgot to tell you. Sunday when you were out, some guy called for you."

"What guy?"

"I don't know. Dave. Don. Dan. Something like that."

"Dan? Dan called? What did he say?" I almost grabbed him by the collar.

"He just asked if you were there. I told him no."

"What else did he say?" I sounded desperate.

"Nothing. That was it. I didn't even think he was going to tell me his name."

"Did he want me to call him back?" Great. He'd called Sunday and it was now Wednesday.

"I don't know."

I mumbled thanks and shut the door behind him.

After he left, I plopped down between the dogs and debated what to do about Dan. Why would he call me? Was it related to Blue? Had he needed something? Was he going to ask me out? Argh. I sank back into the cushions and rubbed two sets of dog ears, going in mental circles.

I eventually circled back around to Miriam. In spite of what I'd said, I was sure she was still there. The place just radiated creepy vibes. No wonder Henry was acting so weird. For all we knew, Miriam was terrorizing him all day long while Evan was at work. Miriam hadn't struck me as the warm-hearted dog lover type. She was probably ticked off that not only had Evan stolen her house, but he'd brought his dog to live there.

Yeah, we had to get rid of her. Maybe finding her killer would dispatch her to wherever it was that she was going. But we really didn't know much about her, besides the fact that she hadn't wanted to give up her house, and the senior group thought she'd been a pain in their respective backsides. It also could have just been a random shooting, although the placement of the whole thing still struck me as odd.

Maybe she had been a really awful person and there was a reason no one was upset by her death. I still found that tremendously sad, but at any rate, she needed to move on so that Evan could make this house work. But how does one dispatch a ghost to the other side?

I finally gave up and went to bed, determined to stop obsessing about this. Alas, Evan was back by eleven thirty, a stuffed duffle bag at his side and a haunted fear in his eyes. Okay, so maybe I wasn't thrilled at being woken up. And maybe I was still slightly irritated about the Dan message thing. And maybe I'd stomped up the stairs harder than was polite. But once I'd calmed my racing heart, quieted the dogs and headed back to bed, I started getting anxious about this situation again. If Evan thought there was a ghost in his house, he might never go back there. Where else would he go? His apartment was gone. I had to imagine his finances couldn't handle his new mortgage payment and a rent payment too. Which left us with what? From the foot of the bed, Addie raised her head and stared at me in the dark. It's like she could read my mind. Yes, we would end up with Evan living on the couch indefinitely.

I was out walking the dogs when Evan left the next morning, but more effective than a note on the table were the jumbled blankets on the couch and his overnight bag sitting ominously on a cushion. He was obviously planning on coming back.

This was no big deal. People have houseguests all the time. I should be planning the menu and putting out fresh towels and small sachets of rose-scented potpourri every day, not plotting ways to get rid of him. I needed to be a better friend. Maybe I'd make dinner tonight, pick up some beer and we could sit and brainstorm how to get rid of Miriam. Kind of like we used to brainstorm work issues together. If we could get back to more comfortable footing, this could be fun.

That decided, I flew into my day, baking, walking, playing and cuddling my furry friends. Everything right on schedule.

When I arrived at Dan's house, Blue was waiting for me in his customary position. I leashed him up, and we zipped up and down the streets around his house, while I thought about how to respond to Dan's call. The call he probably thought I was ignoring. I finally decided to write him a short note apologizing for not returning his call and letting him know I'd just received his message. I left the note next to Blue's leash, preteen anxiety welling up as strong as if I'd just left a note with cute little boxes to check Yes or No if he liked me.

My last client was in a sniffing mood, so we ambled around slowly, bush to bush, wall to wall. I considered, and dropped, at least five different dinner ideas. I felt like a nice salad, but that probably wouldn't go over well with fast-food-Evan. Steaks would be nice, but I don't have a grill. We'd had Chinese last night. He was probably eating Mexican every day at that taqueria by his house. Fish? Chicken? Any way you looked at it, I kept coming back to pasta. Fast, easy, cheap. Done.

By the time Evan got back to my house, I had ziti baking in the oven, the living room was clean and I was a full glass of wine into a comfortable buzz.

"Wow, something smells good," he said, dropping his computer bag onto the rug with a thunk.

"I made some baked ziti, and a small salad," I said.

"Awesome," he said. "We don't have a ton of time."

"What'd you mean?" I asked, handing him a beer.

He took a long drag. "Mrs. Grey is coming tonight. She's going to take care of it."

"Who's Mrs. Grey?"

"She's a psychic or medium or something."

I stared at him for a minute to see if he was kidding, then I added another healthy splash of wine to my glass. I got the sense I was going to need a better buzz.

"Where did you find this person?"

"She's the mail guy's wife's aunt."

I took a small sip of wine. "And she can get rid of Miriam?"

Evan shrugged a shoulder. "I don't know if she can get rid of Miriam. But the mail guy said she could, and what do I have to lose?"

I wanted to ask how much Mrs. Grey was charging. That would be what he had to lose.

He glanced at the clock on the wall. "She's coming at seven, so we have a little time."

I served up dinner and we plowed through the meal like we'd never eaten before. I finished my glass of wine and had just a smidge more. Evan polished off another beer.

"Are you coming with me?" he asked as I was loading the dishes into the dishwasher.

"Oh, I wasn't sure if I was invited," I said. Maybe I shouldn't have had that last bit of wine. I was feeling so tired, yet watching someone get rid of a ghost wasn't something you got to do every day. "Sure, I'd love to come."

We left as soon as I'd cleaned the dishes, Evan driving. It was almost six thirty, and just about fully dark by the time we reached his house. The streetlights were on, but the closest one was two houses down, so his house disappeared into the dark lot. A damp breeze had sprung up, and I wished I'd worn something warmer than a sweatshirt.

I stood on the porch and squinted into the shadows of the yard while he fumbled with the lock. Was that something moving over by the fence? I inched closer to Evan.

"I probably need to get this lock replaced," he said as he jerked and jimmied the key. "Dang it." After what felt like an hour, he fell through the door when the lock finally gave.

I pushed in behind him, ready for the brightly lit safety of a cozy room. Then he hit the light switch, and the dim bulb hanging from the ceiling reminded me where I was. It appeared that he'd done little since I was last here. The room was damp and chilly, a musty smell tainting the air. Maybe it was better that the light was dim; a brighter light on that wallpaper would be blinding.

"Can I get you something to drink?" he asked heading for the kitchen. "I've got Diet Coke and water." I followed behind, not wanting to be left alone.

"Do you have any tea?" A warm cup of tea would be comforting.

Evan raised an eyebrow at me. "No. I've got Diet Coke and water."

"Okay, how about a water?" He went to the sink and turned on a tap, unleashing a torrent of brown. I thought he'd meant a bottle. "Oh. You know, I think I'm okay."

"It'll be fine in a minute," he said, sticking a finger under the flow. "See? It's not that bad now."

"No, really, I'm fine," I said, moving to the window. The only illumination outside came from the security light on the back of the taqueria. I found myself looking for giant rodents, but it was too dark. Any of them that had survived the poison and traps were probably regrouping and plotting their strategy for retaking the house. I imagined beady hostile eyes staring at me from the shadows. "You know, maybe I will have a Diet Coke," I said.

Evan popped the top on a couple of cans. "Come look at the laundry room," he said. "This is where Henry stands and freaks out."

We stood side by side, peering into the dark room. I could hear the bubbles effervescing in the cans. As we stared into the darkness, I felt a chilly breeze blow past. Eyes wide, I looked to Evan. His mouth was open and his eyes were popping, probably mirroring mine.

"What was that?" I asked, looking back into the laundry room.

I turned to Evan, but he was gone. Fighting the impulse to flee with him, I stood still, listening and waiting. Maybe it had just been a draft. I'm sure there were plenty of holes in this house.

Feeling braver, I inched into the laundry room. Shoulders hunched and neck muscles tight, I ducked into the center of the room, halfway expecting a crazed, screaming spirit to come swooping down at me from the ceiling. After a minute of nothing happening, I straightened up. Light from the taqueria was brighter in here, and I leaned over the dryer to peep out the window.

Diego stood outside the back door of the taqueria, smoking a cigarette and staring right at me. I pulled back quickly before I realized there was probably no way he could see into this darkened room. And somehow seeing someone going about their everyday business make the specter of a ghost less scary. I took a sip of Diet Coke and looked out the window again. Diego threw his cigarette onto the concrete, stomped on it and headed back into the restaurant.

I turned away and went into the living room, where Evan stood staring out the front window. Kip was probably looking back from his house, taking notes on Evan's odd behavior.

"Hey," I said.

He yelped and nearly came out of his shoes. "Don't do that!"

"I'm sorry," I said. I would have laughed, except he'd turned so pale I was afraid he was going to pass out. "Are you okay?"

"Did you feel anything?" he asked, turning and looking straight at me.

"Yes."

He blew out a breath and looked relieved. "I've been thinking I'm going crazy," he said softly.

"I don't think you're going crazy," I said. "You don't have a history of crazy in your family, do you?" Might as well find out about his family history. Just for future reference.

"No," he said, sounding highly insulted.

"Okay, just checking." I walked to the other window and looked out at Kip's. His lights gleamed brightly in the dark, like a welcome beacon of safety. I'd bet the inside of his house was a lot cozier than Evan's. Maybe he could come over here and give Evan some design pointers.

"Can you believe that guy has a purple house?" he asked, gesturing towards Kip's. There went that idea.

We stood in silence, staring out towards the street. Every car that drove past convinced us that Mrs. Grey was here. My feet were beginning to hurt by the time she finally puttered down the street, the rickety car weaving from side to side as she scanned the house numbers. She passed by once, unable to find Evan's nonexistent house number. We watched her taillights as she zigzagged away, finally turning around and belching to a stop, just at the end of the driveway.

Kip's curtains flew open, and I could see his face pressed close to the window as he appraised our visitor. She was something to behold as she hauled herself out of the car. As wide around as she was tall, she was completely decked out in sparkly, shimmering purple, with a large turban of the same material wrapped around her head. From the backseat, she hauled a large, bulky bag. Before she'd even made it halfway up the walk, Kip was skipping up behind her.

"Yoo-hoo, hello!" he said. Evan and I walked out on the porch. "I couldn't help but notice your lovely headwear," he gushed. "I just adore purple, as you can see from my house," he giggled and waved an arm toward his house.

"I've always wanted a purple house," Mrs. Grey said, fluttering a hand towards her heart. "But my son, he won't hear of it."

"Well, pardon me for saying so, but I think you should get to decide what color your own house is."

"Maybe you talk to him," she said. Her voice was accented, but I couldn't place the origin. Evan shifted restlessly beside me.

"What's he doing here?" Evan hissed.

Kip and the ghostbuster had started an animated discussion around what kind of material her turban was made from. It sounded like he was considering designing some pillows with a similar look. I thought Evan might have a coronary next to me. I wasn't sure if it was because Kip was there, or if he was afraid Kip would find out why Mrs. Grey was there.

I wandered down the walk, sort of wanting to touch the shimmery material myself.

"Hi, Kip," I said. I turned to the purple lady and held out my hand. "You must be Mrs. Grey."

"I am, yes, Mrs. Grey," she said, taking my fingers in a hand so cold and damp I almost jerked it back. She gave me a weak little finger shake before dropping my hand and turning to Evan. "And you are the boy that works with our Anastasia's husband." Evan looked affronted at being called a boy, but he dutifully held out his hand. She took his fingers in a two-handed clutch, and as soon as she dropped them, he wiped them on his pant legs.

"So where is this ghost you say you have? Hmm?"

Kip nearly danced in delight. "She's here to get rid of Miriam? Oh, heavens! This is marvelous! This, I have to see." He bounced up and down. "I hope you brought the big guns, sister, because you just don't know who you're dealing with."

Mrs. Grey shot him a look. "What is this you mean by that?"

"Miriam was a bitch on wheels," Kip said. "If she's decided she's going to haunt this guy, then fabulous turban or not, I doubt there's much you can do."

"You pay me up front," she said, turning to Evan and holding out her hand. "Before we go in."

"No way," he said, shoving his hands in his pockets. "You get rid of my ghost or do whatever thing you do, and then I'll pay you."

She squinted her eyes, mumbled something under her breath and made a "pfft, pfft, pfft" sound at Evan. He looked scared. I was scared for him. He just couldn't handle any more bad luck. And frankly, I was getting worried about his bad mojo rubbing off on me. I took a couple steps back. Maybe it was like catching germs and you'd be okay if you just kept your distance. Maybe.

CHAPTER FIFTEEN

"I will start with the inside of the house," Mrs. Grey said, shoving a beefy shoulder into Evan as she passed him. He tipped sideways, surprised by the move, but managed to catch his balance before falling over.

"Maybe she *can* take on Miriam," said Kip, following in her wake. Evan and I followed more slowly. My wine buzz was starting to drag at my temples and I wanted to sit down.

"What's up?" said someone behind me. Oh, good. Just what we needed—Wynne skulking around our de-ghosting.

"Nothing," I said.

"Who's that?" She was wearing a long, bulky black sweater that reached nearly to her knees, black tights and a floppy scarf wound numerous times around her neck.

"Someone Evan knows from work." I started up the porch.

"Really?" she asked, drawing out the word into multiple sarcastic syllables. "She definitely looks like someone that dork would work with." I slipped through the front door after

Evan and pushed it shut behind me. "She's here for Miriam, isn't she?" she shouted through the door.

Mrs. Grey had stopped in the living room and was digging through her bulky bag. Her head nearly disappeared inside as she rattled through whatever was in there. What did one need to get rid of a ghost? I guess we were about to find out. Kip hovered so close behind her that she surely felt him breathing on her neck. Evan stood against the wall, staring at the ceiling. I couldn't help but glance up, thinking maybe he'd just spotted a new water stain. No, just all the old ones.

"Good. Good," said Mrs. Grey, straightening up. She held two metal sticks in her hand that looked a lot like bent wire hangers. "First I go and find where we have the problem. Yes?"

"Okay, yes," said Evan. "Are we supposed to come with you?"

Mrs. Grey closed her eyes and started waving her hangers in front of her. "Hummmm," she said, vibrating the sound in her throat. Kip, Evan and I looked at each other, and I bit my lip to keep from laughing. Clicking the hangers together, she shuffled forward, nearly crashing into the wall before cracking one eyelid and moving sideways toward the hall to the kitchen. "Hummmm."

Kip grabbed me by the arm. "Come on. I have to see this." He propelled me in front of him, and I dragged my feet, not wanting to get too close. I didn't really think Mrs. Grey was for real, but what if Miriam's ghost was? I didn't want to get caught in any spectral crossfire. Stepping quickly sideways, Kip fell in front of me and I smiled sweetly at him.

"Sure, let's go." I stayed behind him, gesturing for Evan to come too. He stayed even farther back.

"Hummmmm." We shuffled like junior high kids through

a fright house at Halloween. If one of us screamed, we would all panic. "Hummmmm." Mrs. Grey reached the kitchen and nearly fell over the curled lip of linoleum. "Hmph," she muttered, opening her eyes and stomping down the offending intrusion. She closed her eyes again and began banging the wires together. Click, click, click. She pointed the wires towards the bulging ceiling. "Hummmm." She opened her eyes. "That is bad," she said, looking back at Evan.

"Is that where the ghost is?" he asked. Kip giggled, a high-pitched, nervous sound.

"No. It is ceiling that is falling down," she snapped. She turned towards Kip. "Pfft, pfft."

"Hey!" he said. "What's that? What did you just do?" He brushed wildly at his arms as if trying to rid himself of a spider. "What'd she do?" he asked, turning to me.

I laughed, trying to suppress it, but the nervous tension combined with the wine was doing its work.

"Pfft," she turned, spitting towards me.

Resisting the urge to shake my arms around like Kip was doing, I nevertheless took a step back. Satisfied that we'd been put in our place, she closed her eyes again and shuffled towards Evan's bedroom. Kip crowded close to me, clutching my arms with fingers so tense I knew I'd have a bruise tomorrow.

"Ow," I whispered, smacking at his hands. "Stop it." He let go of my flesh but balled the fabric of my sweatshirt into his hands like a lifeline. I rolled my eyes but moved forward, dragging him along. Mrs. Grey had moved into Evan's room, and I saw her crack open an eyelid to take a look around. With one stick, she poked at a pile of laundry on the floor. This time Evan didn't say anything.

"Dirty," she said, sounding disgusted.

"Ick," said Kip in my ear.

The clicking started up again. It got faster as she got to the closet, and a nervous tingle raced through me. "Hummm-mm." She hummed louder than she had in the other rooms. The wires clicked faster. The faster the clicking, the faster my heart raced. She edged closer to the closet door, hesitating. The wires seemed to be surprising even her, and she opened her eyes and stared at her hands like she wasn't controlling them anymore.

"Humm." Her voice lowered almost to a whisper that made the hairs on my neck stand up. "Open the door," she said to Evan. The overhead light reflected harshly on his face, and he looked pale enough that I feared he might be close to fainting. He moved reluctantly forward. With a quick jerk, he flung the door open and stepped sideways. From inside the closet, something moved, crashing to the floor.

Kip and I screamed in stereo, my hands flying to cover my eyes. Even Mrs. Grey stifled a scream. Only Evan looked unmoved.

"It was just one of the dolls," he said, glancing into the dark space. "They keep falling off the shelf."

I rested my hand against my hammering heart. "I thought you were going to get rid of those."

"You keep dolls?" asked Kip, looking at Evan speculatively.

"I don't keep dolls," said Evan, scowling darkly at Kip. "They were here when I moved in. I want to get rid of them, but they might be worth something."

"I doubt if Miriam had anything that was worth something," whispered Kip in my ear.

I peered around the door and shuddered at the eyes

staring out at us. I looked quickly away. "They still give me the creeps."

Mrs. Grey stood immobilized, staring at the dolls. "These are bad," she finally said after the rest of us had fallen silent. "You must get rid of them. No wait."

I was all for that.

"Not if they're worth something," Evan said, setting his jaw in what I knew indicated complete immovability. "I've got a lot of stuff that needs to be done around here, and I need the money."

"They must go," she said. "Money no worth the risk."

"Maybe we could at least put them outside," I said, meaning maybe Evan could put them outside. I had no intention of touching any of those things.

"They go," she insisted. Her sticks hung limply in front of her.

"Can we keep going?" Evan asked. I should have never told him they could be worth something. What did I know about dolls? Apart from a plastic baby with a frizz-ball of nylon hair that I'd dragged around till I was three, I hadn't really been into dolls.

Mrs. Grey squinted at the closet and gave the dolls a couple of "pffts," then backed away, kicking the door shut behind her. She lifted her wires up, but I noticed they were trembling slightly before she managed to get them going again with a click, click, click. After that, we moved rapidly through the rooms. She'd almost given up closing her eyes, merely squinting as we went, humming more quickly and racing through the house.

We were back in the living room within minutes. Evan said, "You didn't check the laundry room. That's where my dog has his worst reaction. I told you, that's where I think the"—he hesitated, searching for a word—"the problem is."

Mrs. Grey frowned at him. "No to worry. We will cleanse the whole house. I no need to see more." She clutched her large bag to her chest, her turban slipping to the side. I thought she was getting ready to bolt for the door. Instead, she took a deep breath, stuck a hand into her bag, and pulled out a large metal disk on a heavy chain. Stretching the chain with both hands, she pulled it carefully over her turban and let it fall with a thump onto her chest.

"What's that?" asked Kip, leaning forward and squinting at her ample chest. He stayed well out of pffting distance. I found myself squinting alongside him. A rough dragon with a jewel eye rested on her bosom. She ignored us and went back into the bag, pulling out a bundle of twigs and a candle lighter.

"Now we fix it." With a click, she lit the end of the sticks, and a mildew-smelling white smoke began drifting towards the ceiling. She walked slowly around the room, spreading her noxious fumes. At each corner, she waved the bundle skyward, her dragon disc bouncing up and down on its heavy chain. "Pfft, pfft, pfft."

As she passed the front window, I caught sight of Wynne bending towards the window. Mrs. Grey saw her too and gave an extra loud "pfft," waving her glowing sticks at the window. Wynne laughed, pressing her face closer.

"Ugh, that child," said Kip. "Someone should call the truant police."

"School's out for the night," I said, clearly stating the obvious.

"Well, maybe the regular police. She is most certainly trespassing." He flicked a dismissive finger at her. Like Kip was one to be criticizing a trespasser, I thought. Mr. Murder Tour Operator. "That was different," he said to me.

"I didn't say anything."

"I know what you were thinking." Mrs. Grey moved slowly down the hall with Evan trailing along behind her. "I want to see those dolls again," Kip said. "Come with me."

"No way. Those things really give me the heebie-jeebies."

"Come on," he said, the merest hint of a whine marring his words. "I don't want to go by myself."

"I don't know why you want to go at all."

"What if they're lovely and decked out in style? You never know where you are going to find stylish inspiration." He ran a critical eye over my outfit. "Right?"

"You know I have a dog biscuit and dog-walking business, don't you? I think my style is just fine."

"No excuse not to look your best, sweetie. Haven't you ever run into a hottie while you're out and about? Hmm? I'll bet a cute little thing like you could have men falling all over you if you just spruced up your look a little bit." I hesitated, thinking about Dan, and Kip, sensing my weakness, jumped right in. "We should go shopping together. You and me! I could really help you, sister." He tilted his head sideways as if studying a sculpture.

"I don't know." Maybe this wasn't a great idea. I thought I looked perfectly fine.

"These baggy clothes just don't show off your figure. Look." He grabbed the sides of my sweatshirt and pulled out. "Just look! You could fit three more people in there. I'm thinking something more tailored."

"I walk dogs for a living," I said, speaking each word slowly so he could understand me. "And I bake biscuits."

He flicked a dismissive hand. "And I make pillows, but do

you see me hanging around in my jammies all day? No, you do not." Actually, he did look super-spiffy every time I saw him.

"I also need to watch my costs. My business is just getting started."

"All the more reason to look good now," he said. "Who wants to buy gourmet dog biscuits from a slob?"

A slob? One look at my expression, and he rushed to put an arm around my shoulder. "Honey, I didn't mean that," he said. "You are adorable. You know that. I just want to help you. I have some talent in this field." He squeezed my shoulders. "Let's just go take one little peek at those dolls, and then we'll set up our shopping agenda."

I know when I'm beaten. Maybe if I'd skipped that last little bit of wine, I could have resisted. But I was too tired to resist. I could hear Evan and Mrs. Grey in the kitchen.

"Here, wave that smoke under here," Evan said. "I have a rat problem."

"I no do rats," Mrs. Grey said, banging a cabinet door.

Kip pulled me into the bedroom. "Ooh, let's look." He pulled the door open and flicked on the light. "Oh," he said, stepping back. "That is not what I expected."

I looked over his shoulder. Yep. Still lined up in militant rows staring at us with their mean, beady little eyes. The bride doll gave Kip a look that made my blood go cold. Mrs. Grey was going to need a few more flaming stick bundles in here.

Kip slammed the door, throwing his body against it. "Why didn't you tell me how evil they are?" he whispered.

"I tried." His eyes darted around the room, settling on an unpacked box near the bed.

"Drag that box over here," he said. "We've got to lock those things up."

"We need to just get rid of them."

"But how?"

"If I find a trash bag, will you load them into it and haul them away?" I started for the door, thinking maybe Evan had some bags in the kitchen.

"I am not hauling those things anywhere," he said, putting his full weight against the door. "And I don't want them living across the street from me. My God! This is worse than having Miriam living here."

"They're Miriam's dolls," I said. "They lived here with her, you just didn't know about them."

"They have got to go."

"You're going to have to convince Evan of that. I think they're his now, and he thinks he can sell them."

Mildew smoke puffed into the room ahead of Mrs. Grey. Evan slouched in behind her. He scowled when he saw Kip in his bedroom. "What are you doing?"

"Kip wanted to see your dolls."

"They're not my dolls. I mean, they are, but not like you're saying it."

"You need to get rid of those things," Kip said.

"You listen to this one," Mrs. Grey chimed in, waving a smoke cloud towards Kip. Little chunks of ash fell to the floor as she waved her stick around.

"Can you de-evil them?" Kip asked.

She clutched the chain around her neck and took a deep breath. "I no know," she said. "This is more than I have worked before." She closed her eyes. Kip closed his as well and began breathing in sync with her. Evan rolled his eyes and cleared his throat.

"So can we finish this job, please?" he asked.

"I work to finish this job," she snapped back, not bothering to open her eyes. She moaned and rocked, smoke rising in waves from her swaying arms.

I made my way around piles of dirty clothes to the window and leaned toward the uncovered pane. Out of the darkness, a beam of light blasted through the window, blinding me with its intensity.

"Oh!" I screamed, stumbling backwards.

"Ahh!" Kip screamed. Dots of white danced in front of my eyes, and I closed them, trying to stop the assault, but I could still see flashing orange circles against the inside of my eyelids.

"Get off me!" I heard Evan say.

"It's Miriam! It's Miriam!" Kip shouted. "And she's angry!"

"Mother of God!" Mrs. Grey cried, her clothing rustling like cellophane as she moved somewhere near me.

I risked cracking open a lid, but my vision was still affected. Shuffling backwards, I tried to move away from the window. Loose clothing wrapped around my ankles and I lost my balance, falling sideways. Luckily, I landed on something soft.

"Oomph." Uh-oh. I must have landed on Mrs. Grey. I slipped sideways to the floor, trying to get off of her. I opened my eyes again. Slightly better.

"Are you okay?" I asked. She rolled away from me, rolling right over her smoldering stick bundle.

"Ow," she cried, leaping up and swatting at her bottom.

"What was that out there?" I asked. No one answered, obviously afraid to go look. A sudden tapping on the pane silenced us all.

"Turn out the light," Evan whispered. No one moved. I

pushed to my knees and lurched to a crouch, ready to run out of there if I had to.

Tap, tap, tap.

"Hey," came a voice from the yard. "What's going on in there?"

"That's not Miriam," I said. No one moved, obviously having learned a lesson from watching what had happened to me when I'd looked out the window.

"Well, who is it?" Evan asked.

"I don't know, but I'm not risking cornea damage by looking out there again." There was silence outside now, and we all stared mutely at each other. Mrs. Grey's bundle had stopped smoking.

"Do you need to light those on fire again?" Evan asked, waving towards her sticks.

"I no want to do this house anymore," she said. "I burn my nice outfit." Kip moved behind her bending down to look at the damage.

"It's just a little burned," he said sympathetically. A pounding from the front door made us all jump. We shuffled in a clump towards the living room. A light flashed wildly outside the front window.

"Don't look at it," I warned. Smaller spots still floated in front of my eyes.

"Who's there?" Evan shouted through the door.

"It's Arthur McNeil!" Evan looked at me, obviously having no idea who that was.

"Mr. McNeil!" Kip said, pushing Evan out of the way and ripping open the door. "Argh!" He turned back towards us, clutching his hands over his eyes. "Turn it off, Mr. McNeil! Turn it off!"

I'd closed my eyes in self-defense, but even with my eyes closed, I could tell the minute the light shut off.

"Oh, sorry," he mumbled. I risked a look. Mr. McNeil stood just outside the door, a bulb the size of a car headlight dominating the center of his forehead.

"What is that?" I asked. Kip was still out of commission, cupping his hands over his eyes.

"It's a headlamp," Mr. McNeil said.

"I've never seen one that bright before."

"I made it myself," he said proudly. "Those ones they sell aren't worth anything. Puny wattage. Can't see nothing with those."

"What are you doing here?" Kip asked. Tears leaked down between his fingers.

"I saw the smoke through the window. I thought there was a fire," Mr. McNeil said, sounding every bit like he thought we were all idiots. He moved forward through the door, dragging his metal detector along behind him. Poking his nose in the air, he sniffed suspiciously. "What's that smell?" he demanded. "Smells like that wacky tobaccy the kids smoke. That's what causes all the trouble nowadays. Damn wacky tobaccy. You kids need to get a job like I had to when I was your age."

Mrs. Grey muttered under her breath. I don't think this was going quite the way she'd hoped.

"It's not wacky tobaccy," Kip said, finally taking his hands off his eyes. He blinked rapidly against the overhead lightbulb and shut his lids again. "This lady is getting rid of Miriam."

Mr. McNeil looked at Mrs. Grey in her purple getup. "Whaddya doing? One of those whaddyacallits? A séance?" He poked a finger at her turban. "Your hat's crooked."

"I am smudging the house to rid the spirits," she said, putting her nose up in the air and trying to look down it at him. That move would have been more effective if she was taller.

"Smudging, huh? Oh, brother." He stomped towards the door.

"You must be special trained to do this," said Mrs. Grey. "I am special trained. I have the skills and the power to work with the dead."

"Trained, schmained," Mr. McNeil said. "Maybe I'll smudge my house. Get rid of spirits. Light up a cigar and puff it around the house." Mrs. Grey swelled with indignation.

"You haven't said what you're doing over here," Kip said.

"Oh." Mr. McNeil suddenly looked guilty and stepped back outside, swinging his metal detector behind him. "I was just looking around."

"What are you looking for?" asked Evan, finally jumping in. "This is my property. If you find anything valuable, it's mine. And now that I'm thinking of it, I don't want you on my property at all. What if you fall and break a hip? I'm not paying for your hospital bills."

"I'm not gonna fall," said Mr. McNeil. "Dumb kids, think just cuz you get a little older you can't do anything." His hand reached towards his headlight and we all grabbed our eyes and turned away.

"No!" shouted Kip. "Have some pity, Mr. McNeil. Please don't turn that thing on anymore."

"How'm I gonna see where I'm going if I don't have a little light?" He started down the rickety stairs, but he didn't turn his headlamp back on. "What? You want an old man to break a hip?" He stomped across the yard and headed back around the side of the house.

"Hey," Evan yelled. "I told you, you can't just be tres-passing on my property!"

Mr. McNeil muttered something unintelligible and kept right on going, turning on both his metal detector and his giant headlamp. "Why doesn't anyone listen to me around here?" Evan asked. We all ignored him.

Kip turned to Mrs. Grey. "Are you finished getting rid of Miriam?"

She blew out a big breath. "I work hard and the bad spirit, that bad one is almost gone," she said. Her shoulder sagged under the weight of her bag as she reached into its depths. Extracting her candle lighter, she clicked it on and held the bundle in the tiny flame until the ends began smoldering again. "Now we finish."

We followed her around as she smoked all the corners and doorways. Like overtired kids, tired of the current game, we shuffled along in silence. I was ready to go home and go to bed. Even Kip looked like he was losing interest, and I found him staring at me, as if sizing me up for my makeover. I was already regretting agreeing to go shopping with him. Well, it wasn't like we'd finalized plans. I'd just make a break for it before he brought it up again.

The laundry room was last. Puffing herself up like a giant purple parakeet, Mrs. Grey attacked the room with gusto, waving her smudge stick in wild arcs and nattering in a language I didn't recognize. Kip and Evan watched wide-eyed, boredom replaced with fascination. Once around the room, then twice, she circled until the smoke churned like a white cyclone. Sweat glistened on her face and the hair under her turban stuck to her face in dark ringlets. Like a whirling dervish, she bounced off the dryer in her excitement, tripped, and fell to the floor with a last "pfft."

If Miriam was still hanging around, this ought to get rid of her.

CHAPTER SIXTEEN

I t felt as if we were waking from a trance, and we all let out a collective breath. Mrs. Grey lay in a purple heap on the floor, looking nearly spent.

"So, is that it?" Evan finally asked.

"What more you want?" Mrs. Grey asked as she hauled herself to her feet. She patted at a bead of sweat trickling out from under her turban.

"I just wanted to make sure that the, you know, the thing we talked about is gone."

She wobbled towards the door. "You get rid of the things in that closet and you be okay now."

"Okay, well, thanks for coming," he said, intent now on ushering Mrs. Grey out.

Mrs. Grey gathered her belongings, and they headed outside to settle up. She looked a lot like I did after a tough day dog-walking in wet, windy weather. Only I didn't usually end up with burn marks on my butt. I'm not sure what material her outfit was made of, but the small burn mark on her backside had morphed into something the size of a hotcake, and as she walked away, I could see straight through to her large white panties underneath.

"My word," Kip said, watching her go. "That was certainly entertaining. I only wish I'd known earlier that this was going to occur. I'm sure Grammy and her friends would have enjoyed this to no end."

"I don't think Evan would have gone for that," I said.

"He is so uptight, isn't he?"

The light from Mr. McNeil's headlamp pierced through the night like a beacon at the State Fair.

"He never did say what he was looking for," I said.

"Sweetie, knowing Mr. McNeil, he could be looking for a quarter he thinks he dropped the other day or he could be looking for Civil War cannonballs."

"There're Civil War cannonballs in Houston?"

"I wouldn't know myself. At any rate, I need to get back to work. I've got some stunning ideas for my new Mystic Collection."

"Your Mystic Collection?" I asked.

"Yes, isn't it darling! I just thought of it tonight. I'm seeing poufy purple pillows with big bangles and maybe shimmery trim. Oh! And maybe they can be produced in such a way that they can ward off evil spirits." He skipped away from me.

"I hope you use flame-retardant material," I called after him.

"Excellent point," he shouted at me from his front porch. "This is going to be fabulous!"

At least he'd forgotten about my fashion makeover. I looked around for Evan. He stood beside Mrs. Grey next to her car, his head bowed close beside hers. I couldn't hear what she was saying, but she seemed to be speaking with rapid-fire speed. Her hands gesticulated wildly, nearly hitting

Evan in the face a couple times, but he stood absolutely still, staring at her like she was passing him the keys to the universe.

I headed around the side of the house to find Mr. McNeil.

"Mr. McNeil," I shouted as I reached the corner. "This is Jessie. I'm coming around the corner. Could you please turn your headlamp off, or at least face the other way?"

"What?" he shouted back.

"This is Jessie! I'm coming around the corner. Could you please—" The light hit me in the face before I could finish. Luckily, this time my reflexes were faster and I snapped my eyelids closed. Even closed, the light burned through as if I were racing straight towards the sun. "Could you please turn off your light?"

"Sorry," he said. The light snapped off and it went black under my eyelids. I risked a peek. "Darn fool strap," he said, fumbling with the back of his head. The contraption came loose suddenly and tumbled forward with a crash, bouncing off a bush and hitting the ground. I sort of hoped the lightbulb had broken.

I bent forward to retrieve it. With the exception of a large ding in the aluminum saucer housing the giant bulb, it looked relatively unscathed.

"This is quite a device you have here," I said.

Mr. McNeil puffed up proudly. "I made it myself. If you want something made right these days, you gotta make it yourself."

"What are you looking for out here anyways?" I'd noticed he'd sidestepped the question earlier. He shuffled his feet and fiddled with his metal detector handle.

Finally he sighed. "Well, I guess your boyfriend there has a right to what I found the other day." He reached into his pocket and pulled out a small oval medal. "I found this the day we was over here with Kip."

I leaned forward, staring through the darkness at the oblong disc in his hand. "What is it?"

"It's one of them religious medals," he said. "You know, the kind that folks carry around for luck or whatever."

"Oh, like a St. Joseph medal," I said.

"Yeah, like that," he said. "But this isn't St. Joseph, it's St. Anthony." I leaned closer, but the medal was too small and the night was too dark for me to make anything out. "Here, you want to look at it?"

"No, that's okay," I said. "So, what? You're looking for more of these things?"

He slipped it back into his pocket. "Yeah. I checked out this St. Anthony. He's the patron saint of lost things. So I figure, this one is kind of a dud. I mean, patron saint of lost things, but someone obviously lost this, so how good can it be? I'm trying to find one that works."

"Works for what? Are you looking for a particular saint?"

"Nah. I just want a lucky one. I had a buddy in the war, he had a half dozen of them things hanging around his neck, and you wouldn't believe how good they worked. It was like nothing could touch that guy." His gaze drifted off. "Lucky Charlie. I wonder what ever happened to old Lucky Charlie."

"You should Google him," I said. "You might find him."

He gave a snort. "Have ya seen how old I am? Lucky Charlie was even older than me. He'd be older than dirt by now. He's probably dead."

"You don't know," I said. "He was lucky. For all you know, he's still lucky."

"Yeah. Maybe." He didn't sound very convinced. "But

anyway, I was looking for more of these things. I figured they helped Charlie, maybe they could help me too.”

“I think you can buy these online now.”

He snorted again. “You kids just don’t know anything. Lucky Charlie didn’t just get his medals from some computer place. He got them from people. People give you lucky stuff, or ya find it. You don’t just go buying lucky things on the Google like you said.”

He was probably right about that. “Have you found anything else?”

“Nah, just some junk. Bottle caps, like that.” He leaned forward, bracing himself with his metal detector. He looked worn out.

“You okay?” I asked.

“I’m fine. I’m fine,” he said, straightening up.

“Maybe Anthony is your lucky thing.”

He snorted.

“But maybe you shouldn’t be out here looking around at night. Evan’s worried you might trip over something and get hurt.” I should tell him that Evan didn’t want him looking around at all, but it seemed rude.

“I’m not gonna trip.” He made an exasperated sound. “But, I guess I could call it a night.”

We picked our way towards the front yard, past where I’d found Miriam.

“This is where I found her,” I said, sounding like a docent pointing out an interesting architectural feature.

“You don’t say,” grunted Mr. McNeil.

“Yes, she was under the house. My dog found her.”

“Well, Miriam was damn fool enough to end up like that.” He sounded very matter of fact as he pushed past me, swinging his metal detector casually back and forth.

Evan was just coming out the front door as we rounded the corner.

"There you are," he said. "Is that old—" He stopped as he saw Mr. McNeil standing in the shadows.

"Is that old what?" Mr. McNeil asked.

Evan stood shifting on the porch. "Oh, hi," he finally said. "Everything okay?" he asked, looking towards me.

"Yes, everything's fine. Mr. McNeil is going to call it a day."

"Okay, good. I want to get some stuff done in there tonight. It seems so much better since Mrs. Grey did her thing, I'm excited to start making it look nice."

"Great. I'm glad you feel better. But I need a ride home first." Evan stared at me, as if confused. "Remember? Henry's at my place? You brought me over here?"

"I can take ya home," Mr. McNeil piped in.

"No, that's okay," I said. "I don't want you to have to go out of your way."

"It's not outta my way. I could use the company."

"You don't even know where I live."

Evan chimed in. "Thanks. It's not that far from here," he said to Mr. McNeil. He turned and headed for the door.

"I need to get my purse."

"I'll get it!" Evan raced inside and was out in seconds, swinging my bag by the strap. "Here you go. If you could keep Henry one more night, that would be great, Jess."

He headed back inside, the door thumping closed behind him.

I followed Mr. McNeil to a behemoth brown car parked in front of Tiffany and Brian's house. It was the same one I'd seen outside Mrs. Liddell's at Sunday brunch. The dang thing had to be about twenty feet long, and wide enough that I could have stretched out across the backseat without either my head or feet touching a door.

"Wow," I said, struggling to open the heavy door. "This is huge."

Mr. McNeil squared his shoulders and patted the driver's door proudly. "She's a Chrysler Imperial. They don't make 'em like this anymore."

Considering it probably got two miles a gallon, I could see why. I slid onto a split bench seat wider than my couch and reached for my seat belt. It took me a minute to realize there were only lap belts. I pulled the belt over my hips and prayed that my internal organs wouldn't be cut in half if we were in a wreck. Comforting myself with the thought that there was probably more metal just in the front end of this thing than there is in the entire body of most cars on the road, I tried to forget about it.

Mr. McNeil turned the key, and the engine turned over with a deep-throated groan. We surged forward, barely missing the car parked on the other side of the street. I turned my head and looked out the passenger-side window, wondering if I'd have been better off walking home.

I gave him directions to my house, and we cruised along, the suspension system feeling much looser and bouncier than my little CR-V. I leaned back in my seat and attempted to relax.

"Have you had any luck trying to figure out what happened to Miriam?" I asked as the car swayed side to side.

"We've been working on it," he said, scowling at the windshield. "She coulda been killed by anyone who ever knew her. She had a way about her."

We'd come to a cross street, no stop sign in our direction, when Mr. McNeil stomped hard on the brake about four feet into the intersection. The big car burned rubber, and I threw my hands against the dashboard to brace myself. Once we stopped, he hit the horn with two long, loud honks. I looked to either side, but there were no cars approaching in either direction.

"I did my investigation Monday," he said, stepping on the gas. We shot forward again like nothing had happened. I was still clutching my heart with one hand and the dash with the other.

"How'd that go?"

"I think that restaurant manager guy is in this up to his beady eyes."

"Diego?" I asked. He'd seemed nice enough to me, but then again, I really didn't know anything about him other than Evan loved his food.

"That his name? He didn't introduce himself, but I don't like him."

I tried to imagine how Mr. McNeil would have gone about this investigation. "What did he say? Did you tell him you were investigating Miriam's murder?" I was starting to get a bad feeling about these seniors running around poking their noses into this. I mean, that was presumably what had gotten Miriam killed.

He turned and looked at me several beats longer than I felt good about while we were rolling down the street. "Of course I didn't tell him I was investigating Miriam's murder. Whaddya take me for? An idiot?"

"No, no. Of course not," I said, waving a hand towards the windshield. "So, what did you ask him, then?"

He turned forward again. "Well, I didn't ask him nothing at first. I went looking around the back. Because it seems to me that maybe someone over there saw something. I mean, it's possible. Or maybe there were security cameras or something. They have that on TV all the time. Just get the video."

He had a point. I felt dumb that I hadn't thought about that. But presumably the police had.

"I would think the cops would have checked any security videos in the area," I said.

He grunted. "Yeah. If there were security videos."

"Oh. So there aren't any behind the restaurant?"

We'd stopped at a red light, and he looked over at me, his hands still at two and ten.

"Oh, there's cameras," he said. "Only they wasn't working."

"Really? Like they don't work at all? Or they just weren't working then?" I asked.

"They haven't been working since the night Miriam got it." He glanced up as the light turned and we lurched forward.

"So how'd you find this out?"

"Like I said. I was looking around out back. I had my metal detector with me and I was kind of poking around the back alley there. There's no windows back there, so it's not like someone coulda seen anything that way. But the steps to the backdoor are pretty high. If someone was standing up there, they mighta seen something. But while I was checking this out, this guy comes out. Asks me what I'm doing. So I say, 'What's it look like I'm doin'?' And he says 'I don't know, but this is private property and you can't be doing it here.'"

I was starting to think Mr. McNeil heard that a lot.

"What did you tell him?"

"I said I was looking for change. I'm an old man. It's hard to live on Social Security. Said he was sorry to hear that, but I couldn't be back there."

"And that was it?" Here I'd thought my investigation had been a little lame.

"No. Then I asked if those security cameras were working, 'cause someone had broken into my car on the street last week, and I was hoping that maybe they'd captured some footage of who did it."

"You didn't tell him who you were, did you?" If Diego was involved, then I was really getting concerned about Mr. McNeil. He didn't even dignify that with a response.

"He told me that his cameras went out during that big storm last week and haven't been working since."

"That was a heck of a storm," I said.

"Yeah. Well, what I'd like to know is, if them cameras ain't working, how'd he know I was out there?"

I pondered this in silence, feeling like he was on to something. "Might he have just been coming to throw something out? Or maybe he was having a smoke break?"

"Nope. He came out with the intent of asking me what I was doing. How else could he have known I was there if he wasn't watching me through the cameras?"

"Wow," I said. "So at the least, he was lying about his cameras not working. But why? Maybe they were working and there was something on them from the night Miriam got killed that he didn't want the police to see."

"Maybe he popped her and the whole thing was on tape," said Mr. McNeil, braking for a light.

"Why would he kill Miriam, though?" I asked.

"'Cause Miriam was a pain in the patootie," he said, getting animated. "Living right there, she was probably always poking around, making a nuisance of herself."

"Okay, well, great work," I said, feeling a little ashamed of how little I'd found out. "Have you told Kip about it?"

"Yep. He also talked to Esther. She went and saw the bank manager this week." He stepped on the gas. "She was pretty set on him being the one that killed Miriam. Said that Miriam was always up there hounding that man, and he'd probably just had enough."

We were approaching another cross street, and I shifted my eyes left and right, scanning for cars.

"Seems like that motive applies to a lot of folks."

He snorted. "Yeah. But I guess Miriam did go to the bank that night, that last night. Got there right as he was trying to close."

"How did Mrs. Staskywicz find this out?"

"Ah, the old biddy told him she was investigating Miriam's murder. Terrible, terrible way to go about this. Kip shoulda set some ground rules or something." Perhaps he shouldn't have turned this group loose with the directive to investigate a murder. That's what the police were doing, right? "Anyway, Miriam said she needed money and she needed a lot of it and she needed it right then."

"She did the same thing at her old job," I said, finally feeling like I had at least a little to contribute.

"Did she now?" We screamed to a stop midway through the intersection. This time I was halfway prepared for it. *Honk. Hoooooonk.*

"Yes," I said. "One of the ladies she worked with at Marty's Party Warehouse said she was up there Tuesday night too. Asking for an advance on her paycheck or a loan. It sounded like it was a scene. She was even asking the customers for money."

He clicked his tongue against the roof of his mouth. "Such a shame, really," he tsked. "Never did like the woman," he said. "But you hate to see any critter get cornered."

A chill ran across me. He'd nailed that both metaphorically and physically. It still freaked me out that Miriam had been shot in the back and had lived long enough to crawl under the house to hide, only to see her killer ultimately lean down, poke the pistol under and finish the job. It took some cold blood to do that.

I took a breath and shook my head. No need to dwell on that unpleasantness.

"So the bank manager is still on the list?" I asked.

"Nah. He had an alibi. Or at least he said he did. Seems his daughter was at the hospital giving birth to his first grandbaby that night. He was right there with the rest of the family in the waiting room. Guess that wouldn't be too hard to check out."

"Well, I guess we've got at least one off the list, then." I was starting to get used to his driving style, and I'd taken my hands off the dashboard. "Although, it could just as easily be a homeless person or some random person off the street."

"Yeah. Dotty's not having a lot of luck with her assignment. Said her woo-woo only works when it wants to. Nutty as a fruitcake. Kind of like that fruit loop you kids had over tonight."

"Well, Evan's trying to get rid of Miriam's spirit."

He took his eyes off the road and turned towards me, fixing me with a stare. I looked out the windshield.

"Uh, intersection!" I said, my voice rising.

He shifted back around and pounded the horn.

"Yeah. Like I said," he muttered. "Anyway, I have to say, your friend is lucky she's dead. Believe me, if she wanted her house back, she was going to do whatever she had to to get it."

We lapsed into silence, interrupted only by the intermittent braking and honking. Other drivers seemed intimidated by the hulking, honking mass of metal we rode in and kept their distance. We stopped at every cross street, whether we had a stop sign or not, and reached a maximum of fifteen miles an hour. Consequently, it took almost twice as long as it normally did to reach my house.

"Thanks for the ride," I said. "Are you okay getting home from here?" He snorted. I took that for a yes. With a final wave, he shot away from the curb, hit the brakes ten feet later and laid on the horn.

Oh boy.

The dogs were happy to see me, but exhaustion was coursing through my body and I couldn't wait to get in bed. But once there, I kept thinking about Mrs. Grey, her purple turban, and the clicking sticks. Whatever she had done, I hope it had fixed whatever was bothering Evan and Henry.

At 3 a.m., my doorbell rang. Both dogs leapt from a sound sleep, rocketing straight to the top of the stairs and barking loud enough to wake the neighbors two streets over. My heart thudded painfully in my chest, having shot to two hundred beats a minute in under one point five seconds.

I stomped down the stairs, hoping it wasn't Evan. Then again, if it wasn't Evan, who was it? I peered through the peephole, squinting into the dark. The dogs twirled and barked around me. "Shhh." I waved an irritated hand at them.

I could see Evan's head backlit from the porch light. Surprise. I'm slightly ashamed to say I hesitated briefly before opening the door, but I didn't feel right leaving him standing out there.

Henry raced through the door as soon as it opened,

dancing on his short little legs for attention. Evan stood, gnawing his lower lip.

"Hey," I said.

"Do you mind if I come in?" he asked.

I hadn't really noticed that I was blocking the door. "Sure," I said, stepping aside. Addie turned around and headed back up the stairs.

"I'm sorry to bother you," he said. "I couldn't sleep."

"Evan," I said, thankful for the dark living room. "You've got to decide whether you're going to live in your house or not." Henry's tail swished against the rug, the only happy one in the place. The clock ticked away almost a minute of silence.

"Do you want me to leave?" he finally asked.

"That's not what I'm saying. But you've spent more time here than there since you bought it. And if you're really not comfortable there, you need to decide what you're going to do with it."

He flopped down on the couch, and Henry hopped up beside him. "I keep hearing things," he finally said.

"It's an old house. Old houses make noise," I said. Particularly when they're falling down around you. "You're not used to its sounds yet. Or is it more than that? Do you really think it's haunted?"

"I don't know. I really don't believe in ghosts." He hesitated. "I guess. But something keeps waking me up."

My entire body felt limp. I'm not a big fan of 3 a.m. "We can talk about it tomorrow. But really, you're going to have to decide what you're going to do."

I left him sitting in the dark with Henry and pulled myself up the stairs. Shutting my bedroom door, I pushed Addie off my pillow and flopped down on the bed. I felt like a jerk, but

I wanted my house back. Evan had his own house. A horrible house for sure, but he'd done this to himself.

By six, I was staring in the mirror at the dark circles under my eyes. Where had those come from? A warm shower had done little to revive my energy or improve my haggard face. I dabbed a little concealer on the smudges, lightening them from plum to violet. My face looked pale, so I swept some blush across my cheeks, penciled some color around my eyes and stepped back to take a look. It looked like I'd been taking makeup pointers from Miriam.

The downstairs was dark, but I had to get moving. It was Friday, so I needed to visit my distributors, although I really didn't feel up to it. I needed to walk Addie and start baking. I reached the kitchen and threw on the overhead light, ignoring the muffled groans from the couch. I opened the back door for the eager dogs and headed for the coffeemaker, hoping a giant cup of caffeine would help get me through the day.

Evan made his way to the counter, rubbing his eyes with the back of his hand and blinking against the harsh overhead glare.

"What time is it?" he croaked.

"A little after six. Don't you need to get ready for work?"

He gave his eyes a final rub and looked at me. "Whoa!" he said, stumbling backwards into a chair. "What happened to your face?"

I clenched my teeth so tightly my jaw popped. "Nothing happened to my face." Turning away from him, I dumped a pot of water into the top of the machine. It hissed and spat, much like I longed to do. I watched the flow of steaming brown liquid. Okay, maybe I needed to go check my makeup again.

"Oh, sorry," he said, sounding vaguely frightened. "The light must have done something to my eyes. I'm kind of tired today."

"Yeah, well, me too," I said. The coffee was taking its time getting done. Maybe I should think about getting one of those machines with a timer, so it would be ready before I came down in the morning. Now that would make a nice housewarming gift for someone you liked. Maybe Evan could use a plunger. That felt more right.

The last of the coffee burbled its way into the pot and I filled a large mug, wrapping my fingers around the hot sides. Steam billowed around my nose as I blew on the surface. Without turning around, I could tell Evan was still there. Maybe he'd fallen back asleep.

I took a quick peek over my shoulder. Nope, just sitting there staring at me.

"Okay, fine. So I need to redo my makeup," I said, blowing harder on my coffee. "I'm tired too, as you can probably tell."

He sighed. "I know you're sick of having me here." He paused as if waiting for me to contradict him. I took a tentative sip of liquid. Yowza, still too hot. "Anyway, I want to be out of your hair, I really do. And I know I'm being stupid. There's no such thing as ghosts. I know." He picked at a cuticle. "But do you think you could come over and spend a night there with me? Just to make sure. Because if you don't hear anything and you don't think there's anything weird going on, then I'll feel better about it. I promise. And then I'll stop bothering you."

Any other guy and I'd wonder if this was some kind of bizarre method of hitting on me. But it was Evan, and we'd been friends for long enough that sometimes I think he forgot I was a girl.

"I've never stayed in a haunted house overnight," I said from behind my mug.

"It's not haunted. I'm just saying I hear things at night."

"Could be the rats, you know. I'm probably more afraid of seeing a rat if I stay there than I am of seeing Miriam."

He looked up at me and I caught a glimpse of purple shadows under his eyes too. He really was having a rough time.

"Sure. I'll come spend a night in your house and we'll prove that there are no ghosts."

Probably.

CHAPTER SEVENTEEN

I t was eight thirty before I got to Evan's. I wasn't dragging my feet getting there, I was just busy. Really. The day had whirled by as I'd raced through extra batches of biscuits in the morning, visits to my daycare distributors (where I was thrilled to see the empty spaces where my biscuits usually sat), and frisky walks with my dogs. I'd spent an extra two hours baking after my rounds, and had a rousing game of chase the goose with Addie and Henry. We'd decided to leave the dogs at my house unsupervised overnight. I wasn't sure how that would go, but it seemed safer than bringing them along to Evan's house of doggie dangers.

I'd shaken off the exhaustion that had dogged me in the morning, but now as I reached Evan's droopy front porch, it came flooding back with the dragging weight of a wet flannel blanket. I clutched my pillow under one arm and shifted my little overnight bag over the opposite shoulder. Sleepover at the Petty house. Hopefully there would be more sleep than your standard pajama party.

The clear skies of the afternoon had been replaced by

dreary low-hanging clouds, and as I rang the bell, a fine cold rain spritzed against my skin. I pulled my sweatshirt tight and poked the doorbell again.

Evan's head popped into the living room window, squinting at me through the dirty glass before disappearing again as he moved to the door.

"It's cold out there," I said, pushing past him into the chilly room. "Cold in here too," I muttered.

"I think there's something wrong with the heater," he said, running a hand through his dark hair. He looked tired, stress lines etching the corners of his eyes. He was still in his work clothes, the wrinkles in those worse than around his eyes. "Do you want a beer?"

I followed him to the kitchen, still clutching my pillow and bag. I hesitated to put them down anywhere. Maybe I could sleep standing up. The kitchen ceiling hadn't improved since the last time I'd seen it. Small bits of paint flaked off and landed in Evan's hair as he bent and reached into the refrigerator.

We took our beers back to the living room and settled stiffly on the mismatched furniture.

"I really appreciate you coming," he said. "I know I've got to get used to this place." He took a long swallow of beer. "I know I will," he said, his voice rising uncertainly.

"Sure you will." I sounded as sincere as a politician cooing over a baby. "It took me some time to get used to my house when I first moved in. And once you get a little work done in here, I'm sure you'll come to love it." I waited for the lightning bolt to strike, but all that hit was a little rain on the window.

Evan looked around with a critical eye. "If you decide there're no ghosts tonight, do you think you could help me fix this place up a little? So it looks as good as your place?"

Oh, good grief. This place was never going to look as good as my place.

"Sure!" I said, looking around. The floors were nice; well, except for the sloping. "Taking down the wallpaper will make a big difference," I said. "This room should be pretty easy to fix up."

We spent another hour drinking beer and wandering around the house discussing improvements. This place needed a ton of work. There wasn't much I could say about the kitchen. He must have started realizing how bad it was, because we skipped past it pretty fast. By nine thirty I was nearly sleeping on my feet, and the beer was leaving me groggy-headed.

Evan graciously offered me his bedroom. I'd come over in a pair of baggy sweats that I'd planned to sleep in, so after a quick brush of my teeth and a washcloth across my face, I retired to the bedroom and closed the door behind me. Okay, so I'm a little picky about where I sleep. What can I say? But I'd known what I would be up against here, so from my duffle I pulled my silk sleep sack and a micro-fleece blanket. You can't be too careful, and really, did I know how often Evan did laundry?

Settling into my little cocoon with a paperback I'd brought, I began reading, only to realize several minutes later that I'd read the same page over and over. I missed Addie's warm, comforting presence beside me, and I was worried that she was missing me too. I'd never left her alone overnight before. This whole thing was a dumb idea. I tossed the book on the floor and flicked off the light. Addie was fine. But my heart gave a tender tug as I thought of her lying at home waiting for me. I wondered when she'd give up. Tears pricked the corners of my eyes.

Get a grip, I told myself. *It's just one night. She's probably sleeping on my pillow right now.*

Thump.

I sat up. What was that? Heart racing, I sat still, listening for something else to identify what that had been. It seemed close. Sitting bolt upright, I waited for another noise. After several minutes of hearing nothing but my breathing, I flopped back down and pulled my blanket tight around my neck. It must have been the house settling. Or it could have been a giant rat jumping from rafter to rafter in the attic above me. Rats or no rats, ghosts or no ghosts, I needed to get some sleep. I knew Evan wanted me to see if there were ghosts in his house, but if they wanted to get my attention, they were going to have to shake me awake.

Thump.

This time I wasn't as startled, but an irritated curiosity propelled me from the bed. I hadn't thought to bring earplugs, so for any hope of sleep, I had to put a stop to the thumping. It sounded like it was coming from the closet.

I crept towards the closet door and leaned my head against it, listening for any telltale rustlings or rat chirpings from within. Nothing. It could be the dolls, or it could be a rat. Maybe I should just get Evan. Nah. Turning the knob, I pulled the door slowly open and flailed around inside for a light switch.

Crash!

I screamed, slamming the door shut behind me.

"Jess?" Evan knocked on the bedroom door. "Is everything okay in there?"

I opened the door and grabbed his shirt. "I think there's a rat in the closet."

His eyes widened for a moment. "Did you see it?"

"No, I heard it. Something kept thumping in there, and when I opened the door it landed by my feet."

His face relaxed a bit, and he walked over to the closet door and threw it open. I should have left my shoes on in case I needed to run. He flipped on the switch and stared at the floor.

"That's what I thought," he said, bending down. I leaned around to see what he was looking at.

"Oh," I said. The dolls were still lined up on the closet shelves. Three of them lay facedown on the floor, the big bride doll closest to where I'd been standing.

"Sometimes they do that," he said, calming picking them up and propping them back on the shelf. "Remember? I told you that when Mrs. Grey was here."

"Why do you still have them?" I asked. I looked around the closet. Their beady little eyes glared at me from the dim corners. I shifted from side to side, trying to see if their eyes were really following me or if it just seemed like they were. "I thought you were going to throw them away. She clearly told you to get rid of them."

"Shhhhh," he shushed me, hustling me quickly out of the closet. He closed the door and leaned against it. "Don't ever let them hear you say that."

A cold chill ran up my spine as he stared into my eyes with all the passion of a fanatic. "You've got to get rid of them," I whispered. "They're really unsettling. I think maybe they're your whole problem here. Maybe the house isn't haunted by a ghost, it's just those freaky dolls falling off the shelf that's making you think it's haunted."

He herded me farther away from the closet. "I can't just throw them away," he said. "I get the feeling they don't want to leave this house." To normal people, this probably would have sounded insane, but I knew what he was talking about because I could feel that about them too. All the more reason to get them out of here.

"So, what? You're going to keep them forever?" From the closet another thud. "I thought you were at least going to sell them."

"I don't think they like you being here," he said, nudging me out of the bedroom entirely. "Normally they don't fly around like they are tonight."

"Do you want me to leave?" I asked. Part of me was almost too tired to drive home, but the other part yearned for my own bed.

"No, of course not! Maybe we just need to give them a few minutes to calm down."

"Evan." We'd reached the living room and he began walking back and forth in front of the window. "Evan!" He stopped pacing and looked up at me. "This sounds crazy. Don't you think it sounds crazy? They're just a bunch of creepy dolls. Maybe you can get someone to come take them away. Like a collector or something." He pushed a dark thatch of hair away from his forehead. "Maybe they're just ready for a new home."

"That might work," he said, sounding relieved. "I really don't want to keep them here, but I'm afraid to move them." We were still talking in low whispers like they could actually hear us.

"We'll just look online for a doll collector or a consignment shop or something tomorrow."

"Okay. I don't know what a consignment shop is, but if they'll come take them and not throw them away, that would be good." I didn't want to tell him that no matter where they went, he was probably going to have to pack them up. We could just go throw them in the taqueria's dumpster. Then I thought of the mean bride doll. I could just imagine her, refried beans dripping from her head, rising from the dumpster like the monster in a B-grade horror flick. On further reflection, maybe a charity would be willing to pick them up. They could distribute them to poor children all over the city, instilling doll phobias in a whole new generation.

"I'm really beat, Evan. I've got to get some sleep."

"Oh, sure. You going to be okay sleeping in there with them? I can't promise they're done falling off the shelf."

I hadn't noticed a lock on the closet door. No way I was falling asleep with those things flying around just a few feet from my unconscious self.

"Maybe I'll just take the couch," I said. "Just give me a minute to get my stuff." I zipped into the bedroom, grabbed my duffle, pillow, blanket and silk sleep sack and headed back into the living room.

Evan watched me set up my sleep sack. He opened his mouth a couple of times like he wanted to make a smart-aleck comment, but refrained. It wasn't till I was nestled into my crunched-up cocoon that I noticed there were no blinds on the front windows. How could he live in a goldfish bowl this way?

"Are you set?" he asked, as I tossed my pillow around, trying to find room for my head on his noticeably short couch.

"Yep, I'm good," I said brightly. Just needed to get this night over, declare his house free and clear of ghosts, and my world would hopefully get back to normal.

"Okay, then. Good night. If you hear anything, or see anything weird, let me know." He flicked off the overhead light and clumped towards his bedroom.

As tired as I was, I couldn't get comfortable. The couch was too short to stretch out on, and the middle cushion kept slipping out from under me every time I rolled over. And then there were the naked windows. How had I not noticed these naked windows before now? At least with the lights out, I felt less exposed. Flipping onto my back, I pulled my blanket up high and looked out at the clouds moving swiftly across the sky. The rain had stopped and the moon cast a muted glow over the live oak in the front yard. One of its branches scraped the roof, no doubt ripping yet another shingle loose.

I watched the branches move in rhythm to the gusty wind, and had nearly lulled myself to sleep with the hypnotic movements when a sudden rapping on the glass pane above my head sent me lurching to my feet. Tripping over my sleep sack, I fought for balance.

"Hey, it's me, Wynne." She gestured towards the door. "Open up, would you? It's cold out here." The last thing I wanted to do was invite Wynne in. I'd still not fully recovered from her hair-raising intonation that Miriam was still here. "Come on." I could see her hands whirling in circles as if she could hurry me along with the movement. So help me, if she freaked me out with one scary Miriam comment, she was out of here.

I kicked myself out of my sleep sack and headed for the door. This night was not going at all well.

"What are you doing here?" I asked as I cracked the door open. She shoved the door open and slipped past me.

"I saw you in here earlier. How come you're sleeping in here? Have a fight with your boyfriend?"

"He's not my boyfriend. He's just a friend." I cut myself off quickly. What Evan and I were to each other was none of her business. "But back to my question. What are you doing here?"

She plopped down on the couch and pulled my pillow onto her lap, curling her arms around it like a child cuddling a teddy bear.

"I don't know. I couldn't sleep and I saw you over here."

"So you thought you'd drop by?"

"Yeah. Is that a problem?" Even in the dark I could see her pink hair flop forward over her face, like a magician disappearing behind the curtain.

I sat down on the other end of the couch. Now that the adrenaline was dissipating in my bloodstream, I was being overcome by an overwhelming desire to put my head down and crash, ghosts and goth teens be dammed.

"I'm just really tired," I said, curling my feet under me. "I haven't been getting enough sleep."

She sat silently stroking my pillow, obviously not interested in my sleep disorders.

"You know, I was kind of mean to her." Her face was fully hidden by walls of hair now.

"You mean Miriam?" I'm pretty sure I heard a snort, but she reeled it back in.

"Duh," she said. "Who else would I be talking about?" I rested my head against the back cushion. Perhaps she could rant on by herself for a while, maybe work through a little teenage angst before waking me for the good part. "Are you listening to me?"

"Yes."

"You look like you're sleeping."

I opened my eyes. I just hate people watching me sleep. "I'm not sleeping. You were mean to Miriam. How were you mean to her?"

"I thought she was a nosy bitch."

"You and everyone else it seems."

"Yeah, well, she was. But what if she was because she was trying to do the right thing?"

I was getting the feeling there was something specific Wynne was driving at, and I was equally certain one wrong word and she'd shut down tighter than a bank vault at five.

"Maybe you're right. Maybe she did stick her nose in other people's business because she was trying to help in her own way." Okay, so that didn't really jibe with the crazy woman I'd seen screaming at Evan to get out of her house. Maybe crazy was just crazy. I wished I knew what we were talking about so that I could get a sense of how close we were to the end of this little chat. "Did she butt into your business?"

"That's just it. I used to hate how I'd see her always looking out her window at me. Or hanging over her porch rail, trying to see what I was doing or who I was with. It used to make me nuts. Like, get your own life, you know?"

"Sure, that would get on anyone's nerves."

She drew a hand towards her lips and began gnawing on a nail. "But since she died, I've been thinking about it. Maybe she was just lonely. I don't think she had any family, or at least I never saw anyone come visit her."

I was getting the feeling this wasn't going to be a short conversation. My eyelids drooped in spite of my best efforts.

"And like maybe she only butted into other people's business when it was the right thing to do."

"Maybe," I muttered.

"You know, I think she said something to my step-perv." Her teeth clicked away on her nail. "Like when she caught him trying to look in my window."

My eyes opened in spite of themselves. "What are you saying, Wynne? Brian looks in your window?"

"Something like that. Or at least he used to. Until Miriam caught him peeping and took some pictures of him. Caught him right in the act. Maybe she was blackmailing him with them. Who knows? But anyway, I put up some blackout stuff on my window. Now he can't even if he wanted to."

Alarm bells were going off, and I felt like I should call someone who knew what you're supposed to do in these kinds of situations. I sure as heck didn't know. They always tell kids to notify a trusted adult if someone is doing something they shouldn't. Was I Wynne's trusted adult? Good grief, she couldn't have gone to a guidance counselor?

"Wynne? Do you need me to talk to your mother? Is there something bad going on at your house?" I sounded lame even to myself.

"Talk to my mother? Oh, please. She's the one that married him. She'd just be pissed he wasn't trying to peep in her window. Gawd." She punched my pillow and rearranged herself, tucking her legs up under herself and curling into an even smaller ball. "Gawd," she repeated.

"But really," I said, trying to think of the right thing to say. "Is Brian doing anything to you?"

Her pink head turned away from me in the dark. "No. He just used to like to look at me when I was a kid. Freaking perv."

"Is there something I can do? Like, I don't know, should I be contacting child protective services or something?"

Even in the dark, I could sense her eye roll. "He doesn't like the way I look anymore. If you have to contact them, it wouldn't be on my behalf." The baggy clothes and goth look were beginning to make sense. Wynne had figured out a way to take care of this herself. Then I wondered where else his attention was directed these days. And where did this fit with Miriam's murder?

"Do you know if she really had pictures of Brian?"

"She said she did. I mean, I heard them fighting about it."

"When was this?"

"I don't know, a couple of weeks ago." She settled back against the couch cushion, relaxing now. She held a nail up for inspection, although I doubted she could see anything in the dark. "It was kind of weird, now that I think about it. I mean, that was months ago when she caught him outside."

"So why were they fighting about it now?"

"I don't know. It was on the weekend. One of his golf-lesson girls was there." She started gnawing on her nail.

"His what?"

"He has some golf-lesson girls now. He started giving golf lessons."

"What is he, some kind of golf pro?"

"No. He works at some lame financial services company, but he thinks he's a golf pro. So he started giving lessons on the weekends. It's like his favorite thing now. It's fine with me. It keeps him busy."

"So what happened with Miriam?"

"I'm not sure. I didn't hear the whole thing. It wasn't till she started asking him what he was doing, like really loud, and asking who *this* was, that I looked out the window."

"What was he doing?"

"He was just getting ready to go to the driving range with this girl. They were loading their clubs into the perv's car. Sometimes the babes get dropped off at our house, and sometimes the parents meet him at the driving range, I think. I don't know. I don't really pay that much attention."

"And Miriam just showed up?" I could picture the scene that must have been.

Wynne laughed. "Yeah, the girl looked really freaked out. I mean, Miriam was kind of crazy looking." She had certainly freaked me out the first time I'd seen her. "She was yelling at her to get away. Call her parents. Said she needed to run away from the monster."

"Then what happened?" My tiredness had faded as my brain visualized this melodrama with video-like clarity.

"Brian told the girl to get in the car. Then he went after Miriam. He was pissed. I thought he was going to grab her, but she could have probably taken him. He told her to shut her stupid mouth and get off his property."

"Did she?"

"No. She got right up in his face and started screaming that she had pictures of him and she didn't know if the police would be interested or if that girl's parents would be interested, but she didn't think he should be as friendly with young girls as he was." She laughed. "I thought he was going to have a stroke. He said he'd sue her if she didn't shut up and leave him alone."

"Wow," I said. Brian was moving up the list. I wondered how Mrs. Liddell and Miss Potts's investigation was going on Wynne's family. "And that was that?"

"Pretty much. The perv got in the car and they drove off."

"Did you see Miriam and Brian together at all after that?" I asked.

"No, I don't think so." She sighed, sounding as if she was losing interest. But now that I had her, I might as well keep going.

"Hey, did you happen to hear anything the night Miriam was killed?"

She got quiet and I could hear the wind blowing in the trees. "No. The cops asked us that too, but I wasn't home." I gave her a minute, getting the feeling there was more. "Fine, I guess it doesn't matter."

"What?" I asked softly.

"I was out with this guy that night. And he got pulled over for driving under the influence. So they took us both in and they called my mom to come get me."

"Wynne! Geez, do you want to get killed?"

"No, Mom," she said in a singsong voice. "It was dumb, I get that." She dropped back to more serious tones. "But anyway, I was at the police station that night. At least during the time they thought Miriam got it."

"Did they tell you what time they thought she was killed?"

"Well, they said it was most likely during the storm. I guess that's why no one heard anything." I thought back to Miriam's sodden skirts as she lay under the house.

"That makes sense," I said. "And I think her clothes were wet, so that probably factored into their timeline."

"Yeah. Anyway, my mom and I got home pretty much right as the rain was letting up."

"Brian didn't come to get you too?"

"No. Funny thing, he was too drunk himself. I mean, they tried to hide that little fact, but it was pretty apparent when I got home. And then he had the nerve to try and lecture me." She sighed. "So now you know. I'm an at-risk teen." She snorted. "Whatever that means."

We sat in silence for a few minutes. I was trying to process all this new information about Brian. He'd seemed like your perfectly ironed, magazine-model kind of neighbor when I'd seen him. Maybe he was more like the one that neighbors discuss in shocked tones on the local news after a disturbing incident.

"Are you sure you don't want me to contact someone for you? I mean now with Miriam gone, what if he goes back to the way he was again?"

She sighed. "No worries. I'm too old for him. And he hates my clothes and my hair and just about every other thing about me."

"What about your real father?" I asked. It seemed like we were way past personal boundaries at this point. "I mean, can he help you at all?"

"He's great," she said, sounding animated for the first time since I'd met her. "But he moved to Singapore with his new wife last summer."

"Oh, that's too bad."

"Yeah, they talked about me coming with them, but my mother said I couldn't go."

The wind had picked up again, and drops splatted against the bare windows. A tired chill washed over me and the urge to lie down was quickly overtaking me.

"Well, this has been interesting, Wynne. But I'm really tired, and I need to get some sleep."

"You gonna be okay with the ghosts here?" she asked.

"Yes," I said. "I'm thinking maybe they're not as bad as I thought."

I locked the door after her, wrapped up snugly in my sleep sack and tried to get some desperately needed sleep.

CHAPTER EIGHTEEN

Nothing was going to stop me from catching some shut-eye. And I actually made it far into the night before a heavy rumbling noise roused me from the deep. Swimming slowly back into consciousness, I struggled to understand what I was hearing. Was Addie growling in her sleep? I rolled over to pet her and soothe her back to sleep when I slipped suddenly from my bed onto the floor.

Sitting up, I rubbed my eyes and looked around. It took me close to a minute to remember where I was. A crick in my neck made it nearly impossible to turn my head to the left, not to mention the ache that radiated across my lower back. I'd be lucky if I could walk right in the morning. Maybe I could make an emergency appointment with my massage therapist. I fumbled for my phone to check the time—3:12. What was that noise?

It sounded like a Mack truck idling right outside the window. Hoisting myself clumsily to my feet, I hobbled over to the bare window and peered into the darkness. The wind had died down and darkness covered everything. No truck, but the rumbling continued.

Maybe it was coming from the taqueria. I shuffled towards the kitchen and laundry room, fearful of running into a rat or roach. Roaches ruled the night in Houston, as I well knew, and I considered putting on my shoes but lacked the energy even for that.

The rumbling was louder from this side of the house, rattling the cabinets in the laundry room and vibrating the floor. This couldn't be good for the kitchen ceiling. Leaning across the washing machine, I looked out over towards the taqueria. A large delivery truck idled outside the back door. Darkness shadowed the alley, so I couldn't make out if there were any markings on the side. Probably an early-morning produce delivery or something.

It seemed awfully early for a delivery, or awfully late, but what did I know about the restaurant business? Whatever they were doing, I hoped they'd hurry up and get done because I hadn't had enough sleep. I stood staring out for several more minutes until the chill of the night crept up through the drafty floorboards, snaking around my ankles and chilling me to the bone. Even the lumpy couch began to sound good.

I peeked out for one last look, hopeful that they were almost done. I'd never be able to sleep with all that racket. The overhead light in the cab of the truck flickered on and I caught sight of a dark-haired man hoisting something into the passenger seat. It looked like Diego, but I couldn't be positive. If that was him, he certainly kept long hours. A few more heads gathered near the cab, and hope flared that they were almost done. I shuffled back to the couch and shoved the cushions as far back onto the seat as I could. No guarantees that I wouldn't end up on my fanny again, but it was the best I could do.

This lack of sleep was catching up to me. Even my bones felt tired. Tomorrow night, I planned on being in bed by eight. I'd turn off the phone, close up my shutters and I could collapse next to Addie. But tonight, I had a few more hours to get through. The good news was, I hadn't seen any ghosts yet.

By six I was fully awake, trying to work the painful kinks out of my neck. Daylight hadn't even begun to tinge the heavy slate clouds that tumbled across the sky, and spatterings of raindrops tapped against the dirty windowpanes. A perfect morning to sleep in—had I been in my comfy, cushy bed at home. As it was, I just wanted to stagger to my car and head home. Maybe it wasn't too late for that sleep-in thing.

I debated whether to leave a note for Evan or just pack up and go. Pawing through my purse, I couldn't find either pen or paper, so pack up and go it was. Shoving all my belongings into my duffle bag, I shook out my pillow (hoping that any fleas or roaches that might have laid eggs overnight would fall off) and tiptoed across the creaky floor towards the front door. Why I tiptoed, I didn't know. If Evan could sleep through Wynne's visit and the ninety-decibel delivery truck, he surely wouldn't wake to a creaky floorboard.

Closing the door softly behind me, I thought about that. Evan really did sleep like the dead. Why would he even think he had a ghost in his house? Mrs. Grey could have a disco party with all her spirits on his bed, and he'd sleep right through it.

Traffic was light, and I was home in a matter of minutes. By the time I pulled into my driveway, it had stopped raining, at least for the time being, but judging by the ponderous dark clouds that hovered over my house, it wouldn't be long before it came down even harder.

As soon as I opened the door, Addie leapt at me, bouncing off the tile like an overinflated basketball, up and down and up and down until I feared she'd slip and hurt herself.

"Whoa, whoa," I said, trying to calm her down. "I'm so sorry. I guess you didn't like staying by yourself last night. But you did have Henry for company." She planted her paws on me, nearly knocking me off my feet. I knelt down. "It's okay. Really. I'm right here."

I glanced around. Where *was* Henry? I would have expected him to be bouncing right alongside Addie.

"Where's Henry?" I asked out loud. Addie spun around and raced towards the living room, looking over her shoulder at me. Obviously, I was supposed to tag along. As I turned the corner, my mouth fell open. Clouds of stuffing littered the living room, scattered and pulled in every direction like an eviscerated wildebeest after a hungry pride of lions had gotten a hold of it. What had he gotten into? My eyes raced across the scene, searching for the source. Please let it be a pillow. Just a pillow. Not—

But it was. My new couch. My new couch with the cheese stain lay mangled and mauled in the middle of the living room. Henry was nowhere in sight. I walked slowly over to inspect the damage. Addie danced in front of me, whining and pawing at some of the larger chunks. She rolled a loose ball of polyester fiber towards me, then raised her head and stared at me. She seemed almost as outraged as I was.

"Henry!" I called. "Come here!" Right. Like he was that

stupid. I walked slowly around the back of the sofa, inspecting the damage from all angles. He'd done a thorough job, I had to say that much for him. The decorative throw pillows didn't exist in any recognizable form anymore. Small bits of the outer fabric clung to the rug and dangled from the polyfill tumbleweeds. The back cushions had suffered an equally tragic fate, and even the wood frame showed the scars of canine teeth. No possible way this couch could be saved.

Truth be told, I wasn't even that angry. Disappointed—yes. Frustrated that I would have to go buy a new couch and spend time and money I didn't really have—yes. But if I was honest with myself, I wasn't sure I would have gotten past Larry's cheese stain. Maybe a professional cleaner could have steamed it out, and maybe they couldn't, but this saved me years of being aggravated at Larry every time I looked at that spiky, hard fabric nap.

A rumble overhead brought me back to the task of finding Henry and getting the two dogs out before the storm hit. The difference in playing hide-and-seek with a forty-pound dog versus a twelve-pound dog was remarkable. I checked all of the usual spots I could think of: under the bed, behind my reading chair, in the kneehole of my desk. Nada. It took me another ten minutes of calling and poking around before I finally found the little destroyer. Addie had been no help whatsoever. I knew full well she knew exactly where he was, but she either didn't want to rat him out or was enjoying watching me play "Find It" for a change. In the end, I found him cowering behind the laundry basket in my closet. He'd managed to knock a shirt and a towel off the top of the pile, and he'd dug himself a little cave. I missed him completely the first time I looked in there, but the second time I caught sight of a slight movement under the shirt. In spite of his fear, his little tail was wagging. A bit of fabric hung from a side whisker.

"Henry," I said softly. "What happened?" He put his nose under the dirty shirt and refused to meet my eyes. He knew he was in big trouble.

"Well, let's get you outside before it starts to rain," I said. "I'm sure you have to go."

He refused to budge, so I finally just picked him up and carried him down the stairs. Addie jumped and pawed at me, clearly frustrated by the special treatment he was getting. *It's like dealing with a couple of children*, I thought. I plunked Henry down on my small patio, and with one tentative backward glance at me, he ran for the grass. Poor thing. He never had gotten the hang of the doggie door, so I guessed he'd never made it outside during the night. Big plops of rain began spattering the flagstone patio and I turned and trotted through the door, followed close behind by the dogs, who were no more interested in getting wet than I was.

Henry raced past me into the living room and pounced on a destroyed pillow, grabbing what was left of an end and shaking it side to side, killing it all over again.

"Hey!" I shouted. "What do you think you're doing?"

He froze in midshake, clearly having forgotten the angry owner was home now. Turning tail, he raced up the stairs. I looked at the mess and mourned my lost nap. This was going to take a while to clean up. Forty-five minutes later, I'd run out of trash bags. It's amazing how much bigger upholstered furniture is once you let it loose from the confines of its fabric shell. Addie watched my efforts, occasionally sniffing out a pocket of filling I'd missed.

I wondered how I was going to get rid of this carcass. No

charity would accept it. I couldn't even hope someone would take it off the curb with a "Free" sign on it. In the meantime, I covered it with a bedsheet, tucking the edges in where I could. When I was finished, it looked like Salvador Dalí's version of a sofa. Addie hopped up and began stomping on the lumpy sections of cushion, trying to force them into something comfortable.

"Good luck with that," I told her, heading upstairs for a shower.

My phone rang just as I was stepping out. Dripping across the carpet, I raced for it.

"Where'd you go?" Evan asked as soon as I picked up.

"Oh, sorry. I was going to leave you a note, but I couldn't find anything to write on."

"So what do you think?" he asked. "Do you think the house is clear? From—you know?"

"Ghosts?" I hesitated. I didn't really want to mention the creepy feelings I'd gotten while at his house. The last thing I needed was for him to freak out and move back in with me. "I think Mrs. Grey probably took care of any ghosts you might have had. Who knew smudging was the way to go?"

Silence floated through the line. Finally, "Really? Really, Jessie? You think my house is okay?"

"Well 'okay' might be a strong word," I hedged. "I mean, you got that roof problem, and the kitchen is a mess, but I think the other stuff you're worried about should be okay."

"Well, your opinion means a lot to me here," he said. I immediately felt like a jerk. "There really isn't anyone else I can even talk to about this. And not only did you not laugh when I told you I thought there was a ghost in my house, but you believed me. And you've been willing to inconvenience yourself for me." He took a deep breath. He was kind of freaking me out. We normally don't have these kind of conversations. "I just wanted to tell you how much I appreciate your friendship."

"Come on, Evan. Cut it out. This is no big deal. I know buying your first house is stressful, and frankly your experience has been a little more stressful than most people's. But, sure, I'd do whatever I could to help you out with this."

A moment of silence stretched between us. Finally he cleared his throat. "So, is Henry okay? I think I'm ready to bring him back over here. It's his home too, and hopefully he won't be freaked out anymore." He sounded unsure, probably still smarting over my lecture on his doggie caretaker capabilities. As peeved as I was at Henry, I still hated to see him move out to that dump.

"Don't we need to finish cleaning up the backyard before he can move back in? And what about the fence? And the rat bait?" I thought about my ruined couch. Nope. Still didn't want to see Henry eaten by a rat. Or poisoned.

Evan sighed deeply into the mouthpiece. "I know, Jessie. There's a lot of work to do over here. I'm doing the best I can, you know." Our warm-hearted truce hadn't lasted very long. "And you know what I'm up against at work." His voice rose. "But I'm not going to be able to get everything done at once. I need to know when I can bring my dog home."

I glanced towards my closet, where I could hear Henry rooting through my laundry. I should tell him about my couch, but I wasn't sure where Evan's breaking point was. He had a lot to contend with as it was. "Maybe if the rain stops, we can work on your yard this afternoon." I tried not to picture what a sodden mess his yard would be after last night's rain. Then again, maybe the ground would have softened up enough to be able to actually get some of the weeds out.

"They just said this storm's going to blow through fast. Do you want to come over in a little while? I might have to go to work for a few hours later, but we could get some stuff done before that."

What I didn't want to do was go muck around in Evan's yard. But what I did want was for Evan to stop staying with me. I told him I'd be over shortly.

Henry charged out of the closet swinging a sock from his mouth. "Your daddy is a mess," I told him. I closed my eyes and rethought my plans. No time for a nap. No time for couch shopping. I did need to call Frances. How many days had it been since I'd checked in? And hadn't I told her we'd do dinner?

I hunted down Henry, put him in the powder room with a biscuit and a bowl of water, and decided if I worked really hard, I could be home by lunchtime.

Evan was already out back, haphazardly yanking weeds out and flinging them behind him. He'd cleared a swath, like a runway in the jungle, although I noticed he'd avoided the truly overgrown sections along the fence.

"Nice work," I said, squelching towards him.

"Yeah, looks good, right?" he asked, standing upright and surveying his work. He rubbed his back, leaving a muddy streak on his jacket, and swiveled side to side. "It's harder than it looks."

I taped my gloves on and joined him, first gathering up his discarded weeds and bagging them before attacking my own swath of weed-choked ground. The rain had definitely softened the ground and the stubborn weeds began giving up to our efforts. That's not to say they were giving up without a fight, but with a little effort, I was able to get some of the bigger ones up by their tap roots.

"You know, I can work on this part if you want to work on the edges," I said to Evan, eyeing the dense growth in the corners.

He glanced over at the thick vegetation and then back at me. "You know, your gloves are better than mine. Maybe you should have a run at it."

"You could just start chopping things down. Then we could pull up the roots once it's more clear."

He grumbled something unintelligible but grabbed a pair of pruning shears and headed for the thickest corner. If I were him, I would have beat the area with a broom before approaching, but hey, it was his yard.

We worked steadily for what felt like hours, but was probably less. I was impressed with Evan's work. You could actually see through the thicket to the fence now, and he'd uncovered a whole pile of debris that was probably housing a large population of those overgrown rats. I noticed he was careful not to disturb that. I couldn't blame him. In fact, I'd kept a steady eye on him, ready to run if anything shot out.

"I need a break," Evan finally said, looking as if he'd spent the morning rolling around a pigsty. Mud streaked his pants, his jacket and even his face. Gunky leaves clung to his butt, and his hair had a clump of something unidentifiable matted along the side of his head. "And I'm hungry. Do you want to go get something to eat?"

"We can't go like this. Look at us. I'd need to go home and shower and change."

He sighed and rubbed at his legs. "Look, it's not that bad. We'll wash our hands and go next door. If I don't get something to eat, I'm going to die."

I realized how ravenous I was too. Well, if he didn't care how we looked, then why should I? We gathered up our weed bags, headed inside to clean up as much as possible, and were headed for the taqueria in less than five minutes. Forget the salad today, I needed one of those big honking burritos.

CHAPTER NINETEEN

Turned out it was lunchtime, so the taqueria was pretty crowded. We got in line, and I studied the big menu board, trying to decide what to get.

"Excuse me." A woman behind me tapped me on the shoulder. I turned. "There's something in your hair." She waved a hand in the general vicinity of my head. "I think it's moving."

"Get it," I said to Evan.

He looked impassively at me. "It's gone."

I looked back at the woman for confirmation. She shrugged noncommittally. I started to shake my head, swatting at my hair. "Evan!"

"I don't see anything."

"I'm going to the ladies' room."

"You can't get out of line. We're almost at the front."

"Just order me whatever you're getting."

I raced down a short hall towards the bathrooms. Still shaking and flailing, I pulled my hair out of its ponytail holder, nearly knocking down a girl as she washed her hands at the sink. She smiled at me, seemingly unperturbed by my spasms.

"Can I help?" she asked.

"Someone said there was something moving in my hair." I tried to quiet the instinctive mewling sounds that wanted to come out of my throat. "Ick, ick, ick."

"Hold still. Let me look." She couldn't have been more than fourteen, but she was lovely, with round dewy cheeks and a beautiful smile. Her thick black hair didn't have anything crawling in it. She leaned towards me, and I caught sight of myself in the mirror.

"Oh, geez," I said, staring at the mess that was me. "Look at me."

She laughed and pulled a paper towel from the dispenser. "Hold still," she said, reaching towards the side of my head.

One of the mewling sounds escaped then. "What is it? What is it?" She snagged something in the folds between her fingers, then peered closely at it.

"It's just a stick," she said, laughing. Then she looked again. "Oh. Or maybe not." She squished her fingers together, then tossed the whole thing in the trash.

I leaned towards the mirror, looking for any other crawly things. "Thanks so much," I said. "I was afraid I was going to start screaming." I grabbed a paper towel, wet it and scrubbed at a dirt streak on my face. "Geez. I knew we should have never come over like this."

"You're fine," she said graciously. She smoothed her own hair back and headed out the door.

I ran my fingers through my hair, hoping I wouldn't feel anything else, before attempting to gather it back into something presentable. Having reassured myself that I was semi-okay, I hurried down the hall. Halfway along, a door marked

"Private" popped open, and I found myself looking into a small office where a burly guy was hunched over a sewing machine. Diego pushed out of the office into the hall, nearly knocking me over, and pulled the door closed behind him with a bang.

"Can I help you?" he asked.

"No, we're just having lunch," I said, waving an arm towards the dining area and waiting for him to move aside. He stared at me for a minute before making room for me to pass.

Evan had snagged a table near the counter and was mindlessly shaking a yellow maraca with the number ten on it. The young girl from the ladies' room was sitting at a table in the corner with a book open. She waved at me as I slid into my chair.

"Oh, hey, Isabelle," said Evan, loud enough to be heard across the room. She waved at him.

"You know her?" I asked.

"That's Diego's niece. She comes here a lot. Her mom works and is taking classes, so Diego likes to keep an eye on her so she's not home alone."

"That's nice," I said.

"Yeah, he's a good guy." He slid a plastic cup across the table towards me, dark soda fizzing in tiny explosions across the surface.

"What'd you order?"

"Beef burritos. Extra queso," he said. A plastic basket of chips lay in the middle of the table, a white bowl of salsa untouched beside it. I grabbed a chip and scooped some salsa.

"I thought you were starving," I said. He looked at the chips and took one absently. "What's the matter?"

"I'm really worried about work," he said.

"Yeah, I know," I said. "But I'm sure you'll be fine. They need analysts, and you know what you're doing. I'm sure they'll keep you."

"It's not that," he said, leaning forward. "I think they're doing stuff. Like, you know, wrong stuff."

I took another chip. "I have no idea what you're talking about."

"You know they've had me working on some confidential stuff. And I need this job. But, I don't know." He took a chip and began breaking it into bits, the pieces littering the table-top. "They had me running some numbers, and one of the senior managers asked me for a copy of my file."

"So? Maybe he just wants to check that you're modeling it like he wants."

"That's what I thought too. But this is the same project that Karen Atwood was working on."

"I don't know who that is," I said, glancing towards the counter and wondering when our food was coming.

"She was a senior analyst. She knew *everything*. They had her working on this same project. And then all of a sudden, she was gone." He snapped his fingers, leaned forward and lowered his voice. "Someone said they saw security escorting her from the building. She was screaming crazy stuff about how they were setting her up. And how they had planted things in her desk. I don't know. It sounds like she went off the rails."

"Okay, well, you all are under a lot of stress. Maybe she did."

"Maybe." He didn't sound convinced. "But now, I'm working on the same project. And I sort of feel like they're setting me up."

I looked at him, back to evaluating his mental stability. "I'm not really understanding where you're getting this," I said carefully. "What am I missing?"

"Okay. Last night when I was leaving the office, I realized I left my workout bag under my desk. I haven't had time to work out in weeks, but I wanted to bring all my stuff home because maybe I'd have time to work out this weekend." I'd never actually known Evan to exercise, but okay. "Anyway, when I got back up there, I heard voices, and I wasn't really in the mood to talk to anyone, so I hung back and kind of looked around the corner."

He picked another chip out of the basket and began pinching bits off the edges again. Then he hunched closer to me. "They were going through my desk."

I felt the first stirrings of genuine unease. "Who was?"

"That senior manager I told you about, and another one whose team has also been providing data for the acquisition."

"Don't you lock your desk at night?"

"Yes, of course I do!" He huffed and broke the chip in half. "Well, lately I have, since I heard about Karen."

"So, how'd they get in?"

"I guess they have a master key."

"What would they have been looking for?"

"I don't know. Maybe they're planting something in my desk, like they did in hers."

None of this sounded real. I'd used to work at that company. It was a sweatshop for sure, but this kind of thing sounded really implausible.

His voice rose. "What if he saw me? What if he finds out I know something? Look what happened to her."

"Two beef burritos, extra queso!" Diego announced, coming around the counter with our meals. Evan shot up like his seat was electrified, his eyes round and his cheeks red, as Diego slid the food in front of us. "Everything okay?"

Evan stared at the food as if he'd forgotten where we were.

"Yeah, looks great," I said, pulling one of the baskets towards me.

Diego stood, staring at Evan. "And for you? Everything looks okay?"

Evan mumbled his assent without looking up. Diego gave him a half smile, probably wondering why his reaction was so tepid compared to his usual enthusiasm.

"Let me know if you need anything," he said, moving away.

I sliced into my burrito, beef and cheese oozing from the tortilla. "Oh, man," I said, leaning over the steaming mess. I knew I was hungry, so probably anything would impress me at this point, but the spicy mix seemed like the best thing ever. "Aren't you going to eat?" Evan was just staring at his basket. "Evan. C'mon. This is good. Try it." He stuck a fork into his burrito and split it open, letting the steam escape.

"Look, so what if someone was looking through your desk? I'm sure it's nothing. I mean, you're making it sound like some CIA thriller or something."

He finally looked up and scowled at me. "I'm not making it sound anything. I'm just telling you what's happening."

I took a bite, quickly followed by another. This was so good.

"And it's what they want me to do with the numbers too. I just don't think it's right."

"Isn't there anyone there you can talk to? Ask about it?"

"I don't know. Everyone's freaked out. Everyone's just doing anything they're asked to do."

"Well, sure. But if you really think something is wrong…I mean, just be careful." I didn't think he would look good in a jumpsuit, and somehow I could see him being set up as a fall guy.

"That's just it. I think this is the kind of thing that gets people in trouble. It wasn't just that they wanted a copy of my file, it's that they asked me to create two files. With two sets of numbers."

"Well, maybe they're just running different scenarios. That's not a bad thing."

He looked halfway hopeful for a second. Then he deflated. "No, I still think it's wrong. They want me to change the value of some of the long-term deals we have. They gave me new price curves to use. They're totally inflating the value of these deals."

"Are you sure?"

"Of course I'm sure," he hissed, outrage turning his eyebrows into angry slashes. "And they made me sign a confidentiality agreement, so I could actually be fired for telling you this."

"I'm not sure confidentiality agreements cover illegal things."

He poked his burrito. He must really be freaking out if he wasn't eating. His phone buzzed and he held it to his ear. "Evan Petty. Uh, yeah. Sure. Yeah, no, it's fine." He glanced out the window. "I don't know, maybe half an hour?" He mumbled a few more things, then disconnected.

"Problem?" I asked.

"I have to go into the office," he said, looking like he'd been called in to have all his teeth extracted. "I'm sorry. Thanks for your help." He stared at his burrito. Diego waved a to-go container from the other side of the counter, and Evan took it with a mumbled thanks.

After he was gone, I hunkered down over my burrito. I was about two-thirds done and taking a breather when the little bell over the door jangled and Brian Barbieri walked in. He wore khakis and a button-down, with a sweater tied around his neck, preppy style. He was even sporting sockless loafers.

He walked straight to the counter without looking around. Wynne's words from last night swirled in my head. Step-perv. Peeper. I wondered if the police were looking at him at all in Miriam's murder. If Miriam really had pictures of him prowling around Wynne's window, he might have decided to cut short any risk of her going to the police. But then where were the pictures? More than likely Evan and I had tossed them out along with all the other junk in the garage. And really, a picture of a guy standing outside a window of a house he owned didn't add up to much.

I went back to work on my burrito. Glancing up, I saw Brian staring at me, a half smile on his face.

"Haven't we met?" he asked, approaching my table.

I chewed faster, waving a finger in the air to indicate I needed a minute. Swallowing, I gave him a half smile and said, "Yes, I'm a friend of Evan's, the guy that just moved in next door to you."

"Oh, that's right!" he said brightly. "Now I remember." I glanced down at my hideous shirt and rubber boots.

"I'm surprised you recognized me in this getup," I said, trying to make it clear I didn't dress like this every day. Then again, what did I care what this child peeper thought? "I was over there helping him try and clean up the backyard."

"Do you mind if I sit?" he asked, sliding into a chair

without waiting for an answer. "My order'll be up in just a minute. I'm picking some tacos up for Wynne and some tortilla soup for Tiffany. She's sick, and I thought some soup might just clear her right up."

"I'm sorry to hear she's not well," I said, eying my burrito. I really wanted another bite but didn't want to be rude.

"Thanks. I'm sorry she's sick too. We were supposed to go to dinner with some of my clients and their wives tonight. She knows I need her to handle the women." He glanced back towards the counter, looking for his order. "But now I guess I'll have to handle everything myself."

"What do you do?" I asked, more to be polite than because I cared. His eyes had locked on to something, and I casually turned my head to see what he was looking at. Isabelle had moved behind the counter and was laughingly grabbing at a basket of chips as Diego ruffled her hair affectionately. He caught sight of Brian's face and his eyes turned icy. If someone looked at one of my relatives like Brian was, I would probably make that face too. Before calling the cops.

Brian wasn't even blinking, and I fully expected to see drool running over the side of his lip any second. Wynne wasn't kidding. This guy really had issues.

He still hadn't blinked by the time Diego had bagged his order, stomped towards my table and shoved the bag into Brian's chest.

"Here's your food," Diego said in a tone that was both low and incredibly menacing. Brian hadn't noticed his approach, and he bolted up from his chair.

"Great, thanks," he said, clutching the food. His eyes darted back towards the counter like metal shavings flying toward a magnet. He glanced over at Diego and me, only to shift his gaze immediately back to the young girl.

"Do you need anything else?" Diego asked, starting to close the space between them. I took a bite of burrito, trying to finish just in case a fight broke out and my table got overturned.

Brian started unwrapping the bag, then glanced at Diego's face and said, "No, I'm sure I've got everything I need." He walked quickly towards the door but kept looking back at the counter like a junkie being chased away from his fix.

Diego muttered something unintelligible and headed back towards the office. My Spanish wasn't very good, but I was pretty sure it wasn't a word you'd learn in any classroom.

With the drama over, I turned back to my lunch. I couldn't help but think about Brian. He really had a problem. How could his wife not know about this? He'd better watch himself, or I had the feeling Diego would take care of the problem for everyone.

Too full to finish, I wrapped up my trash and carried it with me towards the can by the door. My butt muscles and hamstrings had stiffened up while I sat, and I moved slowly. A lot of the drive I'd had this morning seemed to have leaked away, and I walked slowly back towards Evan's house. I could call it a day and go home. Maybe soak this grime off in a hot bath. Or I could try to finish a couple more sections of the backyard.

"Jessie! Over here!" Kip skipped down his driveway, clapping his hands. "I thought I saw you go by," he said. He was wearing a daisy-splashed apron over skinny black jeans and a neon purple shirt. He rubbed his hands on the apron as he walked.

I crossed the street and met him halfway up his driveway. "Hi, Kip. How are you?" He grabbed my shoulders and held me at arm's length while he looked me up and down.

"Oh, sweetie. What happened here?"

I glanced down at my outfit. "I was helping Evan get his backyard cleaned up."

"And yet, you're still out in public. Well, we can get to that. But first, there's so much I've wanted to tell you."

"Me too," I said. I wanted to get his take on what Wynne had told me about Brian, and what I'd just seen at the taqueria.

"We should have some coffee," he said. "Are you hungry?"

"No. No, not at all. I just ate a burrito. I'm so full."

"Where does a little bitty thing like you hold it all?" he asked. "Well, how about some coffee?"

"That sounds good. Maybe it will perk me up."

"One perky coffee coming up. Only I can't invite you in because Frenzy is in a really bad mood today. I'm afraid he might tear your scalp off. Do you mind sitting out here?"

"No, that's fine," I said, sinking down on the step. Last thing I needed was a cat attack. A cool breeze blew across my face and rustled the leaves on the azalea bush next to me. I wondered if Kip wasn't inviting me in because of my appearance. I couldn't blame him—I was a mess.

I got up and moved to the window, curiosity winning out over good manners. Kip had his back to me and was fussing with a tray. Books of fabric samples towered on his kitchen table, and piles of unstuffed pillow covers draped from the back of every chair. I was nearly willing to risk a cat attack to see his work, but even as I thought it, a stray dead leaf fell from my shirt. I sat back down.

Within minutes, Kip was back balancing a tray that held a French press, two cups, a small pitcher of cream and a tiny bowl filled with sugar cubes.

"Here we are!" he said, setting the tray gently down next

to me. "I wasn't sure how you take your coffee, so I brought both cream and sugar."

"This is lovely," I said trying to decide which cup to take. One said "Closets Are For Clothes" and the other proclaimed "Queen for a Day."

He filled both cups with a flourish, then pushed the "Queen for a Day" in my direction.

"Thank you," I said, picking up my cup and adding a drip of cream. The smell rising from the cup was heavenly: earthy and robust with just the slightest hint of vanilla. I took a sip. "Oh, wow!"

He smiled, joy lighting up his face at my reaction. "I'm so glad you like it," he said, wiggling into a more comfortable position and wrapping his hands around his mug. "So, tell me. Has your friend had any more trouble with Miriam's ghost?"

"No. Not really."

He leaned forward. "So, yes!"

"No, I don't think so. He said he just hears things. I stayed over last night."

"Ooo-la-la!"

"No! He wanted me to stay over and see if I heard anything."

Kip blew softly on his coffee. "And did you?"

"Well, the dolls. First the dolls kept falling off the shelves."

Kip patted his chest. "Oh, I've been trying not to think of those things. They just give me the willies." He gave a small, nervous laugh. "I thought we all agreed they need to go."

"I know. I couldn't sleep in that room. It was too creepy. So I slept on the couch." I took another sip of my coffee. "Wynne came over."

Kip snorted. "I hope you sent her home. I don't care for her."

I started to fill him in on what she'd told me about Brian, and how Miriam had stood up for her.

"Well, that's a fresh development," he said. "I always did get a bad feeling from him. From the whole family, actually. Oh! I haven't told you about Miss Potts and Mrs. Liddell's investigation!"

I settled in, wrapping my fingers around my mug.

"So, they came over here and staked out the house."

"The Barbieris'?"

"Yes. That was their assignment. Remember?" he said, speaking slowly as if I were dim-witted. "Anyway, they followed the mom to work. Guess where she works?"

I thought about it. "Strip club?"

"No! You're bad!" He swatted my arm. "But now that you say that, I could see that too." He took a sip of his coffee. "She works at a spa near the Galleria."

"What kind of spa?" I asked. I'd seen some spas on the news recently, and they weren't far off of my original guess.

"You are terrible today," he said. "Please. Get your mind out of the gutter. It's a day spa. She does facials." He touched his own cheek as if thinking of getting one. "The ladies went in and managed to get an appointment with her. She must not be very good if she had openings like that. But anyway, they asked her a lot of questions while they were there, but they said she wasn't very friendly. Or talkative."

I tried to picture this. "They didn't ask her anything outright, did they? And anyway, she has an alibi."

"How do you know?" he asked.

"I didn't finish what Wynne told me." Actually, I'd thought about not bringing up the whole police station incident. Kip already thought the worst of Wynne, and I was starting to think she wasn't that bad. But the police station was the linchpin of their alibis. I filled him in on where Tiffany and Wynne had been the night Miriam had been killed.

"Well, this is certainly better information than Mrs. Liddell and Miss Potts got," he said. "All they were able to find out was that she has a daughter and she's frustrated that the daughter doesn't want to be a cheerleader."

I tried to imagine Wynne as a cheerleader.

"Yeah, I can't see that, and it's not very helpful in terms of who killed Miriam."

"What about the husband?" he asked. "If he didn't go to the police station, he could have killed Miriam."

"Wynne said he was too drunk to come. I wonder how drunk he was. Like too drunk to hit his target? Or drunk enough to think shooting Miriam was a good idea?"

Kip stared off into space, lost in thought.

"And you for sure didn't hear anything that night?" I asked.

He snapped his attention back to me. "Sister, the only thing I heard was the thunder and the yowling of my cat. And that was only until I got up and put him in the spare room, and adjusted my earplugs and eye mask. After that, it was lights out."

"What time was that?" I asked.

"Now, now, I am Grammy's assignment," he said. "You've already encroached on Mrs. Liddell's and Miss Potts's assignments." He winked at me. "But, as I told the police, it was a little after eleven."

"Wynne said they got home just as the rain was letting up," I said. "What was that, around midnight? And we don't know exactly what time Miriam was killed. I guess the police said she was killed during the storm. So, I don't know. I guess if Brian wasn't too drunk, he definitely could have done it."

"Was he wet when that horrible girl got home with her horrible mother?"

I stared at Kip. "That's a great question. If he'd been out in that storm, he would have been soaked."

"He might have been wearing a raincoat, but still. No way he couldn't have gotten drenched in that monsoon." He glanced towards the street. "Well, speak of the devil."

Brian was walking quickly along the sidewalk, headed back towards the taqueria.

"Oh, I didn't tell you what happened while I was having lunch today." I lowered my voice, as if Brian could hear me, and gave Kip an update on how he was ogling Diego's niece.

"You think he's going to see her again?"

"He would have to be insane," I said. "Diego looked like he was ready to rip his head off."

"Perhaps he really has a problem. Maybe he just can't help himself."

"Or maybe he forgot part of his order."

Kip refilled our mugs with the remaining coffee. "But back to whether you heard Miriam last night," he said. "I thought that turbaned lady got rid of her."

"I didn't hear Miriam. I don't think. But there was a delivery truck in the middle of the night that was really loud."

"Oh, honey, that place is like Grand Central Station with those trucks. Day. Night. Weekends. I wear earplugs because I'm a light sleeper myself."

A flash of movement across the street caught my eye. Brian race-walked around the corner of the taqueria and took a few steps into the alley. Kip swiveled his head to see what I was looking at. We watched as Brian tossed something towards the dumpster, then raced back towards the sidewalk. Just as Brian reached the edge of Evan's yard, Diego roared around the corner after him.

"I tell you once, I tell you again, stop coming around here!" Diego screamed.

Kip and I sat stock-still, watching the drama unfold in front of us. Diego had caught up with Brian, and he grabbed him by the shoulder, spinning him around. He grabbed his shirtfront and stuck a meaty finger directly in Brian's face.

"You leave my family *alone*. Do you hear me? If I see you in my restaurant, or I see you hanging around outside my restaurant, or I see you looking at anyone in my family, *te rompo la cara!*"

"What did he say?" I whispered to Kip. So far neither man had noticed us. I didn't want to draw attention to ourselves now.

"I think he said he's going to romp with his car."

That didn't seem right, but it didn't take a translator to read the fury on Diego's face. Brian must have been crazy enough to go back for another look at Isabelle.

Brian had mustered up enough nerve to shake himself loose. "Don't touch me," he said, his voice an octave too high and his pitch just slightly shaky.

Diego stepped back, but his eyes fixed on Brian's face with the intensity of a pit bull in a fighting ring. "Don't you ever come in my place again. And if I see you hanging around outside, I will take care of you. You understand me?"

"We'll see about that," Brian said as he turned and walked away, straightening his sweater as he went.

"It's hard to look tough in that outfit," I whispered to Kip.

"Oh, don't even go there," he said. "It hurts me just to look at that."

Diego disappeared into the back of the taqueria, and Brian, after taking a couple of steps towards the alley, seemed to change his mind and headed for his car instead. Swinging himself into the driver's seat, he gunned the engine and squealed down the street. Easier to be macho when you're safely locked inside your car.

CHAPTER TWENTY

Kip stood up, brushing at the back of his pants. "We have to go find whatever he threw away," he said. "It's probably important. Why else would he want to ditch it before Diego got a hold of him?" We wandered nonchalantly across the street and stopped at the end of Evan's sidewalk.

"Did you see what it was?" I whispered to Kip. I wasn't sure why I was whispering, it just felt right.

"No. But I think he threw it into the dumpster."

We stared at the dumpster from about fifteen feet away. One half of the lid was thrown back, and even from here I could see bags of garbage piled high.

"Maybe it landed right on top," I said. "Go look. I'll watch from here and make sure no one's coming."

He grabbed my wrist. "Come with me."

"What are you scared of?" I asked, pulling back. "Just look in and see if you see anything. No big deal."

"If it's not a big deal, then come with me."

"Oh, fine."

"What about the cameras?" I asked. "Mr. McNeil said Diego saw him when he was out here last week."

"I doubt he's just sitting there watching now. He's too wound up." We stood in silence. "Well, if he comes out, just say you're getting something out of the dumpster that you threw away by accident."

"Like what?" I asked.

"I don't know. I'm sure you'll think of something if you have to."

Like two kids contemplating a candy bar theft, we huddled close to each other and crept the short distance to the dumpster. From this side of the fence I noticed the giant weeds had migrated from Evan's yard and had slowly begun stretching along the alley. They were knee-high behind the dumpster, and I was suddenly glad for my wellies. Kip tiptoed gingerly towards the opening, his hands on his cheeks like he was primed to start screaming. My own heart had started thudding a little faster, as I crept in close behind him. Hopefully if there were any rats in there, they wouldn't spring out at us or we'd probably have simultaneous breakdowns.

I poked my head next to his and we spent an anticlimactic couple of minutes staring at garbage bags and broken-down cardboard boxes.

"Do you see anything?" I whispered.

"No, do you?"

"Not really." We stared for another thirty seconds. "What if it slipped down between the bags?" I asked.

"That's possible," he said. "We need a stick or something to poke around with." After less than a minute, he found a dead branch near the fence. "Here. How about this?" It was about two feet long, with rough bark that had flaked off in patches, exposing the moldy wood beneath.

He handed it to me, and I inched back towards the dumpster opening. Looking was one thing, but disturbing whatever might be in there was another.

"Here, you do it," I said, trying to hand him back the stick.

"No, that's okay. You go ahead."

Great. I reached over the edge and gave the nearest bag a tentative jab.

"How's that helping?" he asked. I shot him a look.

"If you think you can do better, you just go ahead."

He gave my shoulder a little pat. "No, you're doing fine. Keep looking."

I swung the stick back over the edge and thumped it against the garbage. Might as well scare away anything that might be in there.

"I wish we knew what we were looking for," I said, getting a little braver now that nothing was leaping out at me.

"It can't have been too big." Kip came a little closer and looked in with me. "Did you see what it looked like?"

"No. Geez, for all we know he was throwing his coffee cup away," I said.

"Did it look to you like he was throwing his coffee cup away? No. He was tossing something before the angry man caught up with him."

I stirred the stick around the inside of the dumpster. "I don't see anything," I finally said. Even in the cool air, the smell of rotted vegetables and decaying meat reached my nose. Ick. I turned away. "I guess we'll never know."

"You're giving up? Just like that? What if this is the key that tells us who killed Miriam?"

"How would this be related to Miriam?" I asked. "I think it's just about Brian being a pervert and Diego calling him out on it."

"Yes, and you said that Miriam had found out he was a pervert. What if he killed her? Sure, he's afraid of Diego because he's a big guy. Miriam? Not so much."

I sighed. He could be right. If we didn't find whatever it was, we could be letting the one thing get away from us that could crack this case and put Miriam's killer away. Which could also keep Evan off my couch.

"Here, help me look," I said, turning back. We stared fruitlessly for a few more minutes.

"It might be better if you get in and take a quick look around," Kip said.

"What? I'm not getting in there! You get in and take a quick look around."

He looked down at his shoes, then pointedly at my wellies.

"Honey, I am wearing my Cesare Paciotti's. These are not dumpster diving shoes." I looked down at his feet. He was wearing a pair of short black leather boots. They looked expensive.

"They make your feet look big," I said, feeling irritated that my shoes were indeed the better dumpster diving shoes.

"Here, I'll give you a boost," he offered.

"That's okay," I said. "I can do it myself." I positioned myself next to the edge and pushed up onto my stomach, swinging one leg up and over the side. I was just starting to have second thoughts, when I slipped on the greasy edge and fell sideways into the dumpster. "Ack!" I yelled, my voice muffled by the bags of garbage surrounding me. It was deeper than I'd thought from the outside, and I scrambled to get to my feet, panic surging in my chest.

"Help! Help!" My feet thrashed wildly, trying to find traction, their frantic churning doing nothing more than bursting open the closest garbage bags.

"Oh my God! Are you okay?" Kip's voice was muffled but reassuring. His arm reached in and I clutched at it, gripping it like a drowning victim's last chance at survival. I managed to right myself, and the panic began to subside. "Okay?" he asked.

"Yes, thanks," I said. The smell was much stronger inside the dumpster than out, and I tried to quell the gagging feeling that was quickly building in my throat. Glancing down, I saw that a bag of rotted food had burst, spilling its congealed queso, runny gray refried beans and globs of unidentifiable meats onto my legs. Holy crap. One maggot and I was going to lose it.

"So, do you see anything?" Kip asked, pulling his arm away.

"Oh, right," I said. Yes, I needed to focus. Find the thing that Brian had tossed in here. I held my breath and began pawing at the nearest bags. It was possible that I'd dislodged whatever it was when I'd fallen in. What if it had fallen into the muck at the bottom? I took a deep breath, breathing through my mouth, and began systematically tossing aside the garbage nearest me, hoping that the thing would miraculously appear at hand.

All I could see was garbage. And nasty garbage at that. Most of the bags were tied, but some had burst, spilling their foul contents onto crushed cardboard produce boxes and canvas rice bags. Near the far side, it looked like large spools of thread or yarn had been tossed in and maybe some cloth bags, but it was too dim to see clearly.

"Oh, no!" Kip said. "I think someone is coming! Duck under the other side!"

I heard him scurry around the side, thumping against the corner as he went.

Crap. Crap. Crap.

I held my breath and fought my way under to the closed side of the dumpster. What if someone was coming out to throw more garbage in? I closed my eyes, hunched over and leaned my back against the side. Holding my breath till I nearly passed out, I waited. And waited. Time passed, and I wondered if Kip was still hiding behind the bin. If someone was coming out to throw something away, they should have been here by now. Finally the smell of smoke made its way to me, fighting past the nauseating smells that were nearly strangling me. I generally don't like the smell of cigarettes, but considering what I was surrounded by, it smelled heavenly.

Someone from the taqueria must be taking a smoke break on the back steps. Great. How long was that going to take? Shoots of panic began winding their way into my head again. Claustrophobia and nausea battled for first place, and if that person didn't leave soon, I was going to shoot up from the dumpster like some giant screaming garbage-covered jack-in-the-box.

I closed my eyes and tried to think happy thoughts, but all I could think of were the nasty things that were touching me. Just as I'd reached my breaking point, I heard Kip at the opening.

"Okay, all clear," he said.

I scrambled across, wading through the waist-high bags intent on getting out. I didn't care who had killed Miriam anymore. I didn't care if the only clue in the world was mere inches from my hand. I had to get out.

I got out as gracefully as I'd gotten in. Throwing myself

over the edge, I flopped out, missing my landing and falling in a heap on the hard ground.

"Oh, what's that in your hair?" Kip asked, taking a quick step back. My hand flew to my hair where it sank into something squishy and soft.

"Get it off! Oh, God, what is it?" I batted at my head, trying to fling off whatever it was without having to touch it, but I just managed to spread it farther along the side of my head. Tears welled up and started falling down my face. I wanted to rip my clothes off and stand in front of a fire hose. "Get it off," I said, trying not to sniffle, as that just pulled the noxious smells deeper into my sinus cavities.

"Oh, sugar, don't cry," Kip said. I noticed that while he tried to sound comforting, he was staying at least six feet from me. "Hey, it's not that bad. You just need a little washing up. And guess what?"

I didn't care what. "What?"

"I think I found what Brian threw. It wasn't in the dumpster at all. It was behind the dumpster. I guess he was intending to come back later and get it."

All that for nothing? I struggled to my feet as Mexican rice dripped down my front. At least, I hoped that was Mexican rice. I shook my shirt, trying to dislodge whatever it was. I needed a Kleenex for my nose. I needed a Clorox bath for my body. I was probably going to need my head shaved.

"What was it?" I finally asked. "What did you find?"

"It's a camera." He held it out so I could see it, still carefully maintaining his distance. "A little digital one."

I didn't care about being quiet anymore, and I didn't care about whispering. I stomped my wellies on the pavement, trying to get the chunks to fall off. I couldn't get in my car like this.

"Do you have any clothes I could borrow?" I asked. "Or maybe you could hose me down and lend me a towel?"

Kip's perfect nose wrinkled the tiniest bit. "Gosh. I wish I did, but I don't really have anything that would fit you. It's not that bad. I swear, you look just fine. Divine, really. Nothing a little shower won't fix right up."

He backed down the alley towards the street, still clutching the camera.

"We need to see what's on there," I said, pulling myself together and following him. He outpaced me across the street.

"You know, I forgot. I'm supposed to be meeting a friend. Oh! And I have muffins in the oven, they're probably burned to a crisp! I have to go."

"Hey, what about the camera!" I did *not* go into a dumpster for nothing.

He hesitated, clearly torn. In the end, my putrid state decided him. He set the camera on the edge of the sidewalk.

"Fine. If you want, you could take it with you."

"We could look together," I said.

His nose wrinkled again. "No, that's okay. I'm pretty tied up today. But be sure you come back after you've cleaned up and let me know what I found." He gave a small sniff. "Or, you could call me." He pulled a small embossed card from his back pocket and set that on the sidewalk as well. "And don't forget to pick up your purse. Here, let me help you." He picked up my purse and set it gingerly down about eight feet away, then he sped up his driveway and flew through his door with a bang. I leaned over to pick up the camera and card, and a crumpled square of tissue floated down from where it must have been stuck to my hair. I then retrieved my purse and tried not to think about it.

In the end, I scraped as much of the crud off of myself as possible, then found a crusty old towel in Evan's garage and arranged that across my car seat before getting in. I was still worried about the white things that looked like rice. Periodically, one would fall, and the movement nearly sent me into a panic every time afresh.

I was just pulling into my driveway when I saw Larry step out his front door. Could this day get any worse? I pretended not to see him, but he sauntered into my garage before I had a chance to hit the button.

"Holy crap. What happened to you?" he asked, as I stepped from the car.

"I had a little mishap," I said. "I really need a shower. Was there something you needed?"

"Seriously, you look terrible."

"Yeah, I know." I plopped down on the floor and started wrestling with a boot. "Little help?" I asked, holding a foot up in Larry's direction. He looked at the sole and grimaced.

"Not a chance."

"What did you want, Larry?" Irritation fueled me, and I got the first one off.

"I want you to go to the HOA board and tell them that they should pay me to act as security around here."

I got the second boot off and headed for the door. "No." I waved a hand towards the driveway. "You gotta go. I'm going in."

He hesitated for a second, like he was going to argue with me, then wrinkled up his face like he'd finally caught a whiff of me. "You stink," he said, backing up. "And that blob in your hair looks like something a dog ralphed up."

I hit the garage door button and raced through the back door pulling at my clothes as I went. Addie chased me upstairs, and Henry howled from the powder room. Sometimes you just have to take care of yourself first.

Never in my life had I been so thankful for hot water. I washed my hair four times. And as an added precaution, I washed it again. I lathered and scrubbed my skin till it hurt, and I used the nylon tub-cleaning brush to scrub under my nails. It wasn't until I ran out of hot water that I considered myself done. Thankfully, the cut on my hand had healed to the point it was just a red line now. Otherwise, I would probably be in need of an IV cocktail of antibiotics.

I put all my clothes in a garbage bag, tied it up and put it outside. No way I was ever wearing any of that again. Henry was relieved to be let out of the powder room, and he and Addie romped in circles around my tiny backyard while I retrieved Brian's camera and powered it up.

The pictures weren't quite as interesting as I'd hoped. Sure, there were some blurred shots of Diego's niece, clearly taken without stopping to focus. A couple of them had a finger blocking half the picture, and I could only guess that Brian had been trying to hide the camera as he'd snapped. There was even a clear shot of his nostril and half his chin.

The next was a series of teenage girls at a mall. It appeared that whoever, no doubt Brian, had taken the pictures had followed them for a little while, taking pictures at a food court, then more as they'd window-shopped, giggling and taking selfies. Finally, one of the girls seemed to have noticed him and they all turned and stared directly into the camera lens while one of them flipped him the bird. That was the end of the mall girls.

And the remainder showed photos of young women at a driving range. The camera wasn't made for action shots, so this was just a series of blurred teenaged girls swinging golf clubs. A couple of them looked coquettishly over their shoulders. These must be the golf lessons Wynne had mentioned.

I set the camera down and called the dogs in. That was disappointing. If Brian had been killed instead of Miriam, I would think the photos had some relevance. Maybe an angry father had taken exception to his daughter being covertly filmed. But alas, Brian was still alive and well. Next time I went to Evan's, I would take the camera with me and let Kip take a look. But for the most part, this felt like a dead end.

Next, I placed a call to Frances. I realized with a start that I'd not even spoken to her in a couple of weeks. I was really close to my grandmother, and normally we were well connected, but the chaos of Evan's new house had disrupted my normally well-ordered life.

Luckily, Frances wasn't at all fazed by my absence and was happy for a dinner invitation, even if it was later than good manners dictated. I could only hope I would be hungry for dinner, since my burrito seemed to be swelling to twice its size in my belly.

I spent the rest of the afternoon puttering around the house and getting ready for a marathon baking session tomorrow. It felt good to slow down and get organized. I was ready to get back to my routine, and back to my business.

At 6:27, I pulled into my parents' driveway and slowly drove around back to Frances's house. A steady mist was falling, just barely visible in the beam of the headlights. I grabbed an umbrella but ran with it unopened to the front door. Frances was waiting at the door and ushered me into her warm, dry foyer.

"Nice night," I said, wiping my feet on a neat little Oriental rug. Frances looked impeccable in a silver silk cowlneck top and black pleated pants. Clunky silver bracelets jangled on her wrist, matching the wide buckles on her shoes. She gave me a quick hug and disappeared towards her bedroom.

"I just need to get my sweater, and I'll be ready to go." She was back in a moment, and she picked up an umbrella from the stand and her purse from the console table, and we headed for the door.

"I hope you don't mind, I made reservations at Hopper's Choppery," she said. "It just opened a couple of weeks ago. It's supposed to be very good."

I have to admit, I was slightly surprised. Frances and I generally dined at well-established Houston eateries, where you were most likely to run into other River Oaks folks out for a bite. We saw a lot of khaki pants and blue blazers, and women who'd spent the day at the spa getting their hair and face done just so. I'd read a review of Hopper's Choppery last week online, and it sounded like the dress code would be running more towards miniskirts and leather pants. This should be interesting.

I drove slowly through the misty night, soft classical music drifting from the speakers. I gave her the highlights of what had been happening with Evan and his house, realizing I hadn't even spoken to her since this whole mess had started.

Traffic was light as we got close to the restaurant, which was near the corner of McGowen and Fannin. The thing about Houston is that, unlike most big cities, the city center actually closes down as soon as the office workers escape at the end of the day. Weekends it's like a ghost town, with the exception of the areas near the ballpark and the Arts District. This particular area was a little seedy and scruffy, with pockets of townhouses popping up here and there, like hybrid roses in the middle of a weed-choked parking lot.

A mini traffic jam let me know we were close. The restaurant itself was an old, crumbly concrete block building with no windows. It looked more like a defunct eighties club than the hippest new restaurant in town. Out front, the line for the valet stretched eight cars back. Two limos were double-parked, compounding the jam, and black-vested valets raced back and forth, dodging traffic like squirrels on crack.

"Wow," I said to Frances. "This is quite the scene. How'd you manage to get reservations on the spur of the moment like that?"

"Marne's son is a co-owner," she said, her eyes widening as we watched a valet nearly get mowed down by an irate pickup truck driver. "He said I should stop by sometime and check it out."

"It got really good reviews last week," I said. I drove slowly around the block and back around to get in line for the valet. "Isn't the chef some hotshot from New York or something?"

"LA," she said. In spite of the line, the valets were moving things along quickly. I didn't mind the wait because it gave me a chance to gawk at the outfits that were emerging from the cars. As I'd thought, this was not our normal crowd. Frances, too, seemed to be enjoying the show. Apparently, no one knew what to wear to a place like this, because the styles ranged from club wear to grunge, and all the way to a couple of tuxedos and long satin dresses. Frances and I were going to stick out like sore thumbs in our traditional duds.

The chaos continued on the sidewalk as we exited the car. About two dozen people waited in a messy line on the sidewalk, held in place by a fat velvet rope. A rotund man with a clipboard waited on a small red carpet beside the door. He didn't even look up as we approached.

"Reservations and name?" he snapped, already running

his pen down the list as if certain he wouldn't find us on there.

"Frances Latimer." She had to repeat it twice over the thumping of bass blasting from a car idling behind us.

Finding us on the list, he jerked a thumb towards the door. A couple of people in line booed at us as we walked towards the door. The door was heavy, and I had to heft my weight to pull it open. I shot a look at the rotund guy, thinking he ought to expand his services and open the door for patrons as well. So far, I wasn't thinking too much of this place.

Inside, three hostesses buzzed around a seating chart, looking at the layout and then eying the customers as they waited by the door. As best I could tell, we were being seated solely on the basis of looks. The three of them quickly decided where to seat four hot-looking twentysomethings— they were ushered to a table close to the bar area. The couple in front of us, sadly dressed in jeans and penny loafers, was hurried away towards the bathroom.

Frances shot me a look as it was our turn for inspection. Two of them were pointing after the bathroom customers, but the third squinted uneasily at her reservation book. In the end, there must have been something in there about Frances being a guest of the owner, because one of them showed us reluctantly to a small table in a tiny enclave over-looking the bar, but still somewhat sheltered from the noise.

With a sour look, the hostess handed us our menus and stalked away.

"We can only hope the food is good," Frances said, neatly draping her napkin across her lap.

"Interesting place," I said. And it was. It was a cavernous space, the ceiling all exposed pipes and ducts, from which hung what looked like meat cleavers and motorcycle parts. Chopper squared. Massive chandeliers hung over the dining area, looking like they came straight from Henry VIII's dining hall, and a stained red concrete floor gave the impression of bloodstains. I gave a little shudder and turned to the menu.

"What are you thinking of having?" Frances asked, peering intently at the menu through the bifocals perched on the end of her nose.

I scanned the menu, looking for something normal. "The 'Star Strangled Snapper' might be good. Or maybe the 'Victimless Vegetable Plate,'" I said. "How about you?"

She was still staring at the menu. "Hmm, I truly think there is something wrong with Marne's son. Although, the tortellini might be nice."

"You mean the 'Tortured Tortellini'?"

Our waitress approached, expertly weaving through the crowd at the bar to reach us.

"Good evening, ladies," she said, pulling a notepad from her apron pocket. "Can I get you something to drink while you look over the menu? Or would you like to hear the specials first?"

We opted for hearing about the specials.

"Tonight we're serving 'Road Kill Ravioli' topped with a light vodka cream sauce and oven-roasted tomatoes. That comes with a chopped salad to start, along with garlic bread. Our second special is a 'Death Row Duck,' and that is served with sesame-toasted carrots and a wild rice pilaf. They're both very good."

"I think I'm going to need another minute to decide," said Frances. We each ordered a glass of wine and our waitress rushed back off into the fray. "Seriously. Road Kill Ravioli? Do you think anyone's going to actually order that?"

"It's probably not stuffed with actual road kill," I said, with more conviction than I felt. "I'm sure she would have told us if we'd asked."

"I don't want to know," Frances said, her head still bent over her menu.

I looked at the crowd mingling around the bar and wondered how they'd gotten past Fat-Boy Bouncer at the door. It was packed now, bodies pressed almost up against each other as they jostled for space. The couple nearest our table stared at me with hostile expressions. If they were that hungry, perhaps they should have gone somewhere else.

Maybe it was the décor, or maybe it was the menu, or maybe it was the vibe the owners were shooting for, but I had a vague sense of unease in this place. As if violence was simmering just below the surface, ready to explode at the slightest provocation.

"Did you see this? A 'Hope-the-Heimlich-Works-Hamburger.'" Frances was still poring over the menu.

Just past the hostile couple, I spotted someone who looked familiar. Who was that? I tried to place the face. Someone I'd seen recently. It took me a minute, but I finally got it. Tiffany Barbieri. Only she looked different. Her hair was teased high over her head, new highlights shimmering against the overhead lights, and her eye makeup was dusky and dark, almost making her look like she was wearing a mask.

But it was her dress that was catching the eye of almost every person in the room. It was sheer to the point of questionably obscene. The neckline dipped past her ample breasts to her rib cage, and I could see several men around her mesmerized by the shimmying and swaying, no doubt hoping that one of those breasts would cut loose from its tiny tether. The material itself was a gauzy silver mist, about as dense as a mesh screen, that wrapped around her, dipping just below her buttocks. If she dropped her purse, everyone was going to get a show.

Frances glanced over her shoulder to see what I was staring at. "My word," she said. "That is quite an interesting outfit. I do wonder where she bought it." Then she turned back to the menu.

"That's Evan's next-door neighbor," I hissed, even though the place was so loud no one could have possibly overheard me. Frances turned and looked again.

"That's very nice for Evan, I'm sure," she said.

"Yes, only that's not her husband," I said, finally noticing the man that Tiffany had attached herself to. And by attached, I mean she'd pressed her body up against his stomach and had begun undulating as if doing a pole dance on his leg.

"Oh my," said Frances, shifting her chair slightly so she didn't have to turn her neck so far.

"I ran into her husband at lunch today, and he told me that she was sick and couldn't go to a business dinner with him."

"She appears to be feeling better," Frances said, setting her menu down and pulling off her bifocals. "Much better."

She did look like she was feeling pretty good. She moved in closer to the man's neck and was tracing a line with her finger up and down under his ear. Periodically she'd lean in and flick his earlobe with her tongue.

"Did they ever find out who killed the woman who previously owned Evan's house?" Frances asked.

"I don't think so. Evan hasn't heard anything from the police. As far as I know, they don't have any ideas."

Our waitress arrived with our wine, ready to take our orders, but Frances waved her away, saying she hadn't made her mind up yet and needed a few more minutes. The waitress stomped away, clearly irritated that we were taking up her table and foiling her plan of turning it every forty-five minutes.

"Evan did have someone over to clean out the spirits in his house," I said after we'd clinked glasses. "She smudged it. I'm hoping it worked, because he's been sleeping on my couch most of the week, convinced that Miriam's ghost is still there."

"He's got a ghost in his house?"

I told her what I'd experienced, feeling slightly foolish, but buoyed by her interest. "I'm actually more concerned about Henry getting into some rat poison than I am about Evan being harassed by a ghost. But at the same time, I think if they catch Miriam's killer, I could convince him that her spirit could rest."

Frances leaned across the table, her menu all but forgotten. "Jessica, I know you have ideas. Who do you think killed her?"

"I wish I knew. The problem is, I didn't know her at all. I only saw her that one time. Or twice, if you count when I found her." I took a sip of wine, trying not to think of Addie tugging at the thick skirts.

"But you surely have some opinions. You always do," she sighed.

"It could have been someone she knew, or it could have just been random. From what people tell me, she was first and foremost a busybody. Maybe someone didn't like her meddling in their affairs." I filled her in on what Wynne had told me about Brian, and how the taqueria owner had chased him out of his restaurant for taking pictures of the young woman.

We both looked over at Tiffany, who had moved on to another man and was gyrating enthusiastically against his leg. It was disturbing to watch.

"Evan certainly has some colorful neighbors," I said. "I wonder if Brian knows what she's up to."

"It sounds like Brian doesn't care," said Frances. "He's too busy with his own hobbies."

Our waitress sidled up to our table again, pen clenched in her hand. "Are you ready to order?" She didn't even bother to try to sound polite.

"You know, dear," said Frances, "this is frankly the worst-looking menu I have ever seen. I don't believe we'll be eating here tonight. If you could just give us the bill for our drinks, we'll let you have your table back."

"Fine," said our waitress. "I wouldn't expect you two to understand an awesome concept like this." She smacked our bill down on the table and turned away. I swear if I've ever been tempted to completely stiff a server, this was the time. Lucky for me, I was saved from that sentiment by Frances, who cracked open the brown vinyl check cover, peeled a few bills from her wallet and slipped them inside.

"Are you ready?" she said to me, pushing back her chair. "I'm very sorry for my restaurant selection tonight. It was obviously a mistake."

"Don't worry about it," I said. "I've enjoyed it immensely. And if we hadn't come here, we would have never known what Evan's neighbor is up to."

We reached the crush of bodies in the bar area and began picking our way through. I kept looking for Tiffany, but I'd lost sight of her in the crowd. It took some pushing and maybe a little shoving, but we finally made it to the door, bursting out into the fresh air like swimmers breaking free of the undertow.

The line of cars at the valet stand was even longer than it had been twenty minutes ago, most lined up to come in, very few leaving. I wondered how many people they would pack in there tonight. Well, they could have it. I handed my valet ticket to the nearest black vest, and Frances and I stepped aside to let the arriving couples pass.

"Geez, get a room!" someone yelled from the line near the door. I glanced around to see who he was talking to and spotted Tiffany with her new friend standing behind us, waiting for their car. Or cars, as may be. They were making out like a couple of sixteen-year-olds, swapping spit and groping each other like they were going to rip their clothes off right there.

She glanced around, her mouth still in an open lock on his. Catching my eye, I could see her trying to place my face.

"Hi, Tiff!" I said, acting like I wasn't looking at her tongue slide around some guy's mouth. "You know, I ran into your husband this afternoon, and he mentioned you weren't feeling well. I'm glad you're feeling better."

She disengaged, tugging the hem of her dress into place. "You've mistaken me for someone else," she said, narrowing her eyes at me as if daring me to contradict her.

"No, Tiffany Barbieri, right? I met you and your husband last week. Nice guy." *As perverts go*, I thought. Just then, the valet pulled up with my car. "Okay, anyway, it was nice to see you," I said as I went around to the driver's side. "Tell Brian I said hi."

Frances and I slid into the car, and I pulled slowly out into traffic. Tiffany was still staring after us, no doubt trying to figure out where she'd met me. Women like that never remember because they never bothered to actually notice you in the first place.

"Does she have any idea who you are?" asked Frances as I signaled for a right turn onto Elgin.

"It didn't appear so," I said, switching on my windshield wipers. A light mist had started to fall, coating everything with a fine sheen. I was willing to bet the beautiful people waiting in line outside Hopper's Choppery were going to look a little less beautiful in about five minutes. "She's only seen me once, and I'm pretty sure she wasn't paying any attention to me."

"Well, that's probably good. I enjoyed speculating about who might have killed that Miriam person," she said. "But it makes me nervous to think maybe it was that woman. I mean, if it was, and she killed her neighbor for knowing about her secret life, well, you just made it clear that you know about it as well."

"No, Frances, I'm sure she doesn't remember me at all. There's nothing to worry about. And actually, she's one of the only ones who has an alibi."

"Well, I did not care for her. I hope you're sure of her alibi." She tsked softly. "Cold-blooded. You could see it in her face. Reminds me of my friend Marcy's son-in-law. I met him once at a crawfish boil. That was before he tried to kill his mistress with a board, for threatening to tell his wife about their affair."

I cocked an eyebrow. "You never told me about that."

"It was a long time ago. He's out of prison now, but they never hear from him."

"I guess not."

We were cruising down Westheimer now, very close to

Evan's house. "Hey, we're right by Evan's. Do you want to see his new house? We won't stop or anything, I just thought you might like to see what he bought."

"I would love to see what the dear boy has gotten himself into," she said, sitting up straighter in her seat.

"You probably won't be able to see much since it's so dark," I said. "But you might be able to get an idea of it."

I turned right on Montrose and went up a couple of blocks. Traffic was heavy, and it took a couple of minutes until I got a break to make the left turn onto Evan's street.

"He's the first house here behind the taqueria," I said. Evan's house was dark, no lights in any windows, and his car wasn't in the driveway. "It looks like he's not home." I pulled up to the curb, feeling better about gawking if he wasn't there.

The shadows beneath the live oak were deep, and the glare from a security light on the back side of the taqueria rendered it nearly impossible to see anything more than the basic structure of the building.

"It's cute," said Frances, sounding slightly disappointed. "It doesn't look bad at all."

She was right. In the misty light, the peeling paint, sagging porch and dilapidated roof weren't visible. All the bad parts were softened, and the bones showed through, giving a glimpse of what it could be if someone put the money in to rehab it.

"It doesn't look bad in the dark," I conceded. "It's a whole other story in the light."

"I'm sure Evan can make this a nice little home for Henry and himself. And you have such a good eye for decorating. I'm sure you can help him sort this out."

"I think you're being overly generous on that," I said,

pulling away from the curb. "I think he needs someone with a lot more than good taste to help with this."

"Well, you're a good friend, Jessica. I know you'll help in any way you can. Now, how would you like to go to Tony Mandola's? I'm sure they'll be able to find us a table. And we'll be able to find something normal on the menu."

CHAPTER TWENTY-ONE

Frances had been right. The menu, the food, the atmosphere, the service, essentially everything about Tony Mandola's soothed us after the aggravation of Hopper's Choppery. Most of the staff knew us by sight, and I relaxed as waiters and busboys rushed around, pampering us with attention.

During dinner, I'd filled Frances in on everything that had been going on with Evan and his house, his ghost, and his rats. I'd shared with her how I felt having him stay with me, including the guilt I'd been suffering over hating having him there. He was my friend, after all, and a friend in need at that. But Frances, in her level-headed way, validated my feelings while gently reminding me that we all need someone to lean on sometimes, and perhaps Evan needed me more right now than I realized.

"I have sometimes wondered," she mused over dessert, "just what Evan means to you. I know you're friends, but I've often wondered if it might deepen into more than that."

"Frances!" I nearly choked on my pecan pie. "No. It's Evan. I mean, it's Evan."

"He's a nice boy," she said. "And I'm glad you have such a good friend. But sometimes I do wish you would find someone special."

"You and me both," I said, running my fork through the softening ice cream. It struck me suddenly why the whole Miriam thing had been bothering me so much. The very fact that she seemed so alone in the world was triggering a certain uneasiness in myself. What if I never found a special person? What if I ended up old and alone? And crazy like Miriam?

"Maybe you should let me introduce you to some of—"

"No, Frances. We've talked about this. I don't like blind dates."

"It wouldn't have to be a blind date. You could just attend some functions with me." She dabbed her lips gently with her napkin and took a sip of coffee.

Dan flashed through my mind. "Well." I took a sip of my own decaf. "There is someone that you know, that...well, I don't know why I didn't really notice him when I first met him. But now..."

She sat forward on her chair. "And who might that be?"

"He's one of my dog-walking clients. Dan Harrison? Remember, you referred me to him?"

She looked down at the table, her shoulders sagging infinitesimally. "Yes, of course. He is quite the gentleman, isn't he? I saw him just a couple of days ago, when I was having lunch at the club."

I felt like there was a big "but" coming. Only I couldn't imagine what it could be.

"What? Is he married? Is he engaged? Is he gay? I can tell there's something you don't want to tell me."

"No. No, Jessica. It's nothing like that." She straightened the spoon beside her coffee cup.

"What? Is he dying?" A woman at the next table swiveled her head to look.

Frances smiled slightly. "No. None of those things, but I understand he's taken a job in Dubai. I would have thought you'd known about it, because his parents will be taking his dog, and—well, I guess you're losing a client." She looked up, compassion in her eyes, and she reached across and placed her hand over mine. "I'm so sorry, Jessica. I had no idea you were interested in him."

A surprising stab of disappointment was ricocheting around my chest, and I felt short of breath. I dropped my gaze so she wouldn't see how affected I was by this. Why hadn't he told me? Oh. The phone call.

"Dubai?"

"I understand it's a two-year assignment," she said. "His mother isn't very happy about it. She doesn't want him to be half a world away. His father, on the other hand, is so proud. He was telling everyone in earshot about Dan's promotion."

"Poor Blue," I said, tears pricking at my eyes at the thought of how heartbroken he would be. "And he can't take Blue with him?"

"He said his dog wouldn't do well with the climate over there."

"No. I guess he wouldn't, but he won't do well without Dan either." What kind of person can leave their dog for a job?

"His mother is going to take the dog. She said she will Skype with Dan all the time so he can see how well—what did you call him? Blue? See how well Blue is doing."

"I don't know how he can leave him."

"Sometimes people have to do things that they don't want to do."

"I would never leave Addie. Not for anything."

The waiter came by and slipped the check onto the table. "I know you wouldn't, dear. And I'm thankful for that. I don't know what I would do if you wanted to move halfway around the world."

We were quiet as I drove Frances home, the damp, misty evening a fitting backdrop to the pall of weariness that had begun to envelop me. I thanked her for dinner and drove the familiar streets to my house, feeling an unfamiliar loneliness. But when I got home, I got a mega-greeting from Addie and Henry, and their wiggly butts were just enough to short-circuit the self-pity that had threatened to derail me on the drive.

I slept hard and woke Sunday morning feeling more my optimistic self. It was time to get back to my business and my regular life. Evan was well on his way to settling into his new house. Whether or not the police caught Miriam's killer, I had to believe that Mrs. Grey had banished whatever was left of any spiritual residue that might be hanging around. So everything should be back to normal.

I buzzed around the house for most of the morning, catching up on my cleaning and laundry and other fun things like grocery shopping. At eleven, I texted Evan to ask him when he was going to be retrieving Henry from my house, making it clear that he was welcome to leave the dog with me if he had too much going on.

The phone rang just as I hit send. Dan's name popped onto my screen, and my heart thudded as I swiped to answer.

"Hello?"

"Jessie? This is Dan. Sorry I didn't get back to you earlier."

"Dan! No, I'm sorry I didn't call you back. I didn't get your message that you'd called until midweek."

It was probably better that Frances had told me about his job in Dubai, because even though I knew it was coming, I still felt a surprising sense of trepidation when he said he had something he needed to talk to me about. Without Frances's head's up, I probably would have thought something had happened to Blue. Or maybe from his tone, I'd have thought I was being fired. But, no. Frances was right. He was moving to Dubai, and he was moving fast.

He asked if I could come over and pick up my last payment, but really, I knew he was giving me a chance to say good-bye to Blue. My earlier optimism started disintegrating around the edges, being replaced by a threatening wave of emotion.

Blue was sitting, as he did every day, waiting for me patiently by the back door. His leash hung on its hook like normal, but the boxes strewn about the kitchen were anything but. Dan was in the middle of packing papers into a cardboard box, and he looked up and smiled at me as I came through the door.

"That was fast," he said, setting down a folder. "Can I get you something to drink? Coffee? A beer?"

I knelt down next to Blue and rubbed the thick fur around his neck, leaning in to kiss the smooth plane of his head.

"Maybe a little hot chocolate?" Dan asked, his voice sounding just the slightest bit shaky.

"Hot chocolate sounds great," I said, rocking back on my heels as Blue pushed his head against my chest. I wrapped an arm around his neck and murmured into his ear. "I'm really going to miss you, boy. But your grandma will take good care of you." He whined softly and pulled away, trotting over to where Dan was filling a kettle.

I stood up and followed him, stepping around boxes.

"Big move," I said to Dan. "Dubai. Wow, it's going to be so different."

"Yeah. Yeah. Professionally, it's a good move for me," he said, sounding as if he was trying to convince himself as much as me.

"Do you think Blue knows what's happening?"

He turned and spooned a powdered mix into two big mugs before leaning down to rub the big dog, who was leaning against his leg, making soft guttural cries.

"Yeah, he definitely knows something's up," he said. "I've never heard him make sounds like that before."

I thought my heart would shatter in my chest.

Dan poured the steaming water and mixed each cup slowly, adding a cloud of whipped cream when he was finished stirring. I couldn't believe I'd missed out on finding this guy who added whipped cream to hot chocolate. We carried our drinks into the family room, where a gas fire danced in the fireplace. Houston doesn't get too many really cold days, but a damp raw day like this made me glad for the luxury.

I sat down on an overstuffed leather chair, and Dan and Blue settled on the sofa across from me. Blue skipped his digging ritual, dropped down instead, and put his head across Dan's leg.

"This must be really hard," I said, blowing on my mug to distract myself from the tears that kept welling in my eyes every time I looked at Blue.

"I wish I didn't have to go," he said, so softly I nearly missed it. "I can't imagine leaving him for so long."

"Frances told me your parents are going to take him."

"Yes. My mom will spoil him rotten," he said, laying a hand on Blue's head. "I know she will."

"Oh, I'm sure," I said. "But still. I don't know how he'll do without you. A lot of the dogs I walk are different. They're kind of happy-go-lucky, roll-with-the-punches pooches. But Blue...I don't know. Blue is more a one-man dog."

Dan closed his eyes and took a deep breath. His hand moved rhythmically down Blue's neck, around his ears and back up. Slow, steady strokes, soothing both himself and his dog. "I know."

"But I'm sure he'll be fine," I amended, way too late. I wasn't trying to make him feel worse, I was just worried about the dog. He really was a serious soul, and Dan's departure would be difficult for him. "I brought him a bag of his favorite treats," I said, reaching for my bag on the floor beside me. "I thought it might help when he goes to your parents' to have something familiar."

"That's very kind of you," Dan said, opening his eyes and looking at me so intently that I found my cheeks reddening. "You've been so good to him, and I know he loves you. Would it be okay if I give my mom your number? Just in case he has any adjustment issues. I'd feel better if she could call you, being that I'll be a zillion time zones different."

"Of course," I said. "Anytime she needs anything, I would be more than happy to help."

He let out a breath as if he'd been holding it. "I really appreciate that. You know him so well, and I'll feel better knowing you're around if he needs anything."

We sat, the silence broken only by Blue's soft cries and the popping of the fire. I didn't stay long, just long enough to finish my hot chocolate and say a final good-bye to the big husky. His cries were unlike any sound I'd ever heard him make, and it nearly undid me. As I crouched by the back door, he shoved his head into my chest, hiding his face against me. We stayed like that for a long few minutes, and when I finally stood, I could hardly see the door handle through the haze of tears that clouded my eyes.

"Good luck in Dubai," I said, my voice breaking in spite of my best effort to stop it.

"Thanks," he whispered. "Thank you for loving Blue like you have."

I drove home through a fine cold mist, intent on spending the afternoon curled up with Addie. And, of course, Henry, if Evan hadn't responded. I was pawing through my purse as I pulled into the garage, looking for my phone, when Larry ambled in.

"Yo, uh, neighbor."

I looked up, then resumed my rummaging.

"Oh, man! Do you have pink-eye?"

"No." Why hadn't I put the door down as I'd pulled in?

"Good. That's some nasty contagious funk. So, do you have any eggs?" He leaned against my car and ran a hand across his face. "I had a rough night, if you know what I mean." He belched. "Whoops. 'Scuse me."

I finally found my phone and pulled it out. The little red light was blinking. Evan had responded to my text, letting me know that he was working and that he'd be home after five if I wanted to bring Henry home then.

"So, about those eggs?"

"I don't know, Larry."

He sighed. "Could you check? I mean, I need eggs. I got a hangover like you wouldn't believe. Do you have any bacon, too? I think some grease would make me feel better."

He followed me into the house. Addie's greeting cooled off as soon as she saw Larry. Henry, on the other hand, was delighted to see a stranger, and he began dancing on his hind feet, belting out a series of high-pitched yelps.

"No! No, make it stop." Larry covered his ears and backed away from Henry.

"Henry," I said. "Stop." I went to the pantry and pulled out some dog biscuits. That stopped it.

"Eggs?" Larry shuffled over and slumped down on my couch. "What the hell happened to this thing?" he asked, looking at the misshapen cushions that were left. I pulled open the refrigerator and peeped inside, spotting the carton of pastured eggs I'd bought just this morning.

"No, sorry," I said, slamming the door. "I don't have bacon or eggs." Those eggs were pricey, and frankly, I didn't want to waste them on hungover Larry.

"How do you not have eggs?" he asked. "You seem like you would have eggs." He slid down on his side, then hoisted his legs onto the couch, looking like he was settling in for the day.

"Nope, sorry. You should just take yourself out to brunch or something."

Leaning forward towards the coffee table, he picked up Brian's camera and hit the power button. A faint high-pitched whine sounded as it powered up.

"Dude. My grandpa had a camera like this. Doesn't your phone have a camera?"

"It's not mine."

He forwarded through the pictures, occasionally stopping and holding the screen closer.

"I'm seeing a theme here," he said slowly. "You like young girls."

"That's not mine," I repeated.

"Oh, okay. Right. How are those eggs coming along?" He resumed his scrolling. "Hel-lo!" he shouted. "Who is this little hottie? Tell me you know her and can tell me where to find her." He held the camera up and I could see one of the pictures of Isabelle.

"Larry, that is a child. Geez."

"She's not a child, she's a hot mama." He lay back and continued to stare at the screen.

"You need to go. I don't have eggs, and I have things to do."

He grunted and started wiggling deeper into what was left of my couch. "But I'm hungry and hungover, and if you were a good neighbor, you would help me," he whined.

If he wasn't so heavy, I would have dragged him out like the caveman he was. As it stood, I could tell he was going to be harder to get rid of if I didn't feed him something. I pulled open my freezer and rooted around. Finally, I spotted an old frozen dinner. I looked for an expiration date, but if there had been one, it had long since worn off. I was sure it was fine. I popped it in the microwave. He went back to zipping through the remaining pictures.

"Who's this girl flipping you off?"

"She's not flipping me off. I didn't take the picture."

"You really seem to have a thing for young girls." He waved the camera in the air. "Can I have this one?" He was back to the one of the Isabelle pictures. "Send it to me."

"No! Geez, Larry. Seriously, she's like fourteen or so. Maybe thirteen. Put it down."

He gazed at it one more time before tossing the camera back on the table and laying his head back with a groan. "Do you have any Advil?"

The microwave beeped. "No. But here. I made you breakfast, only you have to take it to go."

He closed his eyes and stuck his nose in the air, sniffing like an animal trying to discern its prey. "What is that? I don't think I like the smell."

"It's breakfast. But really, you have to take it with you." I pulled it out of the microwave onto a stack of napkins so I wouldn't burn myself.

Larry hauled himself to his feet and came towards me, looking suspiciously at the black plastic container. I walked towards the front door, waving the food side to side, as he followed obediently along behind me. At the door, I opened it and held the food over the threshold until he stepped outside. Then I shoved it into his hands, told him to feel better and slammed the door.

The only good thing about Larry's visit is that it had helped dispel the sadness of saying good-bye to Dan and Blue and worked me into an annoyed agitation. So rather than curling up on my bed with the dogs and feeling sorry for myself, I decided to get some work done. I powered through my inventory lists, both for supplies as well as updating my sales figures by distributor. I stamped dozens of bags with my logo and even baked a few batches of peanut butter biscuits to start the week off right.

Before I knew it, the afternoon had flown by. I fed the dogs early and gathered up all of Henry's belongings for his trip home. I was just putting his leash on when my phone rang.

"Hello?"

"Jessie? Oh, thank heavens!" It was Kip. "She's there," he shouted at someone in the background. "She's fine. You are fine, aren't you?" he asked, speaking back into the phone.

"Yes, I'm fine. Why? I was just getting ready to take Henry over to Evan's."

"Well, we're at Sunday Senior Bingo, and Mrs. Johnston has been all atwitter, saying she's getting a message regarding you from her spirits."

"Really? What kind of message?" Henry had grown impatient and was tugging the leash in his mouth. I pulled it from his teeth and rubbed his neck to distract him.

"Well, she's not sure, but she said they're insistent that we needed to check on you and make sure you're okay."

"That's kind of weird, but I'm okay," I said, feeling a slight tingle of unease. "Although, that kind of creeps me out a little."

"I know, it creeped me out a little too," he said. "I guess, just be careful. And try not to worry." His voice dropped to a whisper. "Sometimes she's way off the mark."

"Tell her the rest!" someone shouted in the background.

Kip sighed. "Peter Piper."

"What?" I asked, wondering if I'd heard him correctly.

"Peter Piper. She said I am supposed to tell you Peter Piper."

We sat in silence for several seconds.

"Okay, then. Ah, thanks for the message," I finally said.

"See what I mean?" he whispered. "Anyway, be careful. Take my number and let me know if you need anything. We should be done here in about an hour or so." I programmed his cell phone number into my contacts list on my own cell and loaded Henry and his stuff into the car.

The rain had persisted in fits and starts throughout the day, and now it had settled into a drippy, damp evening. It was barely past five, but the light of the day had faded out behind the steely clouds, and I had to turn on my lights as well as my wiper blades. Henry bounced around the backseat, trying to look out the side, but his little paws kept slipping off the door, and he finally settled for the occasional glimpse of power lines as they zipped by his window.

Evan's street looked eerie in the gray drizzle, and I was semi-thankful to see Wynne standing on the sidewalk, halfway between her house and Evan's. She looked up from her phone as I pulled to the curb and parked, then slowly walked my way.

"Hey," she said as I stepped from the car. Her hair was starting to flatten like cotton candy in the rain, but she didn't seem to care. "You here to check on Miriam?"

I opened the back door and snagged Henry's leash before he could jump out. "No. Just bringing the little guy home." I glanced at Evan's house, which looked dark, although his car was in the drive.

"Oh." She sounded bored. "Have you seen my mom or step-perv?"

"No, this is the first I've been here today." I flashed on her mom locking lips with that guy last night. I wondered if Wynne knew what her mother had been up to, and whether it was a regular occurrence. "How's your mom feeling? I saw your step-perv—um, I mean, I saw Brian yesterday at the taqueria. He said she was sick."

She snorted. "Sick of him probably."

"Hey, I meant to ask you. That night that Miriam was killed and you were out, you said that Brian was too drunk to pick you up. But I was wondering, did you see him when you got home?"

"Yeah. Why?"

"Was his hair wet?" She looked at me intently. "Or were his clothes wet? Maybe muddy shoes?"

"Oh, I get it! You think he was out killing Miriam before me and my mom got home." She laughed. "I wish! I would like nothing better than for him to be the one heading to prison for that. But sorry. He was dry and barely able to stand. He wouldn't have been able to hit the side of a house if he tried. And he doesn't have a gun, so there's that."

Their front door flew open and Brian stormed out and marched down the walk. "Young lady, where have you been? Your mother has been worried sick."

Wynne sighed dramatically, then went back to tapping on her phone.

"Wynne? Did you hear me?"

Tiffany pushed through the door and stomped down the porch steps behind Brian. Her hair was back to the fountain-top ponytail sticking straight up on the top of her head, and the see-through dress from last night had been replaced by a shorty-short pink robe and big fuzzy slippers.

"Where have you been? Do you know what time it is?" she shrieked at Wynne. Wynne didn't even look up.

"No, what time is it?"

"It's Sunday! Almost Sunday night! We were worried sick. Were you with that boy all night?"

I'd frozen to my spot in the street, an unintended audience of some other family's drama. Henry ignored everyone, sniffing at a stain on the street. I didn't know if I should just gather up my stuff and run up the steps to Evan's or stay still and hope they moved inside.

"I asked you a question!"

"That boy?" Wynne mimicked. In the fading light, I could see how washed out Tiffany looked. She must have had a late night after leaving Hopper's Choppery. Even from a distance, I could see her skin mottle with anger.

"Go to your room. You are grounded until I tell you otherwise!"

"Oh, please. Like you're one to talk about not coming home at night." Oh, boy.

Tiffany sputtered, but no coherent words were coming out.

"What is that supposed to mean?" asked Brian, taking a few steps back.

"Why don't you ask her?" said Wynne, pushing past them and towards the front walk.

Tiffany looked from Wynne to Brian and back again. Her arms gave an impatient flap at her sides. "Maybe you *should* go live with your father," she shrieked at Wynne.

"Great! Tell me when I can go and I'm outta here!" She ran up the steps and slammed into the house.

"What is she talking about?" asked Brian, moving closer to Tiffany. "What did she mean about you not coming home at night?"

Henry had had enough waiting, and he let out a bark to remind me that he was still there. Two heads turned towards me.

Tiffany squinted at me, her mouth falling open in surprise. "Oh my God! Are you following me?" she asked.

Brian looked from face to face, clearly out of the loop.

"No," I said, shifting my purse and getting a better hold on the leash. "I'm bringing my friend's dog home."

"Tiff. What's going on? Someone talk to me here." Brian sounded petulant, like a first-grader not invited to play four square.

Tiffany turned in her furry slippers and followed Wynne inside. That left Brian and me.

We stared at each other for an uncomfortable minute.

"Well, alrighty, then," I said, heading for the back of my car to get Henry's belongings.

"Wait a minute," Brian said, walking towards me. "What did my wife mean about you following her?"

"I have no idea."

"She must have seen you somewhere. Somewhere else, I mean."

I sidled closer to my car. "Yes, I saw her when I was having dinner with my grandmother."

"When was this?"

"Last night. I saw her out at a restaurant last night." I generously left off the part about her cleaning out some guy's mouth with her tongue. Henry shook, his collars jangling, as he tried to shake the rain off his back. "Look, I need to go."

I grabbed Henry's bed and bag of food from the backseat and went up onto Evan's porch, out of the drizzle. Brian stood silently staring after me, as if hoping I would change my mind and enlighten him. He was going to have to wait a long time if he thought I was going to step into his familial minefield. After a few moments, he got into his car and drove away.

CHAPTER TWENTY-TWO

Glad that was over, I poked Evan's doorbell and wondered why his house was so dark. His car was in the driveway, so he must be here. I hit the bell again. Henry raced back and forth in front of the door, crying with excitement. Where was Evan? I let Henry's bed fall to the porch and dropped the bag of food with a thump. Digging around in my purse, I fished out my cell phone and saw the blinking red light.

A text from Evan. Shoot. I hadn't heard the ding. "Can you bring Henry over later? Maybe seven? Diego asked me to dinner. Burrito night!"

Argh. I looked at Henry and sighed. I could take him home again, but I really didn't feel like having to make the trip back later. I could keep him a few more nights and make Evan come get him sometime this week. Or, I could go get Evan's keys and just let Henry in. I was guessing he meant that he and Diego were eating at the taqueria.

An uneasy feeling was working its way to the front of my head. We'd pretty much ruled out everyone but Brian and

Diego. Or, of course, a stranger. But if Wynne was right, and Brian was dry, too drunk to hit anything and lacking a gun, then that removed Brian from the list. Which left Diego or a stranger. And Evan was there having dinner with Diego.

I stood uncertainly on the droopy porch. Maybe I could just text him to come home.

"Evan. At your house with Henry. Can you come let us in?"

I hit send and waited. Henry got restless, twining around my legs and whining. After a couple of minutes, I tried again.

"Hey, you there?"

I could tell he wasn't going to answer. In spite of my unease, I told myself that there was nothing to worry about. I mean, just for the sake of argument, let's say Diego killed Miriam. Unless he had a thing about killing the people who lived behind his restaurant, I didn't think there was any reason that Evan would be in danger. Right?

And they were just having dinner. In a public place. I would just go get him.

I left Henry's stuff on the porch and headed next door with Henry in tow. He trotted along beside me, excited to be going for a walk. The drizzle was light and the streets were wet, the red glare from taillights reflecting on their surface.

A large black pickup was parked in the alley behind the restaurant, but the small parking lot out front was empty. The windows were dark, and the restaurant looked closed. I walked up to the door and pulled on the handle, but it was locked. Leaning forward, I used my hand to shade the window and peer in.

The dining area was dark, but lights were on in the back, and the bar area was lit up. I could see Evan sitting on a barstool at the end of the bar, his head resting on his hand as if he was nearly asleep. Diego stood behind the bar, vigorously swinging a stainless-steel cocktail shaker back and forth. As I watched, he swept a lime wedge around the lip of a glass, rolled it in salt, and poured the contents of the shaker in.

As if sensing my attention, Diego looked up and gave a little wave, motioning me to stay where I was. I could see him say something to Evan as he came out from behind the bar. He walked towards the front door, wiping his hands on a bar towel before fishing a large set of keys from his pocket. He picked through an extensive bunch until he found the right one and opened the door. His expression clouded for a second when he noticed Henry standing beside me, but his smile was back as he unlocked the door for me.

"Hi," I said. "Sorry to bother you guys, but I didn't get Evan's message that he was having dinner with you until I got over here, and I didn't want to have to take Henry back to my house and then have to turn around and bring him back."

"It's no problem," he said, waving an arm to usher me in. "Generally the Health Department frowns on dogs in eating establishments, but who's going to know? Right?" I hesitated a minute, not wanting to enter.

"Maybe Evan can just come out for a minute and we could run the dog over to his house. I don't want to be a bother."

He motioned me in. "It's no bother." I edged in, holding Henry's leash close. I would just get Evan and head back out. Diego slid behind me and closed the door, locking it and repocketing the keys. I smiled a tight smile.

Henry was fascinated by the smells along the bar, and he sniffed his way from chair to chair before spotting Evan. He whined with excitement and dragged me the rest of the way until we reached him.

"Hey, Evan," I said. He turned his head towards me, trying to focus. Geez.

"Jesh!" he said, brightening and trying to sit up a little straighter. "Hey! D'ya get my messagh? I'm having dinner."

"Yeah, I can see that," I said, looking towards Diego. Diego gave a little shrug of his shoulders. "How was work?" Play it cool. Act like everything was normal, because for all I knew, everything was normal. Brian surely had more to fear from Diego than Evan or I did.

I thought I heard Diego sigh.

"Oh, Jesh. Oh my gosh. Work. Did I tell you that we're getting bought?"

"Yeah. Yeah, you mentioned that." I looked over at Diego. "How many drinks has he had?"

"Oh my gosh! Diego makes the best margaritas! Did you know that? Hey, Diego, can you make my friend Jesh a margarita? You're gonna like these." He settled his head on his hand again. "I's telling Diego about work."

"That you were, my friend," Diego said, smiling. "He's had a lot to say about it." I was getting the sense Diego had heard more about Evan's work than he bargained for.

"So, you know you have to go to work tomorrow, right?" I asked, wondering if he'd even be able to walk home. "Has he eaten anything?" I asked Diego. Tequila on an empty stomach wasn't the best idea.

"Not yet. He's been talking. Sometimes, I think, a man just needs to get things off his chest."

Evan smiled. "See?" He waved a hand towards Diego. "This. He gets me."

"Okay, good," I said. "I'm glad you're feeling better about

things. But maybe we should get you home."

"No, no! We haven't had dinner yet."

I stood uncertainly.

"I was just going to prepare something," said Diego. "Why don't you join us?" He pulled out a stool for me, and I climbed up, feeling more vulnerable once my feet no longer touched the floor. "Can I get you a drink?"

"No, I'm fine. I'll just stay here with him and make sure he doesn't fall off his stool."

Diego turned and headed for the kitchen.

"Evan." He was staring unblinking at the bar. "Evan. Hey, how much have you had to drink?"

"I dunno. One?"

"Yeah, I don't think so. Seriously, Evan, how are you going to go to work tomorrow? I think we should go."

He reached for the drink Diego had been making when I came in, but he missed it by half a foot. Furrowing his brow and squinting, he leaned forward and tried again. He was closer, but still not there. He laughed. "Look! Didya see that? The glass moved. It was here, then it was there."

I reached out and picked up the glass. "He made this one for me. I think you need to eat something."

Diego reappeared carrying a large orange plate loaded with nachos. In spite of my apprehension, my mouth started watering immediately.

"Here. I thought perhaps an appetizer would help before the main course."

"Wow, those look fantastic," I said as he slid the plate between Evan and me. The chips looked fresh and crispy. Refried beans formed a base that helped adhere the beef and rice to the chips. Cheese dripped across everything, and a mound of chopped lettuce, tomatoes and jalapeños piled on top. Heaps of guacamole and sour cream rose along the edges. I am a sucker for a good nacho.

"Help yourself," Diego said, watching me all but drool on the bar. I reached over and pulled a loaded chip from the side, pushing the whole thing into my mouth.

"Delicious," I said, taking a sip of the margarita that I was still holding. "Whoa. That's pretty strong." I grabbed another chip. "But these are amazing," I said.

He smiled his extra white smile at me. "I'm happy you like them. Would you like to stay and have dinner? I have some mole I was heating."

I really wanted to get Evan out of here. But so far I didn't see that there was anything to worry about. Except of course, the locked front door.

"That would be nice. Thanks." Diego disappeared back towards the kitchen.

"Evan, have some nachos, they're amazing." If I had any hope of getting him on his feet, he was going to need some food.

Evan rolled his head towards me, his eyes flying open as if he'd been sleeping.

"Jess! What time is it? Oh my God, did I miss work?" Hoo boy.

"Here. Have something to eat. It's Sunday, you didn't miss work." Although he was probably going to miss it tomorrow.

He turned to the plate and tried to focus. "Oh, good. Dinner. Did I tell ya I was havin' dinner with Diego?" His words were running together now, the spaces between barely noticeable.

"Yeah, you did." I took another chip, then glanced down towards Henry, who'd been pulling on the leash. "Hold on, boy," I started to say, then noticed he was piddling on the leg of the barstool next to me. "No, no!" I hissed at him. Oh geez, Diego was going to be peeved. We didn't need to give Diego anything to be peeved about. "Oh geez, Evan, hand me those napkins," I whispered at him. He was still focused on his nacho. I grabbed the stack and hopped off my stool, intent on cleaning it up before Diego returned.

I could hear Diego moving around the kitchen, and I hurried to soak up most of the mess with the napkins. "Henry, really." Boy dogs. Addie would never dream of doing something like that.

I looked around for somewhere to throw the sopping napkins, but didn't see a trash can. Still holding Henry's leash, I dragged him with me towards the ladies' room. At least there I could wash my hands as well.

As we walked down the hall, I noticed a stack of white bags in the back hallway near the back door. The pile was nearly as high as my head, and I realized they were rice bags. Why did that ring a bell? My heart started to beat faster, and I ducked into the ladies' room as my brain whirred around trying to remember why I was thinking of rice bags.

I ditched the napkins, did a quick wash of my hands, and stared at myself in the mirror. Mrs. Johnston at brunch. Bags of snow or ice with darkness inside. Kip said she wasn't always right, but what if these were the bags she'd been seeing? What did this mean? So what? It was a Mexican restaurant, of course there would be bags of rice. But that many? And I had no idea what the darkness inside might mean.

I pulled out my phone and texted Kip. "At the taqueria. Mrs. J said bags of ice, but did she mean rice? Evan and I are locked inside. Not sure if we need police?"

They say that women often ignore their intuition at their

own peril. Rather than cause someone embarrassment, they choose to be polite. But really, I was going to feel stupid if I called the police because I was scared of a nice man who was making me and my friend dinner, and who happened to have a stack of rice bags in his restaurant.

There was a tap on the door, and Diego stuck his head through.

"Everything okay?"

"Yeah," I stammered, "I just wanted to wash my hands."

He held the door open for me and, with a mock bow, ushered me back out towards the bar. Henry trotted along beside me, running his nose along the floor like a scent hound.

"Your friend isn't looking too mobile," he said as we neared Evan. It was true. Evan's head was resting on the bar now, and I could hear his snores from six feet away.

"Yeah. You know, maybe I should just take him home. I think work's just been too much for him, and he got a little carried away with your margaritas. They are really good, by the way."

He wasn't smiling anymore. He was staring at me with cold, flat eyes.

"Evan!" I shook his arm.

"Why don't you take a seat?" Diego said to me, gesturing to the barstool that I'd abandoned just moments before.

My legs were shaking as I hoisted myself back up. Henry scooted in between my legs and the bar, as if picking up on my fear.

"Yeah, maybe a few more nachos would be good before I go." I slipped my cell phone under my thigh, hoping Diego didn't see it, and reached for the plate. But it just looked congealed now, and my stomach was doing flips. Was I imagining that there was something going on here? Maybe it was just a rice delivery.

My phone dinged and I cursed myself for not having it on silent. Kip's name and text flashed on the screen: *Mrs. Johnston said get out now!* My heart thudded with a surge of fright, and I just managed to clear the screen when Diego came up behind me.

"What's that?" he asked, his voice even.

"Oh, I'm supposed to be meeting a friend of mine. He's probably just wondering where I am."

"He doesn't know where you are?"

I hesitated, trying to decide the best answer. "I just meant I'm running late. So yeah, I need to be going." I slipped from my stool, my knees nearly buckling under me. "Evan, I think we need to get you home."

Diego held out his hand. "Give me the phone." Thankfully the screen had gone black so Diego didn't see Kip's message. Not that it was going to matter.

"Why do you want my phone?" I handed it to him, still trying to pretend like nothing was amiss.

"You had to dig around, didn't you?" Diego had taken several steps back and was leaning against the wall of the hallway.

"Pardon me?" Playing dumb would be easier if my voice wasn't cracking with fear.

"Your friend doesn't know anything. I could tell talking with him this evening. He's too wrapped up in his own world. You couldn't do the same? Maybe it's a woman thing."

A small spark of anger touched at the edges of my fear. I glanced across the bar to see if there was anything I could use to bash his head in with. Unfortunately, all the bottles were on shelves behind the bar, well out of my reach. The only thing close was the plate of nachos. I envisioned winging it like a frisbee at Diego's head, but it was heavy and unwieldy, and I was sure he would have no problem deflecting it.

Henry whined softly, and I leaned down to shush him. How was I going to get us all out of here?

"You've created a problem for me," he continued. "Now I have to take care of you and your friend."

"I don't know what you're talking about." I hated that I sounded whiny. In my mind I'm braver than this.

"You don't know what I'm talking about?" He mocked my tone, and the anger in me grew a little bit more. He was laughing now, a cruel sound that made me want to launch myself at him like an angry cat. But then I saw the gun in his hand.

He hadn't had it a minute ago. At least not where I could see it. I'd had a small hope that this was really not happening, but it was. A sense of unreality closed around me, shrinking the world to this one moment, to this little space near the bar of the taqueria by Evan's house. And Evan was missing it while he slept peacefully with his head resting on the bar.

I took a deep breath and tried to steady myself. "Look. I don't know what's going on here," I said, struggling to control the quiver in my voice. "Let me just get my friend and go. You'll never see us again. I don't care what you're doing. It's got nothing to do with us."

"You should have thought of that earlier," he said.

"Just let us go," I said again. "I don't care what you're doing. I don't care what you've done." I flashed to dead Miriam.

Diego pinned me with hard eyes. "Really? You strike me as a...what is the phrase? A goody-goody. The last one wanted money. You? You'll run straight to the cops."

"No, I won't. I swear." So it had been about money after all. I guessed Miriam had thought she'd figured out a way to extract enough money from Diego to get her house back.

"Or maybe you want money too. Ay, you don't look as stupid as that one. She thought I would just give her money and everything would be okay."

"No! No, I don't want money. I just want to go, okay?"

He squinted at me. "I saw you looking around back there just now. I saw when you saw my man working on the bags."

It took me a minute to figure out what he was talking about. Then I remembered the man sewing in the office yesterday. What had that been about? He was sewing the rice bags closed. *Darkness inside.* Drugs? Was Diego a drug dealer?

"Look, each to his own, right? I mean, you want to sell drugs or whatever, I don't care. A man's got to make a living, right? Evan!" I gave Evan a hard poke in the ribs.

"Ay, you're *estúpida* too."

"Yes, I am. Really, really stupid. So please." Where was Kip? Surely he'd called 911.

"You think this is drugs?" He laughed, a hard staccato sound. "That pile of rice there?" He waved his hand towards the back. "Do you have any idea how much that many kilos would be worth?"

He stared at me as if waiting for an answer. I'd assumed that was a rhetorical question. "No?" I said.

"*Estúpida.*" He pulled a cell phone from his pocket and began thumbing one-handed across the screen.

"See? I don't know anything. So, I'm just going to take Evan and go."

"I cannot take any chances," he said. "I already had a problem with the last lady. Now I have a problem with you. This shipment is going out tonight. No more problems."

Diego must have found what he was looking for, because he hit the screen and held the phone to his ear. He fired off a rapid spate of Spanish, of which I was only able to make out "*aqui*" and "*ahora*." I did not want whoever he was calling to come here now. My chest clenched with fear.

When he ended the call, Diego turned back to me. "I am going to tell you what I am doing here," he said. "And do you want to know why I am telling you this?"

I shook my head, more a spastic tremor than anything.

"Because right now, you have hope that I'm going to let you leave." He paused, his dark eyes boring into me. "And I want to watch that hope die."

My knees nearly gave out on me.

"This"—he waved his hand towards the back hall—"this is a shipment of guns that is going to Mexico tonight. Do you know how much demand there is for guns there? There's a war going on, and they need guns to fight it."

I wanted to close my eyes, hold my hands over my ears and rock in terror. He was right. The more he told me, the more afraid I was. Where was Kip? Where were the police?

"Guns are so easy to get here. My men gather guns, and when I have enough, we ship them. I have commitments to my customers there. Nothing is going to interfere with my commitments. And that crazy *puta* tried to interfere. She came over the night they were bringing them to me. She told me she needed money to keep her house. If I gave her money, she would keep 'my secret.' I have a better way to keep my secret." He waved his pistol towards me.

I was still staring at his eyes. They were flat, dark and devoid of humanity. I had to try something. Surely he wasn't completely evil.

"What about Isabelle?" I whispered. "Please."

His lips pulled back in sudden fury. "Do not bring my family up to me! This is for Isabelle! They killed her father! The *policía* are so corrupt there. Why do you think my sister has no husband? My niece has no father. This is for them!"

He ran a hand through his hair, clearly trying to regain his control. He took a deep breath and laughed. "And when she saw that she wasn't going to get money, she ran." I guessed we were back to Miriam. "Like a scared rabbit, she ran. But she was slow. I shot her as she rounded the fence. And like the scared rabbit, she crawled under the house." He looked me in the eye. "And then I shot her again."

I took my own deep breath, feigning bravery I didn't have. "I guess you got lucky with that storm. No one heard the shots."

"I don't count on luck," he said. "Don't move." He moved quickly into the back office.

"Evan!" I shook him hard, needing him to wake up and run. He roused himself to a half-sitting position.

"What?" he mumbled. He rubbed at an eye and spotted the plate of nachos. "Oh, yum," he said, grabbing at them. The cheese had started to solidify, and the entire plate slid towards him.

Diego was back. He held up a black cylinder, which he began screwing into the muzzle of his pistol. "No one would have heard those shots."

My heart gave what I was sure was its final thud. A gun is a gun. It can kill you. So why would a gun with a silencer be even more terrifying? I slid down along the side of the bar, into a heap on the floor beside Henry. He crawled onto my chest and nuzzled my face with this nose.

"Get up," Diego said.

I wrapped my arms around Henry, the warmth of his

body the only thing keeping me from passing out, and staggered to my feet.

Diego waved the gun at us. "Move."

The gesture caught Evan's attention and he looked at Diego. "Wha's that?" His forehead wrinkled in exaggerated confusion.

At the end of the bar, my phone buzzed. Diego turned it over and glanced at the screen.

"Who's Kip?" he asked.

"A friend."

"Why is he calling?"

"How would I know?" I sounded testy, but mostly I was terrified.

"Oh, geesh," said Evan. "Is that the guy across the street?"

Diego pocketed my phone. "You're both going to need to come with me."

I thought about refusing, but the silencer waving towards us was convincing.

"Where are you taking us?" I asked. I could hear traffic swooshing along the wet pavement down Montrose. Why didn't anyone look in and see this?

"I have a driver coming for you. He'll take care of this."

I nearly fainted.

"What's going on?" Evan was still trying to understand what was happening, but judging by his lack of coordination, he wasn't going to be much help to me. He took a wobbly step. "I gotta go to the bathroom."

Diego jerked his head towards a door near the kitchen. "Let's go. This way." He backed up a few steps and opened the door, gesturing with the gun. Evan stumbled towards the opening, not even noticing it wasn't a bathroom. "You too," he said to me. I hesitated only long enough for Diego's eyes to cut to Henry. I clutched him tighter, terrified that Diego might shoot him first as an incentive for us to cooperate. I followed Evan through the door and into a small storage room that appeared to be acting as a pantry.

Diego slammed the door shut behind me, and a loud click confirmed that he'd locked us in. Evan turned in confused circles beside me.

"This isn't the men's room," he said, looking distressed.

"Yeah, no," I said, trying to remain calm. "Diego's locked us in a storage room until his driver gets here."

"But I need a bathroom," Evan said, turning around again. He was starting to bounce up and down a little, like a toddler doing a tinkle-dance.

Henry was squirming in my arms, so I set him down, still holding tight to his leash. I looked around, hoping for another way out, or maybe something we could use as a weapon when they came for us. Wire shelving lined three walls, stocked solid with dry and canned goods that you'd expect to find in a Mexican restaurant. A large section was bare, probably where they'd had the rice bags stored before they dragged them into the back hall to be loaded onto a truck and taken wherever they were going to be taken. Along with us.

I sank down on the floor next to Henry, feeling unaccountably bad that he was probably going to be killed too. And no one would ever know what had happened to us. I thought of Addie, waiting for me at home. She was a one-person dog. She was mine, and I was hers. How would she fare without me? Frances and my parents would never get over my disappearance. I'd never see my little house again. Anger flooded my veins, and I stood up, determined to either find a way out or die trying.

CHAPTER TWENTY-THREE

In the corner, Evan turned his back to me and told me not to look. I turned to the opposite wall and began pulling things from the shelves, trying to find something, anything, that could help us get out or be used as a weapon.

"Wha' you doing?" Evan asked, zipping up and turning around.

"We need to get out of here." I pulled at a bag of beans. I wondered if there were any guns hidden in these bags like there were in the rice. Grabbing one, I jerked at the seam, trying to open it. Henry joined in, grabbing the other end and gnawing at the corner. He broke through before I did, and a cascade of dried pinto beans flowed onto the floor. I tipped the bag up, hoping for a gun to fall out. There were only beans.

My eyes darted around the dim space. There had to be something. Evan started to take a step towards the door, then slid on the loose beans and crashed to the floor. He didn't even seem to notice he'd fallen. He just curled himself into a more comfortable position and passed out against one of the bean bags. Great.

I leaned against the shelf, resting my own head on a big jar of jalapeños, and took a deep breath. Surely we weren't going to die today. Right?

From the other side of the door, I heard a phone ringing. Ring. Ring. Ring. I held my breath, listening over Evan's soft snores. Eventually it stopped, and a pang of disappointment shot through me, as if somehow the ringing could save us. After a minute it began to ring again.

I inched over and pressed my ear to the door.

"Hello?" Diego sounded muffled, but I could still hear him. "No. There is no one here. We are closed." Almost immediately, the phone began to ring again.

"Hello?" This time he was louder and sounded more irritated. "No, I told you—" There was a silence. "You're mistaken." Even through the door, I could hear the phone hit the bar. A string of unintelligible Spanish filtered through, and his heavy footsteps thumped back and forth, as if he was pacing by the bar.

Could that have been Kip looking for me? A glimmer of hope shot through me, and I began to look around again for a weapon. Whether or not that was Kip, and whether or not help might arrive before Evan and I were spirited off and killed in a desert somewhere, I wasn't going down without a fight.

I didn't see anything that was going to help me overpower Diego and his gun. I could try to throw some cans at him, but these were all commercial-sized cans, and I doubted I could launch them with any sort of force or accuracy. And Evan certainly wasn't going to be much help.

I closed my eyes and tried to send brainwaves to Kip. *Send help. Send help.* There was something Kip had said earlier that was niggling at my brain. Mrs. Johnston wanted him to tell me Peter Piper. She said her spirits were passing the message on. Why was I thinking of that?

I opened my eyes and found myself looking at the giant jar of jalapeños. Peter Piper picked a peck of pickled peppers. Pickled jalapeños. This was almost as good as having pepper spray. If I could throw jalapeños in Diego's face when he opened the door, we might have a chance. But I had to do it before his driver got there. It was questionable whether it would work on Diego; it was highly unlikely it would work on two men.

I pulled Henry to the back of the closet and tied his leash to one of the metal racks. His little nose twitched wildly, and he strained at his tether, trying to pull loose. Whatever had his interest was closer to the door, but there was no time to let him check it out now.

There were four one-gallon jars of jalapeños on the shelf, each one showing Scoville scales in the light orange range. Too bad they weren't habaneros or ghost peppers. Well, they would just have to do. I grabbed the first one, clutching it to my chest and wrestling the lid off. The pungent smell wafted up as I broke the seal, and I turned my head away. This might just work.

I glanced over at Evan, who was still out cold. I might have been worried that he was dying of alcohol poisoning if I wasn't so freaked out at what was about to happen to us. Maybe he was the lucky one. If this didn't work, he might be dead before he woke up. I, on the other hand, was regrettably sober.

I turned back towards the door. The phone had begun ringing again. I needed Diego to open the door.

"Diego!" I shouted, readying my stance with the open jar. "Diego! Open the door. Evan's really sick! We need help." Like he cared about that. The phone continued ringing. Finally, I heard his shoes clipping on the floor as he approached. He was muttering in Spanish, but I couldn't make out the words.

"Who knows you're here?" he shouted through the door.

I hesitated, not sure what the right answer was. Would he shoot us faster if he knew someone was coming for us? A key scraped in the lock, and I barely had time to ready myself before he whipped the door open.

In one smooth motion, I pulled the jar back, then heaved the contents forward and up, like I was practicing for the county hog-slopping contest. I closed my eyes as the liquid flew through the air, the jalapeños following up in an arc before hitting the floor with a splat.

Diego let out a cry of pain, and I cracked my eyelids to see how much damage I'd done. My aim had been more lucky than good, and he was rubbing at his face with the back of his forearm. But what alarmed me was that the other hand, which still held his gun, was swinging wildly.

"You bitch!" he cried. Henry began to bark, and I yelled at him to be quiet as Diego waved the gun in that direction.

Over Diego's screams and Henry's barking, I nearly missed the honking. Honk Honk. Honnnnk Hooonnnnnnk. I looked frantically around for something I could throw at him before he could pull the trigger. The horn was getting louder. Henry was still pulling at his leash, and I finally noticed what he was trying to get. A black rat bait station was under one of the racks, and judging by the rustling and movement of the box, a rat was inside, having dinner. I *knew* Evan's rat problem had started here.

The honking sounded as if it was almost upon us, and

Diego turned towards the front of the restaurant, still trying to open his eyes, as a giant crash rocked the building. I turned just in time to see the colossal front end of Mr. McNeil's Chrysler Imperial shoot through the windows, smashing tables and chairs in its wake. The horn blared in a steady ear-blasting pitch as the car launched all the way into the dining room, finally squealing to a stop just short of the pass into the kitchen.

I heard Grammy shout, "Good one, Arthur!"

"There she is!" someone shouted.

"Oh, it's the bad man! Over there! Someone get him!"

Like a slow-motion nightmare, I watched as Diego turned, both hands now wrapped around his pistol. He blinked through streaming red eyes, his finger on the trigger as he turned towards the car. In the driver's seat, I could see Mr. McNeil's fingers still wrapped around the steering wheel, his head barely visible over the dashboard.

Silver heads bounced up and down in the windows, like puppies in a box. I caught a glimpse of a neon blue sweater and a merrily waving hand from the middle of the front seat. In the back, Kip clung to the headrest in front of him. His face was the only one that seemed to show any fear at all. He stared at Diego, frozen in place.

"There she is! There she is! Yoo-hoo!" The hand in front waved faster.

Diego planted his feet, his eyes still blinking and tearing from the jalapeños. He took aim.

"No!" I yelled. I grabbed the only thing small enough to hurl at him: the bait box. Grimacing, I flung it Frisbee-style towards Diego. Screams broke from my throat as the rat flew out, the box and the rat soaring independently through the air. The box glanced off Diego's shoulder, but the rat, legs flying wildly, managed to grab a hold of Diego's hair as it hit the side of his head. It twisted and scrabbled, trying to find a foothold. I saw it slip under Diego's collar and disappear in a writhing lump down his back.

Diego twisted, trying to pull his shirt loose from his pants to free the clawing rodent, but before he could, Mr. McNeil hit the gas pedal again, and the car lurched forward, striking Diego broadside in the hip, knocking him to the floor. His gun flew from his hand and slid across the floor. The doors of the car flew open and everyone piled out, scattering across the floor and chattering at high speed.

"Did you hit her?"

"Does it look like I hit her?"

"Where's the gentleman with the gun? Someone get the gun away from him!"

"Jessie! Jessie! Are you okay?"

"I told you. I told you we needed to get here."

I pulled Henry into my arms and sank to the floor. The adrenaline that had been powering me was draining away, replaced by a total body-dropping exhaustion. I was safe. I wasn't going to die. I put my head between my knees, closed my eyes, and faded softly into the relief.

A gentle hand patted my shoulder, and a worried voice floated overhead.

"Are you okay? Did Arthur run you over? Can you move? Kip! Kip, come quick!"

I opened my eyes to a ring of worried faces.

"We need to call the police," I said. "And Diego—make sure he can't get up."

"Oh, don't you worry about him." Was that Mrs. Johnston or Miss Potts? I wasn't sure. "Mr. McNeil has him under control. He's not going anywhere."

I lifted my head to look. Diego was writhing on his stomach about ten feet away. His hands were tied behind his back with what looked like yarn. Mr. McNeil sat on his back, attempting to rope his flailing feet. It didn't really look like Mr. McNeil had him under control.

"Hold still, will ya?"

Diego moaned, a deep, wounded guttural noise that still sounded dangerous.

Grammy walked over and took a swing at Diego's head with her oversized tote. It cracked him squarely on the side of his head with a resounding thunk. He went limp.

"He told you to hold still!" She hoisted her bag up and started rummaging through it. "You better not have broken my bottle of Manischewitz," she told his inert form. "It's hard to find the blackberry flavor."

Kip finally emerged from the backseat, his face ashen.

"Are you okay?" I asked him. With the exception of Diego, he looked the worst of the bunch.

"I could use a drink," he said, sinking to the floor beside me. He must be in bad shape, because this floor was not the cleanest, and I couldn't help but notice the Versace label on his jeans.

"Maybe Grammy will let you have a little of her wine," I said.

"Oh Lord, spare me," he said, his lips drawn back in horror at the thought.

"Has anyone called 911?" I asked no one in particular. No one answered. I cradled Henry's warm body in my arms, his heartbeat a rhythmic comfort against my own.

In the distance, I heard sirens beginning to wail. I guess we didn't need to call.

With Diego still unconscious, Mr. McNeil had finished

wrapping his legs up with a fuzzy pale blue yarn. It looked like a second-grader's art project gone horribly wrong. Mrs. Liddell had pulled her wheeled suitcase out of the car and was busy laying a tape outline around Diego's inert form.

"He's not dead, is he?" I asked Kip. Grammy had pulled up a chair near Diego's head and was taking ladylike sips from her Manischewitz bottle. She stared at him, looking as if she would give him another pop if he so much as cracked an eyelid.

"I don't think so," he said. "But I don't really care either way."

Mrs. Staskywicz pushed her walker through the scattered tables, stopping to take pictures every few feet. She motored around the front end of the Chrysler.

"I have to say, the car still looks pretty good," I said. The bumper had the tiniest of dents in it, although in contrast, the restaurant looked like a bomb had gone off.

A patrol car raced into the parking lot, followed immediately by a second. The sirens blared, echoing off the walls, but the seniors hardly seemed to notice. They all just kept doing what they were doing, albeit at a faster pace. Grammy gave a small kick at Diego's shoulder, connecting with surprising force. If I hadn't been so tired, I might have gotten up and given him a kick in the head myself.

Within seconds, four police officers hustled through the broken window, guns drawn, clearly confused as to what they'd come upon.

"Hands in the air," one screamed. The others aimed their guns one way, then another, taking in the elderly crowd, who continued their random activities. I felt kind of sorry for them. No one was paying any attention to their orders. I watched as Miss Potts pulled her headlamp out of her purse, strapped it on her head and leaned down to examine the dark space under the bar.

"Hands up!" one of the cops yelled. I looked over and saw with alarm that Mrs. Johnston was coming out of the back office with pistols in each hand. My breath caught in my throat.

She wandered towards us, seemingly unaware of her predicament.

"Look what I found," she said, holding her hands out. "They were sitting on some open bags of rice."

"Drop your weapons!" one of the cops screamed. Everyone stopped moving. Mrs. Johnston blinked in confusion, the guns now wobbling in her trembling hands.

"I found these back there," she said, her voice as shaky as her hands.

"Drop your weapons now!"

She leaned forward, and the two guns slid from her hands and clattered to the floor. Two cops rushed forward. One kicked the guns away and the other grabbed her, spun her, and twisted her arm behind her back.

The other two cops shouted at everyone to get their hands up and move slowly into a group. I set Henry down and got to my feet beside Kip, hands in the air like the others. The only one who didn't move was Diego. I noticed his face was resting in a pool of jalapeño juice that had dripped from his hair. No sign of the rat.

The seniors made their way slowly towards Kip and me, hands raised to varying levels. Mrs. Staskywicz kicked her walker along, hands hovering over the handles. Miss Potts had her long arms extended straight up like she was hanging from a clothesline, and Mrs. Liddell touched her hands to her shoulders like she was signaling a play on the field. Grammy gamely tried to raise both hands, but the one holding the wine bottle wobbled under the strain.

"Yoo-hoo, Officer," she said. "This is rather heavy. Could you be a good boy and carry it for me?" She gave him a coquettish smile. His eyes widened in alarm and he glanced at his partner. "You're quite handsome," she said. "You look like that nice young man on that detective show. What's his name?" She turned to Kip. "You know it. The one you and I used to watch. Remember? He had a nice mustache like this one."

She took another sip from her bottle and smiled brightly at the cute officer. More sirens shrieked into the parking lot, sounding as if they were going to follow Mr. McNeil's lead and race right into the building. I couldn't help but notice the cops looked relieved at the arrival of reinforcements.

The next few minutes were a whirlwind of confusion. They seated us all at whatever tables were still upright and told us to stay quiet. Ha, right. Like this group could ever stay quiet.

Two paramedics rolled a gurney in and stooped beside Diego. Without even blinking, one proceeded to cut through the yarn binding Diego's arms.

"Hey," Mr. McNeil protested. "You gotta keep him restrained. He's dangerous. He tried to kill our friend here. Hell, he pointed a pistol at me. He was gonna kill us too."

The second paramedic looked over at us.

"What happened to him?" he asked.

"I bumped him a little with the car. But he was still fightin'. It wasn't till he took a little shot to the head with a bottle that he got quiet like that."

One of the paramedics leaned over his head, pulled up an

eyelid and ran a light back and forth. Diego moaned and flapped an arm, but then went still again.

"What's wrong with his eyes?" the paramedic asked. He sniffed at his gloved hand.

"I threw jalapeños at him," I said.

"Oh geez," he said, extracting a bottle of eyewash from his kit. Within minutes they hoisted him onto the gurney and strapped him down, probably tighter than they normally did. One of the cops followed them out.

"Um, hey," I said towards one of the cops. "My friend is passed out in that little room right there. I think he might have alcohol poisoning." I waved towards the door.

"Yeah, someone's with him now." As if on cue, sounds of retching reached us. Everyone turned away.

At least now we knew who'd killed Miriam. Now she could cross over, or move on or do whatever it was that unhappy dead people did. That would make Evan happy, and I could stop worrying about him living on my couch till he was Mr. McNeil's age.

More police arrived on the scene, and a second ambulance pulled up, two EMT's rushing back with a stretcher to check on Evan.

We sat there for what felt forever. Everyone had to make a statement. I was convinced that they would never actually let any of us go. Of course it didn't help that our stories were all over the map. Henry took another little tinkle on a chair leg. I no longer cared.

Detective Raines arrived, and he had the honor of questioning me. Well, maybe he didn't consider it an honor. I actually felt a little sorry for him because my story was a bit convoluted. I tried. I really did. I wanted to tell this whole thing in a linear fashion but it just didn't come out that way. I would start talking about Evan showing up at my house, and then I'd veer off to the rats or how the dogs were getting along. I wasn't sure how much I should tell him about Brian's propensity for young girls, but I didn't know how to tell my story without telling the whole thing.

Like I said, it took nearly forever, but I finally ran out of steam and Detective Raines finally ran out of questions. The seniors had finished their statements long before I had, but they'd insisted on waiting for me to be finished. Unlike me, they were revved up and ready to roll. Mostly I just wanted to go home, but they would have none of it.

They'd rolled Evan out a long time ago. He was going to be treated for alcohol poisoning and then presumably released. I doubted he'd make it to work tomorrow.

The rain was heavier now than it had been earlier in the evening, and I pulled my jacket tighter, wishing I had an umbrella.

"There she is!" said Grammy, rushing towards me as I crunched my way through the broken glass and out towards the parking lot. She had on a purple plastic poncho, the hood nearly obscuring her face.

"We want to hear everything!" said Miss Potts, plucking at my sleeve. Her headlamp had either burned out or she'd turned it off, but it still bobbed up and down with her head.

"Let's get outta this rain," said Mr. McNeil. "Are we going to the House of Pies or not? I'm starving. Although someone else is gonna have to drive. I don't think they're going to let me take my car back yet."

Kip grabbed me in a big bear hug, the water from his umbrella running down my back. "I'm so happy you're okay!" he said. "To think that horrid man would have killed you. It just makes my blood run cold."

"I want to hear what happened," said Grammy. "But I could use some coffee first."

"Look, guys. Thanks so much. But I really need to get to the hospital and check on Evan."

"Sweetie, he's in good hands. And it might be more pleasant for both of you if skip what they're doing to fix him." He had a point.

"Who's going to drive? Kip, can we all fit in your car?" asked Miss Potts.

Of course we couldn't, since Kip had a normal-sized car. After determining that I was okay to drive after my ordeal, we split the seniors up and headed for the twenty-four-hour House of Pies over on Kirby Boulevard.

I got Mrs. Staskywicz and Mrs. Johnston because I had more room for Mrs. Staskywicz's walker and Mrs. Johnston's suitcase. I also got Miss Potts, who nearly knocked Mr. McNeil over in her rush to my car door.

"I'm riding with Jessie," she said, slapping at his hand as he reached for the door handle. Henry sat wedged in the backseat, looking exhausted.

The House of Pies has been a Houston institution for as long as I remember. It wasn't as crowded as I'd expected. Then again, it was rather late on a Sunday night, and the weather was crummy. We wrapped Henry in a soft afghan that Mrs. Johnston extracted from her suitcase and left him to sleep in the car.

We found two booths across a narrow aisle from each other, and everyone shuffled around, trying to find an optimal seat. Judging from the orange-and-brown décor, this place hadn't been updated since the seventies.

Within minutes, everyone had a cup of steaming coffee. Mine was the only decaf. Kip ordered a "Skinny Caramel

Machiatto" but changed it to a regular when the waitress gave him the eye. I'd barely taken a sip of the steaming brew when they started firing questions at me.

"When did you know who killed Miriam?"

"Why did you go see that taco-rita man if you knew he was a murderer?"

"Was Miriam there tonight? Did she tell you to go?"

"You should have told us ahead of time you were going. We could have come along instead of having to drive through the damn building."

"Did he describe what he'd done to Miriam?" This was asked with just a shade more enthusiasm than I was comfortable with.

"The police told me he was smuggling guns into Mexico. He's helping those drug people kill their own countrymen. Can you believe it?"

"You've got some terrible circles under your eyes. But I have some makeup that might help if you want to come over tomorrow. I can show you how to cover those purple marks."

I picked up a spoon and tried to see my reflection, but fortunately it was so dull I couldn't see anything. "Do I look that bad?" I asked Kip. "I am tired, but I think I'm doing pretty good for what I've been through."

"Oh, sweetie, of course you look bad! This has been harrowing, and it shows. But I'm sure we can do something about it."

I answered the questions as best I could. It wasn't easy. As soon as I'd start answering one question, they'd lose interest in that and veer off into a whole new line of questioning. Or they'd remember something they wanted to tell the group and just launch into their own stories. Within minutes I was able to sit back against the booth and fade out of the limelight.

The waitress staggered over with a huge tray bearing our selected pie slices and Mr. McNeil's corned beef hash and eggs.

"What? I'm hungry," he said, catching Miss Potts staring at him with tight-set lips. "That damn bingo night's gone to the birds," he said, shoveling up his first bite. "Expecting a coupla donuts to be dinner. Donuts aren't dinner. Dinner is dinner."

"That looks like breakfast," said Mrs. Staskywicz.

"That looks like you need to mind your own beeswax," said Mr. McNeil, around an even larger mouthful.

"So anyway," Kip cut in, "I'm glad we were there to save you."

"When Kip read your text about the rice bags, I had another vision," said Mrs. Johnston. "It was terrifying."

"She nearly passed out!"

"I nearly passed out. I could feel you in a dark place. Like a trunk, and you were heading for the desert." Her eyes rolled upward until I could only see the whites, and her eyelids fluttered rapidly. I was afraid she was having a seizure. "It was very horrible."

"She made us quit the game early and go right then. And then she told Mr. McNeil he had to drive through the building," finished Kip, patting his chest with one hand.

"And he just did it?"

"Everyone knows when Mrs. Johnston has a vision, you better do what she tells you." I was starting to be a believer in Mrs. Johnston. "And frankly, it didn't take much convincing on Mr. McNeil's part. I think it's been a long time since he's had this much fun."

Mr. McNeil gave a noncommittal snort over his eggs.

I set down my fork and looked around at all the well-pleased faces. "I cannot thank each and every one of you enough for what you did for me tonight." A small bubble of emotion welled up in my throat. "If you hadn't shown up when you did, and been willing to put yourselves at great personal risk, well, I probably wouldn't be here." Mrs. Liddell leaned over and patted my arm.

"Mrs. Johnston, I don't know how your feelings work, but I think you have a gift. I'm so happy that you do. And Mr. McNeil, I can't believe you were willing to drive through a storefront to save me. I would be more than happy to pay for the damage to your car." I didn't mention that had they called 911, I might have been saved a little sooner.

He lifted a hand and waved me away. "I don't think there's any damage," he said. "Maybe a little scratch, but it gives it character. Don't worry about it."

"Tell her! Tell her!" said Grammy. Everyone looked around the table at each other. Finally Miss Potts cleared her throat.

"We are starting a business."

"Really? That's great," I said, somewhat afraid of where this was going. "What kind of business?"

"We're going to solve murders!" cut in Grammy. "We're calling ourselves Murder Solvers, Inc. MSI!"

"We figured we were so good at solving Miriam's murder that we could do this for money."

"We have some time on our hands. And we have Mrs. Johnston's gift to help us."

"We'll probably make a fortune!"

"We'll probably be famous."

"Did anyone bring a paper? I told you to bring a paper so we can look for our next case."

"I have the paper in my suitcase. Jessie, could you go get my suitcase for me?"

"Don't make her get it now. The girl is exhausted. Can't you see how tired she is?"

"Kids these days. They don't have the stamina that we did at that age. Do you remember being that age? Now that was stamina."

I sat back and took a bite of coconut cream pie. The tension that I'd been holding in my shoulders started to melt out of my muscles. Rain pelted against the window, and the voices chattered on around me. These guys were great. I might have almost been killed tonight, but I hadn't been. And frankly, I was having a better time now than I'd had in a long time. I wondered if I should give up on dog biscuits and join their MSI team.

"We need to check the obituaries."

"Not the obituaries. We need to be looking in the Local section. We gotta find unsolved murders. How many times I gotta tell you this?"

"Murdered people are in the obituaries too. Give me a paper and I'll show you."

Then again, maybe I'd just stick with my dog biscuit business.

CHAPTER TWENTY-FOUR

I peered through the window at the dancing shadows being cast by the late-afternoon sun, and glanced at my watch for the thousandth time in the last fifteen minutes. Next door, the movers were making good progress emptying out the Barbieris' house. I stepped outside onto Evan's rickety porch and looked up and down the street. The doll collector was late. I needed him to get here and pack up that creepy little crew before Evan got home from work.

I'd spent hours pondering a housewarming gift for him. The reality was, what he needed most was a bulldozer. But he steadfastly insisted he could fix this place up, so I'd zeroed in on the one thing he hadn't been able to bring himself to do: I'd found a collector to buy the dolls and get them out of here. And anything the collector was willing to pay for them could go towards one of the zillions of projects this money-sucking house was going to need.

A white panel van cruised slowly down the street. I walked toward the street, ready to wave him over. But it wasn't him. I glanced at my watch again.

"Hey." The voice was so close behind me, I nearly leaped out of my shoes as I whirled around.

"Geez, you scared the heck out of me." Wynne stood just inches from me, almost unrecognizable with light brown hair and sporting a bright yellow sweatshirt over blue jeans. She looked like a normal high school kid. "You look good," I said.

She looked away. "Thanks. What a mess, huh?" She waved a hand at the moving van.

I hadn't seen her since I'd mentioned Brian's proclivities to the cops, and I wasn't sure if there had been any fallout from that.

"The perv's gone," she said, reading my mind. "He packed up his golf clubs and cameras the day after that old guy drove through the restaurant."

"Wow. Where'd he go?"

"I dunno. I don't care. If I never see him again, it'll be too soon. My mom freaked out, though. Everything that he left behind—toast. I didn't know she could be that destructive."

We turned and watched one of the movers throw a box marked "Fragile" into the truck. A tinkle of glass played across the air.

"So where are you guys going?" I asked.

"My mom's moving to Dallas," she said. "She went to high school up there; she said she has a lot of friends there."

"You're not going with her?"

"Nah. I'm gonna go stay with my dad and his wife."

"In Singapore?"

She smiled. Her whole face lit up when she smiled. "Yeah. I've really missed him. They've been great. They said I can come stay with them as long as I want. There's a school near where they live." We both turned at the sound of a diesel engine growling slowly down the street. "I think it'll be awesome."

The truck slowed down, then stopped at the curb.

"I think this is the guy I've been waiting for," I said.

"Yeah, well, I gotta go anyway." We stood looking awkwardly at each other for a second. "I just wanted to say, hey, you know...thanks. Thanks for believing me about the perv. Most adults are useless."

"No problem," I said. "I'm glad you're getting to go stay with your father. Take care of yourself."

She gave me a little wave and walked away. I turned back towards the street, where a buff-looking cowboy jumped down from his Chevy Silverado extended-cab pickup truck. He pulled a battered leather briefcase from the floor and ambled up the drive towards me. Surely this was not the doll guy.

"Hi, I'm Mike," he said, extending a tanned hand. "I'm here for those dolls you called about."

I made a concerted effort to close my gaping mouth and introduced myself.

"You're not really what I expected," I said as we walked towards the house. He laughed, a pleasant gravelly chuckle.

"Yeah, you're not the first I've heard that from. I guess people expect something different," he said, holding the door open for me. "But my grandmother taught me everything there was to know about doll collecting. She pretty much raised me. She didn't know much about raising a boy, but she did the best she could. And now, well, here I am." He bent down and gave Henry a gentle rub on his neck.

"Okay, well, I'm not really sure what we've got here, or how much they might be worth, but it's time to try and find them a new home," I said, gesturing towards the hallway. I was hoping they would be worth a lot. The takeover at Astor Oil had fallen through, so Evan's job was safe for the time-being, but it seemed like every other day Evan found something else around here that needed to be fixed.

Henry raced ahead of us, throwing squeaky toys this way and that like a furry, amped-up flower girl leading the way to the altar. He looked happier than I'd ever seen him. Evan had finally brought in a handyman to find and plug all the holes that had been letting the drafts and the rats in. I guessed the little dog was settling in and feeling more secure.

Once in the bedroom, I flung open the closet door and stood back, looking away. I don't know what I'd expected. They were just dolls, after all. But I'd been halfway afraid they'd be angry at being ousted from their home. After a few seconds of silence, I looked over. Mike stood in the middle of the closet, consulting a memo pad and murmuring softly to the dolls. "Well, aren't you all some of the prettiest little things I've seen in a long time?" He made some notes, carefully picking one or two off the shelf and examining them with care.

The mood seemed to change considerably. Okay, realistically I knew it was all in my head, but I swear those dolls stood up a little straighter and put on some genuine-looking smiles, not those evil-looking grimaces they favored me with. A feeling of relief washed over me; they liked this cowboy.

Although, just as he was turning to check out a doll towards the front of the closet, the crazy bride doll launched herself right at the back of his head. Oh, yeah. I was doing the right thing. These things had to go.

www.ingramcontent.com/pod-product-compliance
Lightning Source LLC
Chambersburg PA
CBHW021810110726
47902CB00006B/1723